THE LAST TRAIN FROM MENDRISIO

THE LAST TRAIN
FROM MENDRISIO

Jon and Lois Foyt

The Book Guild Ltd
Sussex, England

The Book Guild Ltd
25 High Street
Lewes, Sussex

First published 1995
© Jon and Lois Foyt 1995
Set in Bembo
Typesetting by Southern Reproductions (Sussex)
Crowborough, Sussex
Printed in Great Britain by
Antony Rowe Ltd
Chippenham, Wiltshire.

A catalogue record for this book is
available from the British Library

ISBN 0 86332 972 1

PREFACE

International borders, either onshore or offshore, are meant to limit the jurisdiction of one nation's laws, designating a point beyond which its rule may not be imposed. Perhaps it is like the limits to a person's life. For a country there exists a border, and for a person the brink of death – those certain places where each must stop, allowing others to take charge. Yet some countries – and some people – yearn to project their influence even beyond these frontiers.

PROLOGUE

Standing in the entrance to the café in the Swiss border town of Chiasso, Trevor Thomson watched the much younger Count Ambrosiana, a member of Italian royalty, climb into his Maserati. Prominent Italians dress well, he had observed to himself hours earlier when their meeting began, and now in the sunlight he again admired the Count's subtle but expensive jewellery and the successful way his silk tie blended with his tailored suit. Yes, it was true the Italian cut did make a man appear more handsome.

Though he certainly had the money to buy whatever clothes he wanted, one thing Trevor regretted not having acquired during his life was the knack of stylish dress. With his wavy silver hair and clipped white moustache, he might then be hired as a model. Imagine, he thought, being an idol for those younger people who fretted about growing old and about death. But reflecting proudly on his long life, Trevor concluded he would settle for his existing pedigree: a successful, money-grubbing, red-blooded American of Scottish descent and rich as hell.

The Count's sports car, illegally parked during their meeting, predictably bore no ticket. The Count fired the powerful engine, pointing the car's sleek hood towards the border a block away. As corporate treasurer of his family's drug conglomerate in nearby Campione, the Count made this crossing hundreds of times to and from his villa on Lake Como. So it came as no surprise to Trevor when one guard saluted while another automatically raised the thin red and white pole marking this frontier of Switzerland.

Trevor was excited. The Count had signed the papers on behalf of his family, and now his embryonic Thomson-Columbus Museum in the Caribbean, its international status elevated by being endorsed by royalty, would weave another pattern into his own immortality.

Pleased, he wrapped his arm around his other midday companion, the trusted Swiss banker Hans Kubler, and gave a squeeze, remarking,

7

'Hans, with the Count's prestigious support, I now feel more comfortable moving ahead with our project on Grand Turk.'

Frowning, the German-Swiss said, *'Ja,* but spending so much money on a run-down house on some tiny island merely to display rusty artifacts dredged up from an old shipwreck –'

With enthusiasm Trevor interrupted, 'Hans, don't you see how appropriate my idea is? Christopher Columbus – and I realize there's the question of whether or not our find is actually his *Pinta* – was also Italian.'

The younger banker peered at Trevor through his silver-rimmed glasses. Now realizing he should be more in accord with his client's plan, Kubler replied, 'But if you want to gain multinational support you must also have a Spanish connection, because Columbus sailed for Spain.' He thought for a moment and tapped his leather brief-case, his gesture suggesting the solution lay inside in the form of a monthly cheque payable to Samuel A. Thomson, Ph.D. In a tone of voice reflecting proper respect for Trevor's long-deceased wife, he said, 'What about Lillian's son, Samuel – your stepson?'

Trevor replied, 'Yes, I've heard he is a recognized expert on Spanish history in the New World.'

'Ja. So, why don't you include him in your plans?'

Trevor said, 'But all I promised Lillian was to provide financially for him and his sister.'

'It wouldn't cost you anything to go beyond finance and involve your stepson. His scholarly reputation could well bring in Spanish support, maybe even from the royal family in Madrid.'

'Yes, another of your good ideas, Hans.'

Kubler nodded and said, *'Ja,* but you know, Mr Thomson, every month for – how many years now? – I've mailed Samuel and Judith their cheques to Mexico, but I've never known what either of your stepchildren look like. Don't you have pictures?'

'Never carry photos, not even Lillian's – I'm not a sentimentalist. Images developed in the mind are far better.' He laughed and said, 'But Hans, they live in New Mexico – one of our fifty. You must have the right zip code because Sam and Judith always receive their support.'

Trevor thought about geography. Take nearby Lugano. Kubler's branch of the Trans-Swiss Bank was there, not in better-known Zurich or Geneva. Lugano's location as the nearest Swiss banking centre to both Milan and Sicily afforded the city a profitable Italian connection. Its banks were piled high with laundered cash from organized crime and sheltered stashes hidden away by wealthy Italians dodging their own country's income taxes.

Smart money, Trevor mused, always finds its way to the safest haven. In Switzerland safety was embellished with confidentiality; there, money, whether denominated in francs, lire, dollars or Deutschmarks, was calibrated in power.

Another reason he did business with Kubler's branch and not the bank's main office in Zurich was because he needed a man he could trust. From his very first impressions, he had decided Kubler was that man. Kubler could guide him through business dealings in foreign countries with their dissimilar laws and unique customs. But it was different with his other advisors. Over them Trevor exercised raw power.

Through the years the loyal Kubler had assiduously pursued the investment goals Trevor had set. Now and then a risk taker, but only after tedious research, the German-Swiss banker did occasionally recommend a special situation – an opportunity for windfall profits – as he had recently with the Italian pharmaceutical conglomerate Ambrosiana Limited.

Throughout today's meeting Kubler had continuously drunk his creamless coffee brewed by Italian-Swiss experts. Simply inhaling whiffs of the coffee's full-bodied aroma would fortify most Americans enough to go galloping off into the sunset. Tirelessly Kubler had scribbled notes on the lined pad whose cover was embossed with the bank's centuries-old coat of arms, though by the meeting's end it was smudged with the Swiss chocolate he nibbled.

Kubler was saying, 'So, now this museum plan of yours will be carried out, Mr Thomson, as you wished ever since you discovered the shipwreck.'

'Yes, our signatures sealed the deal with the Italian royal family. So I hope the agreement is in order . . . I only read it once.' Reflecting, he said, 'Aren't signatures peculiar things? You can sign your life away with them . . . .'

'And your money, too,' Kubler said, his tone serious.

Trevor was glad Kubler spoke English. He had never decided which of Switzerland's languages to learn, Italian, French or German.

Anyway, with his marine archaeology endeavour now fashionably endorsed, Trevor hoped the wreck was indeed the *Pinta* so he could enjoy tandem immortality with Christopher Columbus. His Thomson-Columbus Museum would be a fitting culmination to his life, and – since he so loved those Caribbean islands – an appropriate use of a slice of his vast wealth. Trevor had always regarded himself as an explorer of new lands – financial ones. Now his name would piggyback the reputation of the 1492 daredevil explorer. Yes, exciting new horizons were unfurling for him after years of being devoted only to making money, albeit cleverly and creatively.

But archaeological projects, whether on land or sea, took a while to excavate, and the ensuing lab work was time-comsuming. Trevor was impatient; he found, as he aged, time became more precious. Passing seventy, Trevor looked forward to the years ahead. Passing eighty, he began to anticipate only months. By now he was down to days – each one more lovely than the last.

On fishing trips, Trevor had often sailed over where the caravel had gone aground in the early sixteenth century. One day while studying aerial photographs of the Caicos Banks, he made out a configuration of blocks lying on the white sand of the shallow Caribbean bottom, and he knew it was the rock ballast from a sunken ship's hull. He shared his discovery with the island nation's Governor, who agreed it could be an important historical find. Together they had formed a non-profit organization, today endorsed by the Italian Count, to oversee the excavation as well as to staff and outfit the museum.

Now, Kubler said, 'Ah, Mr Thomson, one more thing before we part. I must know your plan for the warrants . . . .'

'Hans,' the older man replied, 'just exercise them, and we'll gain control. I trust you to carry out our plan.'

'Ja, but time is running out. And what will Count Ambrosiana and his father say when they find out about it?'

'The Count will keep his position as corporate treasurer – he's too prominent for us to fire. Status is what's important to him. As to his father, it's time he retired. So, Hans, take what action you need to.'

Trevor bid the banker goodbye. Alone he walked along Chiasso's bustling main street, wondering if Kubler thought he had grown callous to life and to the people around him.

'How does it feel to be almost ninety?' some dared ask.

'Like it feels to be sixty or even forty,' he would promptly reply, adding, 'except wisdom continues to grow if you stay fit and challenge yourself mentally.'

Yet younger generations clung tenaciously to society's stereotypes about age, such as, older people are no longer interested in sex, they're over the hill and losing their memory – or their footing – needing help even to cross the street. But their attitudes changed when they found out he was one of America's richest men, with a reputation for shrewdness. He had set up an offshore trust in the Caribbean – a design for his own financial life after death. It avoided probate, with all those attorneys and legal expenses chewing away, not to mention the prying eyes of the press, for it was not open to public view and its assets were safe. The trust enabled him to call out out from the grave, specifying how his money was to be invested and spent, and for whose benefit. His lasting fame would endure for generations.

Despite those stereotypes about ageing, there was nothing amiss with his memory. Testing it, and still tingling with the thrill of the long-ago deal, he recalled outfoxing the world's largest bank.

He had relished those cliff-hanging weeks negotiating the lease on his high-rise building in San Francisco, which the bankers coveted for their world-wide headquarters. After they had finally swallowed his proposals, he compounded his gains by adding the rest of their California branches, designing a pearl necklace which he strung around the Golden State.

Those mid-1950s bankers had snickered when he asked no fixed rent, proposing instead a percentage, albeit minuscule, of every deposit taken in through their tellers' windows. Little had they realized the impact inflation – then barely a disturbance on the horizon – would have on these percentages when it hit the American economy with an incredible force lasting three decades.

His thoughts also went back to his marriage, and a warm glow came over Trevor. Hoping her image would never fade, he visualized Lillian's beauty, and remembered how, during their honeymoon in Nassau, she had sprung the existence of her two small children on him. In their suite overlooking the harbour, lying naked and snuggling by his side, she'd made him promise, since he had no children of his own, to name her handsome little Samuel and her darling Judith his sole beneficiaries.

Her beauty radiating before him, she had whispered sensually, 'Assure me you'll take care of them the rest of their lives.' It was a covenant to which he was easily bound. A few years later, to ease her suffering in her agonizing, painful final days, he had reiterated his vow.

Men of his generation seldom shared financial matters with their wives. Nevertheless he wanted to tell Lillian about his offshore trust. Trying to paint a picture, he said, 'Think of me as a pirate hiding treasure – in this case stocks and bonds and ownership of real estate – in a secret cave on a tiny island. There, my trustee will monitor it while my Swiss banker invests it with all the loving care of polishing jewels.'

Lillian smiled and said, 'But Trevor, you're not a pirate. You didn't steal your money. Is this trust legal? Or are you avoiding taxes?'

She was relieved when he assured her he intended to comply with IRS regulations. He was seeking anonymity only from lawyers and creditors. 'My offshore trust is both legal and moral,' he had told her.

Moving along the bustling Chiasso street, Trevor passed a Swiss mother pushing a double baby carriage. He saw its two little infants and thought of Sam and Judith, by now grown up and living in Santa Fe.

Sam was married, or had a live-in girlfriend. Kubler had once told him the endorsements on Sam's cheques were in feminine handwriting. Was her name Prudence? No, it was Penny. Funny name, and Trevor thought about Ben Franklin's advice – a penny saved is a penny earned. His credo, too.

Since Sam was a scholar of Spanish Colonial history he ought to feel a kinship to the museum on Grand Turk. Maybe Sam should be put in charge. But Charles Fountain, his offshore trustee, had already hired an archaeologist from Kansas with a voice as flat as the American prairie. How Wes Truecoat ever got interested in shipwrecks was a mystery.

Trevor thought he and his stepson might share something in common. Fleetingly he thought about conveying his hopes and dreams to Sam. There was only so much one man could orchestrate during his lifetime. But nothing was going to happen to him. He would be around for ever, courting immortality.

And there was Judith, so far as he knew still single, yet he was sure she must be as striking in appearance as her mother.

Neither communicated with him. Their relationships were akin to the terms of a lease, each party sticking to past commitments.

Past commitments . . . Chiarra. Now, some thirty years afterwards, he felt a deep sorrow. Maybe it was really a regret. Or was he becoming sentimental? She had been so damned innocent, so sincere. Then, if he had wanted to – because people feared his power and would not intervene – he could force himself on a woman and get away with it.

Since he was going through a repentance and cleansing of spirit, maybe he'd call Fountain on Grand Turk. Yes, he would say – although it would not be easy – he wanted to make it up to Chiarra. Both to her and to what was her name? – Felicia – her bastard daughter.

Yes, father or not – forget his doubts – he resolved to call Fountain from the cellular phone in the Mercedes. Never mind the six-hour time difference between Switzerland and the Caribbean. Fountain was always on duty, faithful ever since the incident with Chiarra. The trustee had no choice, Trevor had made sure.

Turning the corner towards his car – and yes, he could remember where his chauffeur had parked it – he looked ahead to the car-park across from the railway station. But suddenly Trevor slowed his pace and abruptly came to a stop. For standing by a kiosk was the same tall man with the square jaw. He looked like a prize-fighter, yet he was dressed in a three-piece suit. Yes, it was the man who'd come up to him earlier as he was entering the coffee house, smiling cordially as an acquaintance would, asking if Trevor wasn't so-and-so from San Francisco.

Annoyed, Trevor had said, 'No, I am Trevor Thomson.' There had been nothing suspicious about the man's apology, nevertheless Trevor had immediately become angry at himself as he brushed past the man, hurrying off into the café to greet Kubler and the Count, for privacy and secrecy were his mottoes.

Then he recalled the puzzling phone call he had taken while his chauffeur was driving along the Swiss Riviera near Vevey on Lake Geneva. The conversation had started out in a normal way, the man saying he was a banker from San Francisco, but the man's voice turned hostile, demanding Trevor annul his bank leases. Trevor was enraged. Indignantly he had stated he would never comply with such a demand and promptly hung up.

He realized now the message had been a serious threat, warning if he didn't return some huge amount of money to the bank – what was the sum the caller had specified, ten billion? – the bank would have to take 'further action'.

And there followed a seemingly chance meeting with the short, plump woman who popped out of a low-slung Citroën at the petrol station in Brig. Reciting a nursery rhyme in a Bavarian accent, she confronted him with, 'You're not a very good boy, Mr Thomson, and you're going to have to put all your plums back in the pie.' She jabbed her car keys at him to make her point, and told him to comply with the demands made by his earlier caller. 'Or else,' she had added, the tone of her voice inflecting an obvious threat.

Surely, Trevor reasoned, the bank wouldn't stoop to violence. But he had second thoughts. Given the near insolvency of their balance sheet – the unpublished one revealing their illiquid condition, which they were concealing behind the façade of his leased skyscraper –

anything, even coercion, was possible. After their real-estate loan losses of the 1980s and early 1990s, he knew the directors were trying to buttress the bank's reputation of rock-solid stability. If they didn't act soon, hordes of customers could descend on the tellers, demanding more cash than an organized platoon of bank robbers. Trevor knew if such an enormous institution failed, public confidence in the economy, even the capitalist cosmos itself, would be severely shaken.

The stout woman had warned, 'I'll huff to the IRS and I'll puff to the CIA and I'll blow your clever little offshore trust across the Caribbean.'

He wondered how she knew about his trust. But, he reassured himself, with more than fifty havens world-wide, the California bank couldn't possibly know which one he was using. Unless . . . . He realized for them to gather such information, they would need to access his tax returns. So much for the IRS's heralded confidentiality.

Trevor began to feel those same apprehensions he had experienced in the World War I trenches in France. He sensed he was facing his biggest ever hurdle. One way or another he would surmount it as he had in France and with every obstacle since. Trying to cope with the crisis, his mind produced a blurred figure. It was Sam. Maybe his stepson was a link beyond the tunnel of death.

The man at the kiosk looked at him, their eyes communicating recognition. Quickly the man turned away. Focusing on his newspaper, he shifted it to hide his face.

The kiosk stood between Trevor and his car. As he started across the street, a speeding scooter, its horn blowing and its driver yelling what was obviously an Italian obscenity, bore down. Frantically he jumped out of its path, his heart beating rapidly.

The other man looked up at the commotion. Rolling his newspaper and gesturing as an old friend might, he stepped off the kerb and moved to meet Trevor.

The scooter incident and the man's movements shocked Trevor. He realized he had miscalculated. He should never have tried to cross the street with the man waiting there, and certainly not allowed himself to make eye contact. He now knew he must escape from this man.

Turning, he saw the entrance to the railway station facing him. It seemed to beckon. Trevor's adrenaline flowed. Bounding up its stairs, he saw a sign, 'Trains to Switzerland'. Another arrow pointed straight ahead. If he chose to follow it, taking a train across the border to Italy, the man could catch him at passport control. Descending two steps at a time, he made the decision to stay in Switzerland.

In the tunnel under the tracks, a sign at the second stairway announced, 'Lugano Express'. Luckily, the train was leaving in less than a minute. And Swiss trains are always on time, no matter what. Thankful he had continued his exercise regimen, he charged up the steps, emerging alongside a red InterCity express. Continuing his brisk pace, Trevor stepped up through the first open door and found himself in the dining-car, totally out of breath. He collapsed into the nearest available seat, even if it was in the smoking section.

Looking out of the window, he saw the guard wave his green and white disc towards the driver, and the train eased into its journey. He felt safe now, though he was drained of energy and his heart beat rapidly.

Numb, he stared absently at the passing countryside. The express, slowing but not stopping, passed through Mendrisio. He saw a bus waiting by the station, its destination marked 'Muggio Valley'. Trevor wondered what mysteries of life, what degree of bucolic solitude such a place, obviously remote from the world of finance and commerce, might offer. He imagined an idyllic valley with medieval stone farmhouses, barns, cattle and small gardens tucked amidst those daunting mountains he now saw rising to the north and east.

He noticed the colourful banner draped across the street, announcing the Mendrisio Easter Pageant, its artwork depicting a solemn procession, scheduled a few days hence. This pageant organized by local villagers ought to be a genuine community celebration, he thought. After ninety years, perhaps it was time he had a religious experience, especially if he was going to repent for his past aberrant behaviour.

The waiter was politely asking him for his order. He chose a beer.

The train sped along the edge of Lake Lugano. Though the bright afternoon sun reflected off the lake into his eyes, he could see its deep blue colour and watch the water lap at the gravel road bed. Together with the rocking motion of the train, the scene reminded him of his pirate galleon plying through the friendly, familiar waters of the Caribbean.

Slowly he sipped his beer, the cool liquid delivering relief from his stress and physical exhaustion. Still weak, he left the right amount of Swiss francs for the waiter. Standing, shaking a bit, he headed for a coach to find a seat, stopping to look out of the window at his favourite lake.

Outside Campione the express slowed to cross the bridge into Lugano.

Suddenly the tall man reappeared, ominously edging closer to Trevor. The woman from the petrol station, his accomplice, was behind him, dark glasses concealing her eyes and her intentions.

Taking charge, she said simply, 'I'll deal with this, Hubert.' To Trevor, her tone suggesting she should not be questioned, she said, 'I'm to witness your signature, Tom, Tom, the Piper's Son.'

On cue, the man called Hubert said, 'Yeah. Me 'n' Helga are from the bank. You're supposed to sign here.' He pressed a document forward.

Trevor felt the thin, sharp edges of its pages. He automatically accepted the ball-point pen which the man thrust at him, adeptly delivering its tip to the beginning of the signature line.

'Why another signature?' asked Trevor, confused, his mind hazy.

'The bank needs it,' Helga directed, her explanation as simple as a mother confirming to a child that it was bedtime.

'Sign.' Hubert repeated his earlier threat, 'Or else Helga and I will be forced to take further action.'

Trevor was afraid this bizarre couple had licence to murder him, and he was terrified.

He saw a crooked smile form on the woman's lips as she reached behind him, gripping the door handle. She must enjoy going to the brink, he foggily concluded. Yes, she and he had a lot in common – effective negotiators, actors playing on the edge.

But to his surprise, she actually turned the handle and pulled the door open. Fresh air hit, reviving him a bit, clearing his mind for a moment. He looked through the open door and saw the white gravel of the track flash past. Abruptly it ended, and there were only repetitious ties affixed to the bridge superstructure. And between, forty or fifty feet below, the blue waters of Lake Lugano.

'He's not going to sign, Helga,' the man said, almost in a whine.

Taking a step closer to Trevor, Helga said, 'Yes he will.' Hypnotically her eyes bored into Trevor's and she said, 'Won't you?' She added with a touch of ill temper, 'This dish is not running away with the spoon.'

Mechanically, pen in hand, his voice feeble, Trevor asked, 'What am I signing?'

Hubert said, 'You're simply changing the Statement of Wishes controlling your offshore trust, Mr Thomson – those instructions to your man Fountain.'

The woman said something about how a fraud would now be rectified by his cancelling the leases and refunding the rent money to the bank. In Trevor's fading vision, her face began to distort amorphously. He felt she was chewing her words and spitting them out at him in a medley of garbled demands.

Shaking his head vehemently, he repeated over and over, 'No, never, no, no!' He was afraid he was in tears as he explained, 'Those leases are my entire life. They're like children to me, my own children, my Sam and my Judith.'

He pleaded, hating himself for doing so, 'Please, my offshore trust is my life's work. It's irrevocable.' Losing control, Trevor repeated the word 'irrevocable' several times.

Raising his hand in protest, surprised at its sudden strength, he emphatically stated, 'You can't revoke my offshore trust any more than you can revoke the accomplishments of my life . . . .'

But now, his body fragile and frail with age, his mind burdened with the weight of memories, Trevor Thomson's strength ebbed. The fear of pain gnawed at him. He dropped the pen, or maybe he threw it, its ball point circling across the page as it left his hand.

The woman, a twisted smile locked onto her face, came towards him. And the man, Hubert, edged closer. Trevor stumbled backwards, trying to escape from both of them and the pain as well.

One of Lake Lugano's frequent passenger boats was passing underneath. He heard screams from sunbathers on the deck. With expressions of horror they looked up, watching as his body plummeted towards the lake.

The splash he made in Lake Lugano was the last thing Trevor Thomson felt before death engulfed him with its nothingness. But for one last brief instant he was happy again, for while it wasn't the warm Caribbean, it was water, and he had always loved the water.

1

Early spring is the best time of year for day hikes in Bandelier National Monument, the remote and mystical wilderness with its ruins and sacred Indian sites near Santa Fe. The snows have mostly melted but the searing heat of summer has not yet arrived to bake the mesas, where pygmy forests of juniper and piñon pine offer scant shade.

This morning the ringing from Penny Bailes's cellular phone not only alarmed her, it disrupted the concentration of the other hikers. Tucked into her daypack beneath lunch, an extra bottle of water, a sweater in case the high altitude weather turned chilly, and her rain poncho, the high-tech instrument emitted several rings before she could dig it out.

'Next time, zipper it into one of those outside pockets where you stow your water bottle,' a male hiker advised.

Maybe after she'd taken part in enough of these treks, Penny hoped, she'd get the drill down right. Embarrassed at the cellular's incessant ringing, she smiled, readily agreeing, 'Yes, Roger.'

'Get things out quicker, too, if you'd trim those long silvery finger nails of yours,' he said and laughed.

'When a woman is in the investment business – a man's field – she should emphasize her femininity,' Penny replied. 'Some men,' she added, looking askance at her companion, 'do appreciate women's little nuances.'

'You mean Sam?'

'Yes,' she smiled contentedly.

'Why doesn't he marry you then?'

'Marriage takes two, so why don't I marry *him*?'

'Because the couple who hike together never stay together?' Roger asked.

'Sam runs. I hike.'

'So, why wouldn't legalizing your arrangement work?'

'He's into books, history, the past, ignores the future.'

19

'Better answer your phone,' Roger advised.

Up ahead, their Germanic excursion leader had continued his gruelling pace, disappearing up the trail. Soon even Roger had left her behind, hurrying to catch up to the others. Penny recalled the leader had pointedly announced there would be respites only on the hour – no unscheduled stops for cellular phone calls, placed or received. The thirteen-mile march out and back was their assignment for the day. Penny was not superstitious, but she knew their destination, the Indian shrine known as the Stone Lions, was a tough challenge.

The phone's little antenna pointed towards the dark clouds floating overhead – fluffy and full of spring rain and, she worried, possibly lightning. The cellular might attract the electricity permeating the sky. In the interests of safety, perhaps life and death, she vowed to cut the call short.

Probably one of her clients, she speculated, who'd checked his Saturday *New York Times* and found one of his bonds dropped half a point. When would her investors realize, she despaired, A-rated bonds were for holding until maturity, not for trading.

'Penny Bailes.'

'Fountain here, calling from Turks and Caicos – Grand Turk Island – Cockburn Town, actually.'

Throughout her several years of both bedtime and balance sheet relationship with Sam, Fountain's name had seldom come up. In his role as Trevor's trustee, Fountain, she felt, dutifully performed in compliance with the legal statutes of the British colony of the Turks and Caicos Islands.

Penny recalled their only meeting, the time the black trustee came to Santa Fe. His task was to inspect Sam's new house before authorizing Trevor's Swiss banker – what was his name? Oh yes, Kubler – to pay out the money for its construction.

Caribbean islanders called themselves by their last name, a carry-over from British colonialism. But in Santa Fe everybody, even the super-wealthy, quickly came to a first-name basis. Sam said it was the four hundred years of written history and ten thousand years of unwritten prehistory. 'Humbled by this diverse heritage, they've dropped the façade of pretentious behaviour,' he would say, 'and are simply themselves.'

'Mr Thomson, please,' Fountain said, his voice demanding.

She wished, just this once, Sam had joined her on this hike. But, she reminded herself, Saturdays were for getting away from both him and her financial clients, her time alone, to herself. And Saturdays were also

20

Sam's for running in his races, the only thing he did rapidly. At forty he was even slow at making love. And as meticulous at it as his library research. Sometimes she felt she was another of his three-by-five cards being lovingly filled out. Even the books he'd authored on Spanish Colonial history had each taken years to write.

Dabbing at the perspiration on her forehead, Penny replied, 'Sam's doing a 10K race up to the radio towers.'

Silence and hesitation from the Caribbean. Confused as to what to say, Fountain uttered an 'ah' followed by more silence.

A frown formed on her forehead. Penny started to speak, but Fountain's voice came through, saying resolutely, 'In his absence, Miss Bailes, I must tell you.' She wanted to correct him with 'Ms' but didn't.

Yielding to the urge to join the others, Penny remounted her pack and resumed the hike, her stride steady, her strong thighs lifting her hiking boots with confidence. Snuggling the phone to her ear beneath her short dark hair, she began to jog slowly along the trail.

To Fountain she managed, 'What must you tell me?'

The trustee's curt reply, 'Mr Thomson's dead,' was as rude a slap at her as a tree branch springing back from a thoughtless hiker.

There was nothing else. No embellishment, no flowery language, no, 'I've some bad news'. Such a warning would prepare the listener for an announcement of death. But there was no, 'I'm sorry to tell you'. No, 'This may come as a shock'. Simply, 'Mr Thomson's dead.'

The thought of flowers flashed across her mind and she mumbled out loud, 'Flowers and death.' Flowers suggested life, blooms, colour, while death must surely be shrouded in a colourless void. Her next thought was to wire a dried floral arrangement to his funeral – fitting, for to her, old Trevor Thomson was, or had been, a long-living, flourishing weed.

Penny wanted to ask, 'How?' Or say, 'That's too bad.' Or philosophize with, 'Well, he did have a long and flamboyant life. How old was he anyway? Ninety?'

But she said none of the above, and Fountain continued, 'He fell off a train in Switzerland – into the lake – apparently after a heart attack. The captain of a tourist boat pulled him out.' The trustee paused and said, enviously she sensed, 'So, it is all yours now – that is, Sam's and Judith's. The money I mean – the wealth.'

Abruptly a jagged lightning bolt struck, zapping a tall ponderosa pine in the Jemez, but also snapping their satellite connection.

The smell of ozone permeated the air. At the same time Penny detected an aroma of resentment from Fountain. Both fragrances lingered as she thought about Sam's future.

For Penny, money had become the goal in life. Money and sex, the latter only after the stock market was closed for the day. And with the time difference in New Mexico it closed early afternoon.

She had attended business school, she could now admit to herself, as a rebellious act against her fanatical left wing parents. Their continual railing against the capitalistic system had translated into a sparse income, poor housing for her while she was growing up and a shortage of food on the table. Not so any more.

Now with Sam's inheritance her advisory fees would escalate. The thought of her income moving well into six figures excited her. Her decision to leave Wall Street and come to Santa Fe, at the time a whim for fresh air and clear skies, was actually going to work out quite favourably. Not bad for eight years out of business school.

She remembered how she'd met Sam on her daily walk one sparkling day in January. She'd come around the corner of the Palace of the Governors into the Plaza. He was sculpting a snowman in the shape of a Spanish conquistador. As he inserted a banner in its arm, Penny had boldly approached him, complimenting him on his artistry.

In one of his few spontaneous reactions, Sam promptly escorted her across the Plaza to the pastry shop in the La Fonda Hotel. Over decaf and a croissant he recited in a half-hour some four hundred years of Santa Fe history. He led her up Canyon Road past art galleries with snow-covered outdoor sculptures to his little studio apartment.

He was awfully horny, she remembered with delight. Maybe it was the fire of piñon logs he built for them in his kiva fireplace. Maybe it was the hot chocolate. Afterwards he remarked it was her magnificent thighs. Imagine. Thighs. For openers he'd hugged them, telling her he was adopting twin teddy bears.

She saw little in his studio other than a powerful and impressive word processor sitting atop his rickety desk-table. And filling his makeshift bookshelves was a library of old and valuable books. Those were the only subtle hints that he was heir to the Thomson billions.

Thinking about their future together, Penny was ready to bet her personal career would ride with Sam's fortune as a warrant instrument attaches itself to a corporate bond.

2

The window in Felicia Fountain's office was tinted to prevent those on the outside from seeing in. Yet from inside she could look out and view the street scene spread before her. Sometimes, especially today, she wished the tinting had been applied in reverse, for she was discouraged. The view never improved, only worsened.

Joanne, the girl in the outer office, called to her, 'Long distance, line one.' Almost immediately there was a second ring, followed by a distress yell from Joanne, 'The new head of the "Bloods" is on line two – mad as hell. Demanding more money.'

'What happened to Roosevelt?' Felicia's voice was full of worry.

'You didn't hear?' Joanne left her post and was quickly inside Felicia's office, remorse on her face, tears in her eyes. 'Gunned down last night by the "Crips" coming out of Fred's Minute Mart.'

Stunned, Felicia lamented, 'And I was beginning to get somewhere with him. I had a grant lined up for his . . . .' Her voice trailed off.

Joanne waited a moment and said, 'Better take the long-distance.'

As she reached to pick up her phone Felicia tried to make sense out of the random graffiti, the only fresh paint in the dismal blocks of austere, unkempt buildings making up her view. She was not impressed by those ultra-liberals who labelled the graffiti an art-form.

How could her brothers and sisters be so bent on negative acts such as destruction and defacing? The black and brown sprayed-on scrawlings blemished even those buildings still occupied, labelling the streetscape a ghetto as readily as a spire with a flashing neon sign. To potential investors and banks, those people and institutions with the capability of financing a rebirth of the inner city, the graffiti signalled instead a grim warning: 'Don't cross our borders'.

In her inner city, she deplored, there was no such capital available. Maybe one measurement of a people's progress is their understanding

23

of the abstraction known as finance. Testing, she said to Joanne, 'Do you know what finance is?'

'Sure, Ms Fountain, that's when you pays for somethin' and you ain't got da money.'

'But you're good for it. I mean, you've got income and you can pay the money back.'

'I got a job, you mean,' Joanne said with pride. 'Why, you need a loan?'

Felicia tried to chuckle, but couldn't. She replied instead, 'It's our neighbourhood. And it needs a whopping loan.'

'But it ain't got a job.' Joanne hesitated and said, 'Leastwise very many, so how can it repay a loan?'

Felicia said, 'Our game is capitalism. But here,' she gestured towards the outside, 'there are no chips with which to play.'

'Them grants from our foundation helps, don't they?'

'Precious little,' Felicia said. 'Only sprinkling a few raindrops in a desert. Moreover the money evaporates with bickering and misuse.'

Joanne looked downcast. Quietly she reminded her, 'Your call . . . .'

Felicia nodded, picking up the phone. She longed for investment capital to put to work in her inner city, and for the power to re-weave the fabric of the neighbourhood she viewed through her window.

'Felicia, it is Charles.'

Ever since she could remember as a little girl on the Caribbean island, her stepfather had always been 'Charles'. She never called him 'Father', for she held the title in contempt, equating it with the white man who had forced himself on her mother.

'The old man is dead,' was Charles's simple message, delivered unclothed in tender language.

News of the morning's second death brought less remorse. Instead she began to galvanize her thoughts.

From inside she watched a drug dealer in the alleyway across the street as he exchanged a small packet with an addict, tucking a wad of bills in his tight-fitting jeans. The scene overwhelmed her with frustration and she began to cry. All she could manage to say chokingly to her stepfather was, 'Charles, I'll be there.' Quickly recovering, and with the firmness a black woman learns to exhibit in order to live and survive in the tough inner city, she preceded her affectionate goodbye with, 'To collect what's rightfully due me.'

Ignoring the gang leader holding on the other line, Felicia punched out the number of her attorneys. Without polite small talk, she said, 'I've just received word of Trevor's death. We'll have a fight on our hands with those privileged adopted free-loaders of his. I want my rightful inheritance.'

Felicia stared at the street scene again and announced, 'My inner city and my foundation depend on us winning the fight.' She added, 'You and your partner get packed. We're flying to the Caribbean.'

3

Penny recalled Sam marvelling about the effect of aerobic exercise on his mind. He said it produced fresh ideas, unveiled new insights and inspired his thought process. So he carried a cellular phone while running, enabling him to call Penny when some new revelation dashed across his mind. Sam would pant out a seminal thought on what to her was some oblique aspect of Spanish Colonial history. And she'd humour him with an 'ooh' or an 'aah' and go back to analysing her bonds. Penny reminded herself normal runners don't jog with a phone.

Her reaction to exercise was just the opposite. It was a time to rest her mind, but this morning she understood what Sam meant. For trudging up from the depths of Frijoles Canyon, trying to catch up to the other hikers, Penny's mind wouldn't shut down.

At the top, the steep ascent behind her and the mesa-top trail now flatter, Penny increased her pace to a slow jog, the fastest she could maintain with a pack. She tried again to phone Sam but her cellular remained dead from the distant storm.

Knowing she must get the word of Trevor's death to him, she debated aborting the hike so she could return to her car and drive back to Santa Fe. But rules forbade her leaving without first seeking permission. If she didn't show up at lunch break, the leader would call out Search and Rescue inside thirty minutes.

She visualized the helicopters whirring overhead and expected to hear the symphony of sounds from the scouts – their whistles and their barking dogs as together they rummaged off-trail, looking for her in the endless canyons of Bandelier. And after an all-night search when they found her next morning safe in Sam's thick-walled adobe home eating blue corn pancakes, having left the hike without notifying its leader, she'd never be allowed to join another outing. Her unreliable reputation would spread around Santa Fe, risking the loss of some of her rule-abiding clients. Penny abhorred risk.

Arriving at the Stone Lions, Penny remembered Sam warning about intruding on sacred Native American sites. The other hikers were following such advice for they were voraciously munching turkey sandwiches outside the circle of chalky antlers and feathered fetishes surrounding the lions.

'Phone call?' the leader asked in a disapproving tone.

Penny nodded sheepishly. After a hungry bite into her sandwich, she tried the phone again, reasoning by now Sam should have finished his race, showered, eaten breakfast and be immersed somewhere in the library.

Perhaps it was the prickle of spicy mustard in her chicken sandwich or perhaps it was the crisp after-storm air, or a message coming to her from these stone lions, for she suddenly told herself Trevor's death could present the opportunity to advance to the next degree of coupling – marriage to Sam. But she'd have to do the proposing. Left to his own speed, Sam would only initiate more library research.

Sam answered promptly, 'Who is it? I'm in a quiet zone. No talking, not even on the cellular.'

'Sam, are you sitting down?' Penny asked.

'I'm in the rare books section trying to decipher a handwritten document narrating one of Columbus's voyages.'

She heard somebody on Sam's end command, 'Shh.'

Penny said, 'Sam, your life is about to change. You can no longer be a recluse hiding in the stacks. Listen to me.'

Penny visualized him running his fingers through dishevelled curly brown hair, a habit to assist his concentration. Often so engrossed in his documents, it took a while for him to change his mental channel. She hated talking to a man who wasn't listening.

His voice low, Sam said, 'The mysticism of the Stone Lions must be getting to you, Penny. You're pontificating again.'

'What do you mean?' Penny said, distracted from telling him the news about Trevor.

'I'm perfectly happy being what I turned out to be.'

'A hermit in a library?'

'I'm simply content with archival records. Why should I change?'

Peeved, Penny now blurted, 'Trevor's trustee, Fountain, just called . . . .'

'Old Trevor been off on another of his fishing trips?' Sam's chuckle was so soft she could barely hear him.

'His last,' she said caustically. 'If he was fishing, he leaned too far out of a train crossing some Swiss lake and fell.' Penny added with finality, 'He's dead. Fountain thinks it may have been a heart attack.'

'Dead!'

She was sure his exclamation ricocheted from stack to stack, probably out into periodicals. Penny didn't wait for the news to sink in. She spoke with hand movements and body language providing italics, punctuation and underlining. She said, 'Listen, Sammy, Trevor's death, though it's a watershed event, can't . . . mustn't . . . won't change our lives.'

Sam was silent as though he were examining a seventeenth-century letter for the first time, contemplating, considering, studying. She suspected he was adjusting his glasses, another of his nervous mannerisms.

Finally he reacted, 'But it will, Penny. Just think of our having to deal with that Swiss banker in Zurich, or is it Lugano?'

'Hans Kubler,' Penny said. 'The one who always signs the cheques. Don't worry about him, Sam, I can handle bankers, even if they are Swiss. He and I'll communicate in an international investment language.'

Sam said, 'Worse, there's Fountain, plus,' he hesitated, 'Felicia, who claims to be Trevor's daughter.'

'Ever met her?'

'No, but her attorneys'll try to prove she's his heir.'

'The important thing,' Penny pleaded, 'is for you and me, through whatever lies ahead, to stick together.'

'Stand united against Felicia, you mean.'

Trying to reassure herself, Penny said, 'I just know she's not his daughter.'

Silently Penny projected how her investment advisory fees would escalate, allowing her to add a high-tech satellite system to her already impressive array of electronic equipment and hire some assistants. And maybe she could manage Judith's half of the estate as well. Who else in Santa Fe, she thought, would be able to tap the London and Frankfurt exchanges and obtain instant quotes on such adorable investments as Danish government Eurobonds denominated in Japanese yen?

Yet Penny sensed how Fountain, with his authority to sign for the trust, could take advantage of Sam and Judith. If she were so inclined, she could do the same with her clients. Naturally, she wouldn't. Not only was it morally wrong but it was also quite illegal, and jail held no allure. But what are the values, she asked herself, guiding men in other countries?

Sam went on as if he were delivering a college lecture. 'You can't tell by looks, because when you mix races, characteristics blend. There's a discourse in my book about the ethnic mix of the peoples of Spanish

28

Colonial New Mexico.'

Sam was luxuriating in his historical knowledge, Penny thought, off on a tangent at a time when he should be thinking about the ramifications of Trevor's death and his own future.

He continued, 'In the sixteen-hundreds, Spanish officers married the daughters of Indian chiefs. Their children intermarried with newly arriving soldiers, some of whom were from Morocco.'

'Blacks from North Africa?' Penny said more in surprise than with any interest.

'Yes,' Sam said, 'and within a couple of generations a whole new colour code developed and nothing remained black and white.'

'How do you know? There weren't any photographs.'

'Drawings and written descriptions. No one knows the archives as I do.'

He paused and to her relief addressed more immediate matters. 'Remember the snowstorm when you read over Trevor's trust indenture? You said there would be no probate. So what difference does it make about Felicia? Trevor's offshore trust automatically transfers everything to me and Judith, doesn't it?'

'Yes, I think so,' Penny said, 'because trusts are a phenomenon of English common law, not recognized in Roman law . . . .'

'The Romans had no trust, you mean,' Sam said quietly, chuckling a bit.

'Under English law, Trevor's estate is a private matter with no legal filing in a court-house for other people to read or challenge,' Penny said, adding, 'but maybe we ought to ask Fountain if Roman law applies here.'

Serious, Sam said, 'Wasn't Trevor smart enough to figure it out? He wouldn't flunk many tests.'

'Even so, Felicia'll try anything,' Penny said. 'Don't discount her and her greedy attorneys. And I'm not sure about where Fountain's loyalties lie either.'

'What can he do? He's bound by the law, isn't he?'

'Which law? New Mexico or Turks and Caicos? Or his own? As far as I am concerned, he's in a position to rewrite the rules, his new version depending on that day's wind direction.' Penny added, 'I mean, suppose for some reason – or maybe there's a loophole – Felicia does upend the trust by proving she's his biological daughter . . . she'll get it all. And you and I and your beautiful sister Judith will be out in the cold of a Santa Fe winter howling along with all those other hungry coyotes because we – you and Judith, that is – aren't in Trevor's genealogical family tree. You know something else?'

'What?'

'We can't let Felicia get her hands on the body!'

'Oh, come on, Penny. Why should she want to touch a corpse?'

'I mean it. Think for a minute, Sam. Her lab people will conduct DNA tests and heaven knows what else. Even if the results prove negative, those attorneys of hers are probably being compensated on a contigency basis . . . .'

'You mean, a percentage of what she gets?'

'Yes, and visualizing a big carrot, they'll bribe anyone for favourable results, or fake them – whatever works. Moreover, we'll have to disprove their evidence. Think of the legal fees, the laboratory bills and doctors' opinions you'll have to pay. Furthermore, there'll be the anguish of it all.'

'They wouldn't act outside the law,' Sam said. 'It's more of your groundless worries. You're always fearing the worst, worrying about corporate disasters, natural or economic.'

'Don't kid yourself, Sam; in estates anything is fair. With money at stake, morals become redefined. Or else they fade as quickly as a wisp of smoke from a cremated body.'

'How awful,' Sam said. Pausing, he asked, 'Has Judith been called?'

'I forgot to ask Fountain.'

'My sister has to know,' Sam said insistently. 'I'll call her first, before I phone Fountain.'

'Try to get more details out of him,' Penny urged.

'Prying facts from Fountain isn't easy. But I'll try,' Sam assured her.

As he said goodbye, she heard him apologize to a fellow researcher for disrupting the library's quiet.

4

The Caicos banks, Turks and Caicos Islands, 1963

It was a pirate ship. At least it appeared to be. Not that anyone had ever seen a real one, only artists' renderings of pirate ships sailing the Caribbean on their missions of plundering and terrifying legitimate ships, captains, crews and ports.

And there were many accounts of legendary pirates, buccaneers who pillaged cities and raped women. Purportedly their origins could be traced to renegade French Protestants on Tortuga, an island north of Haiti near Turks and Caicos where they came to be known as *boucaniers* from their custom of cooking over an open fire, or *boucans* on the beaches – what the Indians called a *barbacoa*, or barbecue. Later they forsook their cook outs and took to ships, becoming the feared buccaneers. During the age of piracy there was even a woman pirate by the name of Anne Bonney.

So it was in character for Trevor to have hired both a marine architect and a boat builder to make over his large fishing vessel into a replicated pirate galleon. Had he been born two centuries earlier, Trevor would likely have been a real ocean-going pirate. Instead he became a financial one, both offshore and onshore, perhaps legal, perhaps not.

For where is the omnipotent judge who will render a truly unbiased verdict? And which country's laws will prevail? Who is to decide in the world of free-market financial imagination what is legal and what is not? Only attorneys and judges. And they could be bought with hard currency or favours, a point of view Trevor would freely share with those who came aboard his fishing boat turned galleon.

On these excursions he revealed his true mind set. Out there alone with him in the isolation of the Caribbean, a visitor could sense Trevor Thomson, as he relaxed on his ship, was as transparent as the shallow waters, forthright with his words and unimpeded in his actions.

Trouble was, most of those invited to come on board were not

31

business men who might themselves profit financially from his discourse. Instead they were women. And being in the Caribbean, often they were black. It was mostly with them he shared his thoughts, ideas, plans, even his business secrets, as he played at the games of fishing and sex, neither very well, but in each contest wanting his own way. The women knew it, but the fish didn't. The women usually complied, albeit giving him a bit of a fight. They made it playfully challenging for him. But the fish, beyond his jurisdiction, seldom performed to his pleasure.

On one particular excursion Trevor invited, or perhaps selected, Chiarra, an attractive girl-woman he had noticed working as a housekeeper in a hotel on Grand Turk. Lured by his reputation for wealth, she had eagerly consented to come.

Seeing the ship at the dock, she hoped for an adventure on the high seas. She might catch one of those big fish, maybe a blue marlin. And her voyage might even take a romantic turn, a man as rich as Trevor giving her some jewellery, perhaps talking sweetly to her, maybe going so far as to suggest she come back again. Dare she hope for romance across the racial barrier, or was it beyond her?

Once aboard, she asked him, her deep brown eyes wide as she showed a childlike admiration for him, how he had become such an important and rich man.

Trevor replied, 'You see, it was after I turned forty. One day I woke up to life's realities and vowed to win the financial game by becoming more clever than the next guy.'

'That's big talk, mon,' she said, still ogling him. 'None ma men friend are so clever.'

'Only way a man can get on top,' he said.

She ignored his lecherous look. 'But how were you clever, mon?' she asked.

His eyes still fixed on her, he said, 'Well, I owned this office building in San Francisco and leased it to a big bank.'

'Lotta money in da bank,' she said, drawing back as he clumsily tried to undo her bikini bra fastener. 'Here now, you don' do that,' she protested, trying to squirm away. 'Just 'cause I'm a black woman, don' mean I'm a loose woman, heah? You tell me more your story . . . .'

Backing off a bit, he continued, 'I told the bank they needn't pay me any rent.'

'Hey, mon, you ain' be no rich mon if you don't take in rent. You be stupid.'

Trevor laughed, the laugh of one who knows the solution to a

multidimensional rubric. And also the laugh of a man on his third beer.
'I made a different arrangement,' he whispered, moving up to her,
rubbing against her body, his mouth next to her ear. He ventured a
nibble before going on.

'Wha' you do?' she asked, moving her head away.

'I told them to simply pay me a tiny, tiny percentage of the deposits
they took in each month.'

'One per cent?'

'No, less.'

'Nuthin' less one per cent.'

He grinned and said, 'I told them, pay me one thousandth of one per
cent. "That's all you need pay," I said, "every month." '

'Tha' aint' nuthin',' she said, 'you must be broke by now. So how you
buy this crazy pirate boat, huh mon?'

Trevor continued, 'This particular vice-president considered himself
quite smart, because my thirty-year lease was going to save him a lot of
rent money, or so he thought. He convinced the president of the bank,
who wasn't much brighter, to go along with my terms.'

'I don' understand,' she said, becoming bored with the subject of
leases and money. A more important question filled her mind – what
was this rich old man going to do for her?

By now, having consumed several beers, they were using first names,
a real accomplishment for a black woman in the company of an older,
rich white man. Yessir, she was making progress.

Chiarra didn't realize there was a problem with the ship until Trevor
reacted. They were a few hours out of Cockburn Town when the
engines stopped. It was quite sudden. First, there was an orgasmic
shudder from deep down in the ship's hull. The make-believe galleon
slowed and soon came to a stop, beginning to drift.

Trevor knew the instant they shut down. His hand was caressing her
thigh as he related yet another episode of his business successes.
Suddenly his eyes and his attention left her and he spoke into the ship's
intercom which he always kept nearby, its cord draped across the
weathered plankings of the deck.

'Dead in the water,' was his disappointed acceptance of the captain's
muffled communication. 'Fix it,' he ordered. Hanging up, he returned
his attention to Chiarra, the boat matter having been dealt with. Or so
he thought. Before his hand could resume its mission, the intercom
buzzed. Irritated, Trevor shouted into the mouthpiece, 'What is it?'

Chiarra waited. By now the clouds had lost interest in the drifting
galleon, moving elsewhere and allowing the sun to beat down fiercely

without relief from the breeze, which had subsided with the almost motionless ship.

Staring blankly across the Caribbean, Trevor listened to the captain. But only briefly before he exploded, issuing instructions, 'Call the US Navy base on Grand Turk. Tell 'em to send a cutter to tow us across the banks to Provodenciales.' He added, 'I want to look at some bare dirt – a development property on Turtle Cove. Might as well take advantage of the opportunity. And send down my young accountant, what's-his-name, Fountain.'

Trevor moved closer, one arm embracing her, the other gesturing to punctuate his conversation. With each movement, his hand brushed her brief swimsuit. He fluffed one breast as if trying to make a bed pillow softer.

'Heah now, you leave me tits alone,' she protested.

Interrupted from making a long string of journal entries, Charles Fountain descended the ladder from the bridge onto their deck. Fresh and neat from being in his cooler cabin, the young man was resolute as he awaited Trevor's instructions. He said respectfully, 'You called, Mr Thomson?'

'Charles, they teach you at the University of London about fasteners on bras?' Trevor asked without hesitating, as if every business executive had an assistant who helped with such matters.

At first Fountain smiled, thinking the question a joke. But receiving no return expression of hilarity from either Chiarra or Trevor, the accountant's smile waned, his eyes narrowed. 'No, suh,' he said, hesitating, backing away from Trevor and Chiarra, concerned some bizarre drama was taking place. A play he wanted no part in.

'Your fingers are more nimble than mine,' Trevor said matter of factly. 'You don't have arthritis.' Looking at Chiarra, he ordered, 'Undo hers.'

Fountain, growing even more distraught, stuttered, 'No, suh, I cannot do that. No, suh.'

'Do it!' Trevor ordered.

Frightened, Chiarra tried her best to wiggle away.

'Now!' was the loud command coming from Trevor as he threatened the young accountant, implying consequences if Fountain didn't assist.

'But Mr Thomson, suh . . . ah . . . gentlemen should not, I mean do not . . . .'

Freeing herself from Trevor's grasp, Chiarra stood up from the chest of ropes and life-jackets on which she and Trevor had been sitting and started to run. With alacrity, Trevor grabbed her and flung her towards Fountain. Automatically the young man's arms extended to receive her and at the same time entrap her. Trevor repeated his order. Fountain complied. Chiarra's yellow halter fell to the deck, her large breasts, strong and expressive, dropping ever so slightly. Trevor's eyes stared at the nipples standing out from the fully rounded breasts of her tall and shapely black body. In their deep purple, they both defied and invited him.

The sight of them ignited him. The fire in his eyes was as bright as a pirate's torch touched to a galleon's wrought-iron cannon. The anticipated spoils of his forthcoming pillage filled his mind, tantalizing, luring, compelling.

Trevor pulled at her bikini, tearing it off.

'Hold her tight, Charles,' the tycoon orderd, 'while I affix my signature. And you, then, must sign as a witness.'

'But Mr Thomson, suh . . . .'

'Shut up and do your job,' Trevor shot back.

Fountain was strong for an accountant. He had been on the rowing team. Crewing strengthens the upper body, and the lower, and the middle, too. Fountain easily contained Chiarra, her struggles useless, her cries for help unanswered. For even if they had been heard, who was aboard the pirate ship who might even think of interfering?

Her belief Fountain might be carrying out an unwilling assignment wasn't any help to Chiarra, who now waited in fright, vulnerable, for Trevor to consume her. Trying to avoid his impending penetration, she moved her pelvis from side to side, but her legs were held by Fountain's and her arms pinned back by his.

Her breasts protruded, resembling ripe tropical fruit, her nipples awaiting Trevor's slobbering mouth, his tongue licking wet lips behind which were bared two rows of perfect teeth.

His trunks, with one swift, adept move, as if he had practised the manoeuvre many times, now fell to his ankles.

'Mon,' she screamed, 'why don' you be nice to me?'

'Niceties are for tea-parties in the Governor's mansion,' he said as his hands grabbed her breasts. Any additional words of justification, explanation or further rationalization were lost as his mouth engaged the first of its targets.

As Trevor attacked, perspiration flowing, and eventually consummated his capture, his eyes locked on those of a reluctant Fountain, the two men remaining in intimate visual contact during the ultimate male moment.

Fountain would never forget those blue eyes, full of fire, boring into his, and the furrowed frown as Trevor's rape was carried out.

From behind, Chiarra felt Fountain's erection through his trunks, and fleetingly wondered if he, too, would take her.

But afterwards, when Trevor was no longer around, there was Fountain's embrace saving her from collapsing on the deck, his hands helping to reclothe her naked, aching body, his words of apology in his acquired English accent trying to comfort her in her humiliation. And later, thankful for Fountain's kindness, she fell asleep in the safety of his tiny stateroom.

5

Provodenciales Island, 1963

It was the next day by the time the pirate ship was towed across the fishing banks to Provodenciales. Composure had settled aboard Trevor Thomson's expedition. Trevor himself was interested only in the enlarging shoreline as he stood at the rail and watched the approaching land with his large topographical map unfurled, jotting notes as he fantasized about making money off the virgin real estate.

Chiarra avoided him, hovering next to Fountain as much as his duties would allow. By now she deduced he had something to do with keeping track of Trevor's money.

Once, she thought about going to the police when the boat docked and lodging a charge against Trevor. But she realized even if she found any sympathy among the all-male force, they'd still believe Trevor. If questioned at all, he would offer his own version of the episode, saying she had invited his intimacy. And everyone on board ship would support him, except perhaps Fountain.

She wondered what Charles would say, how he would reply to the police. But somehow she didn't want to test him, feeling he was her only protection. But if he was forced to choose between her and Trevor, between truth and his promising career following his university education, well, she'd understand. Good jobs for blacks were few, and losing his, especially as he was in Trevor's employ, would mean a bad reputation, no references – never getting a second chance in this white man's world.

So Chiarra said nothing, not even when the police chief, attired in full red, white and black formal dress, accompanied by the mayor of Provodenciales, welcomed Trevor as he set foot on their island dock.

'Allow us to show you the site for our proposed international airport,' she heard the mayor say to Trevor. 'We've finally received the funding commitment from the Pan-American Development Bank.'

'We'll drive you out the Leeward Highway, show you the land you can develop into vacation homes and luxury hotels,' the police chief obsequiously added. He bowed and gestured towards a parked four-wheel-drive vehicle with the official crest of the Turks and Caicos Islands; another uniformed policeman was waiting, inviting, holding the door for them.

She heard the mayor say, 'We have no island income taxes, Mr Thomson. And we can probably waive property taxes for a few years.' Playing the role of an eager salesman, he added, 'And there are no currency restrictions on US dollars moving in and out of the country. What else can we do for you?'

And they left, Charles tagging along, taking notes, ready, she felt, to record Trevor's every question and the answers supplied by the local authorities. Damn him, she thought, rage surging within her. Damn him and damn Trevor, damn the lot of them. What if I'm pregnant? Leaving in the police vehicle goes the man with all the money in the world, and there'll be not one black or white penny from him for me and my baby.

Chiarra worried about her job as she realized, looking at the ship's clock, she should have been at work hours ago back on Grand Turk. Instead she was a hundred miles away aboard a dead ship.

The coastguard cutter was leaving. She thought about trying to hitch a ride on it. She moved her arm in the air, trying to signal for help, but received only waves and whistles from the sailors.

She saw the hand-scrawled sign nailed crookedly to a light post on the dock: 'New! Turks and Caicos Charter Flights'. The sign promised the airline would fly passengers to any of the islands.

In her tattered yellow bikini and top, carrying her little purse, she walked off the pirate ship, half expecting Trevor to reach out from somewhere and grab her, pull her back, rape her again. But he had left and she was free of him, yet would never be free from the memory of his abuse.

From the dock several men eyed her. One was white and wore a shirt with shoulder epaulettes. He shouted to her, almost mockingly, 'Plane ride, baby?' Chiarra ignored him, but he called again, 'On our new national airline?'

Why not? She must get to her job. She smiled and asked, 'Where ya go?'

'Where do you want to go?'

'Gran' Turk.'

38

'Come with me, we'll leave right away.'

'How much money, mon?'

He pulled the cigarette from his mouth and flipped it into the water. His eyes examined her scantily-clad body. Gesturing at her bikini, he taunted her with, 'How much you got tucked away in your bra?'

He came closer so he wouldn't have to yell and said, 'My name's Bill, one of the new pilots. I'm due to drop some cargo in Salt Cay. It's loaded on board, so we can take off right away.'

'But da fare?'

'Don't worry, we'll work it out. Let's go.'

He led her along a dusty, crumbly limestone path past a pair of guinep trees, their little green fruit not yet ripe, for she tried one and it was still bitter. Pretty soon they came to a dirt strip and she saw tyre marks made, she presumed, by the wheels of landing planes. At the far end rested a little airplane, its propeller idle.

Chiarra must have looked frightened for Bill asked, 'Ever been up before?'

'Into da sky, up there?' She pointed upwards and laughed nervously, her white teeth shining in the midday sun. 'No, never been.'

'You climb up here on the wing. I'll get the door.'

Bill helped her inside, both hands firmly on her fanny and legs, steadying her on a small protruding step. He guided her bare foot onto the proper spot on the wing and slipped her into the craft. Inside, there were four seats.

'You can sit in the co-pilot's seat,' he instructed.

Hesitatingly she did.

He strapped her in with the seat-belt, his white hands continuing to handle her. She tried to squirm away.

Bill pushed a button on the control panel and the engine turned over, the propeller beginning its whirl.

He checked a few dials, observed the orange wind sock, taxied, revved the engine, and they began to move down the rough runway.

Lifting off, she felt a sudden panic. But the plane was airborne and she looked down on the receding earth below. Feeling a little bit more relaxed, she noticed the four-wheel-drive police vehicle with Trevor and his entourage standing by it. The mayor was pointing up the short runway showing him where the bulldozers would extend the landing strip. Beside them, she saw Charles busily taking notes.

Flying out over the Caicos Banks, she and Bill were alone, their little plane popping into and out of patches of cloud. Clear water appeared intermittently below. Beneath, the coast-guard boat, poking along, was soon left behind.

Chiarra said, 'You can see da ocean bottom.'

'Yeah,' Bill replied, 'water's pretty shallow on the banks, but over there the bottom drops off, goes thousands of feet down. These islands are plateaus rising from a deep underwater plain. Raise the water level of the Caribbean a few feet and there'd be no islands left around here. Lower it a few feet and there'd be a lot more.' Laughing, he returned to his instruments, recording their readings on official-looking forms attached to a clipboard.

They flew in silence for a while as Bill set a compass or something and twiddled with more dials.

'You work in Cockburn Town, don't you?' he asked. 'I've seen you there.'

'Island small, know almost everyone live there,' Chiarra said and smiled, 'but you new, never seen 'fore.' She added, 'I late for work, need get there fast.'

'Our airline has just been chartered by the government. I signed on last week to fly one of the planes. None of the locals know how to fly, and we hope to get a lot of charter flights.'

'You got work permit?'

'Yes, the special skills of a pilot,' he said, placing his hand on her bare black leg. And he laughed again. Nervously, she thought.

Soon he pointed down and said, 'There's our destination, Salt Cay. You can see Grand Turk a few miles to our left.'

She had never been to Salt Cay. Few people, unless they worked the salt flats they were now flying over, ever went there. The plane was approaching what she hoped was a landing strip. She saw an old stone building below, and a little church and a handful of tiny houses. Bill brought the craft down on the short dirt runway, a cloud of dust trailing their arrival.

Quickly after touchdown, Bill pressed the brakes and threw a few switches on the control panel. The craft bumped along rapidly – too rapidly, Chiarra feared, the end of the short strip fast looming. Terrified, she screamed, but the plane stopped with a few feet to spare, in front of a rocky sea-wall.

Bill patted her on the thigh and said, 'Well, baby, we made it to Salt Cay. You've been initiated into air travel over the Caribbean. It's a thrill, isn't it?' He didn't remove his hand.

She saw no Salt Cay people. There was no terminal building with waiting passengers. No one. There was only silence after he shut down the engine. Instead of getting out of the plane to unload his cargo, Bill turned towards her and said, 'Time for another thrill.'

His jaw was set and his tongue ran along his lips, wetting them. She was suddenly cold. Her muscles tightened. She clamped her eyes shut and shuddered, praying she wasn't going to be hurt again.

She heard him unbuckle his seat-belt; hers was still tightly strapping her in. She felt him on top of her. His hands cupped her breasts, hard and painfully, his sweat dripping down into her face and stinging her eyes. The pungent smell of his white body revolted her and she wanted to vomit, but her throat was dry. She struggled, but couldn't get loose from him or the entrapping seat-belt.

He pulled a lever somewhere and her seat tilted back, and she was fully underneath him. All she heard him say as she screamed and continued to physically protest, was, 'You wanna get back to Grand Turk today? Keep your job? Then behave yourself, ya' hear?'

This time there were no witnesses.

6

***

Sam took off the white viewing gloves required to handle historic documents and returned the primary-source letters to the librarian. Leaving the Palace of the Governors, he donned his stetson and walked along the building's portico, where the Indians squatted on blankets presenting their silver and turquoise jewellery to tourists.

Penny's phone call with news of Trevor's death and her prediction his life was about to change had shocked him into thinking about his future. His senses were already hyperventilating from the stimulus of his ardudous mountain race. He needed an aid station, or better, he needed the comfort of a family.

Most people belonged to families with mothers and fathers, but he was a stepchild who never saw his real father, could recollect only a few years of his mother, and never really knew his stepfather.

He crossed Palace Avenue, dodging the cars, and entered the Plaza. He chose a bench beside the weather-worn American Civil War monument. The Confederate flag had flown here for two weeks in 1862.

The spectre of Spanish conquistadores riding into the Plaza four hundred years earlier danced across his mind. He envisioned their banners trailing in the wind and their horses snorting at the Indians, the strange unfamiliar beasts frightening the Native Americans half to death.

Oh, Sam pined, to be transported by a time machine. To travel back – observing the first intrepid colonists as their oxen arrived from Mexico pulling their crude wooden *carterras* laden with essentials to begin their new colony.

Yes, Sam thought, he and Trevor did have something in common. Each of them would have ridden with those early explorers, Trevor to exploit, seeking gold, scheming to siphon it off from its lawful destination – the Spanish king and his royal court. And he, Sam, to learn the story of what actually took place when European civilization first

42

confronted the culture of these American prehistory peoples.

Sam recalled an earlier visit to the city when he and Judith had sat on the same bench in the Plaza and decided to return to live in Santa Fe, their childhood home. Perhaps the lure was the mud houses, or maybe it was the absurdity of the dirt streets. But for Judith it was the music, the art, the prestige of it all. For her it was a belonging, a warmness they had been without during their parentless upbringing.

His reminiscing was interrupted by the distinctive music of the *mariachi* street band, the melodious sound from its brass instruments and guitars filling the Plaza.

Too noisy here to telephone, so he crossed the Old Santa Fe Trail and bounded up the stairs to the roof garden of the La Fonda, the inn at the end of the trail. From there he could see the still snow-capped Sangre de Cristo Mountains looking down on the Cathedral of St Francis, protecting Bishop Lamy's nineteenth-century architectural concoction.

His mind floated back again. He was a little boy and Trevor was standing over him, speaking. A smaller Judith, her blonde hair tumbling over her shoulders, was clutching his hand as she stood crying by his side. It was autumn in Santa Fe and the white-barked aspen up on the mountains were as golden as Trevor's wedding ring flashing from the bright sunlight as his hand passed in front of Sam's face. Trevor's hand rested on Sam's little shoulder, unremovable, squeezing too hard and too unfatherly.

From overhead Trevor's deep voice reverberated down. 'Samuel, my boy, your dear mother has gone to her reward in heaven. Before she left she asked me to take care of you and Judith . . . financially.'

Sam hadn't known what 'financially' meant, but he knew it didn't mean playing football, or taking walks in the snow together, or picking apples from one of the orchards along the Rio Grande in late summer. And Sam had begun to cry, returning the lonely squeeze from Judith's hand. He remembered feeling lost. He had no mother, no father, and now there was a strange man whom he had seldom seen and barely knew grasping his shoulder. He wanted to die, to take Judith with him, to travel with his mother to this 'final reward' place, to see her again, to laugh with her and feel her love. In the peace of a faraway and serene place he might find his real father. And there Judith could grow to become as beautiful as her mother.

After his mother's funeral and with only a strange stepfather who had promptly left, Sam realized he and Judith would be emotionally on their own. Afterwards they only heard from Trevor when there was a change of governesses. So Sam vowed he would always look after Judith. And he had. And Judith had grown up to be as pretty as he remembered their mother.

Sam often wondered how his mother had managed to trick old Trevor, not telling him she had two little children, and later presenting them as darling little surprise wedding presents. Perhaps Trevor had always wanted children, and Lillian had an intuitive feeling he would accept her children.

Sam punched out Judith's mobile number. She promptly answered, readily volunteering without waiting to find out who was calling, 'I'm in my red Range Rover, driving to La Tierra.'

Sam laughed, amused at his sister. In her mid-thirties, she had had no enduring relationships with men. Material possessions and the impressions they broadcast were important: imported cars, an adobe home on ten acres in a chic new development, its interiors furnished in Santa Fe style and adorned with Acoma Pueblo pottery and contemporary art from the right local galleries. Outward expressions of culture and wealth announced the social heights to which she had risen, reinforcing her self-esteem, difficult enough to nurture when a woman has grown up an orphan.

Likely, he thought, she'd spread the news of Trevor's death and her inheritance to her Opera Guild circles. Given the size of her half of the estate, she'd be invited to sit on the prestigious board of the School of American Research, joining select others of the world-class rich.

'Pull over on the shoulder,' Sam gently instructed as if he were a highway patrolman, 'we've got to talk.' He added slowly, 'I've important news.'

'Sam!' she said, recognizing her brother. 'But I'm late for an Opera Guild meeting, twenty, thirty people coming in . . .' she paused and he could almost see her looking at her Rolex, 'forty minutes. . . . To plan next year's fund raising. Did I tell you, we'll be staging the first-ever opera from Africa – and by a composer with AIDS?'

'Be late. My news is more . . .' he groped for the right word – Judith respected proper vocabulary – '. . . more momentous than your charity.' He added lovingly, 'Lil' Sis.'

'OK, but be quick,' Judith said, echoing his affectionate tone. Giggling, she added, 'But save me from professorial prefaces incorporating centuries of Southwest history . . . .'

So Sam, measuring his words, told her, 'I have just received word Trevor died earlier today.'

Immediately he heard the gravel on the road churn as Judith brought

44

her expensive vehicle to a stop. In Santa Fe prestigious roads were always gravel.

Sam could almost see her reach up, sweeping her silky blonde hair away from her face. He heard her exclaim, 'Jesus, Sam, now we're really rich, not just a lot more rich, but whopping internationally rich.'

After a pause, she said with delight, 'Think of the charitable causes I can champion. I'll set up a foundation for the homeless, another to fight alcoholism on Indian reservations, and,' she thought only for a second before adding, 'one to save the rain forests. I'll become known as the czarina of non-profit organizations. Think of the good I'll do: health clinics, schools for the retarded . . . .'

Her voice drifted into the amorphous orbit of doing good for others. She was anticipating the accolades she would receive from socially prominent locals unable to match her monetary mettle. Sam suspected his sister's altruism was a reaction against Trevor's aloofness. She was supplying affection for others, trying somehow to replace the love she felt was missing from her own upbringing.

Sam explained, 'Fountain called. Trevor fell from a train in Switzerland into Lake Lugano.'

There was an unexpected silence. Judith, sounding as if she were choking back tears, said, 'Poor Trevor . . . .'

Annoyed, Sam reacted, 'Bullshit, "poor Trevor". He was ninety, thirty of which he didn't deserve, giving us a lousy upbringing.'

'But paid for,' she reminded, sniffling. 'Besides, death for anyone is never deserved, no matter how good or bad they've behaved. So I've helped form the Committee to Eliminate the Death Penalty.' Judith added, 'Trevor was quite a prestigious man, you know . . . and now he's dead.' Without pausing she asked, 'Where's the funeral? Switzerland? Or on one of those remote Caribbean islands – what're they called?'

'Turks and Caicos,' Sam answered. 'But I don't know yet. I'm about to call Fountain. I suppose Trevor's instructions will be in his living will.'

'Living?'

'Penny says with a trust, you don't have a normal will – avoid probate. But you do have a living will, setting forth your last instructions – such as not wanting to be kept alive by some machine when you can no longer cheat people out of their money.' Sam forced a sarcastic laugh.

Judith quickly admonished with a loud, 'Sam!'

'And where and how you want to be buried, or cremated, or fed to the crocodiles, or whatever,' he added.

'But what about the offshore trust now that Trevor has passed away?'

'Penny says it's pretty simple.'

'But why did he set it up in such a faraway little place?'

'Apparently he feared creditors and attorneys.' Sam paused, adding, 'And Penny says there are laws in those offshore places protecting privacy. As in your love affairs.' Sam laughed. 'You never tell me about them,' he chided. 'Although during last season's opera you were trying to learn Italian.'

'My business, Big Brother. He was a renowned tenor.'

'I suppose Trevor wanted secrecy, too. Penny says down there it's a criminal offence to even reveal the existence of a trust.'

'Do you mean you can't talk about trusts at cocktail parties?'

'Right,' Sam said. 'But I almost forgot, Penny says since the trust is offshore it is immune from the IRS's long tentacles. Think how much he's saved in taxes down through the years. I mean, the amount is beyond my little calculator's range. And Penny says there are no island income taxes in Turks and Caicos.'

Judith honked the Range Rover's horn in exclamation, and said, 'We'll charter a plane and fly there.'

'They have scheduled airlines. It's a long way across the endless Caribbean.'

'Find out the plans.' Judith thought for a moment and said, 'I hope the funeral's in Switzerland. Lovely weather in the spring, and I'd enjoy sitting in on another board meeting of the International Red Cross in Geneva.'

Sam heard the engine rev as Judith dismissed him with, 'Call me,' adding, 'after my Opera Guild meeting.'

7

Sam searched his wallet for Fountain's number, finding it scribbled on the back of his pass to the University of New Mexico's valuable historic book collection.

Given their infrequent and perfunctory conversations over the years, Fountain remained an enigma to Sam. The trustee seemed detached, impersonal, not sharing Sam's quest for introspection. Yet he appeared fair and just in carrying out his duties. Before talking to him, Sam tried to figure out Fountain's baffling personality.

Their different academic disciplines, accounting and history, might explain some of Fountain's idiosyncrasies. Fountain's career was related to balancing numbers and, Sam suspected, there was little room for exploration. In accounting you either balanced or you didn't.

Geographically and culturally he and Fountain were also at odds. Fountain's Caribbean island with its English heritage reflecting proper comportment contrasted with the American Southwest and its relaxed behavioural patterns. So, Sam concluded, it was logical he and Fountain would approach matters with their own individual cadence.

In his position as trustee, approving the funding for Sam and Judith, Fountain adhered to Trevor's Statement of Wishes, which he would cite the same way a preacher would quote a familiar chapter in the Bible.

Trustees, Sam learned from Penny, had power, legally and about any way they wanted to exercise it, subject to the Statement of Wishes. She was an expert in estate planning, wills, investment strategies – all those esoteric subjects inviting financial planners such as Penny to winter-in, warming themselves with fees as they burrowed into rich clients' billfolds and purses.

Sam guessed he should know about such matters, too, but by the time he'd finished his research, taught his classes in Southwest history at UNM Extension, he'd rather go run. Or pursue his other delight, gourmet cooking.

He had last met Fountain when he requested funds from Trevor's trust to build his home overlooking Santa Fe. In response, Fountain had come personally to verify the plans for the house before authorizing the Swiss banker to make the payment. The visit had been polite, curt and businesslike, affording few answers to satisfy Sam's growing curiosity about Fountain.

Sam and Penny were, however, delighted with Fountain's approval. It ushered in an exciting time in their life. Sam remembered an October Sunday afternoon during the framing stage. In their golden yellows, the aspen covering the Sangre de Cristos shone through the two-by-four wood studs in the wall-to-be. The two of them snuggled next to the roughed-out kiva fireplace in the breakfast nook-to-be, imagining a fire from aromatic piñon logs warming them. They'd drunk a bottle of New Mexico red wine and nibbled organic blue corn chips and what must have been aphrodisiac salsa. For after an erotic rolling romp in a pile of swept-up sawdust, she suggested moving in with him when the house was completed.

And she had, bringing with her cases of female cosmetics plus her array of communications equipment: modems with faxes and even a satellite dish for communicating with financial markets.

After Penny installed herself, Sam began to feel it was he who had moved in with her, for his library, as well as his own private space, paled in square footage to her acquired territory. She dominated the living room, setting a stage for casual but serious business meetings with clients.

Some days, with the whirr and the whizz of global investing resounding throughout his house, he longed for his studio apartment on Canyon Road with its nearby art galleries and coffee houses. Building the house suggested he had bought into the value system of the wealthy from places such as Los Angeles, Dallas and New York who were moving to this remote mountain town. And no matter how much money he spent on his house he hadn't been able to replicate the camaraderie he'd felt living in a neighbourhood of artists and writers.

But now Sam forced himself to pick up his cellular phone and punch the international access code, the country code and even for the tiny island, the trustee's seven-digit number.

Via satellite connection a voice greeted him with a matter-of-fact, 'Fountain here.'

Trying to begin, Sam stumbled out, 'Ah, Mr Fountain, this is Sam Thomson calling. Ah . . . Trevor's son . . . .'

'Step,' Fountain said, instantly correcting, his tone suggesting there was something quite improper about not being biologically related. Sam cringed. 'Step.' In a Pavlovian reaction he felt the knife go in, penetrating his self-esteem once again. His real father had run off somewhere, or died before Judith was born, or perhaps had been a suicide, and out of shame his mother had concealed such an untidy tidbit of family information. Or perhaps he'd run off with a local barmaid. Whatever, his mother had never revealed the true story. Each time he inquired, as a little boy will, her answer was either a new and different story or else she shrugged off his question.

So when the subject of marriage came up with Penny, he would try to offer some simple excuse, backing off, for forming a family meant thinking about having children. And he asked himself, how could a couple take on the responsibility of raising children? Surely their demands would effectively rewrite one's personal agenda. Maybe he and Penny would some day split. Who would care for the kids?

Sam pulled the knife out, recovering his self-esteem, and replied to the trustee, 'Penny told me about Trevor's death . . . .'

'Yes, your stepfather is quite dead.'

The tone of voice in which Fountain confirmed the news made Sam feel guilty. Maybe he had brought about Trevor's death himself across thousands of intervening miles. There had been those times he'd imagined doing his stepfather in, but imagining and doing are miles apart.

'Heart attack, apparently. I told Miss Bailes.'

'Penny is Ms Bailes,' Sam interjected, punctuating the 'Ms'. 'We . . . ah . . . live together . . . aren't married . . . ah yet.'

He thought he heard Fountain's tongue click. The trustee continued, 'Authorities must perform an autopsy.'

Sam read into the trustee's tone a wish for revenge. And he wondered if Fountain was sadistic enough to want to be the one, instead of the examining forensic pathologist, or coroner – or whatever they had in Switzerland – to insert the sharp knife in Trevor's dead white body under the guise of establishing the cause of death.

Penny's advice about preserving the DNA, the tell-tale signs of genealogy, flashed across his mind.

Fountain said, 'His body was in the water only a few minutes. The captain tried to breathe life back into him. I understand he is properly trained, licenced, you know, both by the Swiss and the Italians in CPR emergency procedure.'

Sam asked, 'What're we going to do about a funeral, the body, and

49

the . . . ah . . . final arrangements?'

'You have not read his living will?'

Sam said, 'What's it say?'

'Your stepfather wanted to be buried here on Grand Turk. He developed an affection for this little island.' The trustee went on, 'But, as trustee I feel obliged to advise you to get down here and protect your personal interests. Other people are trying to get their hands on his trust and everything else. In fact, they started in several months before his death.'

'I thought it was against the law to pry around, asking questions without a court order from your court there? At least, I believe Penny said so.'

'Yes,' Fountain said, 'but when there are so many sniffing noses, the local police cannot arrest them all. Our tiny jail is already full of Haitians.'

Sam thought he heard Fountain snort.

The trustee went on, 'But as soon as we arrest one of these prying bankers or the private detectives they have hired, a half-dozen more fly in on next week's flight from Miami. The influx is prompting our immigration officials to question everyone, even snorkelers and those marine salvagers searching for shipwrecks.

'These bankers have become quite clever in their quest, posing as tourists, real-estate developers, fishermen. One even tried to make us believe he was a marine archaeologist. You can identify a banker from ten feet away. Just look into their eyes – most are icy cold. Except, of course, for Hans Kubler. He is a cut above – the reason your stepfather chose him.

'And you can spot the archaeologists, for once off the plane and coming down the stairs, they light up, their hands shaking from being deprived during the three hour no-smoking flight. I suspect they even smoke underwater during their excavations.'

Sam's curiosity arose about the underwater explorations. Before he could inquire, Fountain continued, 'So now our police interrogate every passenger. The other day they locked up an IRS agent who was impersonating an offshore trust client. He thought he could trick us accounting professionals into self-incriminating admissions of tax-avoidance by posing as a tax-dodging American. Foolish, for I thought by now every American realized the long arm of the IRS reaches world-wide.'

'What happened to the agent?' Sam asked.

'When they found out he was IRS, the police immediately released

50

him. But everyone had been alerted, so all he could do was go snorkelling until the next flight out. He returned home empty-handed and heavily tanned.'

'What are these . . . ah . . . bankers after?' Sam asked.

'Your money, I should think,' Fountain replied.

'But why?' Sam's puzzlement mingled with a tinge of fright.

'It is a lot of money.'

Sam asked, 'You know his money. But did you know Trevor well?'

'Who knows who well these days?' Fountain replied. He added, 'My role as trustee is impersonal – not the same as a friend. But I did have a business relationship with your stepfather over a long period of time. So if you want my advice,' Fountain said and paused.

'I do,' Sam said at once.

'Get down here along with your sister and attend the funeral, assuming his remains arrive from Switzerland via the weekly flight from Miami.'

Sam agreed, nodding to himself.

'Oh, and one other matter,' Fountain added, 'you and your sister should file a claim for Mr Thomson's life insurance. The policy is written for a substantial amount. You are each beneficiaries.'

'Uh, yes,' Sam said, not having a clue as to how to go about it.

Before Sam could ask, the trustee said, 'Yes, my advice, Mr Thomson, is to button up your inheritance before something or everything goes awry.'

'The trustee speaking?'

'Yes, I have a legal responsibility under Turks and Caicos law to advise you.'

Sam now knew his future depended on finding out what was really about to take place on a little island in a remote corner of the Caribbean.

51

8

The life insurance company insuring Trevor Thomson was public-relations proud of its architecturally designed skyscraper in Century City. The corporate PR people were fond of reciting its towering strength. Yet its reflective glass façade hid its real internal strife from public view. Recently, hoping to recoup cash drained off by its mounting junk bond losses, which paled the troubles of its rapidly soaring real-estate loan portfolio, it had mortgaged to the hilt, wringing as much cash as it could out of the building's land, steel, aluminium and glass plus its adjacent concrete parking garage.

The fresh dollars provided relief for its negative cash flow – but only temporarily, according to Debra Datsun, armed with an MBA degree from Stanford, thanks to a scholarship programme for Asian-Americans. Her job was to project the company's cash-flow requirements.

This morning Debra paid no attention to formalities or the hierarchy of the company's organizational chart. Even before nine o'clock, the beginning of regular office hours, she barged into the president's office, interrupting a 'planning meeting' he was having with his secretary, Gladys, a meeting requiring them to get their heads, and bodies, quite close together.

'Mr Lloyd,' Debra blurted, 'we've got to scotch this latest death claim or it'll be the company!'

Embarrassed and blushing, Gladys retreated.

Debra went on, 'This old man Thomson's policy is for fifty million,' and she added, scrutinizing Gladys, 'an amount that would pay her salary for years to come.'

Trying to referee, Lloyd said, 'Wait a minute, girls.' Looking at Debra, he said, 'I guess we better hear about this new claim.'

'It's a fifty million dollar crisis. To meet it, I suggest you consider unloading our entire real-estate loan portfolio on some unsuspecting Wall Street brokerage house.'

'So, if we sold the portfolio, how much would we get in real money?' Lloyd asked as he poured himself another cup of coffee from the thermos on his desk, not bothering to offer any to Debra or Gladys.

'Those Wall Street men might pay us as much as ten cents on the dollar if they could put together a quick sale to General Electric Credit Corp.,' Debra replied. 'They're about the only ones left who've got enough capital to speculate there'll someday be a real-estate recovery in this country.'

Lloyd choked on his coffee, recovered, and asked, 'How'd he die?'

Surprised, Debra asked, 'What's the manner of death got to do with it?'

Lloyd smirked and said, 'You've got a lot to learn about the insurance business, my sweet sushi. Let me explain the facts to you. About the business, I mean. How about dinner tonight, my place at seven? My Chilean chef tosses up a special menu for young women . . . .'

Leaving, Gladys slammed the office door.

Offended, Debra said, 'How can you be such a sexist at the same time our company is faced with insolvency?' Remaining as far away from him as she could, she stretched her arm, bending over the desk and handing him the company's summary of Trevor Thomson's life insurance policy and a brief report appended to it.

Lloyd shifted his attention from her cleavage to read the cover sheet. 'Who's the caller wanting a payoff for his evidence?' he asked.

'Some man, said he worked for a bank and was on vacation with his wife. Said he saw the insured jump from the train,' Debra answered, annoyed because she wanted to talk, not about some passer-by's comment, but rather about the company's cash-flow problems.

Lloyd continued reading the report. 'It says here he'll swear the insured deliberately took his own life. Also says his wife will collaborate with his statement which states they were passing between the cars on their way back from the diner, and saw the insured open the carriage door, look down, hesitate only briefly before jumping into Lake . . .' Lloyd paused, 'Lugano? Where the hell is that?'

'The south of Switzerland,' Debra said, remembering her undergraduate studies in geography, 'on the border with Italy.'

Lloyd whistled. 'He wants ten per cent of the policy in return for his sworn statement.'

'Five million bucks,' Debra said, attempting to duplicate his whistle.

Lloyd said, 'Does this policy exclude suicide? Yes, of course it does,' he answered his own question as he read the summary from the policy's terms and conditions. 'By excluding suicide the old goat, well, he wasn't so old when he bought the policy, negotiated a lower premium.' He gazed reflectively out of his office window and said, 'Some people are so sure of their life they know they'll never think about taking it.'

He shook his head in disbelief, turned to her and said, 'Sweetie, pack your little Gucci bag and hop the next LAX non-stop to Europe, corner this guy and his wife, get their sworn statement, pay them a paltry one or two per cent – we've got us a banker who's looking for a little skim on the side – and, of course, do whatever else you have to . . . .'

Debra nodded, agreeing, 'A percentage or two is a lot less than paying the policy in full.'

'Now you're learning the secrets of the insurance business,' Lloyd said, grinning. He walked around his desk. Coming close to her, his arm encircled her petite waist and he whispered, 'A private briefing before you leave? Tonight? A little tenderness before a trip always excites the mind . . . .'

Debra pulled away. 'Look, Mr Lloyd, you don't want a sexual harassment charge on top of the company's money problems.'

'Ah, I'm not abusing you, my oriental doll.'

Growing irate, Debra snapped back, 'You don't get it, do you?'

Ignoring her, he pointed to a geographic name on the attached report and exclaimed, 'Wait a minute! This note says the banker and his wife are leaving Europe and flying off to some weird little island nation in the Caribbean. They must have had a change of plans. So, have our travel department book you there on the next non-stop.' He paused and added, 'Dinner at the airport?'

9

Customarily, large American banks are organized pyramid form with the chairman of the board sitting at the apex, keeper of the sacred torch signifying the highest of banking ethics. Below this august position on the chart sits a box for the president, which in turn tops several other boxes titled for the various vice-presidents.

This chairman of the board, John Smith, acting on his own in the interests of the bank's survival, had set up a clandestine little taskforce, an exception to the rules of bank organization. Its members appeared nowhere on the official chart, not even being recognized by the personnel department. They were paid, not by cheque, but in cash. Members of this crazy cabal were instructed to deny they were employed by the bank.

They were officed in an unmarked Quonset hut in the China Basin district of San Francisco, a neighbourhood where no one expected any bank to have a presence. A seedy lot, they were nevertheless required to wear dark grey suits as they went about their special task of collecting delinquent loans. The few women among them received fashion assistance from one of the chic boutiques on Maiden Lane. Helga Gistelli was the exception. She insisted on buying her clothes at thrift shops, preferring to fit her plump figure with vintage 1950 dirndl skirts.

Their leader was Billy Ray Dumas, recruited by the chairman of the board upon being released from serving time in a Georgia prison for violating consumer collection laws. This morning Billy Ray gathered his taskforce together. Requiring them first to check their weapons, he said, 'Y'awls got yourselves four borrowers to squeeze this week. Pressure's really on from Smith.' He added, 'And it's growin' a heap worse.'

A tough fellow with a wry smile asked, 'Who we get to terrorize first?'

'Well, Sylvester,' Billy Ray replied, 'this-here bank's in such deep shit the big man on top says, "Anything goes so long as we recover the bank's money".' In ecstasy at having been given *carte blanche*, Billy Ray guffawed and said, 'Y'alluns know somethin' else? I think those Mafia brutes must be puttin' a lot of pressure on Smith.'

'How's that?' Sylvester asked.

Billy Ray went on, 'Drug money deposited – why it's skyrocketing the bank's lease payments higher than General Lee ridin' that there horse of his across Stone Mountain.'

'Hey, Billy, whatever happened to our married twosome who flew off there to Switzerland?' The question came from a tall man with a crookedly healed broken nose and pectoral muscles bulging through his Brooks Brothers suit. 'They ever get the old guy to cough up the back rent money?'

'Look, Arnold, I don't have to report to you . . . y'awls reports to me . . . see that there chart on the wall.'

'Yeah, I know, Billy, just curious. Can't fault curiosity, I always says. It's part of the great American spirit . . . we fought how many wars to protect it?'

A secretary poked her head in, 'Mr Dumas, sir, overseas call from Lugano.'

'Who's Lugano?' Arnold asked.

'Shut up, it's a place,' Billy Ray blasted back.

'It's our Mr and Mrs Hubert Gistelli,' another tough nicknamed Delinquent Don said as he waited for the news from Europe.

Billy Ray said into the cordless, 'Yeah.' As he listened his eyes absently examined a pornographic pin-up of a nude bank teller cashing a customer's cheque. Then he exclaimed loudly, trying to project his voice to reach the other side of the world, 'You bungling asshole . . . he did what before he fell? Actually signed the document? What do you mean, "sort of"?'

Billy Ray's face turned red as a beet, 'Listen, Gistelli, you two get your wedded asses down there to Turks and whatever-it-is island and twist that there mother fuckin' nigger trustee's arm till it bleeds money like a producin' mountain still. And you do it rat now!'

10

A dour mood, resonating with the damp incoming San Francisco fog outside, permeated the panelled room in which the bank's board of directors was gathering. From high atop the sky-reaching building in the centre of the bustling financial district, they could, if they were so inclined, look out across San Francisco Bay. On a clear day one could see three dozen miles across the cold waters of the Pacific to the Farallon Islands, those jagged rocks harbouring only birds and migrating whales.

Elsewhere around the Bay, any of the directors could – but none of them yearned to do so – point to raw land, construction projects, vacant office buildings and warehouses on which the bank's loans were about to turn sour, or had already gone bad, ballooning ever larger the financial institution's delinquent real-estate loan portfolio.

And they could also see – if they had the telescope their chairman, John Smith, had locked away in the bank's vault because he no longer could stomach what he saw through it – the branches on which they were paying whopping amounts of rent to Trevor Thomson. In fact, their clever landlord's meter was still running on the bank's world headquarters, the very building in which they were about to meet.

Having called them to order, Smith directed attention to the agenda. First, gesturing to their notepads, he quipped, 'White has replaced yellow, another casualty of the environmental movement.' Next he led their salute to crossed Italian and American flags, solemnly reminding them of the bank founder's humble Italian immigrant beginnings and his faith in the little fellows of the fledgling new state of California with its vibrant gold rush.

'John,' the director from New Mexico said, bringing them to the reality of the moment, 'let's get right to the heart of the matter.' Still wearing his black stetson, he fingered his turquoise and silver bolo tie and asked nervously, 'How many more days can we prevail on the feds to hold off on their takeover?'

'Yeah, how many more days have we got?' asked a California director. He was tanned, having returned from sailing his yacht down to Carmel for the weekend.

An Arizona director with a handcrafted Hopi bolo and a white hat which he kept riding on his balding head urged, 'We better not fool anybody, least of all ourselves. We're each on the hook – legally, I mean, to shareholders, depositors, regulators . . . .' Looking around the large room to make sure the doors were closed, he lowered his voice, confiding, 'You know, I've just set up one of those new asset protection trusts in the Caribbean.' He looked intently at each of them. 'Under the circumstances I suggest you all do the same.'

'Aren't they . . . ah . . . a bit off colour?' the director from the Napa Valley, his suit a shade of chardonnay, asked with hesitation in his voice.

Annoyed, the Arizonian said, 'Listen Sebastian, every man who is a director of a publicly held corporation in America will soon have one. Give you the name of my man – he's at one of the large accounting firms – if you want to talk to him in detail. His fees are not unreasonable considering the gravity of the situation we face here.' His ensuing gesture was meant to take in their meeting room, the bank, the state and all their branches nation-wide.

The Napa Valley man, looking glossy-eyed, said weakly, 'For the sake of our country and our economic system, I urge us to do something.'

Smith injected, 'Otherwise the demise of our bank will drag the American capitalistic system down with it into the boneyard of history, joining communism roasting in a forever hell.' He paused, looking out of the window. Musing, he said, 'God knows what system will replace capitalism.'

A director from Berkeley, a campanile and a golden bear decorating his tie, suggested, 'It'll probably be a state of lawlessness, looting and anarchy.'

A Southern California director, his voice as gloomy as a morning smog attack, asked, 'How will I explain it to my studio people when I have to lay them off and tell them there will be no more movies.' He removed his dark glasses, wiping away a tear.

Arizona Man said softly, 'And my golfing buddies in Scottsdale? They'll never understand.'

The chairman struggled back to his feet. He said, 'In answer to your questions – a week,' appending almost inaudibly, 'at the most. Unless we can offer the feds – with certainty – a source of new money.'

The other directors from Southern California, sitting at the table's lower end, shook their heads in disbelief.

The director from Oregon, umbrella handle hooked over the back of his chair, said, 'Another earthquake could shorten the time with more rubble of uncollectable loans.'

'I want to know,' said a director from Nevada, spinning a silver dollar on the polished wood, 'who is responsible for these bad real-estate loan bets. I've a list here . . . .'

Pulling out a folio, he began to enumerate: 'For instance, our office in Phoenix made a condominium loan on a project beside a desert road leading to the county dump. Every garbage truck in Maricopa County passes it, loaded with stinking shit. There was only one buyer – the manager of the dump. Checking him out, we found he was an illegal alien. So the Border Patrol deported him and his family.'

He went on, 'There's this apartment loan in Fresno. Two hundred units beneath electrical transmission lines from some dam in the Sierras. No one'll rent because those cooky environmentalists have instilled a fear of electromagnetic waves causing cancer. So the entire complex remains vacant no matter how low we drop the rents.'

The chairman made facial contortions to stop him, but the Nevada man insisted on naming another, 'And there's the project south of Santa Barbara – the one your brother-in-law sponsored.'

The chairman grimaced. What was one to do, he thought to himself, when one's wife continually nags about her stupid brother's loan application? Make it and hope for the best. He could think of no other answer.

The Nevada man went on, 'Half of the units are now in the surf because the ocean has continued slicing away at the land. Didn't anybody look at a soils report, or was one even required?'

The New Mexico director piped up, 'Yes, and there's this shopping centre in my state. It's on the opposite side of an Indian Reservation from the freeway. The autonomous tribal governors won't allow the connector road to be built. Something about it crossing one of their sacred sites. We've tried our usual bribes, even physical threats, but nothing works. Those Indians simply stare at us and speak in their native tongues. They dance to a spiritual chant, and money's not one of their tunes. The centre does its only business with barely two thousand reservation Indians, not the fifty thousand customers it was supposed to attract. What're we going to do with it?'

'Give it to the Indians,' someone suggested, 'and take another write-off.'

'Stop!' Smith demanded.

'No, we're going on,' the director from Washington state said. Resembling a husky about to bite, he snarled, 'What about the leases on our own bank properties. Who was the asshole who got us into this mess? We're paying that Thomson fellow a percentage of deposits! Can you imagine? He's worse than a navy of pirates. What with money-laundering from the mobs and inflation burgeoning our deposits, we're being raped daily!'

The chairman sat down exhausted, and answered, 'It was our former president. He's dead now, rest his soul, and maybe I'll soon join him.' He looked skyward and added, 'He and I can trade off up there playing teller and bank robber.'

There was a moment of silence, allowing the current president to assert weakly, 'These loans, gentlemen, are each properly documented . . . .'

'That's the trouble with banks today,' exclaimed a Southern California director, rising to interrupt. 'You bank officers focus on the paperwork and never get out of the fucking office to look at the real-estate.'

'Gentlemen, gentlemen,' Smith tried, leaning forward, the palms of his hands making imprints into the table's polish. 'What if there were ladies present?' he queried. 'Let's watch our language.'

The fog outside the skyscraper's windows began to thicken, turning darker. Passing the fortieth storey the bands of vapour were closing in and filling the air above the bumper-to-bumper cars clogging the nexus of freeways below.

In the ensuing silence, some shuddered as they watched the ominous fog foretelling a threat to their lives, to those in charge of society and the entire capitalist system.

Smith announced, 'Gentlemen, I do have a solution.'

'Let's hear about this solution,' begged the director from Berkeley, his hulk like a bear, his attention warming as if he were coming out of hibernation.

'We're going to get the leases cancelled . . . .'

'That's nice,' said a director from the Peninsula. 'But you already said we're going to have to fold our tents, steal away into the night, perhaps flee to the Caribbean, all within a week. So what good will come from cancelling these leases? It can't help our cash shortage. Not in the short term. And it sounds like there isn't going to be a long term.'

'What's happened?' the Arizona director asked. 'Has that young woman attorney, Vallerie what's-her-name, finally prevailed in our law suit against Trevor Thomson?'

'More than that.' Smith whispered because he had so little energy left. Slowly he said, enunciating his words carefully, 'And better than that.'

His voice now growing stronger with each word as he visualized the solution, the chairman of the board proclaimed, 'We're getting the lease payments refunded.'

'How much is that . . . and how are you going to bring off that miracle?' asked the Peninsula man, the Indian on his tie appearing to dance gleefully.

'How we're planning to force the refund I can tell you,' the chairman replied, 'but precisely how much we're going to recover – I can't until we retrieve the cash.'

'Approximately how many dollars?' the husky director from Washington asked.

The chairman looked each of them in the eye. His sudden strength commanded their fidelity. Slowly as if he were balancing a teller's till at the end of a routine banking day, he said, 'Ten billion.'

Smith made a mental note, adding an exclamation point, that as soon as this directors' meeting was over, he must ring Billy Ray and update himself on the success of those two collectors in Switzerland.

'That's enough to save the bank,' one director said.

Another whistled shrilly.

'And us with it,' the bear-director said softly. Had he a tail he would have wagged it.

11

In Zurich, banks are not housed in skyscrapers but rather in stone structures with markedly horizontal arrangements. The public banking is conducted in historic guildhalls clustered along the Bahnhofstrasse, the thoroughfare leading from the main railway station to Lake Zurich.

Tucked away on quiet side-streets, however, are the private banking offices where the serious millions and billions are managed. Once past the guards who verify identification from clients' passports, customers are warmly greeted by bank officers. Questions are never asked about the source of their deposits. It makes no difference, for example, if the money was cleverly siphoned from the fragile economy of some luckless nation by members of its ruling junta.

It was to one of these inauspicious offices - the head office of his bank, in fact - to which Hans Kubler had been summoned shortly after Trevor Thomson's death, and towards which he now walked on this dark and oppressive spring morning. The rain and cold deepened his foreboding as he turned off the Bahnhofstrasse and walked up Talackerstrasse.

Shaking the rainwater off his big black umbrella and leaving it with the guard, he went straight away - nervously adjusting his silver-rimmed glasses as he rode the Lilliputian elevator - to his second-floor meeting with Bank President Hugo Oberman. He was bemused as he observed how everything in Europe was on a smaller scale than in America: streets, cars, elevators, buildings, but not money.

Notified late the previous afternoon to come forthwith to Zurich, he had barely enough time to catch the last Trans-European Express north from Lugano. Riding in the train, he had figured the meeting would be about Thomson's account. Oberman would want to know if Kubler was still in control now the rich American was dead, or if the heirs were switching to some bank in New York or maybe even Dallas. Wasn't the Texas city the closest financial centre to New Mexico? Hans asked himself as he tried to picture the map of all those states.

But as the swift train threaded through the Alps, Hans worried the president might well have caught on to his scheme to get control of Ambrosiana for Thomson – now his heirs. But even so he hadn't violated any bank rules by buying Ambrosiana bonds with their warrants. He had been within his proper powers as the account's investment manager. Well, maybe he should have cleared it with Oberman since Ambrosiana Limited was a bank customer, but let's be realistic, he said to himself, one doesn't clear every stock and bond purchase with the bank president. Discussing each transaction would be unwieldy.

Still, as the train approached Zurich, Hans began to wonder if Oberman might fire him. But his loyalty was to Trevor Thomson. First. And wasn't fidelity to a client the guiding light for a bank investment officer?

The train arrived in time for him to find a hotel room in the crowded financial centre, but he couldn't sleep. It was not only the news of Trevor's death that saddened him, it was the risks involved in his precarious investment position. For now with Trevor dead, Hans knew he must figure out on his own how to assemble the cash – the billions of dollars of cash – that he would need in order to exercise those warrants and buy the new shares of Ambrosiana stock. It couldn't be accomplished with an IOU or a vague promise to pay at some time in the future. The purchase could only be achieved with hard cold currency – a cheque perhaps, but one that didn't bounce.

Though the Trevor Thomson account was huge, it was fully invested in bonds yielding a substantial income. As well, it was highly leveraged with the account's margin debt having climbed to its maximum permissible ratio. After all, his yield on the portfolio of Eurobonds was almost eight per cent, and the cost of money borrowed from Trans-Swiss Bank barely five. Yes, he'd done his job professionally. Perhaps too well.

And now there was this hastily called meeting, its purpose unknown. He was filled with apprehension, knowing he would have to cope with the diciest gamble he'd ever made – alone and without the benefit of Trevor Thomson's cleverness, strength and insight.

'Just yesterday I was with him in Chiasso and he was alive,' Hans said over and over again during the night as he railed in disbelief against the fates that brought about his client's tragic death. He tried to console himself by asking if death ever arrived, as did the Swiss trains, at a proper time. And, of course, he knew it didn't. Nevertheless he was still reeling emotionally as he arrived at Hugo Oberman's office door.

His inner turmoil hidden behind a banker's stoic façade, he made sure he was presentable for the meeting – posture straight, tie straight, shoes polished, grasping his leather attaché case. Yet he was in a cold sweat. But his credo being to confront every situation coming his way, his face into the wind, challenging it always, Hans Kubler raised his free arm, clenched his fist and prepared to knock.

Before he could strike the polished wood, Ms Schultz, Oberman's matronly secretary, intercepted him with, 'They're waiting for you in the conference room, Herr Kubler.'

'They?'

'Yes, didn't you know? Count Ambrosiana senior . . . .'

The news was a surprise. Hans worried why the head man of the bank's customer was attending this meeting. Now it would all come out: Trevor's account owning the warrants, and with it the plan to gain control of the company. Worse, Victor Ambrosiana might realize his job as president could well be at stake.

Taking out his handkerchief and mopping his forehead while trying to conceal an overwhelming apprehension, he asked, 'And who else is in there?'

A flash of fear darkened her conservatively applied make-up as she replied, 'That awesome man from Sicily. Ms Schultz paused, fearing just saying his name out loud might bring some form of brutal retribution. She leaned closer to Hans and whispered, 'You know, the one people say was seen walking away from that poor Italian banker who got himself hung a couple of years ago from Blackfriars Bridge in London.'

Hans's stomach began to whip into knots as he said the Mafia man's name out loud, 'Angelo Luciano.' He blew air between his teeth. The sound, when merged with his accompanying groan of pain, brought forth the equivalent German sound of 'Oh, my God.'

Why hadn't it dawned on him before? He guessed he'd been too intent on analysing Ambrosiana Limited's financial statements and delving into the sales reports on the burgeoning market for birth-control devices. In his formal investment research, he'd overlooked the real plot – the people. And in this case the people meant the Mafia. They wanted to control the world-wide distribution of the condoms manufactured by this Italian company – keep it all in the family. They wanted to stock each of those little vending machines in rest-rooms around the world, supply the schools with hand-outs. They, too, saw birth-control devices as the next generation of mass-market consumption, the one beyond peddling drugs. If they could promote the idea of a condom in every purse and pocket, they'd have a vast social trend working for them. Yes, damn it, the whole scenario was as apparent as a high-speed train hitting him. He'd been asleep at the switch. What was he to do now?

Perfunctorily he thanked Ms Schultz, turned and walked to the conference room door, this time going in without knocking – afraid to interrupt his forward steps in case he turned and fled to the Bahnhof and jumped on the next train for Liechtenstein.

Inside the conference room, three men sat around a polished walnut table. The only adornment on the dull white walls, which were devoid of creative art or decoration, was a small framed notice, its bold black letters advising any Americans who might be thinking of doing business here 'Not a Member of the FDIC'.

Hans nodded, first at Oberman, then at the others. Perfunctory handshakes ensued, no one bothering to stand. But before Hans could sit, the Sicilian, Angelo Luciano, lit a huge Dutch cigar, performing the task with the flair only hardened Mafia men know how to exhibit.

Having puffed to his satisfaction, he said, 'His death won't be made public for five days. I've made the good coroner an offer he can't refuse.'

Hans visualized Dr Giorgio Giannini, his old friend and the cantonal coroner, hanging limp and lifeless from the little ascension car shuttling between Lugano's hillside railway station and the city centre. But Hans quickly put a different spin on Angelo's remark; Giannini was clever and had probably pocketed a large pay-off. Whatever the scenario, Hans started perspiring again. Financial risk was one thing, but physical danger was a decidedly more fearsome dimension, carrying with it the possibility of being really wiped out.

'I hope that with your offer, Angelo, you kept a copy of the signed document and had his signature notarized,' Count Ambrosiana said with a wave of his hand.

Both his physical size and his position as president of the drug conglomerate instilled fear in most men. Expert tailoring concealed the bulkiness of his ponderous body but when he spoke his flabby jowls jounced, their movement emphasizing his words as power and authority radiated from his presence. His royal status attracted his fair share of Italian women, and even a few in Switzerland.

Hugo Oberman turned towards Hans amd delivered an admonishing stare. It punctured his ego. Hans returned the look, trying to build up his damaged self-esteem. Did Oberman's stare mean he, too, was about

65

to be compromised one way or the other right on the spot? They apparently thought coercing Dr Giannini into delaying the official announcement would somehow prevent the warrants from being exercised. But it was he, Hans Kubler, who would be the one to pull it off – if he could assemble enough money.

Oberman, his words even more fiery than normal, said as he gestured at the other two men and himself, performing a sweeping hand movement, 'Hans, you've gotten each of us, and the bank as well, in a pickle.'

Angelo drew a deep puff on the cigar, brightly illuminating its end. Hans visualized its poker-hot tip burning into his face. In defence he pulled his chair back a bit before he sat down.

The Mafia man looked him in the eye and said, 'You're redundant, Herr Kubler. With this Thomson fellow's death you're in the way, no longer needed.' Angelo's free hand slid to the inside pocket of his hand-tailored suit.

Hans eyed the door and wondered if he should make a run for it, but Oberman restrained the Sicilian with, 'Now, now, Mr Luciano, let's not make a mistake. Sooner or later some journalist from *Der Spiegel* or the European edition of the *Wall Street Journal* would start asking questions.' He gently admonished, 'These days, we in banking, even those of you in . . . ah . . . distribution, must first put everything we do to the media test.'

Victor Ambrosiana, looking at Angelo, nodded agreement.

Angelo withdrew his hand with its manicured finger-nails and ran it over his dark hair as he dismissed his impulsive urge.

Hans let out a sigh.

Angelo said, 'My family's got a lot of lire deposited in your bank, Herr Oberman. Laundered clean and germ-free every day.' He guffawed and sucked again on the stogie.

'Yes, yes, of course,' Oberman hastened to acknowledge. Turning to Count Ambrosiana, he challenged the larger man, 'Victor, in the first place your company should never have issued those bonds with warrants attached. I warned you at the time you could lose control if they were ever exercised in a take-over attempt.'

'But our company was desperate back in those dark days, Hugo. You remember,' Count Amrosiana reminded him, 'how I begged you to loan us money just to keep the company afloat. I promised you the market for birth-control devices was improving, even in Catholic Italy, and certainly elsewhere in the world. But no bank, not even yours, would touch us credit-wise in those days.'

'That was before AIDS became so widespread – turned into an epidemic out of control,' Oberman said. 'Now, out of fear, people are beginning to pay attention to safe sex.' He smiled and added, 'Myself, I particularly like your new line. What do you call it?'

'The Thin-Skinned Tickler,' the mogul replied. 'The latest in latex technology, made in Japan by one of the companies we're about to acquire.'

Oberman nodded with satisfaction. As an afterthought he said, 'Market demand is improving your company's position, Victor.'

Hans inserted a *'Ja.'*

Oberman ignored him and went on, 'Men around the world are starting to view sex as a risk, not a right. . . .'

'And using our products,' Count Ambrosiana said, adding, 'But you miss the point, Hugo. It's the women. They're demanding and getting protection. Women around the world are becoming assertive. Though I'm Italian and Catholic, I realized years ago that sexual values are changing.'

'*Si.* Birth control is in,' Angelo asserted, pointing his cigar at Oberman. 'And now with the threat of AIDS . . . .' He paused to reflect. 'All you've got to do is watch one of those poor guys being interviewed on some TV news show. Next time you'll go in protected.'

Count Ambrosiana's nod vibrated his jowls again. 'And have you heard? The church's position is going to change, too. If you knowingly transmit AIDS to your sexual partner you'll be committing an official sin.'

Hans wondered what they were getting at.

The mogul looked at the bank president and said, 'Don't worry, Hugo, everything'll work out. In a couple of days those warrants – clinging to those bonds like a litter of newborn pigs suckling their mother's unresponsive teats – will expire.' He added, 'Unfed.'

Pointing his finger at Hans, Count Ambrosiana said, 'And no one, not even you, Herr Kubler, with the Thomson billions, can bring dead warrants back to life. An expired warrant is as dead as a Swiss doornail. Aren't I right, Herr Oberman? I mean, exercising our warrants entails more than simply saying you're going to do it. A man's got to pay for the shares of common stock he's converting the warrants into. And he needs money – financing – to bring it off.'

Oberman promptly nodded his head, his expression suggesting such information was common knowledge.

Chagrin in his voice, Hans now spoke up. 'And if Mr Thomson – I mean, if I – let these warrants die, all the money I've invested in buying the warrants will simply be wiped out.' He shrugged his shoulders and added with lament, 'Go *kaput!*'

'Like yesterday's train,' Count Ambrosiana said. His ensuing guffaw shook the room. He added, assuming he was quelling any remaining hopes Hans might have, 'And without our approval' – he gestured around the conference room – 'no one will finance your scheme.' Looking back at Oberman, he said, 'Your boss will see to that. He'll put the word out up and down the Bahnhofstrasse, even tell those Frenchies over in Geneva and those copy-cat opportunists in Vaduz, too.'

Angelo agreed, 'Yes, not even the Liechtenstein royal family will dare touch you, Herr Kubler.'

Oberman said solemnly, 'You're losing, Hans, because by now there's no longer a market for those warrants. It's too late for someone else to step in and buy them from you. So you can't sell them. And you haven't the money to exercise them.' He looked sombre. 'The billions of Trevor Thomson's wealth you've unwisely gambled will drop into your Lake Lugano just like the old man himself.'

In the ensuing silence Hans felt dejected. The investment account he was managing would still own the Ambrosiana bonds, of course, but the loss on the worthless warrants would devastate the portfolio. Hans worried how he could possibly explain such a financial catastrophe to Trevor's stepchildren, Sam and Judith. And what would he say to Charles Fountain?

For a brief moment he was furious with Trevor for dying. 'How could you do this to me,' he wanted to yell out in the hope that his plea of frustration would reach him wherever he was. Maybe Trevor would hear his call for help and resurrect himself long enough to exert his powers and orchestrate the deal . . . and he would be off the hook. But he acknowledged Trevor wasn't coming back. He reminded himself bankers and investment managers were allowed no dreams, permitted no fantasies – such mental larks were reserved for borrowers, those romantics who conceived the world's new ideas.

As he considered his dilemma, a change came over him. Perhaps it was the shock of Trevor's death. Perhaps now he was going to fill the void left by his deceased American client. It was nothing overt. No one in the room could detect this change, but suddenly he felt a bright new hope for the Thomson portfolio. His mental processes having been nurtured over the years working with Trevor, he began to feel more creative. Perhaps some of the Yankee's ingenuity was rubbing off on him.

But his surge of adrenaline was interrupted as Count Ambrosiana stood up, colour draining from his face. With uncertainty he pointed a finger at Oberman and demanded, 'But what about financing our acquisitions? If we don't have the money from the sale of the new shares of stock . . . .' The mogul's voice trailed off. He braced himself against the table, leaning forward with both palms flat.

Oberman waited a moment, allowing his customer's concerns to compound, and said, 'Don't worry, Victor, Trans-Swiss Bank will loan you the money.' The banker rubbed his hands. Calculating the bank's outrageous loan fees and interest income, Hans thought.

In relief, Count Ambrosiana retrieved a kerchief and mopped his brow.

Oberman said, 'With these acquisitions your company will become the world's largest manufacturer. Correct, Victor?'

The mogul nodded. The thought excited him. He smiled and said, 'By far, and our costs of manufacturing the little rolled rubbers – with our new robotic technology – will be driven way down with the increased volume.'

Familiar with the already whopping profit margins of the Swiss drug industry, Oberman smiled knowingly.

Count Ambrosiana added, 'My son, our corporate treasurer, will be most pleased with your generous loan offer, Hugo.'

Oberman said with satisfaction, 'Yes, the three of us must do lunch, as the Americans say. Perhaps a few days from now after the Easter holidays are over.'

Victor Ambrosiana signalled his agreement, adding, 'And our annual pageant is behind us.'

'By then the warrants will have expired,' Oberman added.

'You know,' Count Ambrosiana mused, 'those companies we are going to acquire are poorly managed. If we don't rescue them soon, they'll go under. Think of the thousands of jobs our acquisitions will save.'

Even Angelo smiled. Hans thought he looked proud, probably thinking his Sicilian family would be a player, at long last, in a legitimate and socially beneficial business endeavour.

Oberman looked at Hans and said, 'You see, Hans, we don't want Thomson's American heirs getting control of Ambrosiana.' He added, 'Why, I understand one of them is some sort of a bookish historian. And the other a social butterfly. Can you imagine such a pair running a multinational drug company? Here in Switzerland?' He blew air through his teeth, the whistling sound as high-pitched as a boiling tea-kettle. Pounding the conference table with his little fist, he stated emphatically as an afterthought, 'The company's profits must remain in Switzerland and be deposited in our bank. Don't you agree, Hans?'

'In Ambrosiana Limited's account and our family's account, as well,' Angelo insisted, edged at being left out of the loop.

'Yes, of course,' Oberman replied. 'An oversight on my part. No offence,' the banker nervously assured him.

Count Ambrosiana said proudly, 'Yes, my profits will surely total into the billions over the next decade.'

'And then, having cornered the world market, you'll jack up your prices,' Oberman said and smiled.

The mogul nodded. 'You know, the way things are going in America, I think we should build a high-tech factory in one of their inner cities. Maybe Los Angeles. Lot of people there need work, I hear.'

'But those ghetto people only want to riot and burn. In our American branches we draw red lines around those unstable areas – they're off limits to our lending officers. And we certainly don't tolerate those sorts of people in Switzerland,' the bank president said, holding up his hand as high as a border guard refusing asylum.

'No, Hugo, you're mistaken,' Count Ambrosiana said. 'If you give people a chance, something to work for, life takes on meaning for them.'

Angelo announced longingly, 'Family is important, too. Through our . . . ah . . . valuable family distribution system, our rake-off . . . ah . . . mark-up will be greater than any dope deal . . . ah . . . drug arrangement. And medically helpful, too. Isn't that right? At last our tarnished family image will enjoy a rebirth of its heritage.'

'One long overdue,' Count Ambrosiana commented, fingering another of the cigars from the cannister on Hugo's conference table. He let the cigar go, instructing himself out loud, 'Smoking is unlike sex.'

'How's that?' Oberman asked.

'With smoking the only safe way is quitting, but with sex it must be continued – with vigour and proper . . . ah . . . coverage.'

Angelo's smile was sweet with the taste of money. He said to the drug executive, 'Our family's . . . ah . . . business relationship with your world-wide conglomerate, Count Ambrosiana . . . will mean the dawning of a profitable new day for organized crime. Wait till you see the advertising campaign our new Madison Avenue agency has come up with.'

'For our condoms?'

'Yes,' the Mafia man said, smiling proudly. 'A series of vivid TV spots during this autumn's football season in the US.'

'Those big studs demonstrating?' asked Oberman in disbelief.

'Won't those visuals be effective in creating demand!' the Mafia man exclaimed, laughing loudly. 'And we'll follow up with more commercials during the World Cup.' Angelo raised his cigar in a pledge. 'The world will soon realize drugs and cigarettes are out and condoms and safe sex are in.'

Once again Oberman's eyes bored into Hans as the senior bank official said, 'So, you see, Hans, your little billion-dollar scheme having been found out, you must forget about these warrants. This foolish and secret bet you've made without either my personal knowledge or approval must wait out these next few days like a maiden unspoken for.' The little man was having fun toying with his errant employee.

Reticent to challenge these powerful men, Hans fixed his eyes on the white walls.

'And then, like chips placed on the roulette's double O at the Campione casino,' Count Ambrosiana said, 'those warrants will simply be raked off the investment table by the croupier as the little ball comes to rest elsewhere.' He muffled an ensuing belly laugh by placing a pudgy hand over his mouth.

Patting Hans's shoulder as only a senior bank officer knows how to, reinforcing his authority, Oberman counselled, 'Your client, that is his heirs, will still own the Ambrosiana bonds. After Victor's acquisitions of his competitors the ratings awarded his bonds will advance from junk to gold. They'll become more valuable corporate debt, certain to be repaid upon their maturity in 2006. As a result their price on the Rome Bond Exchange will surely rise.'

Count Ambrosiana smiled proudly.

The bank president went on, 'To boot, the bonds will continue to pay their obligatory twelve per cent interest – a handsome portfolio return in any banker's book. So don't worry so much, Hans. You can cover up your . . . ah . . . little investment mistake so none of Thomson's heirs will ever learn the real story.'

Hans's eyes shifted to the ceiling, their reward continuing to be only a white nothingness. Nor was his mind devising a way out. Again he wished Trevor was back.

'Yes, you'll be a winner, Kubler, in the eyes of the heirs,' Count Ambrosiana said, directing a small, icy smile towards Kubler. He added, thinking his advice was the morning's epilogue, 'Relax, go with the flow, as the Americans say.'

71

Oberman suggested, 'Yes, Kubler, you can advise those American heirs, if they ever ask, it was the bank's judgment not to exercise the warrants. They'll never know anything about the potential profits they . . . ah . . . you gave up.'

The muscles in Hans's forearms flexed and his jaws bulged as he ground his teeth in an effort to compel his mind to function fully.

'And next time, Kubler,' Oberman said, his jovial attitude gone and his reprimand obvious, 'you devise a scheme to get control of a company for one of your investment clients, seek my approval first. Do you understand?'

His face white, Hans nodded. What would he do for a living, he wondered, if he lost his treasured bank job?

As their meeting broke up, Angelo came close. Hans tried to back away, but the Sicilian laid a heavy hand on his shoulder and said sternly, 'Don't worry, Herr Kubler, we always take care of our resident Germans.' Flashing the contented grin of a family man, he added, 'One way or the other.'

Hans stiffened as he wondered what the mobster really meant. All of a sudden, a new wave of confidence bubbled up, and Hans felt stronger. As he left the bank for the international airport north of Zurich on his way to Trevor's funeral on Grand Turk, stung by the freshness of the cold morning drizzle, he resolved not to be beaten.

As his Miami-bound jet lifted off above a Swiss countryside still shrouded in clouds, Hans Kubler looked out at the peaks of the snow-capped Alps poking up through the mist. Soon they were level with his ascending 767.

Trevor Thomson wouldn't have let a slick Sicilian push him around. And now he knew he wouldn't either.

'Ja!' he said to the flight attendant as she passed out the first-class cabin's cognac.

He drew even more strength from the ageless, towering spires of the Swiss Alps. They reminded him of Trevor Thomson, and he resolved not to let his client down.

12

Sam stowed his hat in the overhead compartment and took his seat on the aisle.

Awarded the window seat, Judith harrumphed, advising all around her the rules of civility were being broken right before their very eyes, and suggesting, as a result, the imminent demise of the social order they had come to know and cherish. For she was travelling coach class.

Judith was dressed in a long skirt decorated with an Indian motif. Her pure white blouse was a silken backdrop for her necklace featuring a large silver Zuni pendant. Turquoise earrings and hand-tooled cowboy boots completed her Southwest outfit.

She was still miffed at the airport security guard who had required her to pass three times through the security arch. She had eventually had to remove all her silver jewellery so she could clear it without triggering the alarm.

Penny was in the middle seat. In contrast, she was perky in her business suit. She said, 'No wonder the plane is packed. There's only one flight a week from Miami.'

'We should have flown first class,' Judith reiterated. 'These narrow seats have no leg room, and they're not serving us *hors d'oeuvres* and sherry for the take-off either. Look around us at the riff-raff we're flying with.' She gestured over her shoulder. 'Their carry-ons are merely cardboard boxes tied with string or plastic sacks full of junk food. Why, one woman has nothing but barbecue potato chips.'

Sam said, 'But see how friendly they are. I think they know each other – probably islanders who've been shopping in Miami and returning home.'

'We should be up front with those nattily dressed men,' Judith said. 'They're professionals – attorneys, bankers, prestigious people.'

'Sis,' Sam said, 'just think how many books I can buy for my collection with the money we're saving.'

'We could have rowed over and saved even more money,' Judith retorted. 'What's money for if not to spend, either on yourself or a worthwhile charity?'

'To invest,' Penny said, holding up her finger to make her point. 'A rule of money management.' She opened a copy of the *Financial Times*.

'Your first visit to our islands?' a black woman across the aisle asked Sam. 'You go scuba diving on reefs?'

'Uh, no.'

'Must do. Our island and the waters offshore beautiful. You'll never forget our islands,' she added proudly, her broad smile showing ivory-white teeth.

'Were you born there?' Sam asked.

'Yes, in Provo. But now I live Grand Turk.'

'Provo is Provodenciales?' Sam asked, stumbling over the pronunciation of the long name.

'Yes,' she said. 'We call it Provo for short.'

'The plane lands there first,' Penny said, looking at their itinerary. 'In two hours. And then a short hop over to Grand Turk.'

The woman said, 'I like Grand Turk . . . it's small . . . I know most everybody there. Except the Haitians. Only a few thousand of us, you know, on entire island.'

'Here we go,' Sam said, almost too loudly. 'We're about to take off down the runway. Hold on tight, gals.' His face was white, his hands grasped the chair arm. Wide-eyed, he stared straight ahead.

Once aloft, the steep ascent completed, Sam mopped his forehead and relaxed.

'You were frightened,' Penny said tenderly, her arm encircling his shoulder, her hair brushing his face.

'Ah, me? Of course not. Nonsense.'

'Yes, you were, you dear. It's going to be all right, you stay here, right next to me.' Penny raised the arm rest and snuggled close to him.

'Look up there in first class,' Judith said poking Penny, 'they're getting food and drinks. And there's that odd-looking couple from the waiting lounge. Why doesn't she take off those dark glasses?'

Penny said, 'And who's the tall dark woman with the auburn hair who just stood up to search in the overhead compartment? I wish my hair would shine the way hers does.'

'Getting something out of her Louis Vuitton travel case, no doubt,' Judith said, looking down apprehensively at her own designer bag, which, she fretted, was crammed under the seat.

'Look at her figure,' Sam exclaimed.

'Who's she with?' Penny asked, craning her neck.

'Two men,' Judith said. 'One white and one black. I saw them in the departure lounge. They're either bankers or attorneys.'

Penny turned back to the pink newsprint of the *Financial Times*. A few minutes later she said excitedly, 'Those clever Swiss bankers have devised a new Eurobond. It's a Greek telephone company issue denominated in ECUs, the new European Currency Unit. The interest rate is tied to the London Libor rate.'

Sam yawned.

Penny punched him, 'You haven't heard the best part about these new investment bonds.'

'You receive a free history book of ancient Greece with each bond?'

'No, silly, you get a warrant.'

'Does it give you a free phone call next time you're in Athens?'

Penny looked disgustingly at Sam and said, 'Better. The warrant entitles you to buy shares of common stock.'

Sam spread his next book on the tiny tray table.

Penny continued, 'But you know the SEC, in its protective wisdom, won't allow US citizens to buy these bonds.'

'The Securities and Exchange Commission,' Sam said, 'I've heard of them, but what's the Libor rate?'

'The London Inter Bank Offered Rate of interest,' Penny said, adding, 'it's a benchmark used in Europe, the same way the Federal Reserve discount rate is watched in the US.'

Judith said, 'There's no *Town & Country* in coach. I always read it when I fly. I was written up once, don't you remember?' She looked over at Penny, who had put her newspaper away and was opening a bundle of letters tied with a ribbon. She asked, 'Now what are you reading?'

Sam looked up from his book and said with surprise, 'Those are old letters.' He looked at the postmark on one dogeared envelope. 'Yes, very old.'

Penny smiled. 'They're Trevor's World War I letters.' To Judith she said, 'Remember when you found them among your mother's things a few years ago? I've never looked at them until now. They may help us to understand Trevor a little better.'

'They're fragile,' Sam said, 'like precious documents in the rare book section, so be ginger.'

Penny nodded. 'See here,' she pointed to a still visible postmark, 'this letter is from the 47th Brigade Hospital at Thierry.'

'Why was Trevor in the hospital?' Sam asked.

'Wounded,' Penny replied. 'He writes to his buddy back home about being sprayed with mustard gas.'

'How awful,' Sam said, shaking his head. 'But if Trevor sent these letters to a buddy, the buddy would still have them, wouldn't he?'

'There was a letter from the buddy's granddaughter – she sent them to Lillian after her grandfather died,' Judith said.

Penny said, 'Trevor was so young. And to be wounded right at the end of the war. It was the last few weeks when he finally got into battle. He must have lied about his age, too, caught up in the national euphoria to make the world safe for democracy. I'll read on, see what else he has to say.'

Sam nodded, and in mock alarm, announced, 'Uh oh, the flight attendant is going to draw the curtain. First-class show's about over.' He looked up the aisle. The tall woman was crossing her long legs, her miniskirt exposing a pair of magnificent, trim, athletic thighs.

Before the curtain closed, he heard her fetching laugh as she looked at the man seated in the plush seat next to her. On his lap he had a notebook computer on which he was entering, Sam was sure, instructions issued by her.

'Why do you go to our islands, if not to dive?' the woman asked from across the aisle. 'You go fish?'

'Ah, no,' Sam said and hesitated. 'We're . . . a . . . actually going to a funeral.'

'Mr Thomson's?'

Startled, Sam replied, 'How did you know?'

'Not many white persons' funeral on our island,' she said. 'My name Cassandra.' She held out her hand and Sam and Penny, in turn, shook it.

The drinks trolley came up the aisle and Judith promptly asked for Cabernet Sauvignon.

The attendant replied, 'Sorry, we have only white.'

'Two,' Judith ordered, reaching into her purse for the money. 'Free in first class,' she muttered.

Cassandra leaned around the attendant and said, 'Did he die in Grand Turk?'

'No, actually in Switzerland,' Sam said.

'Uh oh,' she said. 'His body must be on this plane.'

Alarmed, Penny whispered to Sam, 'We were going to do those tests on his body, you know, the DNA, genealogical information, blood types.' She paused, reflected and said, 'That is, unless they cremated him in Lugano. You've got to get up to speed on this thing, Sammy Boy!'

Remembering, Sam said, 'Oh yes, Fountain told me the instructions in Trevor's living will were for him to be cremated.'

With relief Penny said, 'Maybe converting his body to ashes will take care of any claim from Felicia.' She thought for a moment and added, 'But don't be too sure. They couldn't cremate him until after they performed the autopsy. Felicia might still step forward, claiming to be his genetic heir and disputing the distribution.'

'Can she do that?' Sam asked.

'Yes, she'd be trying to enforce heirship under English common law,' Penny said.

'Are you sure he didn't fall off the train in Italy?' Judith asked.

'Why in Italy?' Sam asked.

'Campione, where they found the body, is part of Italy,' Judith replied. 'I know because there's this casino overlooking the lake. I heard about it from the executive director of one of our big charities in Santa Fe. I'm thinking of giving him a rather significant contribution now I've got all of . . . well, half of Trevor's money.' Judith smiled at her big brother. 'And he wants to appoint me to their national board. He's been to Campione, gambling away, having tons of fun . . . .'

'With the charity's money?' Penny asked, abhorred, her green eyes widening. 'Probably flew over for the weekend on the Concorde.'

'Of course not,' Judith said, annoyed. 'You're too sceptical. This executive director's got money of his own.'

'What about this town in Switzerland you say is really in Italy?' Sam pressed.

Judith finished her wine and said, 'Campione is actually part of Italy. My friend says its history goes back to the Bishops of Milan who somehow got title to the enclave from the Pope in the Middle Ages . . . .'

'To pay off a gambling debt maybe,' Penny said, laughing. 'Those daredevil popes and bishops loved to gamble, or so they say.'

'They didn't have a casino then, Penny,' Sam said.

'How do you know?' Penny pressed.

'Well, I don't for sure, I just assumed . . . . Oh, before I forget, there's another thing,' Sam said. 'Trevor's life insurance. Fountain said he had a big policy.'

Edged, her voice rising, Penny said, 'You don't tell me anything, Sammy!'

'I forgot.'

77

'We should file a claim,' Penny said. 'But to do so we'll need a death certificate.'

'How are we going to obtain such a document?' Sam asked.

'If his body's on this plane,' Penny replied, 'the death certificate's got to be with it.'

'Maybe he's in an artfully crafted bronze urn to be sealed away in a lovely vault, like a valuable jewel being placed inside a safe,' Judith said. She emptied the balance of her second wine bottle, assessing her plastic glass with disdain.

Sam said, 'Hey, wait a minute. What is the death certificate going to list as the cause of death? I figure he had a heart attack and fell.'

'Exactly,' Judith said emphatically.

'Or was pushed,' Penny said.

Sam said, his face growing white, 'You think we're on more than a funeral procession here?'

Penny nodded.

Cassandra leaned across the aisle and said, 'You related?'

Sam said, 'Yes, I was his stepson and Judith – by the window – was his stepdaughter.'

'Mr Thomson great man,' Cassandra said, 'always give food 'n' things to us on island. Why, he was even going to build houses for us like they got in Miami. And another medical clinic, too, this one on Grand Turk. But now he passed, poor man. He gone reward. Too bad . . . .'

'Yes,' Sam agreed, being polite, not feeling a loss.

Cassandra said, 'Now he not do big project on reef?'

Sam asked, 'What project?'

'Columbus's ship. He didn't tell you?'

'We . . . ah . . . seldom spoke,' Sam confessed. 'What about this ship?'

'They found Columbus's ship,' Cassandra said. 'Must be full lot gold coin, treasure, you know. Columbus was rich mon. Wish I could find me a rich mon.'

Penny hugged Sam's arm possessively.

Leaning into the aisle, absorbed with the thought he might be on to a bit of history, Sam said, 'Tell me about this shipwreck off your little island.'

Cassandra laughed and said, 'You ought to ask the mon in charge of Mr Thomson's museum – the Thomson-Columbus Museum – where they're goin' display all the stuff dredged up from reef.'

Sam ran his hand through his hair. With interest, a smile forming, he slowly repeated with pride in his voice, 'A Thomson museum?'

13

In a professional way Wes Truecoat, the archaeologist, was looking forward to Trevor Thomson's funeral. To him, funerary procedures, while morbid to most people, offered a key to understanding other cultures. He speculated cremation might mean a particular society placed more value in the spirit of human existence. On the other hand, those people practising embalming or mummifying the deceased felt the body itself would travel to a beyond. Possessions such as jewellery and other symbols of status and wealth were often buried with the deceased for use in the afterlife. In Trevor Thomson's case, Truecoat mused, if the tycoon were to carry his money with him, quite a sizeable coffin would be required.

He lit another cigarette and watched the passengers from Miami deplane. He inhaled deeply as he speculated about the conversation he was going to have with the Swiss banker, Hans Kubler. It would be about his future, which in the aftermath of Thomson's death, he suspected, was umbilically tied to the Thomson-Columbus Museum.

He was worried the museum itself might be aborted. The nicotine gave momentary relief to his uncertainties. He'd grown fond of this remote island and the peaceful ocean surrounding it – free from the clutter and noise of modern American society – and he knew he didn't want to go back to the bleak American prairie.

Here he was in charge of his own show. Except, of course, for the watchful eyes of Charles Fountain and the fiduciary mind of Hans Kubler. In his regular written reports they required him to explain every expenditure for the restoration of the old house which would contain the Thomson-Columbus Museum, as well as the costs involved with the marine excavation.

On their own, his reports would make an interesting archive a hundred years from now should some twenty-second century archaeologist discover them. For one thing, he thought, the reports would reveal how unknowledgeable financial people were about scientific archaeology.

'Why can't you simply scoop the stuff up out of the ocean with a big dredge, spread it out on the beach, photograph it and be done?' was one of their typical questions.

He was obliged to spell out – his twangy Midwestern voice sometimes irritating them – why the position in which each artifact was found was so important to unravelling the mission of the ship and when she ran aground. Stratification, and he was surprised not everyone realized it, meant that the deeper the artifact, the older it was. The rule was one of the first principles of archaeological dating he had learned at the University of Kansas.

Also, their reluctance to approve the expenditures for restoring the 200-year-old house annoyed him. The extent of the decay had not been fully anticipated, and the costs of restoration and improvements to outfit the museum had exceeded his budget.

So it was with trepidation he watched the first passenger off the plane clear island Customs. Extinguishing his cigarette as he walked up to the banker, Truecoat offered his hand. 'Nice to see you again, Mr Kubler.' Trying to hold back his sarcasm, he appended, 'Travelling first class?'

Shaking his hand only because custom required the act, Kubler immediately began to query the archaeologist. 'You have the latest month's figures for me? I hope you've been better at controlling the costs of refurbishing the house and digging up the wreck?'

Truecoat thought the banker was abrupt with his question. He seemed preoccupied with some other matter of greater importance. But Truecoat had never regarded himself as particularly intuitive with people, being much more comfortable in the presence of inanimate artifacts.

Leaving the terminal with Truecoat, Kubler said, 'I haven't much time. I must fly back to Switzerland immediately after the funeral. Business summons. *Ja.* The critical deal is pending.' He felt obliged to elaborate, 'Time is running out.' Absently, almost to himself, he said, 'I must exercise.'

Truecoat didn't answer, trying to sort out what exercise and deals had to do with shipwrecks. He didn't know what the banker was talking about, so he blurted out his rehearsed questions, 'What's the status of the museum and my job now that Mr Thomson is dead? When can we pay our suppliers and craftspeople? They won't work without money.'

'There will be no change in the completion schedule of the museum,' Kubler assured the archaeologist. 'Oh, by the way, you'll be pleased to know Mr Thomson and I – before his death – arranged the support of the Italian royal family. Your museum has been elevated into a world-class category.'

'Hey, that's great,' Truecoat said.

'So, do your job. *Ja*. A lesson for us all. We must always do our jobs. Allegiance to one's employer and one's career is the right way of life.'

Truecoat nodded, apprehension gnawing. He wanted another cigarette.

'*Ja*. The work ethic is the one rule of Western society that should always guide our lives.'

Truecoat fingered the plastic tab on a fresh packet of cigarettes and searched his pockets for a match.

'*Nein!*' Kubler commanded. 'You shouldn't smoke. Why, the president of the company making these little parcels told me just hours ago that if people would use these' – he handed Truecoat a small plastic package – 'as much as they smoke, the world would be a better place.'

'These are condoms,' Truecoat exclaimed, dropping his cigarette. 'You want me to . . .' he paused, 'every time I need a cigarette?'

'*Ja!* Why not? These are the best available – the new Ambrosiana Ticklers. Firm yet thin, fully packed and cool.' Kubler patted the archaeologist on the back and laughed.

Truecoat was reeling. This banker was indeed a strange one. Stymied as to what to say next, he returned to the museum's cash shortage, asking, 'What about my suppliers getting paid?'

'It is only the temporary delay,' Kubler assured him. 'We . . . I . . . need all the money I can assemble right now. But in a few more days things will be OK. *Ja*. To make certain I must fly back to Lugano tomorrow.'

Politely Truecoat said, 'Yes, of course.' But still confused, he asked, 'But is there a will, are there heirs, and who will be in charge of the museum's funding so our bills can be paid? What about probate, lawyers, and all those formal customs of our Western culture?'

'You mean, is there to be a meeting in which some lawyer reads a will so we each know where we stand after the death of the principal character?' Kubler asked.

'Yes, aren't those the proper procedures followed after someone dies?'

Kubler waved his hand, signalling for a taxi, and said, 'Nothing Trevor Thomson ever did followed accepted procedure. Focusing on his own interests is how he made so much money.'

Truecoat nodded uncertainly. 'No will? But how . . . ?'

'Don't worry, Dr Truecoat, you just do your job. Finish the museum and scoop up those treasures from off that reef, all the while trying to control your expenditures.' Seeing the first cab was already booked, Kubler shook his head in dismay. Looking for another, he reiterated, 'You tend the wreck and your little museum, and I'll tend the money.'

Apologizing, Truecoat said, 'I'd give you a lift to your hotel, but my bicycle won't hold two, plus your case.'

'Thanks anyway.' Kubler lowered his arm and looked inquiringly at Truecoat. 'By the way, have you found any gold out there?'

'No,' Truecoat replied, disliking the banker's constant orientation to money. 'But please drop by the museum tomorrow after the funeral and I'll show you our latest treasures.'

Kubler nodded. '*Ja.* Tomorrow on my way to the airport.'

14

A hot island breeze replaced the cool air of the plane's interior as Penny, Judith and Sam emerged from the cabin.

'Caribbean air is so thick you can cut it with a knife,' Judith said.

Taking a deep breath, Penny said, 'I smell the ocean.'

'How do these people survive in this heat?' Judith asked. 'Do you think they have air-conditioning? They surely must.'

Her question was answered as they crossed the tarmac and entered the open-air terminal.

Sam visually followed the movements of the attractive woman from first class who was already through passport control and heading towards the baggage claim area. A group of young men unloading luggage from the tractor-pulled wagon stopped to admire her, too.

'This humidity makes you appreciate the cool, crisp air of Santa Fe,' Penny said, dabbing at the perspiration on her forehead.

'Is Fountain meeting us with an air-conditioned limousine?' Judith asked.

The uniformed official, whose name-tag read 'Robin', flipped through Sam's blue US passport. Looking over its border-crossing imprints as if she were an art critic judging other country's rubber stamps, she asked, 'Here for the funeral, Mr Thomson?'

'Yes, how did you know?'

'Most people on this week's flight are.' She came down hard on his passport with one of the largest rubber stamps he'd ever seen. 'You a relation?'

'Yes, I was his stepson. And this beautiful young woman with me was his stepdaughter.' Sam gestured towards Judith.

'Everyone will be at the funeral tomorrow,' Robin replied. 'Biggest event since John Glenn landed nearby.'

'Really, John Glenn?' Judith said. 'The astronaut? I'm sure he didn't have to clear Immigration.'

Sam thought people should be allowed to pass freely from one country to another. Had the Aztecs exercised such border-crossing procedures, they might have refused entry to Cortez and his army, which in turn would have changed world history. Maybe for the better, he acknowledged. On the other hand, if Immigration and Customs were eliminated, a lot of people would lose their jobs.

Judith demanded Sam find someone to carry their luggage. But there were no porters or carts, so Sam, playing the role of bellhop, joined the queue for Customs behind the husband and wife couple from first class. The woman's face was still concealed by sunglasses.

Sam noticed the signs in the terminal. One read: 'Avoid AIDS, Use A Condom'. Another advised: 'Stick With One Partner'. Another: 'Just Say "No" '. He pointed them out to Penny and said, 'They're seriously trying to educate the natives about AIDS.'

'Yes,' she agreed. 'And the guidelines for safe sex suggest to me an interesting investment opportunity.'

'Luggage up here, please,' a woman official said, her brass name-tag reading 'Moravia'. With her fierce brown eyes she seemed to be X-raying their bags. 'Do you have anything you wish to declare?'

Judith spoke up, 'Yes, I declare that it's extremely hot in here. Don't you have air-conditioning?'

In her government demeanour, Moravia said with all the patience she could muster, 'If you had to pay fifty cents a kilowatt hour, you wouldn't run the equipment either.' She relaxed her formal posture and said, 'Americans have a refreshing sense of humour that should keep them cool.'

Sam said, 'That is a lot more expensive than the ten-cent kilowatt hour in our country.'

'Yes, yet I wouldn't trade places with you. No sir, we islanders may be few in number, and we may have a tiny poor country, but this limestone reef is all ours, and we're in charge here.'

Sam nodded.

Moravia went on, 'We're descendants of your slaves. All of us came over as loyalists to the Crown, still are – we've a governor appointed by the Queen of England.'

'Really?' Judith said, impressed.

'Yes, he lives in the residence.' Moravia added, 'You know, if it hadn't been for the English, we'd have been swallowed up by your country long ago. Can you imagine what life would be like if we were part of, say, your state of Georgia?'

Outside, Sam saw the tall woman again. She was talking to her two companions, one of whom was signalling for a taxi.

Penny asked Sam, 'Do you remember what Fountain looks like?'

Sam forced his attention back to her and said, 'Yes, it's been a while, but I think I could recognize him again.'

'Excuse me,' a handsome man with silver-rimmed glasses wearing a European-cut suit and carrying a leather attaché case, said as he came up to Penny. Tipping his hat and clicking his heels, he asked, 'You were on the flight from Miami?'

Judith said, 'In coach, I'm afraid.'

Bowing slightly, he asked, 'You are Americans? Here for the funeral of Mr Thomson?' His eyes settled on Penny as he asked, 'Are you relatives?'

Unnerved by his searching blue eyes, Penny stumbled out with, 'Yes, are you?'

'*Ja*. But not a relative. Now I must find the hotel.'

Penny said, 'The tour book says there are two – each about two miles north of Cockburn Town. . . .'

'May I share the taxi with you? They have only a few here, and the man who met me was on a bicycle.' The man laughed, the warmth of his smile pleasantly surprising Penny. Reaching into his pocket, he produced a business card.

A young woman interrupted. 'Excuse me,' she said, 'are you the banker couple from California? I'm Debra. . . .'

'No, I can't even balance my cheque book,' Sam said. Turning to Penny, he asked, 'Do I look like a California banker?'

Penny chuckled. 'Californians don't wear hats. And besides, you're a lover, not a banker. Bankers are not much good at things requiring sensitivity.'

The man said, 'But, *Fräulein,* have you ever gone beyond the teller's wicket and sampled the merchandise?'

'I'm an investment manager. I know something . . . .'

'You have been banking at the wrong bank.' He handed her another card. 'I'd like a chance to acquaint you with the services our bank can provide for a nice-looking woman such as yourself.'

Disarmed, Penny laughed out loud. Tucking his two cards in her purse without looking at them, she said, 'I've never spurned good financial service.'

Noticing the group was now too large for one taxi, and impatient to leave, the banker bowed and moved off.

'Bankers do dress well,' Judith declared. 'I sit with several on the boards of charities.' She said to Debra, 'You're not from around here?'

'I'm from Los Angeles,' Debra said, extending her hand. 'Debra Datsun, Universal Life Insurance Company.'

'I know the company well,' Penny said. 'You've lots of real-estate loans. But with problems . . . loans on buildings brimming with asbestos, loans on land contaminated with toxic fill, and no environmental insurance.'

Debra whistled. 'I'm amazed at your knowledge.'

'Here for the funeral, too?' Sam asked.

Judith tugged at her sleeve and asked, 'You know, I've met someone on your board of directors, ah Mr . . . ah . . . I can't remember his name now.'

'I don't personally know any of the board,' Debra replied. 'Our paths aren't likely to cross unless it's at a joint alumni get-together and I'm in the Stanford Singles club.'

'You're a Stanford alumna?' Judith asked.

'Yes, more than ten per cent of my graduating class is Asian-American,' Debra said. 'Thanks to scholarships.'

'I had no idea,' Judith stammered.

'Scholarship money from one of those foundations of yours has served a good student,' Sam said.

'Your being here must have something to do with insurance?' Penny asked.

Debra smiled and said, 'Yes, it does actually. But since none of you is the banker I'm looking for I must be getting along.'

'Insurance on my stepfather?' Sam asked. 'I understand he had a substantial policy.'

'Such information is confidential,' Debra replied. 'Our policy is not to discuss our policies.' She laughed.

'But you do have a policy,' Penny pressed. 'Or else you wouldn't be here.'

'Yes,' Debra acknowledged. 'But . . . well . . . I must . . . .'

'But, what?' Sam said sternly.

'Well, since you are a relative, I guess I can tell you there's a suicide exclusion,' Debra said. 'In the event of self-inflicted death the policy doesn't pay.'

'Suicide!' Sam blurted.

'Shh,' Penny warned, 'everyone can hear you.'

'I don't give a damn,' Sam declared. 'Suicide for Trevor is definitely out.'

Debra said, 'I'm here to question two people who claim to be witnesses.'

Sam watched her hurry over to the couple from first class and introduce herself. He admired her forwardness in approaching strangers.

'Say,' Penny exclaimed, tugging Sam's arm, 'did you get a look at the baggage?'

'Ours?' Sam asked.

'No, I mean did you see if they unloaded Trevor's body?'

Sam said, 'I retrieved our baggage, intent on getting us through Customs.'

'Sam, you've got to get with this thing,' Penny insisted, squeezing his arm. 'We're here on an important mission . . . .'

Judith said, 'And so is everybody else.'

Suddenly Sam decided to be as aggressive as Debra Datsun. He left Penny and Judith and, fortified with new-found fiery male determination, he wove through the passengers, stepping over and around luggage, intent only on meeting the attractive dark woman.

15

'This week's flight just landed, Mr Fountain,' the trustee's assistant announced as she poked her head inside his office. 'Fred called from control tower.'

'Thank you, Marjean,' he replied, holding his hand over the mouthpiece. Speaking into the phone again, he said, 'They are here, Superintendent Hedgepeth. I shall advise the Governor and collect them at the air terminal.'

Punching another set of numbers, Fountain requested, 'His Excellency, please.'

'One moment please.'

To island residents who had known him since he arrived fresh out of the University of London some thirty years ago, Charles Fountain was their elder accountant, a pillar of the community. By reputation, his credibility enhanced the local industry of offshore trusts. Marjean had been with him since the early days. She bragged to friends and relatives what a decent and proper man he was, attentive to his clients from Europe and America.

'Good afternoon, Your Excellency,' Fountain said. 'The heirs have arrived. Everything is on schedule for the funeral tomorrow morning. Superintendent Hedgepeth will collect you first off at ten o'clock. After the funeral, you are scheduled to preside over the formal inquiry into Mr Thomson's death as well as the heirship.'

After a long silence on the other end of the phone, the Governor hesitatingly asked, 'Couldn't we simply have an informal inquiry?'

'No, a decision must be made.'

While waiting for the Governor's response, Fountain's eyes absently roamed the hundreds of seals, one for each of the offshore corporations for which he was responsible. The official stamping devices were stowed on shallow shelves built to accommodate their tall, upright handles. Fountain inhaled deeply. The fragrance from the covers housing the minute books and records of offshore trusts, the bouquet of sturdy old leather, as usual, served to invigorate him.

There still being no reply, Fountain tried another approach with the Governor. 'Maybe you would like to meet informally with the heirs this evening, sir, in your residence?'

'I'll ring you back about that in a minute,' the Governor told him.

The fax machine on the trustee's credenza came alive and began to produce a letter which he could see was on the Arthur Andersen letterhead. Waiting for the Governor to reply, he began to read. The world-wide accounting firm wanted help in setting up an office in Turks and Caicos. The precise signature of John Alexander appeared above his title, Real Estate Property Manager.

Fountain called to Marjean, 'Fax Mr Alexander our basic proposal for office space in my new building and put a note on the fax cover sheet telling him I shall phone later this evening.' He told her, 'They are the third firm to make an inquiry about office space since the first of the year.'

'Maybe you'll get your big building put up yet. By the way, do you want to take the Thomson file with you to the airport?' Marjean asked.

'Absolutely not,' Fountain said emphatically, annoyed.

'I thought since everybody is here on island . . . .' Marjean said dejectedly.

'Our files must not leave this office. You know my rules,' Fountain said, dismissing her.

Damn, what was keeping the Governor this time? Why did he agonize over every detail of every decision?

His annoyance with the Governor lit the fuse that exploded his long-concealed anger at Trevor Thomson. Fountain hoped with Trevor's death he could at last be done with those memories of that appalling episode on the pirate boat. Down through the years barnacles of guilt had clung to him. No matter how disciplined and orderly he conducted his day-to-day life, that awful event back in 1963 was vividly burnt into his mind. Worse, he couldn't pry the guilt loose. Damn Trevor.

All these years he had lived in fear of his part in the deed being exposed. But so well had he concealed his complicity he believed no one else around the island, at least no one with credibility, knew what actually took place.

Years ago he married Chiarra – and he acknowledged he had done so out of a mix of sympathy and guilt. Nevertheless he had been happy, and he was sure she had been, too.

Those among the crew who might have witnessed the rape, or at least heard Chiarra's screams, never told anyone for fear of invoking Trevor's terrible vindictive wrath. Damn Trevor.

From his memory of that voyage, he mulled over those members of the crew who were aboard the pirate galleon. Three had died and one had moved to Australia. That left two in Cockburn Town. One was the grey-haired captain who ran 'The Unlucky Lady'. The other witness was a doddering bearded man called Old Henry. He walked with a cane, waving it in the air, his pet parrot astride his shoulder. Bellowing now and then as if ordering someone down the gangplank, Old Henry made his way up and down the streets of Cockburn Town. The heat forced him back into his tar-paper shack huddled next to the boat dock, and he was seldom seen as the day pressed on, sleeping, most thought, dreaming of his days at sea, others said.

Suddenly all Charles Fountain wanted to do was to telephone Chiarra, or better still, drive the short distance to his house and extend her one of his arms-outstretched, debits-are-on-the-left and credits-are-on-the-right hugs. She loved it when he verbally assigned the proper accounting directions and enveloped her within his embrace. His silliness always cheered her. And himself as well.

At last the phone rang and he heard the Governor's British voice say, 'I should like to interview the stepson tonight, ah . . . Mr Samuel Thomson is his name, right? Yes, perhaps you and he could come round for a chat about eight.'

'Of course, but his sister is also here, sir. And she is an equal beneficiary. The protocol is for her to be invited.'

'Oh dear, not another woman,' the Governor said. 'They can make the most awful disturbances these days.'

'I understand she is quite prominent in charitable circles,' Fountain said. 'And from her picture she is rather attractive.'

'Oh, very well then, we mustn't offend her. And the Americans do have their own proper social circles. Can't really be criticized for catering to them, can we? Tourism and offshore trusts, they're the coin of our little realm. Right, old boy?'

'Eight it will be,' Fountain said, excusing himself to drive to the air terminal.

Before he could leave, Marjean called to him and said, 'There's a banker from San Francisco, a Mr Hubert Gistelli. He says urgent he talk to you. He just got off plane, too.'

'Tell him I am on the other line and take a message. I must leave for the air terminal.'

Marjean was back. 'He says tell you as follows . . . .' She recited Gistelli's exact words: ' "I don' care if he is talking to the head of the United Nations, tell him he must talk to me now." ' With fright in her voice, she went on, 'He yell at me and said, "Or else".'

'Doesn't sound like a *bona fide* California banker to me,' Fountain replied. 'Get rid of him.'

Marjean looked at Fountain closely, hesitated and said, 'Mr Thomson had a lot money, what goin' happen now? You get a share?'

Shocked, he said, 'You know I am not a beneficiary.'

'Yes, but you were faithful to him all these years.'

'All part of the job,' Fountain replied, thinking his remarks settled the matter.

'But you . . .' she hesitated again, 'could . . . if you wanted to, take just a bit for you and Mrs Fountain . . . .'

'Marjean,' he reprimanded, 'do not even think such a thing! Why the whole island – our little country – depends on the honesty of trustees such as myself.'

Testing him further, she said, 'But surely others will try to . . . .'

'Just let them,' Fountain quickly replied.

'Another call,' Marjean said, rushing back to her reception area to answer it.

'Who now?' Fountain said impatiently.

'A woman, says her name Datsun.'

'Charles Fountain,' the trustee said into the phone, its ear-piece still warm.

'Mr Fountain, I represent a life insurance company in Los Angeles. We've written a policy on a Mr Trevor Thomson . . . .'

'Yes, I know about the policy.'

'I wish to see you this evening and discuss . . . ah . . . certain matters under the provisions of the policy pertaining to payment.'

'Such as . . . ?'

'Suicide, Mr Fountain.'

'But Mr Thomson died of a heart attack, didn't he?'

'Not according to a banker and his wife from San Francisco who claim they saw him deliberately jump.'

'Why are you calling me?'

'I need your . . . ah . . . help to confirm their story at the hearing which I understand will be held tomorrow. My company is, of course, willing to compensate you for your . . . ah . . . assistance. I mean, you know the local ropes . . . .'

'Well, I can always talk to you about it. Of course, you realize I'm in a

91

fiduciary capacity.'

'We have factored your position into our . . . ah . . . proposal.'

Fountain was glad Marjean had left and didn't overhear his response. 'Come to my office later this evening, say around ten.' As he left for the terminal, the trustee realized he had a full evening ahead.

16

Penny called out, 'Where are you going?'

But Sam didn't hear. He was several clusters of passengers beyond, his mind charting a course towards his very special objective.

Approaching the tall woman, Sam extended his hand, anticipating her touch. He started to announce his name, picturing himself moving along a procession line to receive another degree at a college graduation ceremony. His voice, however, trailed off into awestruck silence as he looked up into her face. She was an inch taller. Females were supposed to be shorter, but she looked down on him. It took him an eternity to stumble out his name. He wasn't sure if he'd mentioned it only once or repeated it a couple of times.

Her eyes were hazel, augmenting her exciting mulatto complexion. He tried to anticipate what language she would speak. He was reminded of when as a kid he first beheld the stacks of a library. Where should he begin to explore? Truly, he concluded, this woman's character will require thorough research.

Her leather miniskirt embraced her body as fittingly as a romance novel's dust cover. Her thighs waited to be hugged, but with her daunting aura, he suspected invitations were issued, if at all, quite sparingly.

Nervously, he took off his glasses and rubbed his eyes. Her features immediately blurred, so he couldn't tell how hard she was laughing at him, for he was sure she must be. On some occasions, he had found, reality could be less intense if it was blurred. Real-life events often frightened him into taking off his glasses to seek temporary relief. Reinstalling his glasses quickly returned matters to their natural state of clarity.

Struck now by his absurd behaviour, Sam wondered what he was doing standing in front of her, mentally naked. In an overwhelming feeling of fright seasoned with humiliation, he strained to smile. The outcome, he feared, was a silly grin. Exhibiting embarrassment, he fumbled some quickly concocted excuse about mistaken identity, begged her pardon and turned to leave.

'You're Trevor's stepson.' Her voice was not friendly, but the knife didn't go in as sharply as usual at the word 'stepson'.

Her long black wooden African earrings swayed as she turned her head and said to one of the two men by her side, 'Horace, see the man we're up against. He doesn't look formidable to me; what do you think?'

Sam suddenly wanted to become invisible, so he wouldn't be srutinized by this woman and he'd have time to figure her out. Before he could think of anything to say to her, a white Cadillac taxi pulled up. The other man, the white one, picked up her set of matched luggage and helped the driver load them into the trunk. Sam noticed the initials 'F F' engraved on her leather cases.

As she gracefully entered the taxi and tucked herself into the rear seat, Sam forgave her abruptness, dismissing it as jet lag. Briefly he looked into her eyes, her coolness advising him to turn away, to try to forget her. But he knew he couldn't, even if he wanted to.

Suddenly the realization hit Sam. She might as well have slapped him in the face, for he knew without being introduced, without her wearing a brass name-tag, she was Felicia. And the two men were her attorneys.

It dawned on him they must be working to prove she was Trevor's biological daughter, trying to shunt Trevor's billions away from himself and Judith. The money, if they had their way, would flow directly to Felicia's tall, statuesque self, with sizeable slices being carved off in the process for these two hungry-looking lawyers.

Standing in front of the terminal, Sam watched the white taxi vanish from view. Having discovered her, he knew he couldn't allow Felicia to disappear from his life. Her tenacious presence filled his mind.

He walked back to where Penny and Judith were waiting with a black man with cropped and greying curls. He was standing beside a polished Caribbean-blue Range Rover, holding the door for Judith. Sam recognized Charles Fountain. As he rushed up to shake the trustee's hand, Sam noticed Judith's smile, and felt she was now very much at home as she climbed into the vehicle's prestigious chic interior.

'How long's it been,' Sam asked the trustee politely, 'since you came to Santa Fe?'

He replied with the accuracy of an accountant, surprising Sam with, 'Seven years and seven months to the day, Mr Thomson.'

17

Dr Giorgio Giannini had not been in as much hurry to leave the terminal as his old friend Hans Kubler. He held back, allowing the Swiss banker to be the first passenger off the plane. Grasping protectively his box marked 'Fragile' in both Italian and English, he waited for everyone to descend the portable stairs before walking towards Immigration.

The box and its contents were his responsibility, his charge, the reason for his mission to this remote and, he felt as he walked slowly across the tarmac, hot-as-hell island. As the perspiration began to flow from his pudgy body, he thought about the events leading up to his trip. Yes, this autopsy had been the most eventful in his long career as Ticino cantonal coroner.

To begin with, the policeman had interrupted his horseback ride with news of the drowned man and a message he should go straight away to his morgue. Next there had been the question of hegemony over the place of death. For some reason the Italian authorities claimed jurisdiction. But the issue had been resolved when the captain of the lake steamer officially stated his ship was in Swiss waters when he retrieved the body.

Later, at work on the autopsy in his lab in Lugano, he had been interrupted. While he said he was a family man, Angelo Luciano – yes, that was his name – was no relative of the deceased. The visitor had asked him to withhold news of the man's death for five days. When he responded that such a procedure was clearly against the rules, Luciano grew insistent. The caller, coming closer – and now he could again smell his strong, almost nauseating after-shave lotion – had thrust his lighted cigar towards him, reiterating his request. Of course, the decision to comply had come easier as he watched Luciano extract an envelope full of Swiss francs from the inside pocket of his expensive suit. As the man opened his jacket he saw the revolver tucked inside his belt.

Even in the chill of his own morgue, he had perspired with fright. He identified death with the silent cold of the morgue. Most people, fearing a devil, associated death with the burning fires of hell.

Fearful of his own imminent demise, he had responded to the enforcer, 'But, of course, only five days.' Rationalizing the delay, he had added, 'Until after our Mendrisio Pageant.'

After the Sicilian left he realized the importance of the Thomson autopsy. He stopped in the middle of his work and read again the information on the identity tag dangling from the gold chain around the body's neck.

The chain was real gold; the telephone number to call in case of injury or death was in the Caribbean; the man, despite his advanced age, was thin and in good physical shape; he was tanned and not, as were a lot of older bodies, pale white – all those clues signified an important former personage. So he called the number. After all, he'd agreed not to make his report public, but nothing had been said about notifying the next of kin.

Dr Giannini recalled the name of the man who answered the phone – Fountain – for he linked the name with his beloved Trevi Fountain in Rome. After he had conveyed his information, Fountain expressed no regrets, but instead issued a series of quite precise instructions.

When he had protested he could not leave Switzerland, Fountain asked for his bank account number in Lugano, saying quite a sizeable sum would be wired forthwith. Calculating its size, Dr Giannini had concluded the money would more than cover the costs of his laboratory tests on the deceased. The tests Fountain instructed him to make were indeed extensive, including DNA and even one for sterility.

The bank deposit would also reimburse him for his air fare to the Caribbean – to some island he'd never heard of – plus his testifying at the hearing there on the cause of death, and still leave enough money to purchase a stable of horses.

Indeed, Dr Giannini concluded as he presented his Swiss passport to the Immigration official, Robin, Trevor Thomson's autopsy was a memorable one.

As he reluctantly released his box marked 'Fragile' into the hands of Moravia, her X-ray eyes examining both it and him, he felt compelled to advise the Customs official, 'My package contains a funerary urn with a Mr Thomson inside.'

18

Sam rode in the front seat of Fountain's Range Rover, holding his camera at the ready. He was pleased the vehicle was built high off the ground; it was better for taking photographs.

'One must chronicle life's events as much as possible,' he announced, and laughed. 'Just think, if Columbus had brought along his Polaroid.'

Fountain gave him a questioning look.

Judith said, 'Come on, Sam, be serious.'

From the rear seat, Penny leaned over and whispered to Sam, 'There's something wrong with Mr Fountain. He's driving down the wrong side of the road!'

Sam said reassuringly, 'It's OK, Penny Love. They're English.'

'Don't they hit each other head-on?'

'No, because everyone else drives on the left, too.'

'I understand the two sides of the road, silly, but the taxis at the terminal have their steering wheels on the left.'

'But you can still drive on the left if the steering wheel is on the left,' Sam said. 'There's not much traffic.'

'I guess General Motors is stuck on making left-hand drives,' Penny said. 'I remember reading why their results in Japan were so poor – trying to sell cars with steering wheels on the wrong side for Japanese drivers.'

Sam said, 'The moral to your story is that one should adopt to local customs if one is to survive and prosper in a foreign country.'

Judith said, 'So, Mr Fountain, you must advise us how to behave here in your little island so we won't stick out as being foreigners.'

The trustee replied, 'Here, being white or black does not make any difference. Most natives are black but so many whites do business – granters of trusts, investment advisors, bankers – everyone becomes an individual person, not stereotyped by skin colour.'

'I didn't mean . . .' Judith stammered.

'I know. I am just explaining.'

'Please go on.'

Fountain continued. 'Everyone speaks English. And our money is the US dollar.' He looked over his shoulder, making his next point. 'But unlike you, we pay no income taxes.'

'Come on,' Judith said, 'everyone pays income taxes to their own country's government if they have enough income. Don't they?'

Fountain said, 'One of your American misconceptions.'

'How do you pay for government?' Judith asked.

'Fees from trusts and corporations, and import tariffs on hard goods such as computers and automobiles.' He looked over at Sam and added, 'Cameras, too.' To Judith, he said, 'You have really nothing to be concerned about on our island, Miss Thomson. You should feel right at home.'

'I certainly do here in your luxury Range Rover,' Judith said contentedly.

'Yes, it is handy along the beaches and sandy roads.'

Sam observed the island. While poverty appeared pronounced, and there were few cars, the children, walking home from school, were attired in neat, clean uniforms, tidy packs for books clinging to their backs.

Fountain said, 'The next intersection is the divide.'

'Between what?' Sam asked.

'If I turn left we shall go through the poor area. Right is the bypass to your hotel.'

'Right,' Judith said.

'Left,' Sam urged. 'I want to see it all.'

'Spare us,' Judith said, drawing a deep breath.

'But Sis, the best way to see the opportunities for charity work is authentic on-site surveillance.'

Penny said, 'It's getting late in the afternoon. After our long plane ride, I need a shower.'

'Humour me, Penny. Let's take this detour.'

Following Sam's instructions, Fountain steered the Range Rover left. Immediately the road narrowed, turning into little more than a wide dirt path. He slowed to miss a bevy of kids and slammed on the brakes, barely missing a mongrel bitch, her belly dropping in pregnancy. Tiny houses – and Sam realized they were not abandoned but actually being lived in – set on rock piles forming crude foundations. There was no plumbing; Sam saw a little girl at a community fountain drawing water in a jug; behind the houses were outhouses, and he knew there wouldn't be a sewer. Laundry hung from clothes lines. Burros grazed. Few houses had glass in their window openings. Debris, uncollected, appeared everywhere.

Judith gasped.

Penny began to cry.

Fountain said, 'It is not pretty, is it?'

Judith said, 'It's awful.'

Penny said, 'Why doesn't the government float a bond issue? With the money they could build sewers, a water system, housing, and . . . .'

'Give us time and we will,' Fountain said, interrupting her. 'Give us time,' he repeated. 'You should have seen our island before Mr Thomson gave money for the hospitals, the clinics and even some housing. And he had plans for a lot more.'

Penny said, 'These problems require a lot of money to solve.'

'And people who know how,' Sam added.

Judith covered her face with her hands, not wanting to see more.

Their vehicle went on to the city's plaza. Fountain stopped the Range Rover and said, 'I am sorry for the shacks and the poverty.'

'It's not your doing,' Sam said.

'Oh, but it is. I am part of it. Goodness knows, I want to change it. But there is only so much one person can do.'

Sam looked about at the commercial buildings. He noticed offices of world-wide banks discreetly tucked here and there – not many, not large, but their polished presences evident. He also observed offices of international air couriers. 'Yes,' he said, 'this little island is taking on a new importance.'

Gesturing towards the little harbour of Cockburn Town, Fountain said, 'Some say Columbus came ashore here. Our island, not San Salvador, may have been his first landfall in the New World.'

West of Cockburn Town, beyond the beach, an endless Caribbean stretched to the horizon. To the east were the salt beds, flat and austere. Sam reminded himself salt was a preservative used on the caravels and later the clipper ships. He thought salt beds were the same, whether in San Francisco Bay or here on Grand Turk; in neither place did they help the landscape. Yet, without salt, there would have been no explorations. These islands, indeed the entire New World, might still be controlled by aborigines with no written language.

'You know,' Penny said, 'this remote place will soon be known as a twenty-first century financial sanctuary.'

Fountain started up again, driving past restored houses with painted shutters adorning their windows. Brass plaques mounted beside the doorways announced the names of the firms.

Judith said, 'I'm impressed with the graphic art of the signs on these buildings.'

Penny agreed, 'Even the new government building is tastefully signed.'

Judith said, 'Nothing garish, nothing bold, nothing loud, nothing neon.'

'Works of art?' Penny asked.

Judith replied, 'Some of my friends in Santa Fe would say this type of decoration is an art-form.'

In contrast, satellite dishes atop the restored buildings pointed skywards. Sam realized electronic financial messages were being transmitted to and received from the rest of a more tightly regulated, highly taxed and litigious world.

Sam wondered what Columbus would say if he were here now. He'd probably fax Queen Isabella via the satellite dish on the *Pinta,* counselling his queen to create an offshore trust, a safe haven for her riches, out of the reach of those covetous noblemen back in Spain. Rely, the explorer would advise, on the integrity of Charles Fountain, this man who was now steering his sea-blue Range Rover into the gravel parking lot of a small hotel.

Looking at the building up ahead, Judith remarked with delight, 'This hotel's just like those magazine advertisements for upscale Caribbean resorts.'

'It even looks across a white sandy beach at the blue Caribbean,' Penny said, and laughed.

As their vehicle stopped, a man, walking unsteadily with a cane, came up to them. He was mumbling, and the parrot on his shoulder was exclaiming loudly, 'He's grabbing her!' The bird punctuated its message with a series of squawks.

The man greeted them with, 'More English, or are you American, maybe Canadian, or Dutch? Australian now, are ye? Come to bury the dead? Come to dispose of the evil of rich men? But those men are powerful, and they can afford life everlasting – their evil lives on to rule the rest of us, to rule their sons and daughters, to rule the seas around us . . . .'

'Henry, now you be off, don't bother these people,' said a petite black woman who came briskly out of the hotel office.

'He's grabbing her, he's . . .' said the bird.

'Shut up,' the woman said to the parrot. Speaking gently, she added, 'Take your master off to town.' To the old man, she said, 'Go on, Henry,

I'll bring your dinner later.'

She turned to her guests, laughed and said, 'You wouldn't want this place to be devoid of local colour, now would you? Excuse my appearance, I've been playing tennis.'

'In this heat?' Judith asked.

'It's not too bad now, but wait till August.' She smiled and said, 'I'm the manager, Ms Dorchester. English, black English.' She nodded a greeting at Fountain.

'Who's this Henry?' Penny asked.

'Oh, he's our local character. Used to work the fishing ships. He's a bit barmy now and his crazy parrot is simply out of control – keeps squawking about rape. But Old Henry's never harmed anyone in his life. We don't have crime here, no sir, no vices like in Miami.'

Judith walked to the ocean side of the lobby, while Sam filled out their registrations. 'I want an ocean view,' Judith called over her shoulder.

'All our rooms overlook the beach,' Ms Dorchester replied proudly.

Fountain said to Sam, 'As to our plans, the Governor wishes you to visit him in his residence this evening. I'll come by and collect you. Shall we say ten to eight? Now I must return home.'

Ruffled, Sam asked, 'Why are we visiting the Governor?'

Stepping up into his four-wheel-drive, Fountain said, 'He is required to preside over the formal inquest as to the cause of Mr Thomson's death. For the record, you know – tomorrow afternoon – after the funeral, of course.'

'Inquest?' Sam asked, surprised.

'Yes.' Fountain fired the engine. 'On the question of his death. The autopsy will be presented by the Swiss coroner, Dr Giannini, and I understand there are two witnesses who also will be present.'

'Formalities,' Sam suggested.

'Yes and no.'

'What do you mean?' Sam asked.

'There is a claim challenging the validity of the trust.' Fountain added, 'I shall explain later. I must go now.'

The Range Rover moved off, only to be met by a Jeep charging down the road into the hotel parking-lot.

Sam watched as the incoming vehicle spun gravel, coming to a stop in front of the Range Rover and blocking it. The sticker on its bumper read 'Island Rentals'.

A couple jumped out, converging on Fountain.

Penny joined Sam, and seeing the commotion said, 'It's the couple from the first-class section. What are they up to?'

'No good,' Sam said. 'Look, she's shaking her fist at Fountain.'

'And he's got a gun,' Penny exclaimed.

They stood horrified, watching.

The woman sputtered, 'I'll show this Simple Simon, Hubert.'

Sam looked for Ms Dorchester to ask her to telephone the police, but he saw her disappear, carrying Judith's luggage, showing her to her room.

'Come on,' Sam said, leading Penny by the elbow, 'we've got to rescue Fountain.' He started running towards the driveway entrance, the Range Rover and Charles Fountain. Penny followed him.

'Put your travel bag down, Sam,' Penny said, laughing from fear rather than humour.

Sheepishly Sam dropped his carry-on and sprinted as only a runner in training can.

19

Whenever he travelled to a strange town, Hans Kubler went directly to the seediest bar. There he could relax from the pressures of his banking career. This habit satisfied a social curiosity and afforded him excitement. After all, he rationalized, an investment manager should understand all levels of society if he is to invest wisely.

On Grand Turk by asking his taxi driver, George, he discovered the Old Captain's dingy bar.

'You wants the Unlucky Lady,' George said. 'It's inside the old American naval base, north end island. Check in hotel first 'fore I drive you there?'

'Go directly there,' Hans commanded. '*Ja,* I have only one night. By the way, is there a local plane tomorrow to Provodenciales, where I can catch the big jet back to Miami? Otherwise, I must wait a week to fly out of here.'

'Yes, you can get local pilot to fly you there. 'Bout half-hour.'

'Good. So, what kind of place is the Unlucky Lady?'

'Sleazy,' George said. 'Run by an old sea captain, used to work for Trevor Thomson.'

The taxi soon entered an abandoned naval facility, passing through an open gate in the chain-link fence, sections of which had fallen over. Windows in the old guardhouse were broken. Ubiquitous weeds popped up through the disused asphalt street. Paint peeled off the concrete block buildings, once a yellowish military colour. Where sailors long ago diligently performed their duties, there was now a ghostly landscape.

Surveying the site, Hans said, 'It is a bleak eyesore. Why doesn't the government bulldoze this old base, put the island back to a natural state?'

George shrugged his shoulders, not knowing, not understanding, only accepting the ruins' reality.

The Unlucky Lady was installed inside a dank concrete block

building once used as a cabinet shop. Hans could see the faint old sign underneath the more recent hand-scrawled letters naming the bar.

Looking inside, Hans thought for a moment the Unlucky Lady was closed, for it was dark, but the entrance door behind the screen door was open. As he entered he saw a dimly lit bar at the far end of the room, and he made out two patrons sitting at an old chrome-legged table. They watched him come in, appraising his three-piece suit.

Setting his case on the floor, Hans climbed onto one of the empty bar stools and focused his attention on the man behind the bar, who he was sure was the Old Captain. The man looked up and squinted through thick glasses at his new customer. Then he glanced down again, trying in the dim light to read a newspaper.

Behind the bar on a shelf in front of a smudged mirror stood a few dusty bottles of liquor. A filigree of cobwebs bonded each bottle to its reflected twin. Above the mirror a neon sign scrolled the name of Kalik, the beer of the Bahamas. Hans ordered one.

Even if he'd been the Queen of England, Hans thought, he'd receive no special attention from this antique sea captain. At first he ignored Hans. Finally the old man reached down and extracted a sort-of-cold can, not from a refrigerator but instead from an ice chest. Neither producing a glass nor pulling the tab, he wiped the can off with his dirty rag and set it down in front of Hans with a grunt sounding like 'three dollars'.

'Been around here long?' Hans tried.

As he shifted his eyes from Hans to the newspaper in rapid succession, the Old Captain reminded Hans of the back and forth movement of a shuttle on a loom.

The Old Captain nodded and replied, 'Since Columbus.'

One of the patrons hooted.

'I'll bet you were the captain of the *Pinta,*' Hans said, pulling the tab on the beer can. The suds spewed out of the uncold can's key-shaped opening. Watching the foam slide down the outside, Hans issued a hearty German beer laugh.

'You a Kraut?' the Old Captain asked, looking down again and adjusting his glasses. He looked up and squinted at Hans. 'We get 'em from all over the fucking world on this island. But not many come up here to the tip of the island to patronize my first-class bar.'

Hans smiled and said, 'You're no longer a pilot of a ship, now you're the pilot of a bar? *Ja!*'

'Right ye are, mate, and I'm still in charge – nobody forgets it in my bar.'

Hans asked, trying his best to be casual and also wanting to find out more about his former client, 'You piloted Trevor Thomson's pirate galleon?'

'Are you here for the funeral?' the Old Captain asked, avoiding the question.

Hans nodded.

'Yeah, I used to drive him around the Caribbean,' the Old Captain said, and laughed at his own misuse of seaman's language. 'You a relative or a banker?'

'I feel like both,' Hans said. 'I've known . . . knew . . . Trevor Thomson for years.'

'A banker, then,' the seaman concluded.

'*Ja,* in Lugano. A city in Switzerland,' Hans explained, tipping his can, suds running down his arm under his shirt.

'Here's a towel,' the Old Captain said. He tossed the same dirty rag at Hans. 'Another?'

'*Ja.* Why not?' Hans produced three more one-dollar bills. 'And for your friends here, and you, too.' He tossed a twenty on the soiled bar.

One of the black men saluted, scurrying up to collect his early evening treasure. Timidly the other held back, not believing his good fortune.

'Ever get any girls in your bar here?' Hans asked.

'Girls?' The Old Captain squinted. 'You mean women? Yeah, we do, once in a while.'

'When?'

'When I call them up and ask them if they want to come, and let them know if it's worth their while,' he replied, showing irritation.

'Trevor liked girls . . . women,' Hans said.

'Yeah,' the Old Captain muttered.

'We went girl-hopping in Lugano once.'

'Girl-hopping?'

The second man now came up to the bar, edging closer, listening as he slowly downed his beer.

'Yeah, girl-hopping.'

'How's that work?'

'You go from bar to bar and make deals, taking notes on dimensions and . . . ah . . . their financial requirements. Then, after making a half-dozen propositions, you decide on which one.'

'What if she's booked someone else while you were labouring over your decision?' the Old Captain asked.

'You go to number two and so on, back down the list until either you fall asleep – drunk, or get laid.'

'What happened with you and Mr Thomson that night?'

Hans laughed. 'That's privileged information.'

The Old Captain said, 'You know something? I don't believe your story. You're not that kind. And besides, when Mr Thomson wanted something, he took it, or her, right then. He didn't – how do you say – "labour over a decision". You're full of shit, Kraut.'

Hans laughed. 'Makes a good story though – for a banker – especially since we're not supposed to have much imagination.' He asked, 'What kind of women did Trevor fool aroud with here?'

Annoyed, the Old Captain looked up from his paper and said with finality, 'Kraut, in this establishment we don't talk about Mr Thomson's island women.'

'Why not?'

A deep frown furrowing on his face, the Old Captain replied testily, 'Because I'm the captain on this ship and I say so.' He added, 'My word is law here and on the open sea.'

Draining his beer can, the first patron said, 'It wasn't that way on that one fishing trip, they say.' There was a tremble in his voice, suggesting the mention of that day's activities was off-limits in the Unlucky Lady.

A glare from the Old Captain shut him up, and he clanked his can on the counter, having had his little expression for the evening. He turned to leave. As he passed Hans, he said, 'Why don't you ask Old Henry back in town. He weren't the captain of nothin', and he got nothin' to lose. Better yet, ask his crazy bird.'

The second man, throwing barely a glance over his shoulder, hurriedly followed the first, disappearing towards the dark exit of the Unlucky Lady. The tattered screen door banged shut behind them.

From the dim light, to Hans's surprise, another man emerged. He was dressed in a suit and looked familiar.

The Old Captain announced, as if the Unlucky Lady were full of folks and he needed to convey his message to them all, 'I'm closing now.'

Hans turned to protest, but before he could say a word, the Old Captain reached under the bar. Hans watched in horror as he extracted a gun.

Behind him he heard the new man speak in a voice he was certain he recognized, 'Well, Herr Kubler . . . .'

Hans looked round, exposing his back to the Old Captain's waving pistol.

The man said, 'We meet in a different place.'

Recognizing the Mafia man, panic overcame Hans. He jumped off the bar stool and ran towards the door of the Unlucky Lady, passing Angelo Luciano as he followed the still-warm path of the other two men. He hadn't planned to look at Luciano again, but as he drew closer, courage returned, and he stopped, confronting him.

Looking at him was a mistake, he realized too late. But he said anyway, 'How'd you get here, Herr Luciano?'

'Signor, not Herr,' was the correcting reply, and then came the answer, 'Mafia Air. Our family has a fleet of unmarked planes, you know.' His laugh was cold as he added, 'Family values fly world-wide. You should have bought stock in our family enterprise instead of those Ambrosiana bonds.' Raising his voice and projecting it towards the Old Captain, Angelo said, 'He's the man, Cap.'

The Old Captain started muttering. It was mostly gibberish, but Hans thought he heard him say, 'Thomson, you're not goin' get away with it . . . .'

Hans heard a shot and a bullet whined past his left ear. He raced for the screen door, almost reaching safety. Another shot followed. Instantaneously his left shoulder burned and a sharp pain quickly followed.

Slowly the hurt spread down his arm as he fled from the Unlucky Lady, running aimlessly into the darkening evening. Desperately Hans searched for a pay phone from which to call his taxi driver. But there was none, only the vacant and neglected ruins of the sea base. A rising tide of fear swept over him, a terror of the bottomless darkness of death, in an abandoned naval base far away from Lugano and his beloved Switzerland.

Hans Kubler ran as he had never run before, looking over his shoulder for Angelo and the Old Captain, expecting at any moment to hear and feel the pain from another shot. Finally, in the maze of weedy streets, he found his way past the old guardhouse and out to The Ridge Road, the island's asphalt backbone.

Fleetingly he thought the Old Captain's eyesight must be poor, and was grateful. His logical German mind wondered why Luciano was not pursuing him – maybe he was and couldn't see him in the dark – and he ran even harder, feeling the blood flow down his arm.

Seeing the few lights of Cockburn Town in the distance, he somehow continued, now stumbling, now falling, picking himself up, until a Range Rover, its headlights casting his own shadow eerily in front of him, pulled to a stop beside his bleeding, perspiring, reeling body.

20

Two dark-skinned women, the younger one lighter in tone and slightly taller, embraced each other affectionately at the front door of the modest cottage.

'Welcome home,' Chiarra said as she dabbed tears of joy at seeing her daughter again.

Felicia said, 'It *is* wonderful to see you again, Mother, but this island is no longer my home.'

'Come in,' Chiarra said, 'I baked you cookies, chocolate chip, and I fix us coffee.'

As Felicia followed her mother into the tidy interior, she said, 'My home is now Los Angeles.' Chiarra didn't react, and so Felicia added, 'The inner city.'

Entering the small living-room and seeing the familiar old couch with its palm leaf pattern, now slightly more worn, Felicia fondly recalled sitting there on Charles's lap as he read to her.

As they crossed the living-room to the small kitchen, Chairra said, 'But this island is where you grew up.' She ground Caribbean coffee beans and poured boiling water over them in the coffee pot. She motioned for her daughter to sit at the old square wooden table where the two of them, along with Charles, had always eaten their meals.

Tears formed as Felicia remembered their last meal together before she went off to the College of the Bahamas in Nassau. Charles had encouraged her further education. She remembered his exact words: 'Nassau is the beginning. From there you must go on to a real college in Florida, maybe even California.' He had sent her money to help her get by, supplementing her part-time jobs.

As Chiarra spoke again, Felicia realized how great the distance was that separated them, both geographical and educational. Chiarra had seldom been off the island. And there was the question of her mother's mental health. It had always been in doubt. Charles had taken care of her, assisting her through bouts with the black dog of depression. He had also helped her improve her English, although, Felicia noted, her mother still spoke in that rapid native folk shorthand.

Yet Chiarra was her mother, regardless of the circumstances of her conception and the psychological aftermath. The day she left for college, Chiarra told her what had happened on Trevor Thomson's pirate boat. Recalling the grim story, Felicia now embraced her mother in a demonstration of her love and a feeling of pity.

Chiarra said, 'My, you affectionate.'

Felicia replied slowly, her tears freely flowing, 'Mother, I love you.'

'Sit down girl. I bring you cookies. Must be nice for you to see our island again, all its people.'

Felicia watched her mother pour coffee and lift the cover off the plate of cookies. The coffee was dark and intense, the way she'd remembered Caribbean coffee, and the way she felt at that moment.

Chiarra went on, 'Not like your Los Angeles.' She asked, 'How can you call such a place your home?'

'It's where the action is, where the need is, and where I can do the most good for my . . . our people.'

Chiarra shook her head, not understanding, and said, 'You're here for Mr Thomson's money, aren't you?'

'I'm his daughter. I deserve my inheritance. I plan to use it to help my brothers and sisters in the inner city of Los Angeles. They need a place they can take as much pride in as you do in this beautiful island.'

'You want to give Mr Thomson's money away, Felicia?'

'I'm the director of a community foundation. We give money to other charities.'

'How you get the money to give out?'

'Rich benefactors who want to donate to their community, but don't know one charity from the next, give their money to us. We evaluate each local organization, their programme and how they handle their money. We award grants to the deserving ones.'

'You want to be benefactor? So, why you not do the same things here – help your friends, people you grew up with?'

'Here?' Felicia was astonished at her mother's suggestion. 'This place is not . . . .' She groped for a descriptive word.

Her mother supplied, 'Important, you mean.' With indignation she said, 'Any place where is people is important, whether big city or little island like here. We are people just like they in Hollywood.'

'No, Mother, it's a greater challenge. With my work in Los Angeles,

I give money to a multitude of different charities.' Felicia went on, 'We've a business plan worked out as to how to inject ten billion dollars into inner city projects. Just think, Mother, I may turn the tables of urban history, help solve its problems. I may resurrect the soul, the heartbeat of American cities. And I, as executive director, want to meet the challenge.'

'You want to direct other people's lives and have people look up to you?'

Felicia didn't know what to say. 'Let me try to explain. You see, in the inner city it's important to set examples of what folks can look forward to when they do achieve success.'

Chiarra nodded.

Felicia felt she might be gaining her mother's respect, so she went on, 'Those poor souls at the bottom of the social ladder need goals to aspire to, role models to look up to. Not having them has been our problem – with our race, Mother – a shortage of role models.'

'So that's your job, is it? You suppose just look prosperous?'

'It's no ruse, Mother, the role I play. I work hard. In spite of the stress, my life is working out beautifully.'

Looking at her daughter, Chiarra said, 'And you are very beautiful, too.' She added, 'If you making so much money, you soon need one Charles's offshore trusts like he draw up for rich Americans.'

Felicia replied, smiling, 'Yes, they are the rage in LA, especially Hollywood. Why, there are attorneys in Century City who do nothing but set up offshore trusts. They work with people like Charles.'

'You too young, Felicia, to worry about such matters. You just little girl.'

'No, Mother, your little daughter's turned into a grown woman with a responsible job, helping to solve the problems of the poor, feeding starving children, providing food and care for the elderly, homes for the homeless, and cleaning up our polluted air. We need programmes and positive action if we're going to help people.'

Chiarra poured her a fresh cup of coffee.

'Oh, my. Life in your city complicated,' Chiarra said, shaking her head. 'Life here simple.' She paused and said, 'You do charity here.' She hesitated again. 'But you want to stay in Los Angeles because you make big money for yourself?'

Felicia replied, 'Charities don't run themselves, Mother, any more than ships chart their own courses.'

Chiarra said, 'I suppose that true, even for fishing boats.' Her gaze clouded over, and her coffee cup crashed to the floor.

Felicia quickly bent over and picked up the pieces. Glancing up at her mother, she realized how disturbed Chiarra was. She said, 'Let's change the subject. Mother, I flew first class all the way from Los Angeles.'

'First class on big plane?' Her voice trembling, Chiarra whispered, 'I've never flown again – just once, thirty years ago. If I go Provo, I go supply ship. Never fly.' With finality, she added, 'Never.'

Uncertain, Felicia reached across the table, grasping her mother's hand. 'What do you mean? I don't understand.'

'Never you mind.' And then Chiarra was silent. A tear ran down her cheek.

Felicia hugged her mother, and said, 'I'm sorry I brought it up. It's disturbed you. Let's talk about your life – here – today.'

Chiarra gave a little smile and said, 'Well, first, Cockburn Town is bustling. Charles says lots new people from Europe and America coming. Maybe, with my English better, I get job, this time as clerk. Charles says OK I work. I haven't since you born, you know. Thirty years.' Chiarra sniffled. 'But first I must go Houston.'

'Why, Mother?'

'See doctor at clinic. I need treatment, try get over what happened to me, you know.'

Felicia understood. She said, 'It's good you told me about what happened,' she paused, 'when I was conceived. It's inspired me to help others . . . in circumstances like yours . . . and everyone who needs help . . . who has been abused by the white man's system . . . like those poor folks in Los Angeles.'

'Poor folk here, too,' Chiarra said. She stood up, parted the curtain and looked out. She turned back to Felicia and asked, 'Who those two men waiting in Rufus's taxi?'

'My attorneys,' Felicia answered. 'One is white and one is black. Appropriate, don't you think? Together we make a rainbow coalition.' She laughed.

'Why you have attorneys?' Chiarra asked. 'Should we invite them in?'

'I'm just staying for a minute, Mother.'

'You try break Mr Thomson's trust, you can't, no one can. Not children. Not creditors. Mr Thomson clever. Charles smart. Honest, too.' Chiarra smiled proudly.

'I am Trevor's daughter,' Felicia insisted.

Chiarra barely assented, a distant look coming over her face as she stared out of the window, her gaze travelling beyond Rufus's waiting taxi, across the vacant Caribbean and into the consuming dusk.

Felicia hugged her mother again and told her, 'You won't regret giving birth to me. You'll be proud of me. You'll see.'

As Felicia drove off in Rufus's white Cadillac taxi with her two attorneys, Charles Fountain's Range Rover churned to a stop, the loose gravel bubbling under its tyres.

21

Sam jumped out of the Range Rover followed by Penny. Fountain was already at the rear, opening the wide door. Together they helped the wounded Hans Kubler off the blanket Penny had stretched out for his comfort. Their trip along the rutted track, the short cut Fountain had taken off The Ridge Road to his house, had been bouncy and the wound in Hans's shoulder was bleeding. But at least with Fountain's adept driving, they had outmanoeuvred the couple in the Jeep.

Earlier, back in the hotel driveway, when Sam and Penny had run to rescue Fountain, the woman shouted, 'Here comes Jack and Jill. We're outnumbered, Hubert, let's get out of here!' She jumped in the driver's seat of the Jeep, but unfamiliar with its controls, promptly flooded the engine.

'It was almost comical,' Sam remarked as he and Penny climbed into Fountain's Range Rover. They sped off down The Ridge Road, fearing the couple in the Jeep would give pursuit. Sam said, 'The big guy had been driving it, so why did she . . . .'

'What difference does it make?' Penny said, interrupting. 'We've saved Mr Fountain – gotten him away from them. And now he's safe –at least for the moment. But I'm scared the couple will follow us once they get the Jeep started. Grand Turk Island is not that big. They'll find us. And I don't know anything about guns.' As Fountain drove on, Penny asked, 'What did they want from you, Mr Fountain?'

Before the trustee could answer, the Range Rover's lights picked up movement in the roadway, and Sam shouted, 'Watch out, there's an animal or something up ahead!'

Fountain screeched the brakes. Jumping out of the vehicle, he ran up to the Swiss banker and called out, 'My God, it is Hans Kubler.'

The banker was so weak he was stumbling along. He looked at Fountain, moaning a recognition, and fell down.

'What's happened to you?' Fountain demanded.

Coming around the other side of the Range Rover, Penny exclaimed with alarm, 'He's been shot. This poor man's bleeding badly.' Looking more closely, she remarked, 'It's the Swiss banker from the airport.'

Hans braced himself on the asphalt roadway with his uninjured arm and looked up into Penny's eyes. His head weaving, he put his hand gently on Penny's arm as she bent over him. He winced and murmured softly, 'The bullet hurts.'

Fountain asked with indignation, 'Who did this to you, Kubler? Where did it happen?'

Hans smiled at Penny and said feebly, '*Ja*. You are the pretty *fräulein* from the airport.'

Penny smiled back. She said, 'I'm Penny Bailes and this is Sam Thomson.'

'Trevor's stepson?' He shifted his body to look at Sam, and said weakly, 'Finally, after all these years I meet the famous Spanish historian.'

Sam smiled modestly and said, correcting, 'Spanish Colonial. But why would anyone want to shoot a Swiss banker?'

Hans tried to joke with, 'No one likes bankers.'

Penny said quickly, 'Oh, I do.'

Sam and Fountain gently lifted Hans into the back of the vehicle. Penny made him as comfortable as possible, resting his head in her lap. At ease with her sheltered embrace, he soon passed out.

Fountain sped the powerful vehicle along The Ridge Road, repeatedly glancing in his rear view mirror for the headlights of the Jeep. Suddenly he hit a bump, jarring Hans, who cried out in pain.

'Oh, you poor thing,' Penny said soothingly, her concern for the Swiss banker rising. She began a talking jag, trying to keep him awake, keep him alive, save him from slipping away into what she now feared might be the abyss of death. 'What sorts of investments,' she asked him, 'do you . . . ah . . . did you make for Mr Thomson? Tell me about your investment strategy. I mean, what stocks and bonds, or whatever, do you invest in over there in Zurich?'

'Lugano,' Hans murmured. Coming more alive with his favourite subject he went on, 'Usually triple A rated bonds. Mr Thomson, I mean his heirs, are invested in thirty positions – European government bonds, Eurobonds, and multinational corporations.'

Penny was afraid the exertion might do him in, but his mind was off the pain, so her ruse was working.

The banker looked at her and tried to more fully explain, 'You see, Mr Thomson's Statement of Wishes sets the investment goals for me.'

'Triple A,' Sam said to Penny. 'You'd agree with taking such a conservative posture, wouldn't you?'

She smiled, 'Of course, Sam.'

'What else do you invest in?' Penny asked Hans, trying to keep him awake. 'Bonds and stocks of lesser-known countries and companies?'

He managed to reply mechanically, 'The best corporate bonds are triple A, down to single A, followed by triple B, down to single B, and then the Cs . . . .'

'Are there Ds and lower?' Sam asked.

'You mean like triple F?' Penny said, and laughed. 'Those companies flunking Business 101. I'm certain Mr Kubler wouldn't invest in anything so risky?'

'Why not?' Sam asked.

'Well, when you're handling someone else's money . . . .'

'But what if taking risk was part of Trevor's strategy?'

'Well, he would, I suppose, but . . . .'

Hans mumbled.

Penny said, 'Shh, Mr Kubler's trying to say something else.' They strained to listen.

'Ambrosiana Limited. I must . . . if I die . . . you must . . . .'

'But you can't die,' Penny said in horror. 'Ambrosiana.' She slowly repeated the name. 'It's a conglomerate with which I am only somewhat familiar. Isn't it a large Italian pharmaceutical company?'

'It's a company?' Sam asked. 'Sounds to me more like an aftershave.'

Penny said, 'Yes, they do have a cosmetic line as I remember. What about this company?' she asked Hans.

He said weakly, 'Bonds . . . they are . . . they have these warrants attached . . . .'

His voice trailed off and his head slumped to the side, resting on Penny's arm.

'He's passed out,' Penny said.

Fountain reached in the glove box and took out a flask, asking Sam to pass it back. 'This brandy will revive him.'

Penny funnelled the golden liquid into Hans's mouth.

Sam asked, 'Why is he talking about such a risky investment?'

Penny said, 'I'd better do some research on this company, but who has a *Standard & Poor's* on this remote island?'

Fountain said, 'Barclay's bank manager, Fred Allways, may be able to help you when they open in the morning. Tell him I sent you.'

With the stimulus of the brandy, Hans revived and his eyes flashed. Focusing on Penny, he asked, 'Are you into investments?'

'Yes, I mother Sam's money and other people's as well. Bonds mostly,' Penny said. 'But only on a modest basis compared with the size of the portfolios you must manage.' Looking askance at Sam, she said, 'And sometimes I find it necessary to mother my clients, as well.'

Hans looked at her and said, remonstrance in his voice, 'There is the time for mothering and the time for yourself. Mr Thomson always said, "Investments are business. One should invest with their wallet, not their heart."' He tried to sit up, but recoiled in pain.

Penny said, 'I wish I could look at investments with such perspective, but I'm afraid Americans are quite emotional. They continually need their hands held about their dear little nest eggs, and,' she again looked at Sam and added, 'everything else, it seems.'

Hans asked her, 'What sorts of investments do you do?'

'I like Eurobonds. There's a new issue out – maybe you've analysed it – Daimler-Benz guaranteed, denominated in Dutch guilders. Its interest rate floats two points over the Bundesbank . . . .'

Sam interrupted, 'One of these days they're going to tie interest rates to the depth of snow in the Rockies – a much more sporty index.'

'Only for skiers, those foolhardy people who take those serious downhill risks,' Penny quipped.

Kubler smiled, '*Ja,* I ski, too, always at Gstaad. But snow and interest rates don't mix. You make a joke?' To Penny he said, '*Ja,* the Daimler-Benz bond is a good one. What else you want to know? We must talk more about the new Eurobonds being issued these days.'

Penny said, 'Yes, I'd like very much to do so, but you must get well first.'

'*Nein,* business is the most important thing. Money and finance make the world go round.' He drew a globe with his hand, but his face contorted with pain. He quickly asked, 'Is there any more brandy?'

She tipped the flask, and after another sip he whispered, 'My father was a merchant banker in Zurich – a very dedicated man. He taught me a lot about finance and how to invest.'

Penny said, 'My mother and father were revolutionaries. They converted me to a conservative. American children are always reacting against their parents.'

'Ah, you Americans, you've had you Koreas and Viet Nams. We Swiss haven't fought a war this century. We've nothing to revolt against, so we honour our parents, and they us.' Feeling pain, he shut his eyes tightly, opened them and looked intently at Penny, whispering, 'With your know-how you'll understand about the Ambrosiana . . . .'

Fountain interrupted as, looking in the mirror, he exclaimed, 'I just saw the Jeep's headlights flash. It is following us.'

'What'll we do?' Sam asked.

'Hold on, I shall try to lose them.'

Fountain doused the Range Rover's lights and turned onto an obscure track. The vehicle bounced along the rough back road skirting Cockburn Town. Soon Fountain stopped at a modest house atop a small knoll overlooking the ocean, where Sam watched the now-familiar white Cadillac taxi roar away in a cloud of dust.

22

Penny asked nervously, 'Can we get Mr Kubler inside before those people in the Jeep find us?' By herself she struggled to lift the banker. Distraught at her failure, she gave up, admitting, 'With all this turmoil, I'm growing dysfunctional.' She looked downcast. 'My mind is too cluttered with everything going on – I've got to get back in my comfort zone so I can sort this all out.'

Sam offered no relief, watching instead Felicia's vanishing white Cadillac. 'I've seen the tail fins of that antique taxi speeding away from me twice already this evening,' he said dejectedly.

Penny went in to the house to alert whoever might be inside – probably Fountain's wife, she thought – to Hans Kubler's arrival and his wounded condition.

Sam queried the trustee,' What's Felicia doing here?'

Fountain placed Hans's good arm around his shoulder, struggling with the wounded banker's weight as he and Sam helped him slowly towards the house. He replied to Sam, 'Visiting her mother.' Sadly he added, 'And now with this ruckus, I have missed seeing her.'

Sam remembered the initials 'F F' on Felicia's luggage. 'Fountain,' he mused. 'There are enough fountains on this island to rival Italy's Tivoli Gardens.' Almost dropping his hold on Hans, Sam sputtered at the trustee, 'Is she your daughter?' He paused, his voice softer, and asked, 'Your adopted daughter?'

Fountain's reply was a surprise to Sam. 'Why, yes, I thought you knew. It is no secret. All legal, of course, and above board.'

'No, I didn't know actually,' Sam replied. 'But why?'

She must be, Sam calculated, a two-step stepsister. For an instant he wondered where on their family tree genealogists would pencil in this relationship.

Fountain didn't reply right away but instead concentrated on carefully manoeuvring Hans through the front door. Inside, he spoke softly to his wife. 'Chiarra, Hans Kubler has been shot – we must take

119

care of him. Can you begin by putting pressure on the wound, trying to stop the bleeding, while I call Dr Maghool?'

Chiarra nodded, kissing Charles on the cheek. 'Lay him on couch,' she said, her voice as gentle as her command.

Fountain took Sam by the arm, leading him into the kitchen. Motioning for him to sit at the table, the trustee picked up the telephone. As he dialled, he said, 'I have something to tell you.'

Waiting while Fountain spoke to the island physician, Sam saw a plate with a half-dozen cookies. Hungrily he began to devour them.

Hanging up, the trustee began, 'It was some thirty years ago. There was an unfortunate incident on Mr Thomson's pirate fishing boat.'

Sam looked inquisitively at the trustee, waiting, finally pressing with, 'What incident? Why unfortunate?'

Fountain looked down and said hesitatingly, 'Your revered stepfather took unwanted sexual advantage over my wife.'

'Chiarra?' Sam said with disbelief. 'You mean he raped her?'

'That is precisely what I mean, Mr Thomson. Of course, she was not my wife then. I had never met Chiarra until it happened. I had come to the islands only a few weeks earlier after completing my studies at the University of London.'

'And you felt sorry for her?'

'Responsible is a better word.'

'Because you were there?'

Fountain looked dispirited. 'Let me put it another way, Mr Thomson, I – none of us on board his ship – did anything to stop the rape.'

'And so you married her?'

'Exactly.'

'And helped raise her daughter, Felicia?'

Fountain nodded and said, 'No one on the island knows about it except the Old Captain and Old Henry.' The trustee went on, 'Everyone else who was on the ship is either dead or long ago left the islands.'

Sam said softly, 'Poor Chiarra. Poor Felicia.'

'And if people knew, I would be labelled as an accomplice,' Fountain said slowly, despair in his voice.

'But you didn't do it.'

'I was there, wasn't I?' he retorted. 'The Old Captain was, of course, in charge of – responsible for the ship and its passengers. Old Henry was one of the crew. But none of us did anything to restrain Mr Thomson. We were afraid of him.'

Sam felt empathy for the trustee. He asked, 'How long has it been since you've seen Felicia?'

'Several years. She went off to college and was gone too long. Chiarra slipped back into her morose outlook on life. She is not too well, you know, the aftermath of the rape. Men think they can just impose themselves on a woman, and she will get over it, forget it right away the same as they do. But an act as vile as rape has a lasting effect, Mr Thomson, believe me. A woman's dignity, her purpose in life can be visibly eroded, even destroyed, her pride taken away. In Chiarra's case her self-esteem never really returned.'

Fountain paused, poured them each a cup of coffee and said, 'I have lived with her rape for thirty years. On those nights when Chiarra wakes up screaming, I wonder if I did the right thing to marry her. In some ways she has burdened my life, but when I look at her I remember her agony.' He sipped his coffee and said, 'She needs medical – psychiatric – help, but it is not available here. There is a doctor in Houston, but she is expensive and her treatment requires a long stay – expenses much greater than I can afford.'

Fountain's voice was breaking. Sam saw tears forming in his eyes. He suspected the trustee had probably never told his story to anyone before. Sam sensed how a priest might feel receiving a confession. Yet he knew no response which would automatically absolve the guilt. Sam put his arm around Fountain. Together they slowly returned to the living-room.

There, Hans was mumbling, speaking in German. All Sam could make out was, 'Unlucky Lady', followed by another mention of Ambrosiana.

Sam whispered to Penny, 'Did you know Fountain adopted Felicia?'

'He what?' she cried out, her eyes wide.

Chiarra looked up at Penny, startled by her outburst. But her attention was directed to Hans. Gesturing towards him, she said, 'He's been Old Captain's bar.'

'Bad place?' Sam asked, now quite ginger about what he said to her, going out of his way to smile and be polite.

Chiarra didn't answer right away, tending instead to Hans's wound. She said, 'Old Captain probably shot him. He does that if he does not like you, or . . . .' She paused.

'Or what?' Sam pressed.

Chiarra hesitated and said quietly, 'Unlucky Lady worse place on island to go. This man should never have gone there. Maybe he ask question 'bout Trevor Thomson. Old Captain, he not want talk about it, not allow anybody in bar talk about it. No sir, even with Trevor Thomson dead, the Unlucky Lady is off-limits to all us.'

Penny could not remain silent any longer. She blurted out, 'But why did you adopt Felicia?'

Chiarra looked surprised. 'I didn't. She my daughter.'

'No, I mean Mr Fountain. Why did he adopt her?

'He marry me.'

Sam tried to quiet Penny with a stern look, but she went on, her voice incredulous as she said to the trustee, 'Mr Fountain, how can you ethically or legally, or any other way, be the trustee of Trevor Thomson's offshore trust? You're supposed to be looking after the beneficiaries.' She gestured at Sam. 'Sam and his sister Judith. Now the other claimant to the fortune turns out to be your adopted daughter.'

Fountain looked surprised. 'There's nothing wrong with that,' he said. 'Felicia's free, almost white and twenty-one. She's simply pursuing her rights. As for me, nothing will dissuade me from carrying out my legal duties.'

Chiarra nodded and returned to dressing Hans's wound.

Fountain told her, 'The doctor is on his way.'

Sam said, 'Penny, this is a private matter for Mr and Mrs Fountain . . . .'

But Penny didn't buy Fountain's explanation. With disbelief she said, 'Under such circumstances, it's simply not possible for anyone to be disinterested or unbiased.'

Again Sam gave Penny a disapproving look.

Seeing it, she admonished him with, 'Sam, how can you be so complacent? You're being ripped off and smiling all the way to the cleaners.'

'Believe me, Ms Bailes,' Fountain said, 'no one is taking advantage of anyone.'

Trying to change the subject, Sam interrupted, asking, 'What'll the police do about this old sea captain fellow?'

Chiarra said, 'In past, Old Captain above law. But now, if he shoot foreigner, he in real trouble. The police can't let him do that and get away with it. No, sir. Tourists are special here,' she said, emphasizing her statement with a profound nod. She looked at Fountain, 'Now you must report him to Chief Hedgepeth. Maybe you in trouble, too.'

'Why would Mr Fountain be in trouble for reporting a shooting?' Penny asked.

Chiarra didn't answer right away. She only shook her head as she gently applied gauze to Hans's wound. She whispered, 'Old Captain get

Charles in trouble. Over me. I can't tell you more.' She looked at her husband tenderly.

The trustee put his arm protectively around her.

Chiarra said, 'Old Captain tell police. There be official inquiry, lots of talk and maybe Charles lose licence, no longer be trustee for rich folks. Grand Turk won't allow any blemish on his record. No sir, no blemish allowed and still be trustee. That's the law this island. The law of our Turks and Caicos country.'

'What blemish?' Penny insisted on knowing.

Chiarra grimaced at the blood from Hans's shoulder oozing onto the gauze. 'I don' want talk 'bout it. It not your business, anyway. Island business.' Then she was quiet.

The silence was broken as Penny exclaimed, 'I hear a car stopping outside. I'll bet it's the Jeep. We're in deep trouble now. We'll be shot like poor Hans.'

Fountain and Sam rushed to the window.

'Maybe they the ones who shoot this man,' Chiarra said.

'No, it is as you said,' Fountain answered. 'I am sure he was shot earlier in the Unlucky Lady.'

Watching out of the window, Penny said, panic in her voice, 'They're coming towards the house. He's brandishing a gun.'

Chiarra said, fright on her face, 'What we do?'

'This time they will not bungle their mission,' Fountain said. 'Whatever it is.'

Sam said, 'But surely you must know what they want? Why are they carrying a gun, and why are they in such a hurry?'

Without replying, Fountain locked the front door and scurried to the rear of the house. Sam heard him throw a bolt there, too.

Chiarra pulled the window shade, hastening back to the side of the wounded banker.

Frenzy in his voice, Fountain said, 'Oh, my God, Dr Maghool is going to show up, and this couple will be standing there on the doorstep waving a gun.'

'You must call police, it your duty,' Chiarra said, resigned to the consequences which she and Fountain were bound to suffer.

Fountain shook his head vehemently, a determined and negative look on his face. 'I will not involve the police.'

Penny said, 'Perhaps I could talk to this couple, find out what they want, reason with them . . . .'

'You can't reason with violence,' Sam said.

Penny argued, 'Now where in any of your history books is that

123

conclusion written?' She added, 'In the annals of American history there are many stories about smart people out-talking guns.'

'There may be,' Sam said, 'but for each of those stories there are probably a dozen where talk failed and everyone got shot. Don't be a hero.'

'Let me try,' she said simply.

Fountain said firmly, 'No, Ms Bailes, you should not get involved.'

'I think we're all involved,' Sam said. 'Bullets *en route* in mid-air don't stop their projectile and debate the logic or the righteousness of their targets.'

'This is no time to talk like an academic,' Penny told him. 'This is a time for action.'

Sam was more concerned about guns. The guns these people were playing with were real guns shooting real bullets. Not having been in the army, Sam didn't have a clue as to how to load a gun, let alone fire one, and he didn't know what to do when someone pointed one at him. For sure there were no guns in libraries. He wondered how he'd react if the door was flung open and the barrel of a gun was pointed at his face.

There was a knock on the door, the strength of its force frightening. The second time it was even more insistent.

A woman's voice bellowed, 'Come out, come out, wherever you are.'

Fountain looked at Sam who in turn looked at Penny who returned their expressions of disbelief.

A man's voice called, 'Fountain, Helga and I are here from the bank in San Francisco, we've new instructions to you from your client, the old man, before he died . . . er . . . jumped from the train, and also a document you must sign.'

'What're they talking about?' Sam sputtered. 'What document?'

Fountain said, 'A crazy man who told Marjean he was a banker called me earlier, but I thought she got rid of the phony. I guess I shall have to do it,' he said resolutely.

He walked to the entry, strength and determination in his stride. Opening the door with vigour, he confronted the banker couple, saying loudly, 'Look, we are not playing hide and go seek here. I cannot sign a letter without reading it first. And I read documents only during proper hours. Come to my office first thing in the morning before the funeral and I will talk to you about whatever it is you want to talk about, but this is my home and I do not conduct business here. We are having a family reunion.'

Hubert looked confused. He saw Sam and Penny and said whimsically, 'Whites and blacks having a family reunion?'

'Come on, Hubert, we'd better go,' the woman said, tugging determinedly at his shirt sleeve.

'But we've got to report back,' Hubert said, standing his ground. 'Billy Ray's instructions were clear.'

'Come on,' she urged, 'let's bag this one for now.'

'You mean zero in on collecting our life insurance reward?' Hubert said. 'We'll go see the oriental woman.' The thought of money waiting somewhere else, perhaps easier to acquire, excited him.

'Has she any wool? Yes, sir. Yes, sir. Three bags full.' Helga turned, leading him towards the Jeep.

Relieved, Penny asked, 'What's she talking about?'

Fountain said, 'I am beginning to get some ideas, and as Trevor's trustee, I do not like what I am thinking.'

Sam said, 'It sounds like a lot of people are involved.'

Fountain replied, 'Institutions, too.' Before Sam could ask another question, the trustee said, 'Speaking of institutions, we have an appointment this evening with the Governor at his residence.' He looked at his watch, commenting, 'We must not keep him waiting.'

Penny said, 'Me, too?'

'No, I am afraid not, Ms Bailes, you are not . . . a . . . quite family . . . ah . . . yet. The reception is for Sam and his sister.' He looked again at his watch. 'We must collect Ms Thomson at the hotel on our way.'

Sam suggested to Penny, 'Why don't you help Chiarra with Mr Kubler?'

'Thanks a bunch, stud. I'll get out my first-aid manual and my white nurse's cap. Perhaps I've got a few absorbent F-rated bearer bonds in my purse. Instead of papering my wall with them, I'll use them to sop up the rest of his blood.'

'Don't get testy,' Sam said.

'But you'll need me to talk finances if the subject comes up, and it sounds to me as if it will.'

'I do not think so, Ms Bailes,' Fountain said. 'The Governor is concerned only about properly conducting the hearing tomorrow. Routine, more or less.'

'Routine?' Sam asked, hopefully.

'Yes, he is duty-bound to discuss procedure with the immediate family, in my presence, of course, as Trevor's trustee. I suspect that is the only reason he wants to meet with you and your sister tonight.'

Penny changed her sullen expression to smile politely at Chiarra as she watched Sam and Fountain leave. They were quickly replaced by Dr Maghool speeding up in a tattered old Studebaker.

23

Judith was irate. It simply wasn't socially proper. People shouldn't bang on your door, insisting you come immediately to a reception given by the Governor of the country, even if the country was small and the social occasion informal. They should allow you time to dress appropriately and apply make-up. Appearances, she reiterated to herself, were never offhand, never casual. Once on stage, your posture should be that of a star.

'You'll just have to wait,' Judith told her brother as he stood in the doorway of her hotel room. Fountain fidgeted, impatient to keep their appointment. She threw a glare at him and said, 'You men don't understand what appearances are all about, do you? Go wait in the air-conditioned lobby while I get ready.'

Judith took her time. Fountain's the one under the gun, she reasoned, not her, not Sam. Fountain has to live in this island sauna month after month, year after year, engage in its little internal political games, the kind every community continually plays. As a guest, she was exempt, not required to participate.

Once properly attired in a silk dress with soft folds draping her perfect silhouette, sheer nylon stockings and open-toe high-heel shoes, she donned exquisite jewellery, suggesting old money. Judith was ready.

From his jerky handling of the Range Rover coupled with intermittent bursts of speed, it was obvious Fountain was uneasy about their tardiness for the meeting with the Governor.

During the short ride Judith asked if there was a Mrs Governor.

Slowing at the last minute for a curve, Fountain replied the Governor was a widower.

'One must know ahead of time if one is to exchange the proper social greetings,' Judith said.

'Relax, Judith,' Sam advised, trying to allay her concerns about meeting the Queen's representative.

'But how do I properly address him?' she asked.

' "Your Excellency" is appropriate,' Fountain replied. 'Or, if you prefer, "Sir Hugh" is quite acceptable.'

'Sir!' Judith said, her interest growing. 'Tell me more about him.'

'He gave away a lot of his family money – some say most of it – to finance a relief programme for starving children in Africa,' Fountain replied. 'His diplomatic posts have always been in dependent territories or former colonies.'

Judith wiggled and said, 'That is exciting. And he's in charge of this island?'

The trustee nodded. 'But he is not a dictator or a general or a police chief.' Fountain smiled, adding, 'And thank heaven, for he is rather indecisive about making decisions. To enact our island laws, we have an elected legislature.'

'The clever legislation permitting offshore corporations and trusts,' Sam said, repeating what he'd heard Penny say.

'White?' Judith asked, pressing the trustee.

'Of course,' Fountain replied with sarcasm. 'You do not think they would send a black man to be head of a black country, do you? Such an appointment would be too logical.'

Judith said, 'Well, I suppose not.'

'You suppose right,' the trustee said as he braked the Range Rover at the lighted entrance.

The Governor's residence was an English manor house set amidst landscaped grounds. Built of stone, its blocks probably once served as a ship's ballast. By comparison with other homes on the island, Judith marvelled, his elegant house was a palace.

Sam watched the trustee's eyes take in the Governor's residence. He had surely been here before, often. There must be frequent parties, receptions and social events. Yet Fountain, as he surveyed the elegance, seemed envious, or was Sam's imagination over-active?

A uniformed servant opened the Range Rover's door, extending a white-gloved hand for Judith. As she entered the house, its awesomeness transformed into welcome. The interior was elegantly furnished. The gleam of fresh polish sparkled from the furniture and the wooden floors. A portrait of the Queen greeted them. Below stood a Sheraton sideboard. Flickering light from a candle in a brass holder brought out the table's rich patina. Judith felt right at home, as if she herself had designed the interior of the Governor's residence.

The place was obviously cared for by a staff of servants who saw to it everything was dusted, polished and washed. In ceramic vases were flowers freshly snipped from the surrounding gardens. Their sweet fragrance permeated the air. How lovely, Judith thought.

The geometric design of the antique Turkish rug in the entrance added to the pervasive male aura. To her, it was evident a man with taste and English lineage lived here. The gold-leaf portraits of English royalty hummed from these walls, playing background music to the drama unfolding around her. The framed etchings of hunting scenes sang the chorus. On this concert stage she found herself an excited player.

She primped her blonde hair, straightened her shoulders ever so slightly, enhancing her figure, and exhibited a proud stance as she awaited the Governor's entry. She knew he would have a paisley kerchief around his neck, a trim white beard and wavy white hair – as she envisioned her distinguished real father, a father she'd never known.

Standing beside Sam, she whispered, 'Isn't this all quite magnificent, quite Caribbean, quite British?'

Sam nodded.

And then there he was, standing in front of her. The Governor of the colony was tall with dark, wavy hair. He wore British walking shorts, revealing muscular calves, and white shoes. A deeply opened royal blue linen shirt revealed a hairy chest, which she saw right away was adorned with a golden amulet, a caravel charm dangling from a gold chain.

He was inches taller than she, and so she looked up at him, instantly identifying his English social status. His face was ruddy from the playing fields of Eton.

Suddenly she wanted to run her fingertips with their painted and extended nails across his chest, perhaps scratching a little, certainly lingering, ruffling the hairs on his chest, and then to cup his amulet within her palm.

She waited for him to speak, to command her, to inspire her. He could have said, 'Our island is sinking into the Caribbean – we have five minutes to live,' and she would have stood by him, comfortable within these luxurious surroundings, awaiting further instructions, prepared for death by drowning if supporting him required it, for he would be there by her side throughout, and until the end.

Tilting his head downwards, his deep voice welcoming, he said, 'Ms Thomson, I am the Governor, Hugh Broughton-Williams. Welcome to Grand Turk.'

Comfortable yet excited, nervous yet at ease, she nodded, thinking she was smiling. Was she to curtsy or to bow, or to throw her arms around his sun-tanned neck, planting her lips firmly on his? She wasn't sure, so she performed none of these manoeuvres, only thought about each in succession. But she was certain she was smiling as she heard Fountain introduce her brother.

Sam noticed Fountain step back, a bit too far, and he wondered if the trustee was intimidated by the surroundings, for he faded into a dark part of the patterned wallpaper. In the presence of Sir Hugh, Fountain seemed to fear some sort of censure. Surely not from being a little late. Nor was it racial, Sam concluded. Fountain was too sure of himself to let skin colour dictate his behaviour.

Was it, Sam asked, the relationship between the Governor and the governed? Or was it envy for Sir Hugh's titular positon? Sam remembered then that Fountain was worried the Governor would rescind his licence, if word or rumour exposed the awful shipboard episode.

Addressing the Governor, Sam began, 'Your Excellency . . . .'

'Call me Hugh, Mr Thomson. We'll be informal, as people are out there in your American West.'

'I'm Sam,' he replied, being forced, he had to admit, into an uncomfortable informality.

'And I'm Judith,' she said in a warm summer voice floating softly around them in a tone so lilting the Governor appeared to be aroused by it, for he smiled and took her hand. The Englishman bowed and kissed her hand, a social grace mattering very much to Judith.

The Governor glanced at Fountain, addressing him more formally. 'Come, Mr Fountain, join us on the veranda.'

With Sir Hugh Broughton-Williams leading, they moved to a garden room filled with colourful varieties of orchids. A small bar had been set up. A servant, attentive, waited with a tea service, complicating their choice between head-clearing or alcoholic refreshments.

Sam chose to keep his wits, selecting a special herb tea. Judith succumbing to the *ambiance*, said, 'I'll have a scotch on the rocks.' She watched the golden elixir flow across the ice. The first sip of the cool drink buoyed her, and she loved the sensation.

Taking his scotch tall, Sir Hugh said, 'It must be exciting for you, Ms Thomson, to contemplate additional wealth the magnitude of your late stepfather's.'

Judith nodded, the scotch having soothed the tag ends of her nervousness. She replied, 'Yes, I expect to redouble my charitable efforts, giving special emphasis to eliminating the death penalty.'

'But the threat of death is rather a deterrent, don't you think? It dissuades criminals from committing murder and other such capital crimes.'

Fountain now spoke up. 'Blacks in America are usually the ones who are brutally gassed or hanged – they seldom have the money to pay for the complex legal manoeuvres required for a proper defence in your system of so-called justice. Felicia says so in her letters, and she lives there.'

'Now, now, Mr Fountain . . .' the Governor admonished, not even looking at the trustee. 'We don't have such concerns here on our island – only the odd infractions – since I've been Governor.' He smiled, ready to regard the island's low crime rate as a personal accomplishment.

He went on to say, 'Ours is a welcome contrast indeed from all the dope and crime business they're having to contend with back in England. Actually, I expect the Queen will soon formally recognize our enviable record.'

To Fountain, he said, 'But it is lethal injections these days – the method they're using in civilized countries – no more neck-breaking hangings or cruel gas chambers.'

'Your Excellency, any death is cruel,' Judith said. 'Think of our poor stepfather's death, falling off a fast-moving train – at an age when an old man is supposed to die peacefully in bed.'

'There are some who say he deliberately jumped,' Sir Hugh suggested, interrupting.

Her passionate reply made her even more attractive, Sam observed, as she said, 'Who says such a thing?' Her countenance firm, she added, protecting her own reputation, which she now felt was at stake, 'My stepfather had no reason to take his own life.'

Sir Hugh's reply was quite gentle. 'Reason or not,' he said, his tone suggesting ambivalence, 'I understand two people say they saw him jump.' He went on, 'They have, I understand, an affidavit, signed and sworn. After all, affixing one's signature is a sacred act. On the other hand, maybe they're not telling the truth.'

Fountain said, 'Yes, Your Excellency, Mr Thomson left no note, nor had he a history of mental despondency. Far from it. Those of us who knew him would say taking his own life would be the last thing he would ever do.'

Sir Hugh replied with, 'Life is full of surprises. For example, one of these days may come a notice from the Queen appointing me to a major post in some other place. Somewhere . . . ah . . . a bit larger.' He winked at Judith.

Judith blushed.

'Would it be a surprise?' Sam asked.

'Well, actually, no,' Sir Hugh said. 'I am rather expecting it. You see, life here does get a bit lonely.'

Judith said, 'But where would you go?'

Sir Hugh smiled and said, 'I've always held a fondness for New Zealand.' He paused. 'But I'd settle for Nassau. They have casinos, you know.'

Her imagination running, Judith said wistfully, 'Yes, New Zealand is very chic these days – one place I've never been.'

Sir Hugh said, 'One of my cousins is in the Foreign and Commonwealth Office. These appointments, you know, take lots of time and require recommendations, especially political, as well as connections in the particular country.'

Judith nodded. 'And a social agenda, too. Parties and entertainment, I mean.' She waited a moment and said, 'That needs the touch of a woman experienced in the little refinements.'

Toasting her, Sir Hugh said, 'Right you are, my dear.'

'But what is your point, Sir Hugh, about our stepfather's death,' Sam asked. 'Are you trying to tell us something?'

'A lot's at stake here,' Sir Hugh replied, sipping his scotch. 'We must be certain justice is done.'

'Are you telling me . . . us . . . you are going to issue a ruling on the cause of death tomorrow at the hearing?'

Fountain interjected, 'You see, Mr Thomson, the couple – those bankers from California – the ones who came to my house this evening . . . .'

Judith interrupted, 'What couple?'

Answering Judith, the trustee said, 'They called me earlier from the terminal. It seems to me they are playing two games at once – their own and their employer's.'

'How do you mean?' Sam insisted, glad he'd stuck to the non-alcoholic beverage. Even sober he was confused, his mind spinning.

'Well, there was this lawsuit against Mr Thomson,' Fountain began. 'After endless depositions, motions, hearings in court, a long-drawn-out trial ensued.'

'Lawsuit?' Trial?' Sam said, his voice sputtering. 'I didn't know anything about it.'

'You seldom talked to your stepfather,' Fountain said. His tone suggested a reprove.

'He never talked to me, you mean,' Sam retorted.

Fountain continued. 'The trial was in California.' The trustee paused before saying, 'One reason Mr Thomson set up his offshore trust.'

Judith raised her eyebrows, querying Fountain.

'I thought we all understood, Ms Thomson,' Fountain said, 'his motivation from the beginning was to protect his assets.'

Sir Hugh said, 'You see, Ms Thomson . . . .'

'Please call me Judith,' she said, and smiled sweetly.

'Judith it shall be,' Sir Hugh said, and smiled back. Returning to the subject at hand, he said, 'Even if your stepfather lost the trial, his assets would be safe here on our island. The opposition attorneys would have to switch to our legal jurisdiction. Since they are not licenced to practise here, they'd have to hire local attorneys – and pay them up front – no contingency fees are allowed – and, as well, post a huge cash bond.'

Fountain said, 'Yes, but more importantly, they would probably never find out about his trust. Certainly no one here would either confirm or deny its existence.'

Sir Hugh said, 'Yes, for anyone here to do so would mean a jail sentence.'

'But I never heard about a trial either,' Judith said. Taking another sip she added, 'But we wouldn't.' She looked at Sir Hugh and said, 'We seldom heard from him. Oh, Sam and I – together – always sent him a Christmas card. Every so many years we might get one from him – the extent of our correspondence.'

Sam said, 'So why would he suddenly call up and say, "Sam, stepson of mine, I'm involved in this trial – can you fly out here to LA and advise me?" I mean, what do I know about such matters? My discipline is history, not law or accounting. Mr Fountain's the trustee.'

'Right you are,' was the response. 'And I did my job.'

'You went to Los Angeles?' Judith asked.

'No.'

'How could you have been doing your job,' she pressed, 'if you didn't go to the trial?' She looked at the Governor for clarification.

Sir Hugh smiled. His practised hospitality was advancing her to a state of excitement as pleasing as her surroundings, as smooth as her scotch. Judith had never felt so cosy before. She was content to sip, happy in Sir Hugh's presence. Trevor's money was going to be flowing her way with the unstoppable power of an incoming tide, favourably influencing her charitable social agenda.

Fountain said, 'Naturally I would not go, for my presence would

133

reveal Mr Thomson's financial link to our country.'

Judith couldn't understand why Sam wasn't as content, for he pressed with, 'What was the outcome of the trial you're talking about, Mr Fountain?'

Yes, Sam always sought answers. He was a good historian, trained not to take things for granted, to bore into the core of whatever matter was at hand.

Insisting, Sam said, 'Well, Mr Fountain, tell us what happened in a California court room.'

There he goes again, Judith said to herself. Why can't he simply mellow out in the wonderful *ambiance* of this place?

24

They gathered in the exercise room of the small beachside hotel, the only meeting-place affording privacy. The bar and the lobby were too public, and the restaurant was too crowded. Felicia Fountain and her two attorneys, Horace Turner and Jim Stone, were already working the apparatus when the forensic pathologist from Lugano arrived carrying his box marked 'Fragile'.

Goodness knows he needed to work out, the Swiss coroner acknowledged as he looked at himself in the mirrors covering the walls and ceiling. The reflections made the room look much bigger – whereas it was actually quite crowded with equipment – and afforded glances of his pudgy self from all angles, each likeness delivering the same verdict.

Outfitted in body-hugging Southern California chic, Felicia was working the leg press, her trim legs leveraging the weights up and down, the steady repetitions serving to firm her already shapely thighs.

Her black attorney, Turner, in shorts and a Los Angeles Marathon T-shirt, pumped the upper arm machine, grasping the bar with his large hands. Meanwhile her white attorney, Stone, clad in a UCLA Crew shirt and swimming trunks, lay on his back on the stomach muscle-building apparatus, his feet entwined beneath a padded rest for support as he repeatedly lifted his trim body up and down. Dr Giannini's stomach hurt with each of Stone's counts. The attorney didn't stop until he had completed fifty. Worse, with each rise, showing his annoyance at its intrusion into his exercise territory, Stone's elbow deliberately brushed against Giannini's 'Fragile' box.

The coroner realized he was in the way and looked about, but the only unoccupied place was astride the stair-climbing machine. He stepped onto it, and immediately his legs began to move, the machine automatically set in motion by his weight. Startled, he grasped the handle bar with his free hand so as not to fall off while holding his

'Fragile' box under his other arm.

Simply by being there, his legs now moving up and down as the machine's pneumatic shock absorbers functioned, he began to sweat. He was becoming quite uncomfortable as Felicia, her hazel eyes fixed on a mirror image of the Swiss doctor, said, 'Now tell us, Dr Giannini, about this autopsy of yours – the one you did on my father. What did you find out?'

She finished her set, stopped and, looking at him directly, said, 'I mean, as to the cause of his death . . . and anything else . . . ah . . . genetically helpful in establishing Trevor Thomson to be my . . . ah . . . real father.'

Mechanically climbing, he replied, 'You are correct.' He had to gasp for breath. 'I did perform the official inspection of the body.' He nodded his head at the box, gulping air again. 'It was delivered to my laboratory . . . after being pulled from the lake.'

Felicia eyed the box as she said, 'This man – Trevor, my real father – was never labelled as "Fragile" before. Nor did he treat my mother that way.' She clenched her fists at the box.

Restraining her by raising his hand in caution, Turner said, 'Dr Giannini, are you telling us Trevor Thomson is in the box you are holding?'

The coroner nodded, managing, 'Yes, his ashes – within a beautiful bronze urn. I selected it myself.'

'And what did you discover in your autopsy?' Turner asked in the court-room voice he reserved for juries.

'My report will be delivered tomorrow . . . at the hearing,' the doctor replied, hoping to close the matter so he could get off this silly up-and-down machine and return to the comfort of his air-conditioned hotel room.

Stone asked, 'What will your report say was the cause of death? Was there any foul play?'

The coroner replied, 'I understand there are two witnesses who say they saw him deliberately jump.'

'Have you interviewed them?' Turner demanded to know. He gave up the arm machine, admiring his torso in the mirror and asked, 'And if not, why not? Isn't part of your job as coroner – in a case in which the cause of death is controversial – to interrogate anyone who says they know something about the deceased's circumstances immediately preceding death?'

Dr Giannini nodded and said, 'I've left a message at the front desk for them to call me.'

Turner said, 'You're still not certain as to the cause of death?'

'Well, I might change my mind.'

'Well,' Felicia said, 'the bottom line has not yet been written, has it? I mean, it may go one way or the other.'

Dr Giannini nodded, wishing he dared free one hand to wipe away the perspiration.

'He's flexible, Ms Fountain,' Turner said, looking at his client and smiling.

Felicia was silent, pondering.

Stone said, 'I suggest we broach the subject.'

The corners of Dr Giannini's mouth ticked upwards despite the sweat now rolling down his face. He said, 'You can't influence my report . . . if you're thinking of trying.'

'Oh my no, doctor,' Turner said. 'We wouldn't think of such a thing.'

'You see,' Felicia said, 'what we have in mind,' and she gestured to her white and black accompanists, 'really has nothing to do with the cause of death, although we are of course . . . ah . . . interested, if only for me to better understand my real father and how his mind worked.'

Dr Giannini nodded slightly, trying to conserve his energy. Tiring rapidly, he thought about jumping off but with the other three now standing close there was nowhere for him to land. He and his box with its contents were trapped in more ways than one.

Wanting only to end his exercise session quickly, Dr Giannini said weakly, 'What do you have in mind?'

He watched Felicia carefully. There were three of her, two mirror images and the real one. He chose to watch one of the reflecting Felicias, and was not too surprised when she finally said, 'We need to establish genealogy . . . .'

Turner helped, 'You see, Ms Fountain here is his biological daughter, and we must prove it.'

Dr Giannini rushed out with, 'I get the gist of what you're telling me. So she can inherit . . . the entire estate.' By skilfully juggling the box he was able to mop his forehead with his suit sleeve. He added, 'With proof, of course.'

'You've put your finger on it, good doctor,' Turner said, smiling. 'The key is the proof.'

'So, where does that leave us?' Dr Giannini asked, wanting more than ever to climb off the stair-step device.

'It leaves us about to make an entry in your bank account,' Turner said.

Summoning reserves of energy he didn't know he had, Dr Giannini's legs increased their tempo, pumping faster as he anticipated dollars improving his balance. But he said nothing, only waited.

Felicia asked, 'You didn't really answer my question about genealogy, doctor. What did you discover about his DNA?'

'I do have data.'

A broad smile crossed Felicia's face. 'You do,' she said gleefully. 'Does your data show him to have been my father?'

'We'll need more expensive tests.'

Turner said, 'You see, Ms Fountain here was the product of a rape that took place aboard Mr Thomson's pirate ship, some . . . .'

'You needn't reveal my age, Mr Turner,' Felicia said, 'we're not yet in court. And maybe, with Dr Giannini's kind professional assistance, we won't have to be.'

'Yes,' Turner said, 'I'd hate to have to drag the doctor all the way to England to testify before the Privy Council, appealing the island governor's hasty – and quite obviously ill-founded – decision he may make tomorrow.'

Before the coroner could reply, Stone said, 'How large a deposit to your numbered bank account in Lugano, Dr Giannini, do we need to make?'

Turner slipped up from the other side, his arm around the doctor's shoulder, and said, 'Think about it, Dr Giannini, and then tell us the amount.'

Felicia said, 'Of course delivery is contingent upon your testimony being good enough to win for us the grand prize – namely the inheritance. You do understand, don't you, doctor?'

Dr Giannini nodded.

They moved aside, permitting him and his box to get off the dreadful machine, return to the comfort of his air-conditioned hotel room and contemplate his potential new-found wealth.

'Bye, Daddy,' Felicia said, gently touching the box with the tips of her long, slender fingers. As the coroner left, her laugh bounced from mirror to mirror to mirror.

25

As the four sat amongst the orchids on the veranda of the Governor's residence, Charles Fountain replied to Sam's question, 'The trial was held in front of a judge – neither party wanted a jury, certain their peers would not comprehend the complex issues.'

Agreeing with the trustee, Judith nodded and said, 'Juries are so inadequate, so crude, so inelegant.'

The Governor said, 'You're right, Judith. I can't imagine a jury of even my fellows from Cambridge comprehending the legal shadings of such a trial.' He sipped his scotch. 'The San Francisco bank was trying to rescind leases, even if they were indexed to what proved to be inflationary bank deposits . . . .' He hesitated, not wanting to try the case. Instead he said, 'Why, I know economists who don't fully comprehend inflation.' Sir Hugh added, 'So how could you expect the man in the street to be savvy on such an issue?'

Fountain said, 'Mr Thomson was a far-sighted and clever man. But I was not demeaning juries.'

Judith giggled and said, 'All I understand about inflation is our running costs go up each year – even if we don't add staff.'

The Governor smiled and said, 'You must tell me more about your charities, Judith.'

Her ensuing gaze lingered on the Governor. Hugh Broughton-Williams sipped his scotch, in his linen shirt, collar open, amulet dangling.

Sam said, 'But how could the bank's attorneys possibly attack a lease as well written as Trevor's would be?'

'Surely everyone signed, their signatures properly notarized, isn't that true?' Judith asked. 'Certainly there was no duress – I mean, one person can't possibly be accused of "taking" one of the world's largest and smartest banks?'

Smiling knowingly, Fountain said, 'Your legal system is based on what is best for the attorneys, not the clients.' The trustee stood and began pacing the veranda as he added, 'The merits of a case are irrelevant. If the attorneys think they can make a big fee, they sue. They can distort and manipulate evidence, cast a different slant on what may or may not be the facts. Meanwhile their meters click away. The truth has become a disappearing commodity.'

Running his hand through his curly hair, Sam frowned and said, disbelief in his voice, 'You are punching holes in my cherished beliefs about American justice and the courts.'

Fountain said, 'But I am being realistic. Let me put it this way, Mr Thomson: our island is a legal refuge from financial injustice just as your country is a refuge for those who are escaping political persecution.'

The Governor added, 'Mr Fountain's right – we are a haven for the financially harassed.'

Fountain continued, 'Your American lawyers see to it they always get paid, regardless of the outcome of the trial, even if there is a settlement. They are playing on their own turf in a game in which they have written the rule book.'

'And are the quarterback, as well,' Sir Hugh added, pleased with his knowledge of the American gridiron.

'You're cynical,' Sam said, adjusting his glasses for a clearer look at the trustee.

'No, Mr Thomson, I am simply trying to be accurate.' Fountain paused and said, 'Have you ever gone into a police station or a court room in your country?'

'Uh no, I guess not.'

'You should. Let me tell you who you will see there – the minorities. Not that they are criminals by nature. But because they do not understand your system, your laws, your rules. They do not make the rules they are required to live by. Any more than businessmen do. It is the attorneys who do. They make the rules of behaviour, because your state and national legislatures consist of lawyers.'

Fountain continued, 'Businessmen do not make the legal rules. They play a financial game instead – and by its nature it is an optimistic one. The chips of their realm are plans and hopes for future profits.'

Judith re-crossed her ankles, allowing her high-heel shoe to dangle, exposing her high arch. She watched Sir Hugh monitor her movement.

Fountain went on, 'And when a businessman wins, even if it is only one game among the many he is playing, he ought to hide away his winnings.'

140

'Naturally,' Sam said.

'Where some attorney can't get at them, you mean,' Judith said, surprising herself.

Pleased, Fountain looked at Judith, replying, 'Why, yes, Ms Thomson, you made the right entry there. Because otherwise he is going to surely lose them to some attorney who sues on a trumped-up charge.'

Judith smiled politely. 'And that's why your little island is here.' Her voice hinted at a laugh. 'You're the first landfall for the ship of money.'

'Yes, the reason your stepfather came here in the first place,' Fountain replied, his tone serious.

The trustee was growing stronger as the evening progressed, less obsequious to the Governor. Sam's attention moved to the Governor. To his surprise he saw Sir Hugh was really interested in another subject – little sister Judith.

Sam was even more shocked to hear him say, 'Come, Ms Thomson, let me show you my collection of etchings – scenes of our islands, the salt cays, the fishing boats, the ruins of 200-year-old plantations over on Provo . . . .'

He moved closer to her chair, his arm reaching out towards her, his hand waiting to receive hers.

Sam cringed, ready to rush to his sister's defence. But he told himself Judith was certainly mature and needed no protection from him. He could only laugh nervously at Sir Hugh's invitation.

The awkward moment didn't escape Fountain either. The trustee shifted his weight and downed his drink. He shared the moment with Sam, a point in time which they each turned into superfluous pieces of furniture, out of place in the evening's changing programme of events.

Taking the cue, Fountain said, 'I must be going. Come, Mr Thomson, I shall drive you back to your hotel. I have a few phone calls yet to make at my office.'

Missing the hint, Sam said, 'But I'm just getting comfortable.'

Fountain came up with another reason for leaving. 'I must check on Mr Kubler's condition. Dr Maghool may require the helicopter ambulance to airlift him to hospital.'

Turning towards the Governor to bid him goodnight, Sam saw only Sir Hugh's rigidly straight back as the Queen's representative guided Judith across a succession of oriental carpets. Her hand was linked inside the Governor's arm, her body leaning into his at the socially proper

141

degree. Sam watched as they set foot on the thick Persian Bijar stair runner leading to the private world on the second floor of the residence.

26

In the Range Rover, as Fountain steered it down the driveway, Sam broke the silence, querying, 'You didn't tell me what actually happened at the California trial. In Los Angeles, I mean.'

'No, I am afraid I got up on my soap-box about minorities and the law. I have been swayed by Felicia's letters. She is quite opinionated on the subject. To answer your question, your stepfather lost on a mere technicality, so he promptly appealed against the verdict to the next highest court.'

'What happened there?'

'There were more depositions, hearings, counter-suits, the whole basket of legal eggs.'

'But now he's dead, so what will happen from here on out?'

'More legal manoeuvrings, obviously. The appeal and subsequent appeals, no matter who wins or loses the next round, may take years to play out.'

Sam chuckled and said, 'The prehistory peoples didn't have attorneys, only medicine men.'

'And they were happy, I guess,' Fountain said.

Sam nodded, thought for a moment and changed the subject. 'So, the Governor can be replaced by edict of the Queen, but you must stay . . . .'

'Not must, want . . . .'

'You wouldn't leave the island?'

'Where would I go and what would I do?' Fountain replied. 'There are opportunities here for me.'

'To make big money?'

The trustee's reply was less direct as he said, 'Simply to expand my practice, hire an assistant or two, broaden my client base – those kinds of opportunities. I would not label it as "big money".'

Fountain drove past the airport. Sam remembered Penny saying airports were essential for economic growth. Except for its beacon

143

revolving in the night, the runway lights were turned off. He asked the trustee, 'Won't the island's growth be curtailed by lack of natural resources and power?'

Fountain answered, 'Our growth will continue in the one-dimensional respect of financial havens. Offices don't use as much electricity as factories.'

Sam asked, 'Don't you personally want to profit from the growth?' He could tell from the way Fountain's grip on the steering wheel stiffened he was annoyed by the question. But Sam went on, 'Real-estate investments, for example. Penny tells me anywhere there's a limited supply of land – an island such as Grand Turk – and there is also economic growth, the price of land must go up. Supply and demand, she says.'

There was no reaction from the trustee.

Sam went on, 'Perhaps I should buy land here, wait for it to go up in value – sell it – maybe make a lot of money.'

'I thought you were more interested in history.'

'Yes, of course. I don't understand much about money except for its influence on those who make history. I'm only thinking of a hobby.'

'When money becomes a hobby, Mr Thomson, you can't expect a profitable return.'

They passed a weathered sign stuck crookedly into a large parcel of vacant land. Absently Sam read out loud, 'New office building coming soon'. The telephone number looked familiar. He said, 'Someone's going to build on that piece of vacant land. I've had experience building a house, as you know, so maybe I should get into construction here.'

'Foreigners cannot buy land in Turks and Caicos,' Fountain said, quoting from a local statute.

'Didn't Trevor once develop a hotel, or was it condominiums, over on Provo?'

'Yes, but that was before our law was passed.'

'But if I become a resident, I can speculate in real-estate?'

'In brief, yes. But it is not easy to become a resident.'

'You mean, you want my money but not my body? No Statue of Liberty – or even Columbus – welcoming immigrants here, is that it?'

'It *is* our island, Mr Thomson. We have our rules.'

'You mean it's a black island.'

'Is the Governor black?'

Sam shook his head and followed with a 'no'. After a pause, he said,

'You've got a good thing going here, haven't you? A seven-mile-long dot in the Caribbean – your own laws, and half the world's rich people wanting you to hide their money.'

'Only half?'

Ahead of them in the island dark, picked up by the Range Rover's headlights, Sam made out a moving bicycle. The light from its wobbling headlamp danced a weak pattern on the asphalt. He warned, 'Watch out for the bike.'

'I see him – it is Dr Truecoat. His is the only bicycle on the island.'

As they passed, Sam waved. A cigarette glowed from Truecoat's mouth. 'What's he do here?' Sam asked.

'He is organizing the new Thomson-Columbus Museum,' Fountain said. 'I have not had a chance to tell you about your stepfather's plans for excavating the shipwreck on Magnolia Cay and housing its artifacts.'

'A woman on the plane was telling me a little about it before we landed. Supposed to be the *Pinta*?'

'Well, maybe. At least that is the speculation.'

'I must chat with Dr Truecoat – stop,' Sam ordered.

'What, here, now?' Fountain was annoyed.

'Yes, and honk while you're at it.'

'He will be at the funeral tomorrow. I shall introduce you then. We are in a bit of a rush now.'

'No, now, there may not be time tomorrow.'

Fountain grudgingly applied the brakes. Sam got out, shouting, 'Dr Truecoat, we must talk if you have a moment.'

The bicycle pulled up. Even in the dark Sam could see it was rusty, the front mudguard gone, the wide handlebars old-fashioned, and there were no gears.

'Who are you?' the archaeologist quizzed Sam, who might as well have been a marine artifact he was studying.

Sam introduced himself.

Mention of the Thomson name brought a responsive smile, revealing teeth stained with nicotine.

'You want to see my . . . ah . . . our museum, or the beginnings of it?' Truecoat said with pride in his voice. He took a final puff, and to Sam's relief, discarded the cigarette.

'And talk to you as well. I've heard about my stepfather's foundation and your project.'

'I'm going home to dinner. Too late now.'

'How about first off in the morning?'

Truecoat said, 'I go to work at an early hour because of the heat – our air-conditioning isn't installed yet. You'll have to come early. Mr Fountain can direct you – nothing's very far away here on our little island.'

'See you – say about seven?' Sam suggested. In the dark his hand found the archaeologist's, pumping it excitedly.

Back in the Range Rover, Fountain said, 'It is your stepfather's money, you know, funding the museum, so do not let Truecoat keep anything from you.'

'Would he?'

'Not necessarily,' Fountain said, 'but you know how close-mouthed these academics are – never want to tell you something until it's been proven both ways and back again.'

As the trustee stopped the Range Rover in front of his house, Penny came running out, waving her arms. She shouted, 'You two shouldn't have left . . . Mr Kubler's dying.'

Fountain looked shocked. 'He cannot die, not from a shoulder wound. What does Dr Maghool say?'

'He left to get the coroner.'

'The coroner!' Sam exclaimed.

'He's a doctor,' Penny said, 'a pathologist from Switzerland, the one who did the autopsy on Trevor. Dr Maghool wants his opinion, or help, or something, because he's not had any experience with bullets, removing them, I mean. Nobody gets shot here, apparently. I guess the bullet's in pretty deep.'

'We could transport him by helicopter to Provo,' Fountain suggested.'

Penny said, panic in her voice, 'Yes, exactly what Dr Maghool said, but he wanted to consult first with doctor . . . ah . . . I can't remember his name, the one from . . . .'

'Dr Giannini,' Fountain said.

Sam saw headlights coming towards them. Dr Maghool's old Studebaker stopped behind the Range Rover. Not bothering to turn off the lights, Dr Maghool and another man, each nodding only curtly, hurried past Sam and Penny and into the house. The other man carried a box marked 'Fragile'. Sam and Penny followed.

Within a few minutes Sam realized the trustee wasn't there. Curious, he peered outside, but saw only Dr Maghool's car – a 1953, Sam thought as he tried to remember the various styles and match them with years gone by.

Moonlight flooded the island, but Sam saw no Range Rover. Perhaps Fountain's putting it away in the garage, Sam thought. He went outside to turn off the Studebaker's lights – don't want dead batteries on a doctor's car, Sam reasoned. But the little house had no garage and neither Fountain nor his vehicle were anywhere in sight.

He remembered Fountain had said something about making phone calls from his office. He reminded himself some people worked in offices located away from their homes. And he toyed with the idea of hinting to Penny about the doctrine of separation of work and home.

27

On the little island nothing was really very far from anything else, and Charles Fountain's office was not far from his house. Entering its darkened interior, he switched on a light over his desk, allowing him to see the telephone so he could place his call to John Alexander at Arthur Andersen.

Fountain wasted no time getting to the point. 'As I faxed earlier, I am building a new office complex here on Grand Turk. I do have space available for your firm. How many square feet do you require?'

'When's the completion date?' Alexander asked.

'Four, maybe five months,' Fountain said, admitting to himself he was nowhere close to completing the building's design, let alone starting construction.

'And the price per square foot,' the man from Dallas asked, 'triple-net, I presume?'

'Let us make certain we understand the terminology,' Fountain said cautiously. 'It differs, you know, from place to place.'

'By triple-net,' Alexander said, 'I mean you furnish the shell – walls, roof, foundation – and stub out the plumbing and electricity. We'll pay for the interior improvements and bear the cost of fire insurance, pay the monthly utilities . . . .'

'Electric is expensive here, you know.'

'So are the fees to our clients. Don't worry, we'll be able to manage the costs,' Alexander said, rather condescendingly, Fountain thought. The Dallas man went on, 'You insure the building's exterior – that's all.'

Fountain was pleased. If they were to sign a lease in advance, their commitment would be the break he needed – a large recognized international firm wanting to occupy his building. He knew he could now interest Barclay's Bank in financing the construction.

'How long a lease do you have in mind?' the trustee asked, holding his breath, wanting a term long enough to satisfy his lender. 'I need at least ten years,' he said, hoping for an affirmative answer.

'Ten years . . . .'

'I shall give you renewal options, of course,' Fountain assured.

'Two additional ten-year terms?'

'Agreed,' Fountain said, breathing relief. But a new worry came across his mind. Perhaps since he had talked to his bank – it had been exactly six months ago to the day, he quickly calculated – they might have stiffened their requirements. Banks were always changing their minds.

'What is your rental rate per square foot?' Alexander asked.

Fountain fumbled, not being conversant with the formula. Thinking quickly, he asked, 'Did you say how many square feet you require?'

'No, I guess I didn't,' Alexander said. 'We'll need five thousand square feet, net of rest rooms and hallways.'

'Half for debits and half for credits,' Fountain said, and laughed at his forced joke while trying to gain time to think what rent to charge for his non-existent office building. Reminded of Trevor Thomson's cleverness with the Californian bank, he tried in vain to conjure up a formula.

The trustee fixed his gaze on the wall. To attract construction financing, he had commissioned an artist in Provo to draw a coloured picture of the structure so he could show it to his banker, hoping to excite the man's imagination. The effort had been in vain, of course. But Marjean proudly hung the sketch on his office wall. Her choice of locations turned out to be where the picture received the direct afternoon sunlight. Its reality had faded with its colour. At this moment he hoped looking at the painting, though it was four years old, would galvanize his mind. Finally he decided he needed more time to sort out a viable formula. So he said, 'Let me calculate the rate. Then I shall fax you a proposal.' As an afterthought, he added, 'There will be views of Caribbean white sand beaches from every window.'

There was a blustering knock at Fountain's outside office door.

'Fair enough,' Alexander replied, 'but we want our people to pay attention to their work and not sit idly looking at ocean views, at least during office hours.'

The knock was repeated, harder this time, and Fountain heard a woman call out his name.

'Our people are hard workers here – never fear,' Fountain assured him.

'I'm not worried about your people – it's the ones we'll be

149

relocating from Miami and Atlanta. By the way, what are your rules as to work permits? Our personnel people will want to know.'

'Not easy to come by, unless – as in your case – you are bringing people in who have skills not available here. For example, we have only a few local accountants. The authorities will review each application. But do not worry, I can help you through our island red tape.'

The commotion at the outer door grew louder.

As Fountain concluded his conversation, he heard the woman shout, 'No, Hubert, it's glass, don't . . . .'

Fountain hung up and rushed to his outer entrance in time to see a hulk, shoulder raised, charge the door, hurling his entire weight against it. The glass broke, but the frame held. The razor-sharp jagged edges of the remaining glass raked the man's torso as his body passed through it.

The woman screamed, 'Hubert, my God, you're bleeding.'

Behind her, outside, he saw the headlights of a car pulling up next to the parked Jeep. Curious, he watched as a shapely young woman got out. Must be the insurance woman from Los Angeles, he concluded.

But his attention quickly returned to the bloody scene before him. What a fool this Hubert person was to physically charge a glass door. And to go careering around the island, waving a pistol and yelling. And all the while calling himself a banker from San Francisco. Despite his concern for the man's condition, Fountain couldn't help but laugh at the burlesque scene.

The woman accompanying him glared through the void left by the broken glass in the still-locked door. She demanded to know, 'What's so damned funny, Fountain?'

The comely lass entered, and Fountain called out, 'This man has been injured, blood all over – better stand clear.'

'I can see he has, Mr Fountain,' Debra Datsun said with alarm as she surveyed the bleeding and by now groaning Hubert. 'I'm from the insurance company in Los Angeles,' she said simply.

'Yes, you called from the airport. Excuse me for a moment – I should fetch our island doctor.'

Debra said, 'Can I be of assistance?'

Hubert moaned, his eyes appealing to his wife, and said, 'Help me, Helga.'

Helga, hovering over Hubert, looked up and said to Debra, 'You can pay us our ten per cent fee . . . ah . . . reward, the money your company owes us. You bring cash?'

'I don't carry five million in cash on me,' Debra said. 'I must make certain your statements are valid and the autopsy won't refute what you've told us. Only then can I pay you. My job's on the line.'

'Well, if you don't have the cash with you, how can you pay, whether it's today or tomorrow?'

'Ever hear of cheques?'

'Yeah, ones that bounce.'

Hubert moaned again.

Fountain returned. 'The doctor is on his way. Two emergencies on Grand Turk in one night.' He shook his head in disbelief.

Helga looked at Fountain and demanded, 'You got any towels, bandages, those sorts of first-aid supplies?'

Fountain unlocked what was left of the broken entry door, letting in both women and pointing to a nearby door labelled 'rest room'.

'But our cheques are good,' Debra said.

'For what?' the woman quipped as she helped Hubert towards the rest room sink, his lacerations dripping a trail of blood on the carpet.

Debra, waiting for the couple to get out of hearing distance, said, 'Mr Fountain, you do accept cheques for your services?'

'I've been known to do so.'

Debra whispered, 'In that case, how much is your fee for assuring a suicide verdict at the hearing tomorrow?'

Fountain looked aghast. 'My fee?'

'Why, yes, we don't expect you to . . . .'

'Assist for free?'

'Exactly.'

Fountain considered the proposition. He thought about how long he'd dreamed of constructing his office building, and how its new tenants, the mainland accounting firms, would bring in even more money and jobs for his adopted home and country, his island nation. He reviewed the high cost of Chiarra's medical treatment in Houston. And he thought about his duties as trustee. He tried to sort out an ethical stance for himself. The answer to his knotty question was not as clear-cut as he hoped it would be.

'Half in advance, and half after the verdict?' Debra asked, looking at him inquisitively.

Half of what, he wondered. To his surprise and dismay, he heard himself say, 'I cannot guarantee anything. It is the Governor who makes the decision, and I do not necessarily have him in my pocket.' Perhaps, he thought, there had been just too much going on here on his peaceful little island since the big plane from Miami landed. His code of values

151

was blurring, becoming difficult to define.

Fountain had to constrain himself, but somehow the thought of all this money – Trevor's, John Alexander's, Universal Life Insurance Company's – danced before him in the form of a sensuous woman. Lust and money intertwined in his mind and across his vision. Tempted by the she-devil, he was succumbing. Stop, he yelled at himself, but in this nightmare, he could not do so.

'And how much money will half come to?' Debra asked as she extracted from her brief-case an envelope marked, 'Insurance Company Cheques'.

'No, dear.' Once again Fountain found himself uttering things he'd never dreamed he could say. 'You do not understand. This transaction of ours must be in currency.'

Debra exclaimed, 'What's happened to trust and contracts?'

'You want to give me a demand note, a formal obligation of your company?'

'Well, no, I can't produce that kind of documentation out in the field.'

'Then use the greenbacks,' Fountain said in a fatherly tone, his mind already visualizing an attaché case full of paper money.

'But what's wrong with a cheque?'

'Insurance cheques are drafts,' Fountain explained, using his tutorial voice. 'They are payable only *through* a bank, not *by* a bank.'

'What's the difference?'

'Plenty,' the trustee replied. 'It means the cheque is not honoured until the bank presents it to your treasurer back in Los Angeles. He has the option to refuse to pay it. And I fear your treasurer might renege in order to conserve company funds.'

'Our treasurer's a she.'

'Even worse.'

'But I'm not carrying such a large amount of cash,' Debra protested.

'I suggest you telephone your head office and have the funds wired into my account.' Fountain looked up at his wall where four clocks were mounted. One was labelled, 'Switzerland', and showed the time there, another read, 'Turks and Caicos – same as New York', the third, 'Santa Fe', and the last, 'California'. Looking at the West Coast one, he said, 'There is still time to contact your office.'

'How much?'

'Maybe you'd better include the fee for this banker couple, as well. Or they will be all over you like they have been me. They apparently

152

will not give up.'

'You don't believe their suicide story?' Debra asked.

'Do you?'

'I must, don't you see, from the point of view of my insurance company employer.'

'Save a lot of claim money for your company.'

Debra Datsun nodded.

'Here is my bank account number at Barclay's and their wire transfer code,' he said, writing the information on his note pad and handing it to her with one hand while extending the telephone with the other. 'Dial the international code first, the area code, then your office number . . . .'

'Yes, I know how to do all that,' Debra said, a little put out. 'One has to be up to speed on telephone technology in order to survive in the business world today. But how much money?'

'Mine is . . . ah . . . a hundred thousand. Of course, I do not know what the Gistellis are charging.'

Debra thought for a moment and said, 'I better go back to the hotel and organize my thoughts before I telephone. It's important for me to make an intelligent and coherent verbal presentation to our president.' She looked at her watch. 'Mr Lloyd'll have downed a couple by this time and may not be too savvy. I am sure he's making arrangements to entertain Gladys at a Hollywood bistro so he'll be impatient to get on with the evening's agenda. My argument must therefore be short and to the point. I'll need to write it all out on my laptop before phoning.'

Lust for this young woman now overcame Fountain. He asked himself how he would feel to be a student again attending the University of London. Courting her. He thought about making love to Debra Datsun as he watched her movements and listened to her soft voice. Maybe he should try to seduce her, although he realized his technique would be rusty. But afraid of failure and rejection, he did nothing.

He said only, 'I have another, a private office you may use. I am preparing it for a new assistant. To hire, I mean.' He heard himself say, 'And if you can . . . are successful, I mean . . . which I am sure you will be with your president, I shall be glad to feed back to you twenty per cent of my hundred thousand.' He reminded himself once the apple of sin is bitten into, its lure turns to compulsion.

Debra looked at him, exclaiming, 'Personally, you mean?'

'Of course. For your services,' he said, moving closer to her. 'One should share the wealth these days. I mean, in these difficult times, spread it around.' He tried to encircle her with his arm.

She edged away. 'Sharing has a hidden agenda.'

'It is simply that I should like to get to know you better.'

'So would Mr Lloyd,' Debra replied. 'What is it with you men, can't you simply do your job and be satisfied?'

'Dessert,' Fountain said simply remembering a phrase Trevor Thomson had used. Quoting it he said, 'Men like a little sweet after their main course.'

Debra said, 'Men eat too much as it is. So you're going to have to look elsewhere, Mr Fountain. My advice is to watch your intake of calories.' As she left, she said, her smile perfunctory, 'I'll call you later.'

Fountain felt stupid. For relief, he forced himself to focus on the money. Debra Datsun's little consulting fee, he reminded himself, would immeasurably improve his prospects for getting the loan and constructing his new office building. Maybe his real-estate project was going to turn out to be a substitute for sex in this chapter of his life. Well, it was going to be a very sexy building, he thought as he again looked at the faded sketch.

28

Dr Maghool and the Swiss coroner were a study in contrasts, the island doctor diminutive, quiet and courteous, the Swiss coroner the shape of an oak barrel, arrogant and brash. Setting down his box marked 'Fragile', the coroner went to the kitchen and scrubbed up.

Returning, Dr Giannini started to examine the wounded man who had passed out. He began with the bullet wound, dictating his observations the same way he would an autopsy report, 'Shot in the shoulder with a small-calibre weapon.' As he moved his eyes from the wound, searching for other body penetrations, he came to the victim's face and exclaimed, 'Why, I know this man. He's my friend, Hans Kubler, from Lugano.' Baffled, he asked, 'Who would gun down a Swiss banker?'

Dr Giannini retrieved smelling salts from Dr Maghool's medical bag, and putting the bottle to Hans's nose, he said, 'Hans, Hans, it's me, Giorgio. Can you hear me?'

No answer was forthcoming.

Devoid of a bedside manner, the coroner slapped Hans on the cheek several times, trying to revive him.

Penny inquired, 'What's so fragile in your box?'

Dr Giannini replied, 'That's Trevor Thomson.'

Penny gasped.

Chiarra recoiled.

Sam felt ill. Eyeing the box, his old feelings of resentment against his stepfather returned, joined for the first time by curiosity, along with a new feeling of kinship for the Thomson-Columbus Museum.

The coroner explained as he roughly jabbed a needle into Hans Kubler's arm and depressed the built-in plunger, 'His ashes, inside a beautiful bronze urn. Selected it myself.'

Observing this manhandling, Penny said in disapproval, 'This man's alive, not a cadaver. Can't you be a little more tender with your needle?'

The Swiss doctor ignored her and said, 'Probably a loss of blood.' He added, whispering to Dr Maghool, 'If you've a hospital service station on the island, we better tow him there for a refill before he runs dry.' He uttered a coroner's cold laugh.

No one joined in his medical merriment.

Agreeing, Dr Maghool phoned Provo for the helicopter ambulance. As soon as he hung up, the phone rang.

Sam answered. It was Fountain who told him about Hubert Gistelli and his bloody encounter with the glass in the office door. Sam handed the phone to Dr Maghool. Befuddled, now with two emergencies, Dr Maghool hesitated and conferred with the Swiss coroner.

Overhearing, Sam suggested, 'I think Dr Giannini can handle his countryman – why don't you drive over and see how badly this fellow's been hurt?'

Dr Maghool nodded and said, 'The pilot'll land on the road. He knows these islands like the back of his hand, and he's got down lights. But just so he's sure to see the house,' he said to Chiarra, 'please turn on all your electric lights.'

'But the expense,' Chiarra said, shaking her head. Nevertheless, with Penny's help, as Dr Maghool left, she went from room to room flipping every switch.

Alone with Sam and the unconscious Hans, Dr Giannini whispered, 'Are you the heir to this considerable fortune I'm hearing so much about?'

Sam nodded. 'And my sister Judith, too.'

'Any other . . . ah . . . natural heirs?'

Sam shook his head.

The coroner didn't hesitate, saying, 'Someone's claiming to be.'

'How do you know that?'

'She told me herself.'

'You mean Felicia?' Sam said slowly, worry in his voice.

Returning, Penny said, 'She isn't. Forget her. Even if she could prove her genealogy, she'd have to undo Trevor's offshore trust. There are two hurdles in the way of her even approaching "go" and collecting the money.'

'Her legs are long enough to overcome any hurdle, and she's got two attorneys,' the coroner said. 'That's one for each obstacle. And she's also got the looks to sway a judge.'

For the first time Sam tried to cope with the idea of not having unlimited wealth. Intellectually, he told himself it made no difference. Yet ever since he was a little boy he'd thought of himself – and Judith –

as Trevor's heirs, taking the wealth for granted. But now the monarch was dead and the prince of the realm was told there'd been a mistake, he had been misborn, and barred by a plebiscite from being king, and in addition banished.

Sam didn't like rejection. With a distant stepfather he'd suffered too much from emotional set-backs all his life. Reflecting on his prospects for financial survival, he considered his minuscule salary as a teacher plus the trickle of royalties from his books. Combined, he realized they wouldn't be enough to support his life-style. For years he'd relied on the sizeable monthly amount paid from Trevor's investment portfolio, each cheque signed by Hans Kubler. Sam realized he'd have to sell his house in Santa Fe and he wondered where he'd live. Well, perhaps a move wouldn't be so bad – he could try to find a studio apartment somewhere on Canyon Road.

Except, he lamented, everyone would know about his plight. His students. The librarians. They'd snicker in the stacks behind his back. And Penny would leave him – no fees left for her in managing his paltry salary. Yes, money did make the man, or his image. As it had with Trevor.

Worse, he reflected, Judith would be distraught, unable to adjust to a lesser life-style, disgraced among contemporaries, downgraded socially. She'd be hard pressed to continue her socially prominent life of charities. Reality, he railed mentally, is the bane of happiness.

For Judith's sake, if for no other reason, he'd have to solve this inheritance thing, as Penny called it. It was his responsibility to take care of his little sister. Yes, he'd make certain she got what was rightfully hers. It was his duty as her big brother.

The coroner was saying, 'Yes, Felicia is quite serious, Mr Thomson. I'm willing to bet a lot of money on her intentions.'

'Bet?' Penny said. 'Sounds like we're in the risky futures market.' She shuddered at taking such gambles.

'That's exactly where you are,' the coroner said.

There was finality in his voice, and Sam ran one hand through his hair, simultaneously adjusting his glasses. 'What exactly are you getting at?' he asked, pressing the coroner.

'I'm simply asking you,' Dr Giannini said, 'if there are any higher bidders?'

'For what?' Penny said with a flush of anger.

'For my professional services,' the pathologist said, his impatience showing. 'Don't you see? I did the autopsy and conducted certain medical tests on the deceased. I have certain . . . ah . . . evidence –

157

medical documentation which can, if necessary, be expressed in legal testimony. But there are, of course, costs, expenses, professional fees, if you will, involved.'

'What do you mean?' Penny's voice rose in irritation.

'For instance,' Dr Giannini replied, 'my professional analysis and interpretation of these medical tests, not to mention the deep-freeze storage necessary to protect the evidence – those sorts of things.'

'You mean Felicia has offered to reimburse you for all your . . . ah . . . expenses?' The tone in Sam's voice reflected a disbelief life could permit such antics. 'Is that what you are saying? And now you want to know, since these costs are escalating, due of course to circumstances beyond your control, if I'd be willing to help defray . . . .'

Penny said, 'Sam, get off your professorial podium. Say it simply. The doctor's trying to extort . . . .'

The coroner interrupted, perhaps, Sam thought, not wanting to hear his bizarre intention exposed out loud. 'You get the gist. Things are expensive in Switzerland these days.'

'What things and how expensive?' Penny asked.

'Preparing and evaluating the medical evidence. Lab tests. And my . . . ah . . . storage costs. It's not simply a matter of putting a couple of vials on some shelf. They have to be properly refrigerated, the temperature surrounding them controlled day and night. Why, let the temperature rise and, whiff, there goes your evidence and your inheritance with it. I have a specialist who watches over such matters.'

Sam envisioned a high-tech laboratory and people in long white coats going about with clipboards.

'You see, we Swiss deal more in percentages, less in absolutes. In facilitating transactions we're accustomed – perhaps you might say we're bred – to take . . . er . . . earn commissions. What we call a small fee, leaving the portfolio . . . the estate intact for the heirs.'

His indignation growing, Sam said, sarcasm in his voice, 'Sounds to me, doctor, you'd enjoy more dissecting the trust corpus.'

'What percentage?' Penny pressed as she surveyed the box marked 'Fragile'.

'Can't do much for under ten these days,' the doctor replied, smiling, casting a glance at Hans in case the banker moved or said anything, whereupon he would need to resume acting as a medical doctor.

'The bleeding seems to have stopped,' Sam said, sensing he was the one about to be bled.

'Only ten per cent,' the coroner reiterated.

'Of what?' Penny asked. 'Let's get specific so there can be no misunderstanding as to the terms of your extortion . . . .'

Dr Giannini winced. But he repeated himself, 'The corpus . . . of the estate . . . of the total amount you receive as your inheritance, I get ten per cent, up front.'

'In return for what?'

'My testimony at the hearing tomorrow.' He smiled and went on, adding, 'You'll receive favourable interpretations from my autopsy. I'll simply state Mr Thomson, at the time of death, was sterile. And also, from my tests on his DNA and blood type, he could not possibly be the father of Felicia or anyone else. I'll conveniently forget to mention the evidence stowed in Switzerland. Ergo, I won't have to produce it, thus allowing you to win the jackpot of the century, less of course . . . my modest percentage.'

Penny demanded, 'Favourable interpretations . . . compared to what?'

Dr Giannini straightened up, shifting away from Hans. In a quieter voice he said, 'Look, my naive Americans, the key here is genealogy. Mr Thomson,' he said, 'you are a stepson and your sister, what's-her-name, is a stepdaughter. Felicia is, or claims to be, his natural daughter. I'm the one preserving the evidence which can part you from your money, or conversely snuggle it up to you for ever. That is, if you don't later blow it on wine, women and fast motor cars.' He laughed, his belly shaking. 'I can't spell it out much clearer, can I?'

'What is this other evidence you're talking about?' Sam asked, confused. He was shocked when he heard the reply.

'Sperm,' Dr Giannini said simply.

'Sperm?' Penny said, dumbfounded.

'Sperm from the deceased. Frozen. Stored in my . . . ah . . . secret laboratory.'

'What will that tell . . . ?' Sam didn't finish, visions of vials, cold vials in storage in Switzerland filling his mind.

Penny said, 'You mean you can tell . . . and you're saying you know . . . whether Trevor could have fathered Felicia or not?'

'Yes,' Dr Giannini answered. 'A miracle of modern high-tech lab work.'

Penny wanted to kick both the coroner and the box containing Trevor Thomson.

Sam was growing depressed with how the human purpose runs amok. No one was behaving as he thought they should. What was Fountain up to? And when would the air ambulance come to lift Kubler to the hospital? The idea of sleep appealed to him, to be followed early in the morning with a run on the beach before his welcome visit to Truecoat's fledgling museum. Viewing the artifacts and his run were the two events he now looked forward to.

He'd call a cab and take Penny back to the hotel. Judith was set for the night, so why shouldn't he and Penny . . . ? Suddenly he worried about Judith. Perhaps he should rescue her from the lecherous clutches of the Governor. He knew she was delighted with her surroundings. But what if she wasn't enjoying the Englishman as well?

They heard the helicopter and watched it settle on the gravel road. Leaving the house, the wind from the turning blades whooshing around them, Sam and Penny helped the medics load Hans Kubler into the craft. Sam noticed the name on the side. It read: 'Thomson-Provo Emergency Medical Services'.

Trevor's money. Trevor's charity. The woman on the plane had referred to his good deeds. He realized his stepfather was a benefactor of the island. Suddenly Sam yearned to have known his deceased stepfather better. He wanted to get inside the box that Dr Giannini continually clutched, add water to the ashes and hopefully resurrect his stepfather right there on the spot. But it was too late to develop a father-son relationship, now only his urn and his money were left to think about, to hate, or maybe to grow fond of.

Sam watched Dr Giannini climb on board, carrying Trevor Thomson's remains. He wondered what to do about the coroner's proposal. He should talk it over with Penny and maybe Fountain. As trustee, Fountain was supposed to be on his and Judith's side. But a red flag waved somewhere under his curly locks, and Sam told himself Fountain was no reference librarian, someone you could consult with, asking all your questions.

Observing the coroner carrying his 'Fragile' box onto the helicopter, Chiarra said, 'Mr Thomson's making his last trip Provo.' She appeared relieved he was gone. Sadly she said, 'But he back tomorrow for funeral.'

The air ambulance rose from the gravel street and darted into the dark sky off towards Provo. Since Fountain hadn't returned, Sam called a taxi. It came quickly. Sam nodded politely and bid goodnight to Chiarra.

As he helped Penny into the taxi, he caught a glimpse of Chiarra scurrying about the house turning off all the lights.

29

Dr Maghool arrived in Fountain's outer office to find Hubert and Helga Gistelli huddled together on the white couch. It was spotted with blood.

Ignoring the doctor, who promptly went about dressing the collector's wounds, Helga said, 'Fountain, about this matter . . . .'

The trustee asked, 'What matter are you referring to?'

Helga asked her husband, who moaned again, 'Hubert, where'd you put our letter?'

'Inside pocket,' he mumbled, wincing as Dr Maghool extracted another sliver of glass.

'Had a tetanus shot lately, Mr . . . ah . . . .'

'Gistelli,' Helga recited to the doctor. 'It's Italian, San Francisco Italian, not Pakistani.'

'Indian,' the doctor retorted, a hint of antagonism on his face as he yanked another glass fragment out of Hubert, who cried out in agony.

The woman tried to reach into Hubert's pocket, but the doctor deflected her arm. 'I'm attending this man,' he said, 'and I'm afraid you're interfering, madam. Please wait your turn.'

She withdrew her arm, pointing it instead at Fountain. 'Anyway, Fountain, we have a signed document.'

The trustee asked, 'Signed by whom?'

'Trevor Thomson, who else? It instructs you as his trustee to return billions to the bank, less, of course, our . . . Hubert's and mine . . . ah . . . commission.'

'You have a document with those instructions?' Fountain said in disbelief. 'Impossible, Idiotic. I am certain Mr Thomson would make no change in his Statement of Wishes without first discussing it with me.'

'Life is full of surprises,' Helga said. 'Remember, the cow jumped over the moon. So, you can't fiddle around any longer.'

'You're not making any sense,' Fountain responded.

'Our little document is perfectly clear.'

He said, 'Let me get this straight – you're trying to collect a commission from the insurance company in return for your testimony stating Mr Thomson committed suicide.'

Helga said flatly, 'Not trying . . . we will!'

Fountain went on, 'Second, you're being paid by the bank to reverse thirty years of lease payments . . . .'

'Not trying . . . will!' she said, her voice even stronger.

'You're working both sides of the street,' he said in disgust.

'That's why there are two of us.'

Hubert groaned again.

Dr Maghool said, 'There, he's fully bandaged.'

Hubert stood up. He was groggy.

'Here's some pain-killer,' the doctor said, handing Helga a handful of capsules. 'Give him another of these in an hour – it'll soothe him.' He paused, looked at his watch and added, 'That'll be a hundred and fifty, plus thirty-five for the medicine, fifteen for the gauze, and forty-five for the tetanus shot. That comes to two hundred and forty-five dollars.'

'I can add,' Helga retorted, 'but I need a written statement.' She fished a roll of bills from her handbag, counting out six fifties and handed them to him. She added, 'So I can be reimbursed by Personnel. The bank's group medical people won't pay without paperwork. On your letterhead, too.'

Grumbling, Dr Maghool found a pad of his imprinted prescription forms. He wrote out a bill, scrawling with one swift movement an illegible signature across the bottom. He gave it to her along with one of her fifty-dollar bills. 'You paid me too much, but I don't have change, so here's one more five-dollar pain pill.'

Pain shooting through his shoulder, his face contorting, Hubert retrieved a bloody sheaf of papers from his inside pocket. 'See here, Fountain,' he said, turning to the last page, 'it's the old man's signature and mine and Helga's as witnesses. It gives all the money back to the bank. Thomson signed, then jumped from the train. Me 'n' Helga witnessed it all.' He added with determination, 'You've got to pay back the money right now.'

'What he's telling you,' Helga said, 'is the mouse ran up the clock and now is the hour, the moment, the minute when you must write a cheque for . . . .' She paused and hicupped, then asked her husband, 'How many billions is it, Hubert?'

30

There wasn't even a hint of morning outside when Penny punched Sam and turned on the light by their bed.

'What time is it?' he mumbled.

'Forget about the time – wake up. This thing's going to get away from you . . . from us.'

'What thing?' He sat up, clutching the covers. 'You're always talking about "This Thing" as if it were a monster from outer space. Can we turn off the air-conditioning? It's cold in here.'

Penny jumped out of bed, stark naked, and went to the unit mounted in the window, fiddled with it and finally switched it off.

He admired her body, his eyes lingering on her thighs.

She opened the door. Warm air rushed in along with the sound of the ocean.

'They run those waves all night, even when people are asleep?' he asked. 'Can you imagine hearing the sound of an ocean in quiet, land-locked New Mexico? There used to be an ocean there millions of years ago.'

'Listen, Sammy,' Penny pressed, 'you've got to do something. Everyone is conniving to get their hands on Trevor's money.'

Sam nodded, grabbing colourful shorts, a race T-shirt and running shoes from his travel bag.

Penny said, 'Good idea, I'll go for a hike later. Maybe the exercise'll clear both our minds.' Taking neatly folded walking shorts and shirt from her luggage, she dressed and set about her morning cosmetic prep.

'I'll wait for the first light of dawn,' Sam said, peering outside. 'It's only moments away.'

'Think about this thing, though,' Penny insisted.

'Define "thing",' he said.

'I mean this whole thing,' she replied. 'Fountain's playing a double role, stepfather and trustee. I don't like it one bit.'

163

'Define "it".'

'I'm worried.'

'I can tell you are,' Sam said. 'Why don't you share your worries with someone like me, since I'm the only other one in this cold hotel room overlooking the ocean beach.' He stole her lipstick, faking his escape.

'That's my new Caribbean Coral,' she yipped, vaulting across the bed to retrieve it. 'Say, what happened to your little sister last night?'

'She's playing art critic to the Governor's etchings.'

'Bedding the Governor of the island!' Penny exclaimed. 'Wow! I guess if you're going to do it, you might as well go all the way to the top. But isn't he a little old for her?'

'I didn't say she was, or he was, did I? What's age got to do with it?'

'Your implication was pretty plain,' Penny said. 'And as to his age, I haven't seen him, of course, but governors are always sixty-plus, aren't they?'

'You're jumping to conclusions again, Penny, just like you are on this whole island "thing".'

'Look, you oblivious historian, when a woman falls for that old etching line, everybody knows the outcome is going to be beddie-byes. That's not jumping to conclusions, that's being realistic.'

'Judith fancies herself an art critic . . . .'

Penny laughed uproariously.

'. . . and Sir Hugh said they were rare . . . done by some Caribbean artist . . . .'

'While in prison, likely serving time for having pulled off a con game,' Penny said. 'Remind me to query Judith when I see her at the funeral. Among other things, I'll be interested to know how old things are hung.'

'You've got things on your mind.'

'A lot of things.'

'It's getting light.'

'Yes, so you go on and do your run thing, but give me back my lipstick first. Oh, by the way, his ten per cent, so-called "token payment",' she said, forcing a chuckle, 'symbolizing your affection for that overweight Swiss coroner . . . .'

'Yes?'

'. . . won't solve anything.'

'Why not?' Sam asked. 'We'll pay him some money and he'll testify

164

Trevor's sperm is out of print. The solution is simple enough.'

Penny frowned. 'Like an old book? No, there's more to it. You see, even if Trevor was sterile at the time of his death, his condition thirty years ago may have been otherwise. He still might have fathered Felicia.'

'Yeah, maybe you're right. Good thinking, Penny.'

'And then there's Chiarra?'

'What about her?'

Penny frowned again. 'She can testify Trevor was the father. She can say she had sex with him nine months, give or take, before Felicia was born.'

'Admit the rape? She'd be too intimidated, wouldn't she? Maybe she was promiscuous. Who knows?'

'I'm sure she didn't ask for it,' Penny said disgustedly.

'Well, it is possible she had sex with two white men.'

'That's why we need his DNA,' Penny said with insistence.

'Look,' Sam said, 'if this coroner fellow is as pliable as he seems, the facts of the case don't make any difference,'

'Facts must prevail,' Penny said.

'Not necessarily,' Sam replied. 'It's like history. What's important is what people say happened, not what actually took place. Truth gets lost in a pre-dawn fog.'

Penny frowned, 'Yes, maybe you're right. Investments have similar traits. Rumours run the market. Facts are nice, but it's the hearsay. What others think is going to happen compels investors to actually buy or sell.'

Sam looked out of the door. 'The coast is clear.'

'Go, have a good run.'

Sam said, 'Oh, I just remembered, I've a meeting with the museum archaeologist at seven. Want to join me?'

'More history stuff?'

'No, like I said, it's archaeology – a separate discipline, you know.' Sam winked at her.

'Like bonds are different from stocks?'

'I wouldn't know.'

'Yes, you would, damn it,' Penny said. 'But I'm hungry for some breakfast.'

'Blue corn pancakes topped with blue berries, served whilst sitting by the blue ocean?'

'We're oceans away from blue corn. But think about things as you run.'

'I always do,' he said, and left.

31

Sam burst forth onto the beach. The white sand reflected the light of the beginning dawn. He didn't know which way to run. He chose to bear right, the beach seeming to lead for ever. He stopped and took off his shoes and socks. Running barefoot, he splashed in the fingers of waves as they clawed at the island shore. The salt water beaded on his strong legs, and he revelled in the consciousness of an ocean.

It was so much fun he shed his shorts and T-shirt. Resuming his run, he felt the warm breeze caress his body. The ocean surf tingled his genitals, making him spin in a whirlwind of excitement. He heard symphonic music setting an imaginative mood in the brightening dawn. He visualized Pheidippides, the naked messenger running from Marathon to Athens bringing news of the Athenian victory over the Persians. Conjuring up the Greek idol and appreciating his own body with its natural beauty, he picked up his pace.

Perspiration flowing profusely in the humidity – the opposite of dry New Mexico – he ran on, his feet imprinting the virgin sand.

A large wave swirled around his legs, reaching up to his crotch. Sam yelped. For a moment he regarded the ocean as a living thing, displaying its own personality; a troubled person whose problems were continually rolling in on the beaches of time, all the while daring the onlooker as a student of history to seek solutions to its enigmas.

Looking ahead along the beach, Sam made out the dim outline of a figure. He couldn't tell if it was coming towards him or not, but it was running, first ploughing through the surf for a trice, then bounding happily back to the hard sand.

He ran on. The figure came closer. Sam was naked, his running clothes back down the beach. What if it were a woman? What could he do? Turn and run, he supposed. But what if she were faster and caught up?

Glancing down, he saw a large wave coming at him. Adeptly vaulting away, he avoided most of it. Looking up, he saw the figure's outline –

narrow waist with curvaceous hips, long hair trailing in the warm breeze, a fully deployed sail. A woman. In the brightening dawn she was coming towards him.

Sam panicked, turned, trying to increase his pace. As he made the move, he slipped in the sand or tripped over his own feet, he wasn't sure which. But he fell to the soft sand, sprawling awkwardly. Pulling himself together, he looked up and saw a lithesome figure looming over him. She was laughing. It was Felicia. And all the ocean's problems descended upon him.

'You took a tumble, big fella,' she said, her laugh lingering like the island heat.

Sam saw he was covered with sand. Worse, she, too, was taking everything in. He wanted to be anywhere other than here, but he was here, naked as the day he was born. And she was here, a delivery doctor mentally photographing him for her album of absurdities.

Totally embarrassed and not knowing what to do or say, he offered, 'Out for a run?' In the growing light, her dark skin radiated a mystical patina. It was polished mahogany. He yearned to touch her.

Felicia leaned over, brown breasts shapely in the top of her tan body suit. In the grey light with her brief attire, she appeared nude to Sam, but of course she wasn't.

Kneeling at his side, she said, 'So, Mr Rich White Man, Mr Stepson of Trevor Thomson, Mr Unentitled I shall label you, or should I call you Mr Unclothed?'

Sam thought about throwing sand over himself up to his neck and emulating a buried sand crab while he waited for her to go away. He said, 'The ancient Greeks ran naked. It was the thing to do.'

'I suppose you think the women peeked from behind bushes, ogling them. Well, you'd better stop wallowing in your historic myths. Women are no longer passive, sitting idly by while men do the running.'

Lying on the sand next to Sam was a large periwinkle sea shell. Felicia picked it up and idly examined its conical whorls, its hidden recesses suggesting to Sam the mysteries of her mind.

'Why do you dislike me?' Sam pleaded, looking up into her hazel eyes.

'I don't – any more than anyone who's had an easy life paid for by someone else.'

'What do you mean?'

'You're a free-loader, Mr Sandy Sam. You wallow in money you don't need. And the money you are about to receive you deserve even

168

less.'

Sam wished he had the *savoir-faire* of Trevor Thomson. He'd jump up, exert himself and seduce this woman, satisfying his innermost desires. He'd be clever, dominate her in the way real men are supposed to. Instead his temper rose, as much with himself as with her. He said, 'And I'm white, too, is that it?'

'Yes, if you must know, Mr Uncoloured. White like my dead father, your lecherous stepfather.'

Sam said emphatically, 'Oh, my God, I'm really sorry about what happened.' He paused. 'I heard about it last night from Mr Fountain.'

'But if you were to undo that deed, I'd vanish from your sight this instant – depart like a ghost.'

'Done deeds are history,' Sam said. 'Were either of us offered the choice of parents?'

'I say birth is one big lottery in which the stork always delivers the winning ticket in the form of more important and valuable babies to rich white neighbourhoods.'

Sam smiled and said, 'I heard with all us babies coming after World War II they had to change the system because the stork couldn't keep up.'

Felicia tossed the tropical shell into the surf close to him and said, 'I don't need this discussion.' Picking up a handful of sand, she threw it at him, saying, 'Be serious. Tell me, what are you planning to do with more money? Buy another library? Being a historian, have you ever researched the Buffalo soldiers? For your information they're the black cavalry who won the West from outlaws and Indians for you rich white folks.'

'Yes, I've read about them. But what's that got to do with you and me?' Sam wanted to throw sand back at her, and maybe do even more. His wild thoughts, his animal instincts urged him on. But he fretted he would get an erection while she watched.

'You and your socially prominent sister are in my way,' Felicia said sharply. 'In the way of progress for my people – that's what it's got to do with.'

He said, 'Your people? Judith and I are in their way? Come on now.'

'Yes, Mr Naked, you're preventing my father's money from going to work where it should.'

'Into your pocket . . . er . . . purse?'

'No, Mr Unpoor, not for me personally, but for my people in LA.

169

Since my dear father extracted his money from there, it should now go back – returned a hundredfold – to change the lives of the needy, make history for us, the black minority.'

Sam said, 'What makes you so certain he *was* your father?'

Felicia responded quickly. 'Women know such things.' Growing upset, she said, 'Are you saying my mother slept around – but only with white men?'

'Ah, no, of course not.' Sam thought he should get up and make a break for it. Instead he said, 'People, not money, make history.'

'Don't shroud yourself in mystique,' she chided. She laughed and said, 'But you should shroud yourself in something, Mr Circumcised.'

Sam winced. 'Jesus, Felicia, show a little empathy . . . .' He'd better get out of here before he was arrested for indecent exposure, flashing, exhibitionism, lewd conduct, and probably ten or twenty other violations of the laws of this conservative island nation.

'Actually, you are a respectably equipped dude.'

'Ah, thanks.'

'For a white man.'

'Really?'

'Not that I've had the opportunity for much research.'

'But some,' Sam said with a smile.

'You don't think I'm a thirty-year-old virgin, do you? And you're wrong about history.'

'I'm an historian.'

'I don't give a damn if you're Arnold Toynbee, you're still wrong.'

'About what?'

'About history – money makes history, and the people must go along with it. Money charts the course, my naked ape. But those with money – like your white self – want the rest of us to think it's politics. But it's not.'

'So, you mean your money – or Trevor's money – really my money, you think, is going to change the history of the cities?' Sam chuckled. 'How laudatory.'

She threw two handfuls of sand at him.

'And in the interests of changing history, how much of an override are you going to skim off? Personally, I mean. Ninety per cent?' He laughed, adding, 'For promoting your personal career. Your reputation will grow. Who knows, maybe they'll put you at the head of the Smithsonian or the Ford Foundation. The white male establishment would have a two-fer with you.'

'You're full of shit, you know.'

He ignored her remark. 'You could really change history – divert those billions to the problems of the cities, forsaking medical research, experimental educational programmes, archaeological explorations, outer space . . . .'

'Stop. I don't like you. You're beyond reality.'

The sun's rays struck Sam's body, the tiny sand granules glistening. He stood before her, brushing his arms and neck. The sand was sharp, scratching his skin. He'd be wise to run, he concluded, but didn't want to leave. Lingering, he asked, 'How are you going to do it?'

'Do what?'

'Get Trevor's money.'

'Where are your clothes?'

'Back up the beach.'

'I'll race you to them.'

She led the way. Sam exerted himself and caught up. He asked, 'Who are those two guys with you? Lovers?'

'Yeah, every red-blooded woman should carry at least two with her at all times. Preferably one of each colour for when her mood changes.'

'You're on the fifty-yard line.'

'What do you mean?'

'You can go either way.'

She kicked sand at him. Coming close, she pushed him in the surf. Without hesitation, without considering the consequences, now next to her, he grabbed at her.

As she eluded him, her ensuing laugh was sexy, encouraging him while at the same time expressing a stand-offish air. Sam couldn't decide which was dominant.

Reaching the spot where he'd shed his shorts and shoes, he stopped to dress and said, 'You mystify me.'

'Good, let's leave it at that.'

Sam pulled on his shorts, discarding his socks and slipping rapidly into his shoes. 'No,' he announced strongly, 'you and I are going for a little run through Cockburn Town. I'll be your tour guide.' His fingertips touched her elbow, directing her.

She laughed, an enigmatic laugh. 'Lead on,' she invited.

Side by side they paced each other, one testing the other by sprinting ahead, only to have their challenge promptly met. Sparring with one another, their legs rising high with each stride, the pumping of their arms carrying them forward with alacrity, they began to race towards an imaginary finishing-line – wanting to be the first to break the ribbon they envisioned stretching across the beach. Sam loved seeing Felicia's long hair jounce as the tips of her running shoes kissed the sand.

Soon they were crossing the plaza of Cockburn Town. It was too early for anyone else to be out and about. Side by side they entered the poor section, slowing now, for dogs were running about, pregnant bitches sniffing for food. And kids. Black kids watching in awe this two-coloured duo. One little boy, and then another, held out their palms. Sam met their greeting with his own outstretched palm. The children laughed, the laugh of little boys on an early morning adventure.

Suddenly Sam stopped. He picked up one of the little boys, hoisting him onto his shoulders. Sam felt the boy's skin on his body. Sam ran on, and the little boy cheered.

Felicia laughed as others followed. Soon Sam and Felicia were leading a group of boys and now some little girls, too, along the unpaved streets. In the early morning, on the day of the funeral.

Sam said to his boy, 'What's your name?'

He leaned down below where his hands were holding Sam's forehead, looking into Sam's face and replied proudly, 'My name Edward.'

Now Felicia stopped. She picked up one of the laughing little girls running beside her, lifting her onto her shoulders. Little sea shells were attached to her braided hair.

More kids swarmed around, each wanting rides.

'What's your name?' Felicia asked her passenger.

'Sherry,' was the timid reply.

'Yours is a lovely name.'

'Mommy say like hotel.'

'Sheraton?'

'Yeah. Where you from?'

'America.'

'My hotel there.'

Felicia smiled at Sherry.

As they ran, watching the kids and observing the hovels in which they lived, the dogs with which they played, the conditions of their lives, Felicia said, sorrow in her voice, 'I had no idea the poverty was so bad here.' She asked Sam, 'Do you think it's this way on other islands in the Caribbean?'

'Yes,' Sam said, slowing his pace as he dodged boys running in front of him, trying not to lose his hold on Edward in the manoeuvre.

'Trevor tried a bit to help, I understand. Had he lived longer he would have done more.'

'You think so? But you didn't know him.'

Sam laughed. 'He'd define the problem first. Then figure out a solution.' Looking at her, he said, 'That's the white man's way. At least it was for his generation.' Sam stopped, putting Edward down.

'You run Olympics?' the boy asked.

'No, but if you train, you could,' Sam said.

Surprised at Sam's sincerity, Felicia said as she redeposited Sherry on the sandy street, 'You really mean it, don't you?'

'Of course.' There was no hesitation in Sam's reply.

'Could you change this island, like you think Trevor would have? The schools, the housing, the social programmes, like I'm trying to do in my inner city?'

Sam looked at Edward and asked, 'Could I, could we, change this island?'

'You train, you could,' Edward said, and laughed. The children surrounding them nodded, agreeing with Edward.

Felicia looked at their tattered clothes and their meagre homes and her heart went out to them.

Sam said, 'Yes, with an outreach programme here, and someone like you to run it.'

Felicia was keenly aware of her surroundings. It reminded her of Los Angeles and yet it was different. There were no cars here, no noise other than the children and their dogs. In fact, in the background she could hear the surf. She turned to Sam and quickly retorted, 'I'm empathetic, but my job's in LA.'

Now at the edge of the shanty town, they began to run again, back towards the beach, in silence. Then, at the beach, Felicia turned and said prophetically, 'I shall prevail, Mr Running Historian, and I'll have my father's money to work with.'

As she ran in the direction from which she had come, the theatrical spotlight of the bright sun followed and illuminated her. As Sam watched, he saw an assertive woman splashing in the surf of her own determined agenda.

Sam thought how alluring she was, wanting to know her, really know her. He shook his head and told himself he shouldn't be thinking such things. Instead, he was going to have to outsmart her if he was going to keep Trevor's money. For him such a task was going to be as formidable as trying to go to bed with her.

32

As he often did on his early morning walks, Old Henry talked to his parrot. The bird rode on his shoulder as the old seaman slowly made his way around Cockburn Town. A good conversationalist, the parrot interjected a few words here and there along with an occasional fragmented sentence.

'Rape. He raped her,' the bird suggested.

'Yes, Old Pal, but we mustn't tell anyone. He'll kill us if we let on we know. We must keep quiet.'

Old Henry's pace was slow. In the warm breeze his tattered clothes blew and his beard puffed proudly. Yes, he did savour his early morning walks. As a sailor he had preferred early mornings for the swabbing of the deck. Now as he watched the sunrise out there in the east over the Caribbean, the crimson rays lit up the waters of the dark sea. As the sun rose higher, its increasing brilliance let him know once again his island was still reassuringly underfoot. Yes, this day there'd be no island sinking into the sea, Old Henry mused.

Persistent memories of sailing the Caribbean continued to rattle around in his mind. Today was the funeral, Old Henry suddenly remembered. Fleetingly he hoped to bury his memories along with Trevor Thomson.

'Rape,' the bird insisted.

'Shush,' Old Henry urged, 'today's the funeral. We must allow the dead to rest in peace.'

The bird's claws dug into Old Henry's shoulder.

'Especially this old man.' Old Henry swatted at the bird, playfully so as not to hurt his companion. He'd not know what to do if his bird died.

The bird fluttered its wings and hopped from Old Henry's right shoulder to his left.

Old Henry said as he plodded on, 'His deeds will be buried with him and they'll rot in the soil along with his body.'

The parrot rode on his shoulder, a captain commanding from the bridge, supervising their course.

'You know, Old Pal, it's fitting he's not going to be buried at sea, for he'da liked it there, slid proudly into the deep, he woulda – out from beneath his pirate's skull and crossbones. 'Stead, he's goin' to be stuck for ever on this little spittle of an island where the woman still lives. The unlucky woman. Fitting, I says.'

'Rape,' Old Pal reminded him.

'That's punishment enough, I guess.'

'He's grabbing her,' the parrot continued.

33

Charles Fountain's best time was in the morning. He liked his sex then, because he was fresher, and he felt more potent. The previous day's accounting entries, benefiting from a night's sleep, had finally quieted down, settling into appropriate slots. Visualizing Debra Datsun, he was making love to Chiarra.

But there was an interruption, a pounding on the front door, a rusty voice breaking the quiet of the island dawn with the command, 'Fountain, open up! We've matters!'

The trustee recognized the creaky voice of the Old Captain. His pronunciation of 'matters' connoted both a plot and sentence structure familiar to each of them.

He rolled off Chiarra as she whispered, 'Charles, the Old Captain's ranting again.'

From outside the old seaman's voice croaked, 'The old man's dead. There's no one left for you to hide behind. Open up!'

'I get shotgun,' Chiarra said as she slipped out of bed, throwing a flimsy negligee around her still shapely body.

'No!' Charles commanded. 'If I shoot him, the police investigation could bring everything out.'

'But Old Captain going to talk around town,' Chiarra insisted, 'now that Trevor dead. He'll involve you and me. Worse than police asking questions.'

'No,' Charles insisted. 'People think the Old Captain is like Old Henry, demented and living in his own make-believe world.'

The Old Captain banged again, yelling, his voice furious.

'He'll show up at funeral today, maybe even da hearing,' Chiarra said, her voice filled with foreboding.

'Not "da". It is pronounced "the",' Charles corrected.

Chiarra responded slowly, enunciating each word slowly, 'Yes . . . I . . . am . . . too . . . excited.' Immediately she reverted to her rapid chatter, 'But I can't talk slow like you ed'cated folk.'

176

'Ed-u-cat-ed,' Charles corrected with impatience.

The Old Captain had been silent, but now they heard him bang at the back door. 'Fountain, open up! You can't hide any more.'

'Maybe he leave now,' Chiarra said, with hope in her voice.

'I better talk to him,' Charles said.

'Suppose he got gun. He shot that Swiss banker man last night – he might shoot you.' She hugged Charles.

'No, he keeps the gun at the Unlucky Lady.'

'How you know?'

'He told me. Once when I was there with a client the Old Captain joked about his gun, said it really owned the bar. It lived there, he said, and would never leave. It was a recluse, he said, afraid of the outside world.'

'But can you be sure Old Captain doesn't have it?'

'No.'

'Don't go, call Chief Hedgepeth.'

Pulling on his robe, its grey colour as sombre as his look, the trustee shook his head as he left their bedroom. With one fist clenched the Old Captain was about to bang again on the front door when Fountain opened it.

The trustee's defiant attitude turned to icy fear as he stared into the barrel of the Old Captain's revolver.

34

Sam was late in returning to their hotel room.

Penny greeted him with, 'Long run?'

'Uh, no, not really,' Sam said, debating with himself if he should tell about Felicia. But being dedicated to truth – in both history and in life – he blurted out, 'I ran into Felicia.'

'Oh?'

'On the beach.'

'She running naked?'

'Of course not, why do you say that?'

'Felicia being in her birthday suit would have gotten your attention, I should think.' Penny's tone was sarcastic.

Sam said, 'She claims she's going to get Trevor's money.'

'How?'

'By being smarter than we are. She says she needs the money to change inner city history in America.'

'You're kidding me,' Penny hooted. 'No one is that altruistic. Sam, the broad's bullshitting you. Can't you see that? Men are so naive,' she concluded, shaking her head.

Sam looked sheepish. 'I'll shower,' he announced. 'Say, have you got some ointment for my scratched feet?'

'I'm on my way to the bank,' Penny said as she tossed him a tube of lotion, 'to see if I can find out about this multinational corporation Hans Kubler talked about last night.'

'He seems to know quite a bit about bonds,' Sam said. 'You two have a lot in common.'

'He is clever.'

'I hope he's on our side.'

'Somebody needs to be,' she said as Sam turned on the shower and climbed in.

Hiking at a brisk pace, Penny soon arrived at Barclay's Bank, where she knocked on the glass door. The man who unlocked it said, 'Mr

Fountain asked me to meet you, Ms Bailes. I'm Mr Allways, the manager. How can I help?'

Her white hand shook his black one. Smiling, she said, 'I need to investigate an Italian company. Do you have any investment books?'

He pointed to a shelf of *Standard & Poor's* corporate reference books behind his desk. Selecting the first volume, she sat in the leather chair he offered her and paged through the As, finding Ambrosiana. She read the basic information: a large Italian conglomerate making cosmetics, drugs, sanitary towels, birth-control devices, disposable nappies – not biodegradable. Its largest factory was in Milan, but its corporate offices were in Campione. They had floated a bond issue a few years earlier, and indeed there were warrants attached. But it quickly became obvious to Penny that the information in the reference book was only a starting point for her research. She needed current information – scuttlebutt, in other words, the grit of investment decisions.

She found Allways at the fax machine and said, 'I need to make a phone call. I've a credit card.'

'Please help yourself,' he said. 'Dial 9, the international code, the city code, your number, then your credit . . . .'

'I know the drill.' As she punched away, she asked herself, how could this little device digest so many numbers? She heard a human voice say, 'Bonds Italiana.'

'Tony, please,' she said, not trying her Italian. 'Penny Bailes calling.'

'*Momento.*'

Tony came on, 'Penny, where are you?'

'Turks and Caicos.'

'Is that a place or a bar?'

'An island country in the Caribbean,' she said, rushing on to ask, 'What can you tell me about Ambrosiana Limited?'

'Do you want the thirty-second sketch or the five-volume summary?'

'I need both, but let's start with the sketch.'

'Their bonds are attractive, a twelve per cent coupon.'

She heard him strike keys on his computer.

'Bid at 90, asked 101,' he told her.

'With the warrants attached?'

'You do know something about this company.'

'Yes, I've read the S & P here at Barclay's, but I want the latest news, especially the rumours.'

Tony hit the keys again. 'With. Bonds with warrants to purchase common stock are unusual. Apparently the underwriters thought they needed a sweetener in order to interest investors in buying at the initial public offering.'

'When did the bonds come out?' she asked.

'Several years ago. Brought to market by a small family,' he laughed quietly, 'investment house in Milan.'

'Family,' she repeated. 'Like Mafia?'

She couldn't see his ensuing nod, only heard a 'Shh'.

She asked, 'What's happened since?'

Silence while Tony read his computer screen. 'That's funny.'

'What's funny?'

'There's an unknown holder of a large block of the bonds.'

'Unknown?'

'Yeah, Europe is not like the US,' Tony said. 'There's no Securities and Exchange Commission here.'

'No regulation? And no required reporting of holdings greater than five per cent?'

'Exactly,' he said, 'so mysteries and rumours abound.'

Penny waited while Tony paged down to the next screen.

He said, 'The company's expanding.' Lowering his voice, he added, 'It says here they expect to become the world's largest manufacturer of condoms. They're even buying a rubber plantation in Malaysia.'

'Condoms?' Penny exclaimed, her voice loud. The tellers and Allways turned towards her, their surprise followed by frowns. She blushed and looked away.

'Yeah, we Italians are big users, you know,' Tony said and laughed.

'No, I didn't know that,' Penny said, 'but I do know the market is expanding world-wide, thank heaven.'

'Biggest growth industry around.' He laughed again. 'Things are looking up indeed.'

'Will you stop. Tell me about the warrants attached to the bonds. And what is the rating on the bonds?'

Tony paged down again and said, 'Let's see. The bonds are rated single C.'

Penny shuddered. 'Not A?'

Tony said, 'But look here, this other information is interesting.'

Unable to see the screen, Penny waited.

'The final date for exercising the warrants is a couple of days away.'

'You mean these warrants will then become worthless?'

'As yesterday's ticker tape.'

Penny thought and asked, 'So, what's the story? How much common stock do the warrants convert into?' Waiting for his reply, she located a note pad and pencil on Allways's desk.

Tony read her the number. She wrote the figure down.

'How many shares of stock are outstanding?'

He read another number.

Penny paused to calculate. She whistled and said, 'The way I figure it, if these warrants are converted to common stock, the new shares will constitute a majority – and that, my Italian friend, means whoever exercises the warrants will control the company.'

'Yes, I figure it the same way,' Tony said. 'So, are you buying or selling today?'

'Look, I know you're busy, and frankly I don't know which I want to do, if either.'

'I'll need to know if I'm to place an order,' Tony said. 'Oh, and there's one other bit of information on my screen.'

'Yes?'

'US citizens are not allowed to own its bonds or stock. I mean, the SEC hasn't approved shares for sale to US citizens. You can, of course, own them through an offshore trust or corporation domiciled in another country. No problem, but I can't sell them to you for a US-based account. Aren't you glad Big Brother in Washington is looking out for your nest egg?'

'And into it, too,' Penny said. 'In my country we enjoy about as much financial privacy as a Fourth of July parade.'

Tony laughed and said, 'Yeah, I'm glad I expatriated ten years ago. I really enjoy being back here in my parents' home country. I've got dual passport status – US and Italy. I'm making a lot of money while having fun with the European financial markets.'

'And the pasta?'

'*Mamma mia!* Great sauces, too.'

'What else can you find out for me about Ambrosiana, given your restaurant connections?'

'Tratoria more than restaurants,' Tony corrected. 'They're less formal.'

'Whatever, I need to know more as soon as possible.'

'Penny, we're not a research firm – we're a brokerage company making money buying and selling. You should consult with one of those firms that goes around asking penetrating questions of corporate officers.'

'Look, you expatriate stud, I give you a lot of business. Now I need a favour. You speak the language and you've got contacts. I'll pay for your dinner – put it on my account. I'll get back to you in . . . say . . . about five hours. That'll give you time for an evening meal of spaghetti in olive oil and garlic. As you twirl the pasta with someone who really knows something, you can ask a menu of questions. From the answers they serve up, you will know a lot more than either you or I do now.'

Tony transmitted a grumble from Rome to Grand Turk.

Penny pleaded, 'Tony, confirm my suspicions about the mysterious bond holder.'

'I'll try,' he promised.

Penny rushed out of the bank to tell Sam that Hans Kubler appeared to be gambling with his inheritance.

35

Sam figured he would walk to Wes Truecoat's museum and save the taxi fare. It was barely a mile, and though he was already late for his meeting with the archaeologist, he set out, breathing in the ocean air and the island fragrances. As he walked briskly past the salt flats, it suddenly struck him there was no noise. At first the stillness seemed oppressive, but as he listened, the void of hubbub and background commotion engulfed him. He found himself savouring the silence.

Santa Fe was a relatively quiet place – no freeways crossing town, no jet planes – but there were plenty of tourists with cars. Together they generated a certain noise level drifting up to his hillside house. Down in town, it even seeped into his library stacks, disturbing his research.

But here, apart from the occasional car or barking dog, and the once-a-week jet from Miami, the island was as serene as his favourite place of solitude – remote Lake Kathryn high up in the Sangre de Cristo Mountains. There in the magic, running along his high-altitude mountain trails, Sam was awarded a glimpse of immortality, and he wondered if living here would give him that same gift. Dr Truecoat, he speculated, had apparently made such a choice.

In the heat, from time to time, Sam took off his stetson in order to wipe his forehead. Even the persistent perspiration felt good.

The museum was located in an old West Indies style house consisting of two storeys with a sea-facing veranda the length of its façade. It appeared at first to be pretty dilapidated, the paint peeling off its clapboard siding, its few windows unpainted with many panes broken. But then Sam saw piles of construction material and realized the house was in the process of being restored. Outside a freshly lettered sign read 'Thomson-Columbus Museum'. Seeing it, Sam experienced a rush of pride.

Truecoat must have seen him approaching, for the archaeologist came out, and without a formal greeting quickly explained, 'We're putting this old house back to what it was a hundred and fifty

183

years ago.'

Truecoat gestured at the structure. 'Trevor's Swiss banker, Mr Kubler, doesn't understand how we can spend so much money. He's all over me about construction costs. Mr Fountain is a tad more sympathetic, knows restoration is not cheap. But Mr Kubler's the one who writes the cheques.'

Sam nodded, although he'd never been involved in the restoration of a building. Restoring an interest in history for his students, yes. Absently he asked, 'They both must approve your expenses?'

'Not each bill. At the outset we agreed on an overall budget by category of expenditure. Mr Kubler compares the actual costs with the budgeted figures for each part of the restoration – air-conditioning, roof, walls, lighting, interior exhibit cases, flooring – there are more than forty categories including rest rooms.' Truecoat asked, 'Want to see the figures?'

'No, that's not necessary. I'm not much with figures. I'm more anxious to examine the artifacts you've assembled.'

Truecoat hesitated, reaching for a cigarette. Seeing Sam's look of disapproval, he reinserted the package into his pocket and said, 'Uh, yes, but could you speak to Mr Kubler.'

'About what?'

'Well, he's not paying the bills, and with Mr Thomson – your stepfather – now dead, maybe you could influence him. I mean, aren't you sort of in charge? We're running thirty, sixty, even ninety days late. Some people are no longer shipping supplies to us, and a lot of tradespeople aren't showing up. I worked my way through graduate school as a carpenter.' He smiled modestly. 'I'm doing a lot of things myself. But I can't do everything, so the work is progressing slowly.'

'Does Mr Kubler think you're too far over budget?'

'Well, given the run-down condition of the house when we started – your stepfather looked over the building and approved its restoration. He saw firsthand its condition.' Truecoat pointed, 'See here how the foundation is crumbling and the window sills have weathered. And look at the roof – the shingles need replacing. In fact, everything needs attention. Even on Grand Turk work requires money.'

'And workers who know how,' Sam said.

'Yes, people's skills are essential,' Truecoat said, adding, 'whether it's for offshore trusts or plumbing.' He paused and said, 'But I think Mr Kubler's trying to conserve cash. It's as if he has other uses for the money. He said something about it being a temporary condition.'

'I can't imagine him running out of money,' Sam said.

'I suppose everything has its limits.' They moved along to the one room of the museum where construction had been completed and the museum fixtures were installed. The curator gestured. 'Let me show you what we've brought up from the deep so far.' He switched on recessed lighting, illuminating display cabinets containing artifacts.

'See this cannon,' Truecoat said, pointing to a rusty old iron weapon. 'It's quite long – fifteenth-century technology,' he said. 'These didn't work too well. The sailors didn't like to fire them either. Want to know how we know that?'

'Please.'

'The entire lot was found in the ballast, meaning they were stored below deck. In firing one of these, it could blow up in your face. A lot of Spanish sailors were killed in such explosions. They obviously didn't want these cannons up on deck where they'd be ordered to set them off.'

Truecoat pointed to another display case in which were mounted shards of pottery. 'Palmetto ware,' he said, 'made by the Lucayan Indians who once lived in the Bahamas and the Turks and Caicos – the peoples Columbus encountered.'

'Any descendants today?'

'That's the tragedy,' Truecoat said, 'they were wiped out within twenty-one years. We think there were at least fifteen thousand of them, actually more people than we have living on these islands today.'

Sam said, 'Yes, I recall reading how the Spanish mistreated them. Forty-eight years later Coronado marched into what became Santa Fe, and the Spanish continued to make the same mistakes with our Pueblo Indians.'

'The Spanish did the same thing with the Aztecs,' Truecoat added. 'But wiping out the Indians was not entirely their fault. European diseases killed a lot.'

Nodding, Sam examined the artifacts. Finally he asked, looking Truecoat in the eye, 'Is it the *Pinta*? Give me your best guess as of now.'

'Well, there's more data we must assemble and analyze in the laboratory. It's really too early to tell . . . .'

'Your best guess,' Sam insisted.

'We haven't found Columbus's log or his personal collection of credit cards in an old leather billfold.' The archaeologist laughed.

'And?'

'And it's a caravel, likely the oldest Spanish shipwreck yet discovered in the New World – obviously late 1490s or first decade 1500s. So the time is right, but . . . .'

'But what?' Sam wanted to know. Looking at his watch, he realized he'd have to be going to Trevor's funeral.

'But what would Columbus be doing with leg irons?'

'To contain dissidents,' Sam said. 'I don't have a problem with that.'

'I do.'

'Why?'

'Eight sets?'

'That is a lot.'

'Yes,' Truecoat agreed.

'A slave ship,' Sam said.

'Yes.'

'A Spanish slave ship run aground on the submerged cay?'

'My thoughts exactly,' Truecoat said. 'But we need more data. There are lots of things remaining to be done, and lots of marine archaeologists to pay so they'll retrieve those artifacts still lying under the water out there on Magnolia Cay. Those are some of the reasons why we need the money.'

'But my stepfather set up a foundation for the museum.'

'Yes, of course,' the archaeologist replied. 'With the backing of the local government, and now the Italian royal family, so Mr Kubler says. Everybody's in place. We're sitting here like a maiden waiting for Prince Charming. An archaeologist is born to dig, like an excited dog trying to find a buried bone. We're no good at public relations, raising money, promoting museums and abstract causes.'

'Like historians – born to research.'

'Yes, but you've got – and now you'll have even more – money and prestige. People'll listen to you, do what you say. You'll be regarded as sanguine and clever.' Truecoat laughed, adding quickly, 'Not that you aren't respected already.'

'So?'

'So you could really help us here – help the Thomson-Columbus Museum, I mean. Maybe even be here and play an active part. Certainly in promoting it around the world.'

'You mean by moving here permanently.'

'Why not? Don't you like it here?'

'But my research?'

'Oh, you could keep on with it.'

186

Sam hypothesized what he might be able to accomplish, especially with Truecoat's able assistance. He said, 'Yes, we could turn this museum into a tourist drawing card, really document Columbus's presence in the Caribbean. It could become a focal point for group tours from the Smithsonian and university alumni associations.'

Truecoat beamed and added, 'And with the Spanish heritage, you could arrange a grant for the museum from the King and Queen of Spain. Publicity for an endorsement such as theirs would attract tourists from across Europe and Latin America, as well.' Truecoat was excited and wanted a cigarette.

'We could say it was the *Pinta* even if it isn't,' Sam said, and laughed, quickly adding, 'I'm only joking, of course. Because our motto will be "Truth in the Caribbean – the real story". And we won't allow any national interests, Italian or Spanish, to colour our interpretations.'

Truecoat smiled, still excited. 'But you know, I'd personally like it to be the *Pinta*. Just personally, you understand. Give the island a real boost, and my career as well, although I have no thoughts of leaving Cockburn Town.'

Sam said, 'Couldn't it be the *Santa Maria?*'

'No, you see our ship is a caravel. The *Santa Maria* was a different type of vessel.'

Sam said, 'I remember now. The *Santa Maria* was a larger ship, used for supplies – old technology, couldn't keep up with the two faster caravels, the *Pinta* and the *Niña,* as the three ships crossed the Atlantic.'

'Moreover,' Truecoat said, 'the *Santa Maria* was wrecked. Its frightened crew disassembled it in order to build a stockade and protect themselves from the hostile natives.'

'What about the *Niña?*'

'Went back to Spain.'

Sam looked at his watch. 'I've got to run – the funeral, you know. You going?'

'Of course,' Truecoat replied. 'It will be the biggest island event since John Glenn came down in his little capsule offshore.' Locking the museum, Truecoat followed Sam into the warm air and bright sun.

Sam said, 'I'm excited about the museum. I'd like to be part of it, involved in its planning. I've always loved to immerse myself in the details of antiquity, interpret ancient articles – display them for others to see, all the while seeking their true significance.'

Truecoat asked, 'And pay some of the bills?'

The two men left the museum and walked together towards

Government House.

Reflecting on their conversation and the tour of the museum, Sam realized Truecoat had given him another reason for coveting Trevor's wealth – to use it supporting the Thomson-Columbus Museum, an altruistic cause, perhaps even more meaningful than keeping his own cheque book filled with large numbers.

As they walked past the bank, Penny came running out, shouting, 'Sam, wait.'

He introduced her to Truecoat. Taking the initiative, she shook his hand. Sam thought archaeologists, emulating the lifestyle of Basque sheep-herders, isolated themselves from society by spending so many hours alone in some dig. Maybe such a description fit historians, as well. Sam pondered the matter, trying to put his own self in perspective.

'We've got to talk to Mr Kubler,' Penny said with urgency. 'It's very important. I must phone over to Provo. I'll use the phone in the bank. Allways let me use it already.'

Sam said, 'We're due at the funeral.'

Penny said, 'But don't you see? The warrants must be exercised right away or they'll expire.'

'Gracious,' Truecoat said. 'We can't let them die? What are they anyway? Some sort of endangered species? I've always heard exercise prolongs life.'

'No, no,' Penny said, 'you've got it all wrong, but I haven't time to explain. I must talk to Mr Kubler.'

Sam said, 'Penny, calm down, there's a funeral about to start. Respect for the dead, and all that sort of thing.'

'Yes, it's accepted cultural behaviour,' Truecoat reminded her.

Ignoring them both, Penny turned towards the bank. 'Coming?' she asked Sam.

'No, you go on. Dr Truecoat and I are headed for Government House. The procession's starting from there.'

They heard the cacophony of musical instruments tuning up, discordant notes drifting towards them. Members of the band, not yet in formation, wore red uniforms with black and white panama hats, leather straps under their chins. Their white-gloved hands held brass musical instruments.

Stopping to admire them, Sam exclaimed, 'I like their snappy uniforms.'

Truecoat said, 'The island's pride and joy. It's a real honour for Mr Thomson to have them march on his behalf. He was well thought of on the island, you know.'

Sam concluded the more he knew the less he knew.

36

Returning to Barclay's, Penny telephoned the Thomson-Provo Hospital. She asked to speak to Hans Kubler.

The nurse demanded, 'Are you a relative?'

Thinking fast, Penny overrode her innate compulsion to tell the truth. She lied with, 'Yes, I'm his sister from Lugano. I am telephoning from Switzerland. A Charles Fountain called me – middle of the night here – said my brother had been shot. I am very concerned. Please. I must speak to him.'

'Name?'

Penny gave her real name and asked, 'What is his condition?'

'Stable,' the nurse proclaimed after a pause to look up Kubler's record.

'What does that mean? Good or bad?'

'Neither,' the nurse replied. 'But I can't let you talk to him without his doctor's permission.

'Let me talk to Dr Giannini. I'm sure he'll say it is all right.'

There was a pause and Dr Giannini came on the line.

She said, 'This is Penny Bailes, doctor, I must talk to Mr Kubler. How is he doing?'

'The bullet must have been a shock to his system. He doesn't seem to be responding like he should. The doctor here is taking charge. I'm just on my way to the airport to catch the inner-island plane so I can attend the funeral and the hearing.' He laughed, and said, 'They can't have the funeral without my box or hold the hearing without me.' He added, 'I've got to go now. An airport taxi's waiting.'

'I need to ask him a question.'

'No, I don't want him disturbed. I'll leave a message for him to call you when he wakes up, Ms Bailes. What is it you want to tell him?'

Penny was reluctant to explain to Dr Giannini about Ambrosiana. Instead, she asked, 'He's not coming back over here for the funeral?'

'No. Ms Bailes, this man is recuperating from a gunshot wound. And now I must go.'

'OK, I'll see you at the funeral.' And Penny hung up.

Waiting a few long minutes, she called back, this time informing the nurse Dr Giannini had given her permission to speak to Kubler.

At first she thought her ruse was working for there was no protest from the nurse. But after a pause the nurse came back on the line and said, 'His phone is busy. He's talking.'

'To whom?'

'He's made a number of calls.'

In surprise, Penny asked, 'A number of calls?'

'Yes, first to Zurich, two or three to New York and, oh yes, several to Frankfurt. I know because I had to place each call for him. We don't have direct dialling into the rooms yet.'

'Who's he talking to?' Penny asked.

'I'm not an eavesdropper.'

'Sorry, I didn't mean to suggest . . . .'

The nurse said, 'I'll put you on hold.'

Silence.

Frustrated and wondering, Penny waited. And waited, not wanting to hang up.

After a while she heard the Swiss banker's voice say, 'Kubler here.'

'Hans, it's Penny.'

'Ja,' he said with a spark of recognition. 'You rescued me last night. I remember looking up into your heavenly green eyes. But I don't remember thanking you.'

'You had more important matters on your mind.'

Hans said, 'I'm afraid I did babble away before I passed out.'

'The main thing is, how are you feeling now?'

'Much better, thanks to your call.'

Penny blushed. The attention he paid her came as a pleasant surprise. She said, 'Actually I was very interested in what you had to say last night. That's another reason why I'm calling.'

'You mean you want to talk further about Eurobonds?'

'No, more about Ambrosiana. Last night you wanted me to do something about the company's bonds and you mentioned its warrants. You were quite concerned and kept repeating the company's name. So what can I do to help? I do know a little about the company.'

'You do?' he said with surprise. 'This is a situation involving high finance.'

Penny answered back, 'Look, I realize I live and work in what to you must be the unsophisticated American Wild West, but I do know about high finance.'

'I underestimated you. I am sorry.'

'You're in trouble, aren't you? There's something funny going on here, isn't there? I can feel it. Explain it, if you like, as a woman's intuition.'

Hans said, 'Intuition is necessary in investments.'

'So what is the problem? Is it you don't have the money to exercise the warrants? To pay for the shares of stock these warrants entitle you to buy? Hans, please tell me. You've been shot, and you're probably out of commission for a while. Maybe I can help you.' Penny wanted to add, 'Poor dear.'

Hans was silent.

His reaction confirmed her fears. She pleaded with the Swiss banker, 'Hans, please let me help you. For example: A – do you need financing in order to exercise the warrants? B – do you need investment advice as to whether to lay out all this money for what I understand from my research will give you control of Ambrosiana? C – or are you unsure of their product lines?' Penny wished she hadn't said that, but she added, 'Please make the multiple choice.'

'For an advisory fee?'

Penny laughed and said, 'In finance everybody gets paid, even women, but I'm not calling you to earn a fee. I'm genuinely concerned, because I think . . . well, you're a very nice man, and you've been loyal to Mr Thomson all these years, and now you need some kind of assistance.'

Hans was silent.

So Penny tried, 'Is the problem caused by the pressure of time? You've got to exercise your warrants within a couple of days, or else they'll be worthless and the bonds will drop in value as the warrants expire. Am I not right, Hans?'

Hans replied in a surprised voice, '*Ja.* How is it you know all this?'

'Research is the key to making good investments.'

'*Ja,* I always say so, too,' Hans said. 'But this situation involves more than making an investment decision. It is the life-and-death matter. You see, there are people who want these warrants to expire. And even me as well.'

'Oh, dear,' Penny said and meant it. 'You are certainly being loyal to

192

Trevor's goals. I think if you are successful in this endeavour, you'll deserve not only a bonus from Trevor's portfolio but also a reward from Ambrosiana Limited.' She added, 'Maybe they should retain your services.'

'Not a bad idea, Penny. You should be the one advising me. *Ja.* Conversations with you I find to be most stimulating.'

'Really?' she said. 'But Hans, you should not get too excited. You must recover quickly. You have a big task ahead of you.'

'*Ja.* I will rest a bit. But, promise me you will call me again, soon.'

As Penny hung up she realized a certain Swiss banker was beginning to tug away at her personal portfolio of emotions.

37

Charles Fountain was afraid. The Old Captain was not a stable man. He really might do most anything. While there was a certain predictability about his many eccentricities, everyone knew he could go off at a tangent from time to time. Seldom was he violent, but hadn't he shot Hans Kubler the night before?

The Old Captain had been unstable since that day on Trevor Thomson's pirate galleon. Oh, he had made another trip or two as captain of the ship. The change coming over him was not abrupt. Rather, over the ensuing months, it was gradual, Fountain remembered. One day he walked away from the galleon, never to pilot it again. And after the American naval base was abandoned, he opened the bar. Charles Fountain knew why he had named it the Unlucky Lady.

The Old Captain never had any money, and some asked how he was able to pay for opening the bar, meagre as it was, and buy his stock of liquor. Fountain guessed it had been Trevor Thomson who either loaned or gave him the money. Gave? But if Trevor did in fact loan him the money, he knew he would never get his money back, let alone interest on it. Therefore, the trustee concluded, it was more likely the Old Captain had blackmailed the tycoon.

As time passed, the Old Captain grew increasingly abrasive, tending his bar only sporadically, sulking around the island. Occasionally after downing several beers he would brandish the gun in his bar, but he had never fired it at anybody until the incident last night. Now he stood at Fountain's door, pointing the sinister weapon at the trustee.

'Captain, look . . . .' Fountain began.

'No, ye look, laddie,' the Old Captain said, his voice as creaky as the rigging of a mast under stress. 'The old man is dead. Ain't no one around to protect ye no more.' He added ominously, 'And ye can't no longer hide.'

Fountain was afraid to say anything more for fear one wrong word might ignite a spark of anger, causing the Old Captain to pull the

194

trigger. But he had to try. 'Perhaps I could help you with your bar,' he said. 'How much do you need to spruce it up – a fresh paint job – you know, refurbish it?'

'Ah, now ye are making sense.' The Old Captain spoke with barnacled words, each having to be pried one at a time. He lowered his voice but not his gun and said, 'Ye know, back then – thirty years ago – ye shoulda gone to the police.'

'I married her didn't I?' Fountain responded, his anger growing as he thought about how his own life had been constrained.

'How would ye like me to go to the Governor with the story?' the Old Captain blurted.

'Look, Captain, what is it you want? Money? Or forgiveness for your own weakness in not standing up to Mr Thomson?' Now becoming more bold, his fury fortifying him, Fountain grew oblivious to the gun barrel and went on, 'We were as guilty as Mr Thomson. None of us raised a finger to intervene, and afterwards, none of us dared speak about it, talk to the police or to each other. It has been our lifelong cover-up. You and I, and yes, Old Henry, have tried to suppress what happened, tried to forget. But none of us can. Not even that old parrot of his.'

He watched the Old Captain's face as he spoke, afraid he would pull the trigger at any moment. Nothing happened, so Fountain added, 'And what about Chiarra? She has had to live with the horror of being raped. She has never really been the same, you know.' Fountain's eyes darted from the Old Captain to the gun and back again. Raising his voice, he went on, 'Leave it alone, Captain, forget it. Making an issue out of it now will not help any of us.'

'Ah, but ye're wrong. Very wrong.'

'What do you want?' Fountain insisted. He heard Chiarra behind him, but dared not take his eyes off the Old Captain to see if she was holding their gun. If she shot the Old Captain – and he did not know if she knew how to aim it or even pull the trigger – he would have to call the police. The whole scandal would come out.

If the Old Captain did not back off, lower his gun, and leave, Fountain was going to have to physically attack him. But he resolved to make one more verbal attempt before his suicidal move. He said, 'How much money do you want?'

The Old Captain waited a long moment before replying, and Fountain's hopes rose. He said, 'A thousand will do nicely, maybe two, maybe three. I need to paint the Unlucky Lady, get a refrigerator to replace my leaking ice chest. Yes, three thousand will do quite nicely.'

What the Old Captain said next came as no surprise to Fountain: 'That'll be for openers . . . to get us away from the dock and out into the harbour. You and I'll have a little sailing partnership going, laddie.'

Without warning and from behind, Fountain felt a surge of heat rush past before he heard the shot. And he saw the Old Captain slump in a heap in front of him, blocking the entry to his house.

38

For Trevor's funeral, the Governor's official island band, in their pressed ceremonial uniforms, marched solemnly towards the grave. The drummer beat in a slow, methodical rhythm. Now and then, the trumpet sounded a mournful cry. At appropriate intervals the French horn added a melancholy note.

Sam joined the procession. Some thirty years as Trevor Thomson's stepson were over, a song of the blues passing in to history. He promised himself he would build a future as broad as the Caribbean horizon. He would not look back.

Moravia, the Customs official, came up to him and nodded a polite greeting. She grasped him by the hand. Squeezing gently, she said, her voice comforting, 'The reason we have funerals, Mr Thomson, is so those of us who are left can get on with the rest of our lives. It's not an end, but rather a time of beginning.'

Sam smiled. How could she know what was going through his mind? Customs officials were really perceptive.

Two little girls walked behind the band. Each held a handle ring of the bronze urn. They tried to match their steps to the rhythm of the music, swinging the urn between them. Sam took their photograph. One smiled at him, but the other was seriously dedicated to her assigned task.

Sir Hugh Broughton-Williams followed, Judith by his side. Behind came the sorrowful townsfolk. Slowly the procession made its sombre way up the incline separating Government House from the cemetery.

Felicia and her attorneys walked in the midst as did Wes Truecoat. Penny was right up front. Old Henry shuffled behind, trying to keep up, his parrot intimidated into silence by the solemn proceedings.

Sam looked around for Charles Fountain and Chiarra, but they were not in the group.

The island's small cemetery rested atop a slight rise. An old picket fence wanting paint defined its perimeters. At the final resting-place for Trevor Thomson's urn there was no marble crypt in which to gently and lovingly entomb it. But there was a section with pre-cast vaults. The one waiting to receive Trevor's urn was rimmed with rocky soil.

Sam moved to its edge, joining Judith, who was already standing there with Sir Hugh. It was appropriate, he felt, to be by her side. Penny came up and held his hand.

The mourners were now assembled. The drummer delivered a final drumroll. Silence fell across the cemetery. The collage of citizens of Cockburn Town bowed their heads. Discreetly Sam photographed the scene.

The island cleric began to recite recognized Bible passages. When he finished the Governor stepped forward and said a few words about the debt the island nation owed to Trevor Thomson for building the modern medical facility on Provo and aiding other local needs.

When the Governor concluded, Superintendent Hedgepeth came forward, relieving the two little girls of the urn. The uniformed police chief gently and slowly lowered it to rest for ever.

Quietly Sam said to Penny, 'A pity his ashes aren't going to be scattered onto the sea.'

But Penny whispered back, 'No, the pity is on us, I'm afraid, for not being on top of his affairs before his death.'

Sam whispered back, 'If we knew when a person was going to die, we'd all gather round the about-to-be-deceased and sort things out in a proper manner. If there was no will we'd draw one up and have the person sign it. On cue, they would die in peace.'

Penny said, 'With your scenario, attorneys and estate planners would be selling pencils and apples on street corners. Your idea will never fly.'

'Nice if it would, though,' Sam insisted.

'It would also be nice if no one died.'

'The world would get awfully crowded after a while.'

'Makes you wonder about overpopulation in the life hereafter, doesn't it?'

Sam introduced Penny to the Governor. He put his hat back on and edged around the vault, which two workers were already beginning to cover with the limestone soil.

Dr Giannini walked up, perspiration dripping. Sans his 'Fragile' box, it seemed to Sam one of his body parts had been amputated. The coroner whispered to Sam, 'Just got off the puddle-jumper from Provo in time to hand over my urn to those two little girls.'

Sam asked, 'How's Mr Kubler doing?'

'His vital signs are fine, but he professes to be quite tired. I'm not sure I believe him.'

'I think I'd be tired, too, if I'd been shot.'

'Yes, that's true. I've never been wounded either, and I hope never to have the experience, although I've delved into a lot of people who have.'

Sam held his stomach.

The coroner added, 'Ms Bailes called to talk to him.'

'Penny did?'

'She said it was vitally important she speak to him.'

'To Penny everything is a crisis,' Sam said. 'I've grown accustomed to her periods of panic.'

'Living with someone does that, they tell me,' the coroner said, 'but no one's ever lived with me.'

'Coroners are probably not at the top of a woman's wish list,' Sam said, chuckling. 'Right down there with historians.'

Nodding, the coroner said slowly, thinking the baring of his soul might ingratiate himself with Sam, 'Yes, every time I get close to being intimate, I think about the last female autopsy I performed, and then, well, you know, I can't.' The coroner edged closer and whispered, 'Any more thoughts about my little stipend?'

Annoyed, Sam rebuked him, saying, 'We're here for the funeral of my stepfather. We shouldn't be talking about money.'

'Maybe so, but the world's business, my boy, goes on day and night whether we want it to or not.'

'But I'm not obligated to play,' Sam said, leaving the coroner looking after him, agape.

A few steps on, a smartly-dressed but sinister-looking man approached him. He kept looking around the crowd, searching for someone. This strange man certainly didn't fit with the mourners. To Sam he demanded, 'Where is Hans Kubler?'

Surprised, Sam said, 'He was shot last night.'

'I know that,' was the curt reply. 'I was in the bar when it happened.'

'Who are you?' Sam asked.

'Angelo Luciano,' he replied, and grabbed Sam's arm and squeezed. His voice rose as he demanded, 'I want to know where he is now.'

Sam said, 'In the hospital in Provodenciales.'

'Where the hell is that?'

Reacting with annoyance, Sam said, 'It's the bigger town on the other island.'

Without another word, the man left and hurried down the hill. Sam watched him climb into a waiting taxi on the plaza.

Spinning with the abrupt episode, Sam wondered why he wanted to find Hans Kubler. He thought about asking Penny, but then he saw Felicia. Gaining his composure, he walked up to her and said, 'Well, another chapter in our lives is history, isn't it?'

Coolly, she replied, 'I view it more as a preface.'

'Either way, your life and my life will go on.'

'One poorer – that's you; and one richer – that's me.'

'And the poverty around us,' Sam said, 'whether here or in America will also continue.'

'The difference is,' Felicia explained, 'I intend to do something about it. Whereas all you'll do with more money is stuff it in your already deep pockets.'

'You're wrong. Trevor's setting up the museum here has convinced me wealth should not simply sit idle,' Sam replied. 'I'm thinking about applying Trevor's money towards altruistic goals. If we made the Thomson-Columbus Museum the centre of a Caribbean interpretive park dealing with the history of all of these islands, everyone the world over will know what happened here with Columbus, the natives, everything.'

'Yeah, the pursuit of the white man's history, you mean. Digging up old shipwrecks, stocking museums with the white man's concocted story,' she said, her tone belittling.

Sam smiled and said, 'True history isn't a concocted story, and you're smart enough to know that.'

Her eyes searched his face. At first she said nothing, then, 'I have my mother to help take care of, too.'

'Mine's dead.'

'Sometimes I think mine wanted to be.' Felicia dropped her head to hide a tear. 'Men are so cruel. Are you cruel like your stepfather?'

'Would a cruel person sponsor a museum?'

Felicia hesitated. 'I don't know. I just don't know.'

'Let's face it,' Sam tried, 'even Trevor's billions aren't enough to address every social need, are they?'

'That's not the point,' Felicia replied, her voice firm. 'It's what each of us, rich or poor, do with what we've got or will get.'

Sam asked, 'Does it matter where, I mean geographically?'

'One life saved, one life made better is one life, I suppose,' Felicia acknowledged, 'whether it's in Los Angeles or on some isolated

Caribbean island such as here. Yet . . . .'

'Yet what?'

'Yet, let me tell you the secret of charitable organizations, Mr Suddenly Altruistic. You and I live in a media age. And one's dedication gets more attention when it's a media event. And that's more likely to happen in LA, or New York where the media are headquartered. Their reporters don't have to travel so far, and the public relations people located there can promote their clients' causes. Here, they each must fly in on a once-a-week flight from Miami.'

'What about Mother Teresa? I hear her organization's in Albania and India.'

'Maybe she has good PR.'

'So, we'll hire the best,' Sam said.

'We're not selling anything, are we?'

Sam said, 'We will be selling the need, how you and I address the need, and our solutions.' Tauntingly he added, 'That's the white man's way.'

Felicia's ire blossomed. 'You'll make progress when you quit tuning into the white man's programme and listen to the real world. You let me know when you've changed channels. And not before.'

'I was only joking. But if that's your requirement . . . .' Sam hesitated and smiled. He kissed her on the cheek, adding, '. . . I'll be happy to push the remote to any programme you want.'

39

Charles Fountain bent over the Old Captain. The seaman's grimy clothes were bloody from the shotgun wounds. Sticking out from an inside pocket of his tattered jacket Fountain saw the corner of an envelope. Gingerly, trying to avoid the Old Captain's blood, the trustee reached for it.

'Don't touch nothin',' Chiarra pleaded.

Fountain paid no attention as he extracted the blood-spotted envelope. 'It is from an international courier,' he said in surprise, gesturing at the distinctive envelope. Examining it more closely, he said, 'It is addressed to the Old Captain, care of the Unlucky Lady.'

'I'm the unlucky lady,' Chiarra said.

'Yes, I know,' Fountain said, one arm encircling her in one of his bear-hugs.

'Today I double unlucky, shooting Old Captain.' Tears bubbled in her eyes as she asked, 'I go prison, Charles?'

'No, Chiarra, you fired in self-defence.'

'I kill him. Maybe we just bury him our back yard. No Chief Hedgepeth, no explain police.'

'I do not know if he is dead.' Fountain felt for a pulse. 'I have no experience with violent death. We must call Dr Maghool.' The concern in his voice growing, he said, 'Chiarra, we cannot cover up a shooting.'

'Mr Thomson cover up hurting me. Cover up thirty years.'

Fountain nodded. Yes, he thought, rape is worse than shooting an intruder. And this morning the Old Captain was an intruder, robber, thief. He threatened to kill me. He wanted money from me. And God knows what he would have done to Chiarra. But Trevor's rape was worse. She has had to live with rape. You do not live with death.

Chiarra threw her arms around her husband, clinging to him desperately, tears rolling down her face. She said, 'I saw Mr Thomson's

202

face. I shoot gun.'

'I know, I know,' he said gently. Then, realizing he was still holding onto the envelope, he opened it, extracting a photograph and a wad of hundred-dollar bills. The picture was of Hans Kubler.

'Charles, look, money,' Chiarra exclaimed. 'Maybe he paid to kill you.'

'Not me – Kubler,' Fountain said. He looked at the envelope, searching for a sender's name. 'Here,' he announced, pointing, 'the envelope has been sent from Italy, from Milan.'

'Who send it?'

'There is no name, only the air courier's dispatching office.'

'Why they want to kill our nice Mr Kubler?'

'Kubler manages Trevor Thomson's money, his investments . . . .' His voice trailed off as he tried to think of a reason.

'And Old Captain try to blackmail you for even more money,' Chiarra said.

'Yes, Chiarra, money can distort a person's values.'

40

Rushing to Barclay's to use the phone to call Tony again, Penny found the bank closed. In fact, as she looked around, she saw everything was closed. In honour of Trevor Thomson's funeral, she concluded. She saw the pay telephone box next to Government House. She hoped it would connect her to Tony in Rome.

But there he was, leaning up against the box – the sailor with the parrot. As she walked towards the phone, she remembered he was called Old Henry. She saw him eye her and feared harassment, distracting conversation or physical contact. And she worried the bird would squawk while she was trying to listen to Tony.

She searched for an alternative telephone, her eyes taking in the little town centre. On one side were the barbed-wire walls of the jail, on the other the salt flats, and there was Government House. Perhaps there was a phone inside, but with the hearing about to start, the place would soon be crowded and she didn't want to be overheard. This phone would have to do.

Old Henry, not moving, said, 'Mornin', Miss.'

Penny smiled and said, 'Good morning, Henry.' The bird was silent, thank heaven. 'I'm going to make a call,' she said, hoping he would take the hint and move a respectable distance away.

He didn't and continued to lean against the box. The ocean breeze was refreshing but it blew his obnoxious body odours right at her. She tried to shift, tried not to breathe, but his smell engulfed her.

She punched out the long string of numbers including her own credit card code, waiting for the miracle of world-wide telephonic communications to perform. She watched the bird. It was a cute thing. Colourful too. Its eyes watched her but its claws dug into Old Henry's thick shirt.

At last Tony answered with, 'Penny?'

'Tony,' she said, relieved to hear his voice.

'You won't believe what I've found out.'

'Try me.'

'Well, remember I told you this Ambrosiana outfit was into condoms
. . . ah . . . I mean into making condoms?' he said, trying to stifle a laugh.
'Well, this outfit is out to corner the world's condom market! They've
options to buy the other major manufacturers, one in Japan, one in
Thailand and the other in the US. In order to pay for these acquisitions
they'll use the money they receive from the conversion of the warrants
into common stock.'

'Rape. He's raping her,' the parrot squawked.

'What's going on there?' Tony asked, alarmed.

'He's grabbing her,' the bird insisted.

'Penny, are you all right?' Tony's voice was concerned.

'Rape!' repeated the parrot.

Penny said, 'Shut up, you stupid bird.'

Old Henry straightened up, forgetting his cane. It fell by his side.
'Nobody calls my pal stupid.' He moved closer to Penny.

She pulled on the telephone's short cord, extending it as far as
possible from the box, another foot at best. Old Henry's wrinkled
fingers encircled her arm. Penny looked around for help, but the streets
were deserted. Everyone was still up at the cemetery, milling around
after the funeral.

'Henry, let go, please,' Penny insisted. 'I'm sorry I called your bird a
name, but I'm trying to talk to Italy. Can't you give me a little room
here, some quiet.'

Old Henry harrumphed, loosening his grip on her arm.

The bird said, 'Be nice me, Mr Thomson. Be nice me. Not do that.
Rape. Rape.'

Penny said, 'What's he talking about?'

'Rape. Mr Thomson raped Chiarra. My pal knows, my pal tells
everybody about it. But no one cares, no one listens – they all think my
pal crazy.'

Penny said, 'When did this alleged rape take place?'

'Thirty years ago,' Old Henry said.

'Where?'

'On his fishing boat, the pirate galleon, I was a member of the crew.
Me and my pal here – we saw it all. We saw it happen, but no one would
tell, certainly not me – we were all afraid of Mr Thomson. Except him.'
He gestured at his pal whose beak remained closed.

'Penny, who are you talking to? What is going on?'

'It's OK, Tony, I have a kibitzer with an opinionated parrot . . . .'

'Well, it's your lire, but it's my evening, so do you or do you not want to know about Ambrosiana?'

'I do,' Penny said. 'Excuse the interruption. Go ahead, please. What about the warrants?'

'Well, if the warrants are exercised, the exercisor will automatically control the world market for safe sex.' Tony laughed uproariously, and Penny heard a female titter in the background.

Tony added, 'They can raise the price on a package of condoms, French Tickler and Regular, as well. Can you think of a better money-making scheme than ringing the cash register every time there is sex in the world?'

'No, I can't actually,' Penny said.

Tony went on, 'I mean, one need only pop the price a penny on each rubber sold and you'd have your annual salary and bonus guaranteed. This is the greatest money-making scheme since brokerage commissions were conceived.'

'How do you know all this,' Penny asked, her tone sceptical, 'and no one else does? I mean, the price of the bonds is only at par despite their high coupon yield and their common stock is in the doldrums – nothing exciting is happening to the company, no one is bidding their securities up in anticipation of an announcement, either. Where's your inside information coming from?'

Tony laughed.

Penny heard him take another drink. She said, 'I've always dreamed of being on the inside, knowing before anyone else, making a killing like the big boys and girls on Wall Street, the ones who've got the smart bartenders and shoe-shine boys who whisper the word. I've always wanted to feel clever, smart, and laugh at the world because I was in on something before anyone else. But I'm experienced enough to believe the goddess of inside knowledge will never smile my way.'

Old Henry nodded his agreement.

Tony said, 'But my information is reliable.'

'Where's it coming from?'

'Her bedroom,' Tony said, and laughed again.

'What are you – an official product tester?'

'Seriously, Penny, it's the truth. She's Ambrosiana's cute little secretary, confidential secretary.'

Old Henry leaned close to hear both sides of the conversation. The stench was unbearable. Even the parrot, still on his shoulder, stank up a storm.

'Rape,' said the parrot.

'Who's that?' Tony asked.

'A witness,' Penny explained. 'So, it's in somebody's best interest these warrants not be exercised. Whoever it is wants them to die like fish out of water. And whose best interest is it?'

'Ah,' Tony said, his voice travelling all the way from Rome, 'that is the sixty-four billion dollar question.'

'Well, what's the answer?'

'I don't know. Unless . . . . Five years ago when old man Ambrosiana sold these bonds with the warrants attached he needed the money desperately, just to keep his company afloat. So, maybe Count Ambrosiana thinks he's got another way of financing these take-overs – perhaps through private money sources, or perhaps the banks. Either way, he's still going to corner condoms.'

Maybe the Mafia, Penny thought, and said so out loud.

Through his beard Penny could see Old Henry grimace.

'And who owns this large chunk of bonds with the warrants attached?' Penny asked. 'The warrants having a life of only a few days before they are cremated?'

'Ah, that much I do know. At least I can tell you where the rumour arrow, having been spun on the gameboard, is now pointing.'

'Where?'

'To your sidekick, your lover, your client, whatever the relationship is you have going there.'

'What are you talking about?'

'Sam Thomson.'

'My Sam? You've got to be kidding. He's just a historian, a nut for old things, books, libraries, archaeology, what have you. He doesn't understand warrants and such things.'

'But you do, and you'd better get hold of those warrants and get them exercised. It's a damn sight more important than exercising your dog, believe me.'

She whistled and said, 'My God, Tony, this means Sam could be one of the richest men in the world.' She added wistfully, 'Maybe now he'll propose marriage.'

'Why would you want to get married, Penny? Take it from me, it's more fun this way.'

Ignoring his comment, she asked, 'Can you help me convert the warrants into the common stock?'

His answer was drowned out by the sound of a helicopter landing nearby. She shouted into the mouthpiece, 'I can't hear you, Tony, there's a helicopter . . . .'

Tony shouted back, repeating, 'No, you've got to do that directly with the corporate office in Campione.'

The helicopter noise rendered conversation impossible. As it lifted off towards Provo, Penny said loudly, 'OK, but who's got the warrants?'

'Well, the information took a little doing, a little convincing,' Tony replied, his voice lower with the ensuing quiet. 'And it turns out Trevor Thomson's money manager is the man with the clout in this scenario. He's a banker from Lugano.'

Penny exclaimed, 'You mean Hans Kubler!'

'How did you guess?' he asked.

'I didn't. He told me. After he was shot.'

'Shot?'

Penny replied with, 'You'll have to excuse me a minute.'

She looked the parrot in the eye, then Old Henry. 'Would you like to have a nice bath, Henry?'

'Forgot how to take one,' he said, slowly stroking his chin whiskers.

'Here, take this key and go to my hotel. If anyone stops you, tell them I said it's OK. You take a bath. You'll find some clean clothes in Sam's suitcase. Hurry now, so you can get back for the hearing at Government House. Now go!' She shoved him.

Old Henry hesitated in disbelief. But he accepted the key, winked at his parrot, nodded and left. The wake of a ship couldn't rival the stench following Old Henry.

To Tony, she said, 'OK, I'm back.'

He said, 'But why hasn't this man exercised his warrants? The business decision is to go for it.'

'He's worried.'

Tony asked, 'Has somebody gotten to him, persuaded him to back off?'

'You mean paid him off? I can't see him taking a bribe. Furthermore, he'd lose his job at the bank if he were found out.'

Tony suggested, 'You've an opportunity to talk directly to him?'

'He's in the hospital over at Provo,' Penny said. 'Yes, I could fly over there and see him.' Trying not to reveal her eagerness, she added, 'Judge the man by the look in his eye and the cut of his jib.'

41

Sam thought the air-conditioning was turned on in Government House but he felt only hot air circulating amongst the multitude of locals and visitors beginning to crowd into the hearing room. He'd rather have returned to the peace and isolation of the white sand beach, or the quiet challenge of the rudimentary Thomson-Columbus Museum and its inanimate artifacts. In either place he would feel more comfortable.

Looking around the large room, Sam saw Felicia and her two attorneys standing in front, waiting for the proceedings to start. She was in a black chiffon dress with lace here and there – appropriate, he thought, for a dress of mourning. But Sam knew she wasn't mourning. Rather she was yearning to be declared Trevor's heir. She was probably planning how she'd celebrate her victory.

Beside her, Horace Turner mopped his brow and appeared worried. But Felicia was smiling, the same smile Sam had seen at dawn when she looked at him lying fully disclosed on the sand.

Judith entered arm in arm with the Governor, Sir Hugh Broughton-Williams, both displaying the same perfunctory smile as they greeted the islanders. Sam envisioned her being the white queen of this black-populated island – the first lady of this crown colony.

His little sister had left the nest, and Sam felt a burden being removed from his life. At last he was relieved of a childhood, then an adolescent, and what had grown into an adult obligation to care for her, to look after her, to guard her from evil people and unwelcome happenings. He was proud of his sister and smiled back at her as she and the Governor passed by.

Despite his fixed smile, Sir Hugh appeared pleased with the gathering, for it signified his own importance, which was now buoyed even more, Sam thought, by Judith's charm.

Sam saw Felicia was carefully observing his sister's display of affection for the Governor. Her smile of victory quickly evaporated into the muggy air, a frown forming instead. As she noticed Dr Giannini pushing through the crowded room, trying to get Sam's attention, Felicia's frown deepened to a scowl.

She left Horace Turner and moved towards Sam, but quickly changed her mind, turned and sat down. Sam wished she'd come. He started in her direction. But unsure of himself, he hesitated, stopped and only looked at her.

A fantasy filled his mind. Felicia was on the beach in the sand, naked. He was beside her. Felicia stretched her arms to welcome him. Music played in his ears as he desperately – no, gently – complied, lowering himself, ready to become part of her, embracing her, and she him. Tenderly she accepted him, her body and his entwining.

He heard Columbus and the crew of the *Pinta* cheering him on from the deck, the banner of King Ferdinand and Queen Isabella flying from its mast. He heard the Sanish word *bueno,* and laughed out loud, Felicia with him. She moaned with pleasure.

A sailor on board the *Pinta* shot off a cannon, one of those long ones. Sam responded with a wave of his hand, acknowledging their cheers. He and Felicia rose from the sand. Arm in arm they frolicked in the surf, splashing each other as Columbus sailed off on the high tide, heading back to Spain.

Sam's eyes were glossy with his day-dream as he stared into the infinity of the hearing-room. So, he didn't respond right away when Felicia, now standing by his side, quietly called out his name. The tone of her voice was gentle, matching her demeanour in his day-dream.

To make certain she had his attention, Felicia poked his stomach and laughed, 'You day-dreaming, Sam, my Mr Clothed Historian?'

He was surprised her voice was more friendly. Pleased, he stammered and said, 'I was imagining.'

She said, 'What, Mr Rich Man?' But the hostility was there only jokingly, he thought. Or was he just hoping?

He looked into her eyes and said softly, 'Being on the beach again with you, if you must know.'

Felicia exclaimed, 'You're a funny fellow. You've already been on the beach with me once today. Do you go through life repeating episodes, or are you more adventuresome – seeking new experiences?'

Sam said, 'I'm comfortable with the known, but challenged by the unknown.'

'And I'm the unkknown?' she asked. Her hand came forward again, her palm barely touching Sam's Caribbean multicoloured shirt. 'But I feel I know almost everything there is to know about you.'

Sensuously, she averted her eyes. She said, 'Look, Sam, whatever happens here today, I want you to know I don't personally hold anything against you.'

'Well, you didn't this morning when I needed something.'

'That was this morning – a long time ago.'

Sam said, 'Don't mislead me, Felicia, you want the money. It's that simple. You needn't get esoteric about it. Give me more credit.'

'With your money you don't need credit,' she said, removing her hand from his chest.

He thought he'd said something wrong, for her hostility seemed to be returning. Without thinking, he reached out. Touching her shoulder, his strong hand gently and slowly spun her back towards him. He said, 'Please understand, I meant no offence just now.' He paused and slowly suggested, 'Money's in our way, isn't it?' They stood facing each other, silence surrounding their twosome world. Finally he said, 'I've never cared much about money.'

'Because you've always had it,' she retorted, showing her exasperation as she removed his hand from her shoulder. 'My people in the inner city care, because they weren't born with a silver spoon in their mouths. So, since you're more interested in other things like your white man's history and your white man's books, give them your money. Go your way and let us go ours.'

The fire in her eyes was fitting for the temperature of the room. Maybe, he thought, she alone, with her heat, was the one cancelling the building's air-conditioning.

He said, 'Look, Felicia, I realize this is real money we're toying with . . . .'

'Toying?'

'Well, yes. You see, I guess I'm not orientated to making money. I yearn to explore the truth of the past.'

Felicia said, 'Look, could we talk about this without our façades getting in the way?'

Sam didn't know what to say. He wanted to look up an appropriate response in a reference book on human behaviour – no, make it the 'S' volume for sexual relationships. He tried, 'I'd like very much to do so. But when? The hearing is about to start.'

Felicia's eyes seemed to be alive as she said with a hint of a smile, 'Afterwards.'

Sam nodded slowly, his gaze riveted to her black-clad lithe body as she moved away from him to insert herself between her two attorneys.

42

The Governor banged a gavel.

Sam saw Charles Fountain enter the room, brief-case under his arm, Chiarra by his side. The trustee looked harried, but nevertheless went immediately to Felicia who, seeing him, stood up, and father and daughter embraced. Sam wondered why neither he nor Chiarra had attended the funeral. He had no answer until Fountain approached him.

'Mr Thomson . . . .'

'Call me Sam.'

Fountain hesitated and said, 'Clients must be addressed with formality.'

'I may not be a client after this hearing.'

'I may not be a trustee much longer when the police find out what has happened.'

Sam looked puzzled. 'Is someone impugning your reputation?'

'Not yet, but they will.' Fountain hesitated again. He said, 'Mr Kubler was shot on purpose last night. I mean, someone paid the Old Captain to try to kill him. Fortunately the Old Captain's eyesight is poor, or else at the critical moment he could not bring himself to take proper aim.'

Sam whistled softly and asked, 'How do you know?'

Fountain told him about the morning's incident and the envelope with money, concluding with, 'Chiarra's aim is not too good either.' Fountain went on, 'We have helicoptered the Old Captain over to the hospital on Provo.' He paused, looked forlorn and said, 'The local authorities will not like all this violence. And,' his voice rose with concern, 'you may also be in danger. There may be someone else lurking around the island.'

'Really?' Sam said in surprise.

'A lot of money is at stake.'

Sam thought about the pseudo-mourner who had been looking for Kubler following the funeral. Hadn't he said he knew about the shooting? Maybe he'd put the Old Captain up to it, and was now going to finish the job himself. 'We should warn Kubler,' Sam said.

Fountain nodded.

'And the police?'

'We have already involved them too much,' The trustee looked across the room at Chiarra. She was covering her face, obviously crying. He said, 'Excuse me, I must comfort her. She is quite upset.'

Old Henry came up. Good Lord, Sam thought, the old seaman's as clean as a whistle, freshly shaven too, and wearing a very familiar shirt. On his shoulder perched the parrot, looking frightened with all the people. Old Henry said, 'Thanks for the clothes. Your woman said I was to help myself.'

'My woman?'

'Penny, I think's her name.'

'He's grabbing her,' the bird said nervously.

'She sent me to her hotel room for a bath and your clothes. Said I was to look presentable at the hearing.'

Dr Giannini, wiping his forehead as he came up to Sam, said seriously, 'How much will you pay for my favourable testimony?'

'You're not subtle at all, are you?' Sam said, trying to focus on the coroner while searching the room for Penny. He felt adrift facing the hearing alone and needed her by his side.

'It's too late for innuendo,' Dr Giannini replied. 'Now is the time for hard currency and action.'

'I don't know what to tell you,' Sam said. 'I really need to talk to Penny first.'

'I must know,' the doctor whispered, 'before my testimony. What I say depends on what you tell me now.'

'But I've no cash on me to pay you even if I wanted to,' Sam said, adding, 'and frankly, I've forgotten how much you were asking for.'

'Ten per cent,' the doctor replied, his patience evaporating. 'An easy number to remember.' As the Governor's gavel came down again, he said, 'Your credit is good with me. Yes or no, now! Just sign here.' He produced a perspiration-soaked letter from his inside pocket, holding it for Sam to see. Quickly he uncapped a ball-point pen and pressed it into Sam's hand.

Sam said, 'Once I've signed, you'll take this document down front and convince Felicia to raise her bid. You must think I'm awfully stupid.'

'On the contrary, smart,' Dr Giannini said, exhibiting his cold coroner's smile. 'You don't want Trevor Thomson's wealth, your inheritance, to become a forgotten history lesson, do you?'

Sam saw the short woman helping her taller husband, bandages wrapping his arm, shoulder and neck.

Dr Giannini saw them too. He said, 'The local island doctor must have used up his entire supply of gauze last night.'

A younger attractive woman, carrying a brief-case, sat down with the couple.

Sir Hugh spoke into the microphone. It didn't work. He tapped it and looked for help from Superintendent Hedgepeth. The police chief switched a tiny button on the microphone's stem, smiling sheepishly.

This time the Governor's voice boomed throughout the room, 'It is time for us to begin our hearing.'

'What are you going to do?' Dr Giannini said, grasping Sam's arm.

Perhaps it was the feeling of the coroner's pudgy fingers, perhaps it was intuition, perhaps it was because Penny was not there to advise him. Or his own moral values asserting themselves. Maybe it was all of the above. But Sam replied, 'I'm not going to sign your paper or pay you any money, Dr Giannini. You go ahead and testify. If I don't agree with what you tell the hearing, I'll say so publicly, right here today, and we'll get another professional opinion to refute your testimony.'

The coroner laughed. 'You'll be too late. This hearing's not going to recess, research and reconvene. Today will be the final word.'

'I'm used to historians not agreeing on what has happened. Our situation is no different.'

'Medical evidence, my boy, is irrefutable,' the coroner insisted. 'It's fact, and fact is different from history.'

Sam wanted to change his mind, pay the man off, but sensed it would be the wrong move. Why did he have to confront a crooked coroner? Why did things have to go wrong? Why couldn't truth prevail? But, he asked himself, what was the truth? There were no right or wrong answers. Just events unfolding, their nature – even as they occurred – subject to historical interpretation, depending on the agenda of whoever was making the observation.

His eyes surveyed the people in the room, the faces mostly black, or shades of black, or were they shades of white? Even on that point he wasn't sure. His gaze settled on Felicia, and he wanted to take her up on the offer of a quiet chat. But could they? So far each little talk had resulted in a confrontation. Sam wanted answers, but knew life was not so simple as to automatically provide them, each properly indexed in some reference book.

The Governor was no help to Sam's feelings, for he announced, 'There is a question of the manner of death of Trevor Thomson. We are assembled here to accept relevant evidence. This will be an informal hearing. Certain people have asked to speak and I will call on them in turn. Belinda,' and he gestured at a court reporter sitting by his side,'will transcribe what is said.'

Superintendent Hedgepeth, his uniform pressed and perfect, his demeanour disciplined, stood and said in a loud, deep voice, 'Dr Giannini, will you please come forward.'

43

Watching the crowds of people enter Government House, Penny inserted a coin into the pay telephone in the booth across the plaza. With Old Henry gone, she could more easily concentrate. When the hospital in Provo came on the line, she identified herself as Hans Kubler's sister, asking to speak to him again. 'I called earlier,' she reminded the receptionist.

There was a pause. The duty nurse said, 'He check out already. Said he catch Miami flight, go back Switzland.'

'What? But I'm sure Dr Giannini hasn't released him! When did he leave?'

The nurse hesitated. 'I remember now. He said something about Easter pageant, mention town, name Mend –' She paused and Penny heard her ask another nurse, 'How he pronounce?' She was back on the line with, 'Mendrisio – yes, that's it.'

A different voice came on the line and said, 'Ms Bailes, I am the head nurse, Ms Maguire. Mr Kubler said you would call. He asked me to read you a short letter when you telephoned again.'

Penny was surprised and said, 'Yes, please do,' adding, 'by all means.'

Clearing her throat, Ms Maguire began, carefully enunciating her words so she would faithfully deliver the message:

'Dear Penny – if I may be so familiar – please forgive my hurried departure from Turks and Caicos and using this impersonal way to convey to you my gratitude. I appreciate your offer to help me with the Ambrosiana warrants. As you know, there is very little time remaining to exercise them. And I am convinced the shares of new stock would be the proper investment move for Sam and his sister, Judith. I know Mr Thomson wanted me to follow through on our plan. I would be very pleased if you would join me in

Switzerland to work with me.

'Another reason for your coming is the beautiful Mendrisio Easter Pageant. It is to be held on Maundy Thursday in a little medieval town a few miles south of Lugano. For me and my friends marching in the procession has been a tradition over the years. I would be honoured to share this event with you, my new colleague.'

Ms Maguire added, 'And he has signed it, "Affectionately, Hans".'

Penny exclaimed, 'But he was shot last night. When I talked to him earlier the poor, dear man felt weak. He can't have checked out, taken a flight to Switzerland. He can't have left the hospital.'

Head Nurse Maguire replied, 'No ma'am, but he did. Oh, I almost forgot. There is a postscript.'

'Yes?'

'It says: "Look for Pontius Pilate".'

'Who, for God's sake?'

'That man is not for God's sake,' Ms Maguire replied, her words more rapid, her tone indignant. 'He is the man who had our Lord crucified.'

'An Easter pageant,' Penny said to herself. She asked, 'What time did he leave?'

''Bout half ten.'

'When was the flight? Has it left yet?'

'I don't know. I'm no travel agent,' Ms Maguire replied, irritability creeping into her voice. 'But I heard a big jet plane roar overhead about ten minutes ago. I'm sure it was the Provo turn-around flight going back to Miami.'

Penny was disgusted with herself for always playing catch-up.

Leaving the phone booth, Penny rushed across the plaza and into Government House. She entered the hearing-room just as Dr Giannini was beginning his testimony.

The Swiss coroner faced the audience and said, 'Your Excellency, you have asked me to render my professional opinion as Ticino Cantonal Coroner concerning the cause of the death of Trevor Thomson last Friday in Switzerland.'

Penny located Sam, grabbed his arm, and whispered, 'Hans Kubler's left – gone back to Switzerland. We've got to follow him. Something about a pageant, and his meeting Pontius Pilate.'

'Penny, what are you talking about? Pontius Pilate must be dead by now.' He chuckled, 'In fact, I think I clipped his obituary for our file labelled "Famous Christian Religious Personages" at the library.'

'Be serious, Sam, it's Ambrosiana Limited. That's what this whole thing is about.'

'What thing?' Sam asked, a little irritated. 'Shh, Dr Giannini is testifying about the cause of Trevor's death.'

'Did you pay him off?' Penny asked. 'He's as crooked as a dog's hind leg, you know?'

'No, of course not, and certainly not without you to advise me. By the way, where have you been?'

'I just told you. I've been talking to the hospital.'

Sam thought he saw Dr Giannini wink at Felicia, but he couldn't be certain.

The Swiss coroner continued: 'Based on evidence from witnesses on the train and from my examination of the deceased's body, it is my opinion Trevor Thomson died by deliberately jumping from a moving InterCity Express train into Lake Lugano. Death was caused either by the trauma of falling, although at his age – had he lived – he would surely have died of drowning within moments of hitting the water. Witnesses have told me he was despondent over having to sign some document. So it is perfectly clear to me in my official capacity, Trevor Thomson's death was a suicide.'

Helga Gistelli applauded and eyed Debra Datsun's brief-case.

Trying to raise his arm in celebration, Hubert cried out in pain from his injured shoulder.

Sam watched Debra hand Mrs Gistelli an insurance company three-page form, which she flipped through without reading. She showed it to Hubert, who nodded. Since his arm was out of commission, Mrs Gistelli signed and gave it to Debra. Acting for the insurance company, Debra extracted a packet from her brief-case and slipped it to Mother Goose, who gathered the little gosling into the folds of her skirt.

Fountain edged back to Sam and Penny. He said quietly, 'If I were you, I would instigate a lawsuit against the insurance company. My advice is not to acquiesce to this verdict.'

Penny nodded and said, 'I think the company's almost broke anyway.'

'All the more reason to get Sam's claim on record,' the trustee suggested. 'You know, the company could lose its licence for a lot less.'

'But the testimony?' Sam said.

'Challenge it,' Fountain said. 'Aren't you Americans the ones who don't take "no" for an answer?' He returned to comfort Chiarra.

Superintendent Hedgepeth called for Horace Turner.

Felicia's attorney stood to address the Governor. 'Your Excellency, we also have the matter of heirship to determine here today.'

'Proceed,' Sir Hugh said.

The attorney said with finality in his voice, 'The evidence makes it perfectly clear. Felicia Fountain is Trevor Thomson's daughter. Her mother, if called to testify, will confirm she had an affair with Mr Thomson.'

Old Henry's parrot squawked, 'He's grabbing her.' And as the audience turned towards Henry and the bird riding on his shoulder, Old Henry nodded his agreement.

No one snickered at Old Henry for he was clean-shaven and properly attired. He looked respectable as he called out across the hall in his rusty voice, 'Yes, I must tell about it now – it was rape, like my pal here says.' He gestured with his weathered hand towards the parrot. 'He and I were there.'

'Rape,' the bird repeated.

Chiarra hid her head.

Felicia's eyes moistened.

Penny punched Sam in the gut. 'Do something, say something now. You can't sit here and watch it all go by like a chapter in one of your history books. You're a player on stage, not some long-dead personage.'

Dutifully Sam stood, but before he could say anything, Horace Turner continued his argument, his voice booming, 'Therefore, under island laws, Felicia Fountain is entitled to Trevor Thomson's entire estate. As his natural daughter and his only child, her claim preempts any provisions of the deceased's trust because Trevor Thomson did not specifically exclude her by name – either in the written document or in any subsequent amendment.' He added, his voice dropping, 'And we are prepared to subpoena the trust document if necessary in order to substantiate our position.'

Forcing himself, Sam bellowed out, 'Your Excellency.' He waited for recognition from Sir Hugh. He saw his little sister's eyes fix on him. And he stumbled out with, 'My stepfather,' and he paused. Accustomed to speaking before students, he had never been under litigious stress. And he always spoke about matters he had researched and about which he could abstractly theorize.

'Yes, Mr Thomson,' Sir Hugh said, 'go on.'

Remembering to remove his hat, Sam ran his hand through his hair, ruffling it even more, and nervously blurted, 'My stepfather was sterile. He could not father. He was gassed in the trenches in World War I in France. His wounds rendered him infertile.'

Felicia gasped.

Looking at her, Sam perceived she might cry, and he was very sorry for her. He didn't want to hurt her. He wasn't at all comfortable. He thought about sitting down, letting the matter alone. Or perhaps running over to Felicia and saying, 'OK, you take the money, and I'll go back to my history.' But he knew events were really beyond his control. And he had no choice but to continue.

Chiarra, her face wet with tears, eyed Sam in dismay.

Fountain looked aghast at him.

Horace Turner was stunned, but finally said, 'You have no proof Trevor Thomson had such a medical condition.'

Taking his cue, Dr Giannini stood and said, 'I have medical evidence Trevor Thomson was not sterile. Further, from DNA tests I have made on the deceased, I am prepared to back up that statement. I have scientific proof in my laboratory outside Lugano.'

Felicia began to smile, relief showing on her face.

Penny whispered to Sam, 'The letters, tell about Trevor's letters.'

Looking down at her, Sam said, 'What letters?'

Frowning at Sam, Penny whispered, 'I wish you were as perspicacious as our friend, Hans.' Abruptly she stood, pulling a bundle of yellowed envelopes from her purse and waving them in the air for everyone to see.

In her loudest voice, Penny said, 'Your Excellency, we have Mr Thomson's World War I letters written to his buddy, Al Jeep, back in the States. They were mailed from the US Army hospital in France.' She pointed to the postmark on one envelope. 'They clearly reveal the . . . ah . . . nature and severity of his war wounds.'

Sir Hugh's eyes rolled, dismayed with the hearing's growing complexities. He looked at his watch and asked, 'Does Mr Thomson quote a medical diagnosis?'

'Yes,' Penny said. 'In these letters he writes to this Mr Jeep how scared he was that he was sterile and could not be a father.'

Felicia's eyes bore in on her attorney.

Horace Turner pointed his finger at Penny. 'That's neither medical verification nor vaild evidence. If you can't produce his army medical records – and I know you can't because the Veterans Adminstration had a fire at their storage facility in St Louis, and most of those World War I records were destroyed. You have only Dr Giannini's testimony to go on. And he says Mr Thomson was able to father. I say Trevor Thomson did, and she is here, Ms Felicia Fountain.' He gestured dramatically at Felicia as he went on in his loud barrister voice, 'And Ms Fountain is entitled to Trevor Thomson's entire estate.'

Mrs Gistelli stood. Sam wondered why. She said, 'Forget it. There is no estate, no inheritance.' She reached inside Hubert's jacket. As he winced with pain, she extracted a document stained crimson with his dried blood.

Waving it in the air, at Turner, Sir Hugh, Felicia and finally at Sam, she announced, 'I have here a signed amendment to Mr Thomson's Statement of Wishes addressed to his offshore trustee – an amendment to his trust agreement. See here,' she said, pointing at the document, 'it directs Charles Fountain to return all the lease payments, some twenty-five years' worth – I think the amount comes to eight billion dollars – to the bank in San Francisco.' As if it were a dishrag, she again fluttered the document at Charles Fountain.

Penny whispered to Sam, 'Oh-oh. Now you're in trouble. It looks like there will be no life insurance payout, no inheritance – nothing but insecurity for you from here on out.'

Stunned, Sam sat silently, searching for some sense in the developments.

Penny added, shaking her head in disbelief, 'That does it for Ambrosiana, the Thomson-Columbus Museum, Felicia's sanctimonious philanthropy, and Judith's hopes for recognition among national charities. And my financial advisor fees just floated away on the afternoon tide, as well. This is turning out to be a bad day on the cay.'

'One of the worst,' Sam acknowledged, 'since the day of that early sixteenth-century shipwreck.'

44

With incessant banging of his gavel, the Governor pleaded with the unruly audience for quiet.

Not waiting for order, Charles Fountain was on his feet. 'Let me see that purported signature,' he demanded.

Horace Turner craned his neck trying for a closer view of Helga Gistelli's document.

'No, if I give you the letter, you'll rip it up,' she protested.

Sir Hugh struck the gavel and said, 'I'll examine that document, Mrs . . . ah . . . .'

'Gistelli,' she said. Reluctantly she handed it to him, announcing, her voice content with her own cleverness, 'I've made a photocopy.'

'Is this Trevor Thomson's signature?' Sir Hugh asked no one in particular.

Fountain volunteered, 'I am certain it is not.'

'Have you looked at it?'

'No, Your Excellency, but . . . .'

Sir Hugh held the paper out.

The trustee walked up to the dais, looked at the document and defiantly proclaimed, 'It is not his signature.' With conviction in his voice, he added, 'I have seen Trevor Thomson's signature many times during my thirty years of association with him as his trustee. This line with a curlicue running off the page is not his signature.'

'But there are two witnesses – me and Hubert,' Helga insisted. 'It's his writing, we saw him sign. Fountain, you've got to give Thomson's money back to the bank.'

Hubert Gistelli nodded his agreement, pain registering on his face as he stood up. He said, his voice weak, 'What Helga says is true. We both are witnesses – on the train before he jumped.' He added, 'Your Honour.'

'Excellency,' Fountain corrected, but no one else was concerned about protocol.

Sir Hugh sat in silence, indecision preventing him from either asking another question or rendering a decision. He put on his glasses and examined the signature again, tilting the paper to gain a different light on the scrawl strewn across it. Viewing from a different angle, he thought, might help him decide its authenticity.

Fountain produced several letters from his brief-case and handed them to Sir Hugh. He said, 'See here, Your Excellency, Mr Thomson's signature on these letters is quite different. He has . . . had a precise way.'

Sir Hugh examined the letters, commenting, 'He begins each signature with a fancy "T", like the signature on this document Mrs . . . ah . . . Gistelli has produced.'

'Anyone, Your Excellency, could forge at least that much of a signature,' Fountain insisted. 'If you were to pass out paper and pen to everyone in this room, I am certain ninety per cent could make a "T" the same way, and then add a few curlicues to it, calling the result Trevor Thomson's signature.'

'Are you saying I forged it?' Helga said, her voice dripping with incredulity.

Hubert, still standing, turned to Fountain, clenching his good fist and demanding in a loud voice, 'No one calls my pretty little wife a liar! You take that back!'

For protection Superintendent Hedgepeth moved closer to the trustee.

Judith tapped the Governor's hand and whispered, 'Hugh, it can't be his signature. Why would my stepfather forfeit his life's work, his life's earnings? There was absolutely no reason for him to do so. If he did, it was under duress. And the lawyer for our charity in Santa Fe says if we raise money under duress, especially from older people, we may have to give it back. Duress isn't legal.'

'I gave up most of my family fortune – to those African charities – in hopes the Queen would appoint me to an important post,' Sir Hugh replied quietly.

Judith said, her fingers now sensuously tracing along his bare and suntanned arm, 'But in return you were rewarded with a prestigious position, a good salary and a lot of perks. My point is you received something of equal or greater value, at least in your own mind. Trevor got nothing in return – if he did indeed sign that paper.'

'Maybe it's the reason he jumped,' Sir Hugh replied. 'He realized what he'd done and became despondent.'

'What are you two talking about?' Helga asked, her impatience obvious. She added angrily, 'This is supposed to be a public hearing; no private conversations.'

'Yeah, make your ruling, Governor, I've got to call California,' Hubert said, turning away from Fountain. He added, 'To tell the bank they're getting their money back.'

Horace Turner and Felicia's other attorney, Jim Stone, stood, both talking at once. 'Your turn,' Turner said to Stone.

Stone said, 'Your Excellency, the evidence and testimony presented here is conclusive. Let me review it briefly for your benefit.'

Sir Hugh was relieved.

As Sam and Penny sat down, he whispered to her, 'We're in a box, going to lose everything, either to the bank in California or to Felicia. We've no attorney representing us, and I thought this hearing was to be informal. I didn't understand how utterly important it was for us to prevail here today.'

'How dire the outcome might turn out to be, you mean,' she replied dejectedly.

'Yeah. What can we do?' he asked.

'You should have paid off the Swiss coroner,' Penny said sullenly.

'But that wouldn't refute the paper with Trevor's signature.'

Sir Hugh hit the gavel on the table again, demanding quiet.

Suddenly Sam whispered to Penny, 'But what about the money. If we have to give it back to the bank, where'll it come from? I mean, where is it now?'

'That's Hans Kubler's job,' Penny said. 'He manages the portfolio. And he's put it all in . . . .'

Sam interrupted, 'I forgot to tell you – Mr Kubler is in grave danger.'

'He's already been shot. How can he be in any more danger?'

'This strange man at the funeral – says he was at the Unlucky Lady when Kubler was shot – is chasing over to Provo after him. I guess to finish the job.'

'But I told you Hans has flown back to Switzerland.'

'You did? Oh yeah, the bit about Pontius Pilate.' Sam shook his head in disbelief. 'So Hans is safe.'

Penny said, 'And we know from my conversation with Tony that Hans has bet most or all of the money on those Ambrosiana bonds . . . .'

'Maybe that's the key.'

'What do you mean?'

224

'Leaving,' Sam said, 'especially when he's been wounded – he has to be doing something quite important, more critical than his own recovery.'

'I told you about the warrants . . . .'

'Yes, but I didn't really understand all that,' Sam said, removing his hat and running his hand through his curls.

'But you do now?'

'Yes, I think so.'

Jim Stone was speaking. 'Your Excellency, we clearly have an heir to Trevor Thomson's estate . . . .'

Suddenly Sam said to Penny, 'This circus has gone far enough . . . .' He stood and shouted, 'Your Excellency, I ask for a recess in this hearing.'

'On what do you base your request?' Sir Hugh asked, his tone leading Sam to believe he was enthused about the idea.

Sam shouted back, 'Because the proceedings have gotten out of hand. And my sister and I are not represented by legal counsel. In addition, there are many issues being bandied about, causing our discussion to hopscotch from one subject to the next and back again.'

On the dais, Judith whispered to the Governor, 'He's right, Hugh, you personally can't go out on a limb by making a ruling today. You don't want adverse publicity in London. Think of your career.' Her voice even lower, she said, 'Also think of our future together . . . and my half of the estate. How many billions will I receive?'

Sir Hugh looked at her, a hint of a smile on his face, and said, 'Are you suggesting . . . ?'

'I am,' Judith said, smiling demurely.

Sir Hugh Broughton-Williams was ignited. To him, Judith had as much as said, 'I do.' Hesitating no longer, he stood. Taking a deep breath, he banged the gavel and bellowed in his loudest voice, 'This hearing is now recessed.'

Sir Hugh hit the gavel again and said, 'We will reconvene at a later date after I've had a chance to review our island laws and discuss the matters raised today with advisors here and in London.'

Turner and Stone rose to protest.

Helga yelled at Hubert, 'Do something!'

'Come on,' Penny said, 'let's find out what Hans Kubler's going to do with Ambrosiana and those warrants.'

'But,' Sam asked, 'how are we going to get out of town? The next scheduled flight to Miami is not for several days.'

'Charter one,' Penny urged. 'Let's go. Those warrants are the key to the fortune, and they're about to expire.'

'But . . .' Sam began and then hesitated, 'I should check with Judith.'

Pulling Sam towards the door of Government House, Penny assured him, 'She's in good hands. Let's go.'

Sam looked back and saw Felicia conversing with Dr Giannini. And he said to himself, 'Felicia's not in good hands.'

45

Inside the Grand Turk air terminal, Sam and Penny inquired of a few people, 'Can we charter a plane?'

Moravia, the Customs official, came up to them and said, 'Yes, you can fly with our local airline.'

Sam looked around but saw no local airline counter. 'Where?' he asked.

'Ah, they don't really have a booth. Wait here while I go find one of their pilots.'

She soon returned with a tall, greying white man in tow. He wore a shirt with epaulettes and a peaked cap cocked a bit to the side. Pinned crookedly to his shirt, a brass name-tag read 'Bill Garrett'.

'Where do you want to go?' Bill Garrett asked, pulling a cigarette from his lips and blowing smoke at Sam and Penny.

'Uh, Switzerland,' Sam stammered, coughing. 'And we're in an awful hurry.' He added, 'There's two of us.'

Bill laughed. It was a coarse laugh, suggesting callous humour. He ground out the cigarette butt with his shoe.

'Why are you laughing?' Sam asked, his patience fading.

Penny said, 'Don't you know the way?'

'Honey, I know the way, my plane knows the way, but unless you have arranged to refuel me in mid-air, I'll pass up your transatlantic journey. A Lindbergh I ain't.'

'Where can you fly us in your little plane?' Penny asked.

With trepidation, Sam asked, 'And how big or little is this plane?'

Penny said, 'We need to get to Miami first. Can you fly us somewhere where we can get a jet to . . . .'

'How about Nassau?' Bill said, explaining, 'you can connect there to a flight every hour on the hour to Miami.'

'Sounds great. How much?'

'How much you got?' Bill said, and guffawed to everyone in the terminal, though there was hardly anyone there.

'Surely you have a published tariff . . . .'

'One hundred fifty per . . . .' Bill said automatically.

'That much?' Sam said. 'You serve cocktails and a five-course meal?'

Bill frowned his annoyance and started to walk away.

'Hey, wait a minute,' Sam pleaded.

Turning back, Bill said, 'Cash.'

Sam said to Penny, 'You got any money on you?'

'Not much. We're stuck.' Turning to Bill, she said, 'Don't you take credit cards?'

'There'll be a surcharge.'

'How much?' Sam asked.

'Twenty per cent.'

'Twenty! Jesus!' Sam exclaimed.

'Takes a while for the airline to get its money that way,' Bill said, 'and those banks charge a fee to process credit card slips.'

'Surely not twenty per cent,' Penny said.

'I gotta get paid for flying and I gotta get paid for all the other stuff, too,' Bill said, lighting another cigarette.

Penny said to Sam, 'We'd better do it – everything's riding on our getting to Mendrisio.'

'Is that another Caribbean island?' Bill asked. 'I thought I knew 'em all after thirty years.'

Ignoring his question, Sam fished out a credit card.

'I'll have to write this transaction up,' Bill said. He took a final drag on his cigarette and tossed it, half-smoked and still lit, onto the linoleum floor, signifying, Sam thought, he was ready to fly them to Nassau.

'OK, but let's get going,' Penny pleaded.

Bill took care of the paperwork and, leading them towards the tarmac, said, 'Follow me and bring your luggage.'

At the little plane, Penny hoisted herself onto a small step built into the wing, opened the door and manoeuvred into the rear seat. Sam followed and sat up front with Bill. Settling into her seat, Penny's head drooped and she was soon asleep. Sam reached around and strapped her in.

Bill removed his cap in order to mount headphones across his grey hair. As they taxied off the tarmac and onto the airport's main runway, he spoke a few words into a tiny microphone. Sam worried they were intruding on commercial airliner space. Nevertheless, gathering speed, the small craft quickly lifted off.

As they gained altitude, Sam looked down on Grand Turk, feeling he really knew the island and its people. The recent events flashed across his mind. He saw the cemetery, The Ridge Road, Fountain's house, the Governor's residence, the plaza of Cockburn Town with its adjacent Government House and the Thomson-Columbus Museum. And as the plane flew out over the Caicos Banks and he could see Grand Turk no more, he felt sure he would return, and not in some afterlife.

Looking below, he searched the reefs for tell-tale signs of ancient shipwrecks, but whiffs of clouds expanding into blankets beneath soon reduced his view to now and then glimpses of the ocean. And he thought about Felicia and their pilgrimage through the poor area, images now blending in a sort of future challenge.

Bill asked, 'Were you here for the funeral?'

Sam found it hard to focus on his question but nevertheless nodded.

'The old fart hung on a long time.'

Sam said nothing, his annoyance precluding a polite response.

'Liked women, I hear.'

'I suppose that's natural for a man,' Sam said.

'Yeah,' Bill said, smacking his lips. 'I've had some pretty good pieces of ass over the years here in these islands. Black is beautiful, you know. They're especially cooperative when I get 'em up in the plane.'

Sam was taken aback. 'You do it aloft?'

'Well, no, that's too dangerous,' Bill said, turning his head towards Sam. He laughed. 'They might kick the controls.'

Sam noticed the 'no smoking' sign above the controls and hoped Bill would abide by it. But he didn't, offering a cigarette to Sam.

Shaking his head, Sam said, 'Would you mind not smoking during our flight? It really bothers me, might even make me sick, and I know it'll wake up Penny, and she's awfully stressed out.'

Bill looked upset. His hand shook as he lay the unlit cigarette in the ashtray, which Sam noticed was brimming with crumpled, discarded old butts and ashes. Sam wondered if Bill could wait until they landed.

'How do you lure these women into your plane and entice them to throw themselves at you? Are pilots so sexy?'

Bill beamed, his grey eyebrows rising, a macho smile forming. He said, 'It's simple. I offer them a free ride.'

'A free ride?' Sam was glad he was accompanying Penny. No telling what Bill might do if he weren't here to protect her.

'Yeah,' Bill went on, checking his controls, 'and I tell them if they want to get back on land, they need to . . . ah . . . cooperate.'

Sam was appalled. 'You're kidding?'

Bill continued, 'And if the little thing protests, I feign a problem with the plane. Like some control is broken or there's a leak in the gas tank and we may have to ditch, you know, something like that.'

'That's frightening.'

'Yes, they turn cooperative real quick. I set down on some little cay – lots of 'em around here got rudimentary dirt strips – and have my cake and eat it, too.' He guffawed so loud Penny stirred.

'Where are we?' she asked, and promptly went back to sleep.

'But don't they file charges against you when you fly them back to Provo or Grand Turk?'

'File what?'

'Charges . . . go to the police?'

'They're so glad to get back, they thank me. Also, they've had a good time.'

'You're that good?'

'Man, there's nothing to it. Women want it, are always looking for it. Just takes a little persuasion, a little patting in the right places, a little grabbing and massaging here and there, you know. And they're all over you, or want you to be all over them.'

Sam didn't know how to react. He doubted women desired that kind of behaviour from men.

'I mean,' the pilot went on, 'we men have a responsibility to perform, don't you think?' He issued another guffaw.

Sam wanted to express his doubts, but he didn't and they flew in silence. Sam thought about such behaviour, and eventually concluded the pilot was not being truthful. He said, 'So, tell me about one.'

'One?'

'Yes, narrate one episode. We've time before landing in Nassau. I'm younger than you, less experienced and sure could use some pointers as far as women go. Name, place, how you worked it, how you . . . ah . . . scored with her.'

Bill looked surprised.

'Just to pass the time,' Sam said, the tone of his voice encouraging Bill's response.

The pilot scratched his head, reviewed his controls once more, and noted certain readings in his log. He began, 'Well, there was one time that really stands out. It was years ago and I was new on the job with the airline.' He gestured at the plane. He proclaimed, 'It was my first, actually, among many. Airborne fucking, I mean.'

Sam nodded, trying to hide his doubts.

230

'She was black as midnight, tall, and built like Venus de Milo. She'da made it in Hollywood if she'da been white. You know, legs, boobs, butt, come-here look in her eyes.'

Sam was appalled anyone would describe a woman in such a way, but acknowledged some men did so. He suspected these men had inferiority complexes, and degrading women was the only way they could cover up their own foibles.

Bill went on, 'She approached me in Provo. I was at the docks watching this fishing boat come in – the one that old guy redid to look like a pirate galleon. Ever seen it?'

Sam froze. He didn't answer. He wished he'd never brought up the subject. He wanted to push some button on the plane's control panel, change the channel or insert a new tape, something other than listen to Bill unfold his story.

But Bill went on, 'Her flimsy yellow bra was sort of rumpled, her boobs bouncing out, inviting my hands. Her hair was dishevelled like she was ready for a romp in the hay, if there was hay anywhere around. And that walk of hers – the sway of her hips – and her bikini practically falling off, just waiting to be yanked down. Boy, she was really asking for it. All you had to do was look at her and know. And I did, look her over, I mean. She said she wanted a ride back to Grand Turk, so I gave her one. We landed on a dirt strip on Salt Cay. And did it right there where you're sitting.' Bill nodded towards Sam's seat, and added, 'At the end of the runway.'

'Right here,' Sam repeated. 'But didn't she resist?'

She was strapped in,' he said, and guffawed again. 'She was really glad to get back to Grand Turk, actually thanked me, you know, after we'd landed – it happened right after they'd paved the strip.'

Sam didn't know what to say. He looked around and saw Penny was wide awake, staring at the pilot, her eyes full. To Sam's surprise, she asked, 'Did the woman ever come back for more? Take more airplane rides? Want a repeat performance?'

Startled, Bill said, 'I thought you was sleeping.'

'I was.'

Bill stammered, 'Ah yeah, she came back, coupla times, became a real buff for flying.'

They both knew he was lying. But they sat in silence, wanting to talk to each other, but afraid to.

A big Delta Airlines plane, waiting to take off, watched as they landed at the Nassau airport. 'One every hour to Miami,' Bill said, motioning at the much bigger craft. 'I'll drop you off at their terminal.'

Sam couldn't wait to be released from Bill and his cabin. But first he said, 'May I snap your picture here by your plane – a memento, of course.' He wished he'd taped the pilot's confession as additional evidence to accompany his photograph.

46

Sam spoke to the uniformed woman at the Delta counter. 'Two tickets to Miami on the next flight – coach. And do you have information on connections from there to Zurich?'

Her brass name-tag, pinned over one of her substantial breasts, read 'Daisy'. Consulting her computer screen, she said, 'You might still connect with the Swissair flight . . . .'

'I'll bet that's the one Hans is on,' Penny said.

While the woman made out the tickets, Sam whispered to Penny, 'Do you realize our pilot, Bill Garrett, could well be Felicia's father and not Trevor?'

Daisy said, 'But I doubt it, by the time you change gates – it's a big airport.'

'What's the next flight?' Sam asked.

Penny said, 'I think it puts the whole issue of who is Felicia's father in doubt.'

Daisy's fingers, with her painted nails, rushed across the keyboard. She concluded, 'Not till tomorrow, I'm afraid.'

Penny said, 'But we can't prove it. We need evidence, Trevor's sperm, his DNA.' More urgently, she added, 'Sam, we've got to get to Mendrisio – find out what Hans has done with the money. If we can control the money we can somehow dodge Felicia – at least for a while. Hans said the town was in southern Switzerland.' Addressing Daisy, she asked, 'How about Milan?'

'Clever routeing,' Sam said, smiling. 'We'll ride the train from there. But what are we going to do once we get to Mendrisio?'

Penny didn't answer. Instead, she tugged at Sam's sleeve, asking, 'By the way, what was the medical helicopter doing this morning?'

Sam told her about the Old Captain being shot by Chiarra and the money and photograph coming from Lugano.

'You mean, Mr Fountain thinks the Old Captain was paid to shoot Hans?'

'Yes, and he says I may also be in danger.'

'Oh, poor Hans. But who are you in danger from?'

'Ah, that is the mystery, isn't it?' Sam said, smiling.

'This is not a humorous matter, Sam,' she said, her voice rising in alarm.

'You may be able to connect with an Alitalia flight,' Daisy said after her series of keyboard caresses. 'But you'll have to rush to make it and,' she added, 'to make our flight, as well. Remember, you've got to clear US Customs here in Nassau. And,' she warned, 'be sure to get on our flight and not Air Bahamas – they leave the same time as we do.'

'Customs?' Sam said.

'And Immigration, too,' Daisy added. 'Your people have already invaded the Bahamas.'

'Book us into Milan and step on it,' Sam said as he surveyed the terminal, trying to see how long the US Customs line was.

'First class or coach,' Daisy asked.

'First class,' Penny inserted.

'Penny, we can't afford to fly first class,' Sam said. 'It's expensive enough buying tickets on the spot without the advance purchase discount.'

'But I need a free drink,' she retorted.

'I'll buy you one here and pocket the savings,' Sam said, laughing.

'No drinking going through Customs,' Daisy warned, adding, 'coach, then. Open return?'

Sam gave her a 'yes'. A ticket to return to the Caribbean electrified him.

Daisy complied, imprinting Sam's credit card and handing them their tickets, advising, 'Hurry.'

The US Customs official, seeing they were white adults and US citizens, waved them through. But at Immigration the officer, sensing they were in a hurry, gave them a suspicious stare. 'What was the reason for your trip?' she asked.

Without thinking, Sam gushed, 'I just shot a pilot and rape.'

The official must have pushed a hidden button, because Sam saw two uniformed Bahamian police exhibiting suspicious stares come towards them, hands on their heavy leather gun belts.

'And an attempted murder. Oh yes, a funeral, too,' he added before Penny could seal his mouth with her hand.

'You involved in this crime spree, too?' the Immigration official demanded to know, looking at Penny.

'Ah, no, just him,' she said before she could think through her response.

Recovering and removing Penny's palm, Sam said, 'No, no, you see, we went to Grand Turk for my stepfather's funeral. And the question of heirship cropped up. The answer involved an alleged rape the pilot of our little plane seemed to know something about. So I shot his picture. And the Mafia tried to shoot this guy in a bar . . . .'

The official, now flanked by two guards, looked at them incredulously.

'Please,' Penny said, 'we've got to make this flight so we can connect to the non-stop to Italy – there's this Easter pageant across the border in Switzerland we must attend.'

The official asked, 'Are you part of a pageant? Is it the one in Mendrisio?'

'Yes, it's the one,' Penny said with both surprise and relief.

'It's a beautiful pageant, very moving,' the official said, a governmental smile forming on her face. 'I watched it two years ago when I was visiting relatives in Lugano.' Offering a 'sorry', she ran their passports through the electronic scanner. When nothing untoward showed up on either, she waved them through, the two uniformed officers parting as they passed.

'Our government is watching us all the time,' Sam said as he ran, pulling Penny towards a ground-level gate marked 'Miami' which the attendant was just closing. 'Wait,' he yelled, 'we're ticketed.'

47

Settling into the comfortable Delta airliner, Penny fastened her seat-belt for the flight to Miami. When the flight attendant came by, Sam ordered two chardonnays.

Sipping, Penny said, 'I keep hearing that parrot squawking about rape.'

'Shh, someone'll hear you,' Sam said. Reflecting on Bill Garrett's story, he said, 'You know, thirty years ago poor Chiarra was raped by two different men.'

'Yes, on the same day.'

'Either man could be Felicia's father.'

'And with his World War I wounds,' Penny said, 'Trevor's the least likely candidate – a logical conclusion from reading his letter from the hospital in France.'

Sam said, 'But Felicia's attorneys raised an objection because Trevor's letter offered no medical proof.'

Penny said, 'Think about this: your mother gave birth to you and Judith, so she was obviously fertile. Yet being with Trevor – and still in her child-bearing years – she never became pregnant.'

Sam said, 'Maybe Trevor used the latest in condoms.'

'Be serious. My point is valid. Maybe he really wanted children.'

'Yes, I suppose you're right. He did adopt Judith and me. Setting the fertility issue aside, however, explain again why our final destination is Mendrisio.'

'Two reasons – legal and financial,' Penny said. 'Legalwise, it means getting hold of the Swiss coroner's evidence and having it analysed by independent medical authorities.'

'The DNA vials in cold storage? But how are we going to get them? Dr Giannini is pretty covetous of them. We'll have to pay him off.'

'And even if we give him money, he still may not release them to us,' Penny said, worrying.

'Why do we need them?' Sam asked. 'Sir Hugh said he would make a ruling – eventually.'

'But he's not a judge. And I'm not sure which country's jurisdiction governs.'

Suggesting an answer, Sam said, 'I suppose it would be the United States, where we live, that is Judith and I . . . and you and Felicia as well . . . or, maybe it's Switzerland, where Trevor died, or I suppose it could be Turks and Caicos, where his offshore trust was – what do you call it – domiciled.' He added, 'And where his remains are buried.'

'Or Italy?'

'I thought we eliminated Italy,' Sam said with surprise.

'We did,' Penny said, 'but now it's back, because Ambrosiana Limited is headquartered there.'

'In Campione, isn't it the little town Judith mentioned?'

'Yes, I think it is. But as far as determining heirship,' Penny said, 'I think the real jurisdiction is not geographical. Rather, it's the expensive world of attorneys. From here on out, it's going to be their call.'

Penny took a sip of wine and went on, 'Trevor's fortune – as large as it is, assuming Hans is successful in preserving it – could flow down the litigation drain into the yawning reservoir – like pockets of lawyers.'

'That's a lot of legal fees. I should have gone to law school.'

Penny ignored him and said, 'We're smart enough to hire the best legal minds and let them gnaw on these issues, bury themselves in those reference books in law libraries.' She added after an icy chuckle, 'And drain us with their ongoing legal charges.'

'I like research.'

'By comparison yours is uplifting and has – or so you keep telling me – a social purpose.' Penny paused and said, 'But now what is really important is clear to me – the money – it is what we much watch.'

'But if we lose the estate,' Sam said, becoming dejected, 'Felicia and her attorneys will take the income and the bonds and everything away from us. We've got to hire our own attorneys to assert our . . . that is, Judith's and my position.'

Penny said, 'But you're not going to lose your inheritance, at least for a long time. You see, under the law in Turks and Caicos, Mr Fountain must follow Trevor's trust document and immediately pass title to you and Judith.'

Sam thought for a moment and said, 'But we ought to be asking ourselves what Fountain's motivations are.'

'I think he's too duty-bound to do anything illegal,' Penny said. 'He and I are alike in that way, I've come to believe.'

'Yes, I think you're right.'

'It's possible the Governor's eventual decision may be upended later by some court – and I mean way later – but meanwhile the assets are yours and Judith's. Remember, there is no probate.'

'Why is so much time going to pass?'

Penny smiled, 'Because the Governor, after a long recess, is going to issue a favourable ruling, unless I miss my guess. And while it may be appealed, the appeal process will be tied up in the courts for ever.'

'Do you really think we'll get a favourable decision from Sir Hugh?'

'Did you see you little sister?'

Sam cringed, and said, 'I've left Judith in the hands of a lecherous old man.'

'Relax, Sam, let her go.'

Slowly Sam nodded. 'But what about the bank in California?' he asked. 'They may force Fountain to return Trevor's assets because of the document Trevor is supposed to have signed before he jumped or fell . . . .'

'I don't think he signed it,' Penny said.

Sam looked at their wineglasses, saw they were empty and buzzed for the flight attendant, ordering two more.

Penny popped a peanut from the comlimentary package into her mouth and said, 'But it's not so much what the California bank is trying to do – because they can be put on hold by the right lawyers . . . .'

Sam said, 'One other thing, Fountain says we should press Trevor's claim with the Los Angeles life assurance company.'

Penny nodded. 'Yes, good advice.' She went on, 'But the main point I want to make is that beyond these legal gyrations, which will drag on, controlling the portfolio itself is the most important thing we must do. Remember, possession is nine-tenths of the law.'

She began her second glass of wine.

'Now you're into part two. Do we get an intermission?'

'You can visit the loo if you want,' she said. 'But don't get into a poker game back there, because the financial part follows.'

'There's that "F" word again,' Sam said as he stood up to walk down the aisle. He was back quickly, not wanting to miss her second chapter.

Looking at him from her window seat, Penny said, 'What I'm saying is: with Hans's help we can exercise those warrants and get control of Ambrosiana. It'll be the mainstay investment of the portfolio. Over the next several years we'll make a mint of money while a roster of attorneys play their legal games in courts around the world.'

Sam said, 'You mean, follow the dollars. But how're we going to monitor the portfolio?'

'We must grab on to the coat-tails of Hans Kubler. He's our financial saviour.'

'Hans is loyal,' Sam said, believing it. 'But you're the one who is going to have to watch it – not me. I wouldn't know what I'd be looking at,' he said, paying the flight attendant for their second round of drinks.

'It's free in first-class,' Penny said, mimicking Judith. More seriously, she said, 'Look at it this way – what are our priorities?'

'Catching the flight to Milan?'

'I mean after we arrive in Italy and zip up to Switzerland.'

Sam waited.

'Finding our wounded friend, Hans, so we can help him exercise the warrants. They're the centrefold to gaining control of Ambrosiana.'

'But I don't know how to run a corporation.'

'Neither do I. That's not the point. The company has qualified management who were clever enough to have lined up these acquisitions, and they'll continue to run things. They don't need our help. We'll simply bank our interest from the bonds and the dividends from the stock. Clip coupons, as they used to say, although these days payouts are made by computer, not scissors.'

Penny continued, 'You see, if we've got the money, somebody's got to try to take it away. Not easy to do. Gives us time to hide it in an offshore trust.'

She looked out of her little window at the blue-green Atlantic beneath. Nearer now to the Florida coast, she could see the ocean bottom beneath the clear water. She remarked on it to Sam.

'Yes, it's shallow here,' he replied. 'During the ice-age the land extended quite a bit farther east. There are supposed to be a lot of archaeological sites down there, habitations of the prehistory Florida folks.'

'Really,' she said. 'Well, that'll give us something to do during the next ice-age – dig them up.'

'Don't be sarcastic about our heritage.'

'Money's my heritage. Hans understands that.'

As he returned his seat to its upright position in preparation for landing, it struck Sam that men and women with similar interests are attracted to each other. Wishing Felicia would be there, he said, 'On to Mendrisio.'

48

As soon as the Delta captain shut down the engines, Sam said, 'Grab your bag. We'll make a dash for Alitalia.'

'Where's their check-in counter?' Penny asked. Looking around, lost, she said, 'By comparison I liked the little terminal in Grand Turk, even if it wasn't air-conditioned.'

'Here's a directory,' Sam said. Finding Alitalia, he announced, 'They're in terminal C, next to B.'

'Where are we now?'

'In A. Hurry, Penny,' Sam urged, pulling at her. 'It's a long walk, like Daisy said.'

'Is there a connecting high-speed tram?'

'By the time I figure it out, we'll miss the flight.'

Carrying their cases, they ran up to the security check-point, where Sam asked for his camera to be manually examined. 'I don't want to lose my pictures,' he explained.

'Don't tell him you've shot a pilot or we'll never make it out of here,' Penny whispered.

They arrived at the Alitalia gate as it was closing. The attendant looked at her monitor and said, 'There are two seats left in the non-smoking section.'

As they passed along one of the aisles through the huge plane, Sam noticed a row of vacant seats in first class. They located their two coach seats – across the aisle from each other. Perspiring, they slumped into them.

The pilot announced their impending departure, but broke off, saying, 'Just a moment, folks, we've a few more passengers coming down the jetway.'

Penny said, 'Must be for first class – those were the only vacant seats I saw.'

As the 767 waited in line for control-tower permission to rumble down the runway, the big craft's engines droning and its crew routinely instructing passengers on the use of seat-belts and life-preservers, Sam fell asleep.

Overhead television screens offered the latest news and soon, as Penny watched, the stock market report came on. To her dismay she learned the bond market had crashed. She held her hand to her mouth. As usual, the report was cursory. The commentator, getting it all wrong, tied the day's sombre bond market performance to a decrease in the consumer confidence index. Bonds should react in the opposite direction, their price rising with no threat of runway consumer demand, Penny said almost out loud.

As the news switched to a series of murders, Penny reached for the inflight telephone and dialled Tony in Rome, ignoring the man sitting next to her who would obviously listen in. But then she realized with the time difference – it was the middle of the night in Rome – there would be no answer. She tried her New York brokers, but Wall Street had closed, too. All she received for her efforts were unanswered rings.

Across the aisle and fast asleep, Sam, in his dreams, tried to snuggle close to Felicia, but a parrot on her shoulder kept flapping its wings and getting in his way. He engaged in a heady discussion with Christopher Columbus as to whether the world was flat or round, Sam holding out for flat.

'No,' the seagoing explorer advised, 'the world is round, formed like Felicia's breasts.' The explorer urged, 'Why don't you see for yourself? You'll discover you can go completely round it.'

'How do you know?' Sam asked. 'There's no historical record to support your theory.'

'My motto is: Explore Everything in Life. It's too short as it it. Go for it.' With Columbus waving from the deck, the *Pinta* sailed off into a sunrise.

Sam's dream went on. Felicia was standing by his side. He looked into her eyes, and she into his. With gusto she immediately began ripping his clothes off, and he hers. Her lips descended onto his, then parting, her teeth nipping at first his tongue and then exploring, biting away at his now naked body. Sam's erection was so large it actually hurt and he moaned.

The flight attendant nudged Sam, instructing, 'Please place your seat in its upright position, we're landing in Milan.' Looking down, she tried her best to stifle a laugh.

Penny, leaning across the aisle, tugged at his arm. She tittered and whispered, 'Sam, wake up, get control of yourself.'

Sam blushed as his hands flew into a protective position.

241

49

At the Milan airport everybody tried to stand as soon as the captain had taxied up to the jetway and turned off the 'Fasten Your Seat Belt' sign. After the long transatlantic flight it was a chance to stretch.

Penny said, 'There must be three hundred people in coach, business class and first class up there in front of us. It'll take for ever to get out of here.'

Still sleepy, Sam said, 'What's the rush? I'd like to get a hotel, shower and shave, and get a little . . . ah . . . shut-eye.'

'And a little something else, too, I suspect,' Penny said, her eyebrows raised. But her look quickly changed to resolute and she said, 'But our mission is to find Hans. We can't become side-tracked.'

'And if we choose to ignore our mission?'

'You want your little inheritance, don't you? So, we'll find the Milan train station and hop on the first express north into Switzerland.'

Sam nodded in agreement.

Penny said, 'That is, if we ever get out of this airplane. Can you imagine what it'd be like if there was an emergency?'

Sam shuddered, thought for a moment and said, 'It'd be all right, they'd open more doors.'

'Just the same,' Penny said, 'I'd rather be up front in first class close to the pilot's door.'

'You should fly with Judith and not me.' Sam grew sullen, pining, 'I wonder how she's managing by herself. I've left her, really for the first time in my life. She's never been on her own like this before.'

'Relax, silly,' Penny said. 'She's going to save the day for us with Sir Hugh.' She hesitated and began, 'Speaking of . . . .'

A passenger pushed Sam from behind. 'Are you staying on this jet all day?' the rude man asked, shoving again. 'Let's get out of here, buddy, I'm getting claustrophobic.'

Sheepishly Sam apologized, moving forward, Penny following as the passengers finally began to exit.

Sam saw Felicia up ahead. Trailing behind were her attorneys, Horace Turner and Jim Stone, plus, of all people, Dr Giannini. The coroner appeared agitated, the palm of his hand on Stone's suited back, pushing him towards the terminal.

They must be the ones, Sam remembered, for whom the captain had waited. But how'd they fly from Grand Turk to Miami? He recalled the Delta clerk, Daisy, mentioning an Air Bahamas flight leaving Nassau at the same time as their flight.

Inside the terminal Felicia was standing next to the coroner, who was speaking into a pay phone, waving his free hand emotionally in the air. Sam approached her from behind. Undetected, he reached his arm around her midriff and whispered into her ear, 'You're under arrest for fortune-napping and illegal entry into Italy.'

Felicia shrieked. Recognizing Sam, she flashed an uncontrollable smile. But then working at a show of resistance, she pouted, pulling away ever so slightly.

Sam worried he'd made another mistake.

But momentarily she allowed her smile to freely express itself, suggesting she was happy to see him again. 'You were on the plane, too?' she said in surprise. 'That's funny, because I've been thinking about you, Sam.'

He was thrilled by her tender pronunciation of his name and he said softly, 'And I you.'

Felicia said, 'It was a long flight, and I've had some time to review all these matters.'

The hubbub of the people in the terminal and the loudspeaker announcements of flights arriving and departing faded into a background din as they stood close.

Felicia pulled back and said, 'But don't scare me that way again.'

Sam wondered if he should offer an apology. With hope in his voice, he tried instead, 'Are you hinting I might have other opportunities in the near future?'

She ignored his question and said, 'Crossing the Atlantic I thought about our little tour of the poor areas. You know, these challenges are world-wide, aren't they? I mean, we must try to elevate people's lives beyond just a base existence. There has to be more to life for them.'

'Like for us?'

'Yes, I mean we're all people.'

'Like you and me,' Sam said.

Hanging up the telephone, Dr Giannini interrupted, 'They did indeed raid my office in Lugano. But my vials, the deceased's vital fluids, remain safely hidden.'

Sam said to Felicia, 'Look, airport terminals are not the best places to talk.'

She nodded to Sam, but Dr Giannini went on with, 'I'm too clever for them.'

Felicia asked the coroner, 'Who are "they"?'

Dr Giannini didn't answer her right away. Instead, seeing Sam, he said, 'You on Alitalia, too?'

'Yes, in coach, couldn't afford first cabin.'

Dr Giannini looked at Felicia and, lowering his voice, said, 'The Mafia.'

'But why are they after you?' Felicia asked.

'No time to explain now, come on, we've got to get through Customs and Immigration,' the coroner said.

Felicia turned back to Sam. Her ensuing smile was alluring. She said, 'Next time let's meet some place without so much distraction.' She pulled out her US passport from her handbag and led her *entourage* on to the glassed-in Immigration booth with its waiting Italian official.

Sam looked for Penny and saw she was talking at a differnt bank of phones, her back to him, and he wondered who she was calling.

50

'Switzerland is a country of conformity, proper behaviour, established procedures, and wealth,' Sam said, gesturing out of the train window. 'Its orderliness and rigid behaviour patterns would never go over in America . . . well, maybe in places such as Indiana or Wichita.' He chuckled.

'Don't knock it,' Penny said, 'stability is the foundation of a healthy bond market and the basis for a nation's currency. And this country is pretty stable.'

Leaving the railway station, Penny said, 'I don't see where this Easter pageant is to be staged. Hans said he'd meet me there. From here, Mendrisio looks like any other Swiss town cluttered with late afternoon traffic.'

'For one thing, the cars seem to be new,' Sam said, looking around. 'Not so old as they were on Grand Turk. In fact, everybody appears pretty prosperous. Even the dogs look rich.' Sam pointed to a colourful banner strung across the street in front of the station. 'Look up there, Penny, there's a banner proclaiming the Pageant.'

'OK. We'll ask at the local tourist office for directions,' Penny said, pointing to a big 'i' sign at the far end of the depot.

'We're closing,' the uniformed woman attendant announced, 'for the Easter Pageant.'

'Which way is the procession?' Penny asked.

The guide gestured towards a busy street and said in accented English, 'You must go up the road from the station into the old town.'

A crowd of tourists, off a train from Lugano, gathered and now followed Sam and Penny as they set out on their quest.

Soon reaching a major interjection, Sam looked both ways and asked, 'Which way do we go?'

'I don't know either,' Penny said.

Sam blurted out, 'Penny, there's Dr Giannini getting out of a taxi.'

'How'd he get to Mendrisio?'

'Probably up the autostrada,' Sam said.

Coming towards them, Dr Giannini called, 'Hello, again. Here for Easter? Looks like we've all gotten religion at the same time. Must have been the heat in the Caribbean that did it.' He pulled his jacket around him, shuddering in the coolish evening. 'What is it you Americans do for Easter? Hunt for coloured chicken eggs? Strange custom indeed.'

Sam tried a smile.

The coroner asked, 'How's your money supply holding out?' He added, 'Matters aren't decided, you know. About the genealogy of Ms Fountain, I mean. There's still time for me to discover new evidence, run more extensive tests.' He went on, 'The number of laboratory examinations one can conduct these days – what with advanced technology of medical science – is virtually endless, but, of course, quite costly.' His voice was demanding as he said, 'So, what am I offered . . . to . . . ah . . . cover my costs?'

'Not a damn thing,' Sam said, annoyed.

'Why are you in Mendrisio?' Penny asked.

'It's Easter, my dear,' he said, dismissing her with, 'where's your bonnet?'

Sam said, 'Let's get out of this intersection before we all become autopsies.'

Suddenly a black Mercedes sped down upon them.

'Watch out!' Sam yelled, grabbing Penny and pulling her with him. The car thundered past, its velocity spinning the coroner onto the pavement.

Sam rushed up to him. 'Are you hurt?'

Struggling with his bulk, Dr Giannini slowly got up and said, 'Doctors understand death, so it's not so frightening.'

Nevertheless Sam saw he was shaking and the colour had left his face.

'They meant it to be close, but not fatal,' Dr Giannini said weakly.

'They?' Penny asked, fright in her voice.

'Yes,' the coroner replied. 'It's probably their last warning. That's the way they work these days. Adds to their sport. They enjoy the chase. It's more challenging than out and out murder. More fun for them. They're trying to gain a new image.'

'What are you talking about?' Sam said.

Startled tourists gathered around. Some offered assistance.

'But what are they warning you about?' Sam asked.

Dr Giannini straightened his jacket and said, 'You see, they wanted me to withhold the news of your stepfather's death, and I didn't. I took a . . . ah . . . gratuity from them, telling them I would. Well, actually I made only one phone call – to your Mr Fountain in Grand Turk. They weren't too happy.'

'Why didn't they want the news of Trevor's death made public?' Penny asked.

'I don't know, they didn't confide their reason in me,' the coroner said. 'Come on, we'll miss the Pageant.' As he began to walk with them towards the centre of the old town, he said, 'Now's a good time to tell me how much you will pay for my corrected testimony.'

'But the hearing's recessed,' Sam said.

'It'll reconvene, and you'll be needing my expert opinion.' He picked up his pace. Gesturing ahead, he said, 'The Pageant's up this way. Follow me.'

The crowd was enlarged by later travellers arriving from Lugano and Milan. The sightseers amassed along the pavement, engulfing Sam and Penny and separating them from the coroner. The throng moved beyond the portable barricades placed by police to block vehicular traffic. There the visitors spilled into the street, joining local residents, all walking towards the old town to witness the historic Holy Week procession.

Sam said, 'Come on, Penny, let's join in the way to Calvary.'

51

As Sam and Penny entered the medieval section of Mendrisio, Penny pointed overhead and exclaimed, 'Sam, aren't the murals beautiful?'

Sam looked up to see compositions of different biblical events painted in rich oils. The canvases were stretched on wood-framed cases spanning the narrow street at measured distances, joining seventeenth-century shops and houses. Inside each case a dim light illuminated its scene, enhancing the antique hues. These religious tapestries cast their spells along the winding and now crowded streets. Raising his camera, Sam tried to capture the artistic spectacle.

'Too dark, Sammy,' Penny said.

'It's so special, I must try,' he insisted. 'The full moon will provide light.' He began to sing, composing as he went, trying with his untrained voice to sing a lilting lyric of his own origination, 'Moon over Mendrisio . . . .'

'You've a lousy voice,' Penny said.

Giving up at her derisive comment, Sam observed, 'The Medievalelians must have enjoyed this old town in the Middle Ages.'

'The who?'

'That's what they were called. They wore T-shirts inscribed with "Welcome to Medieval Times". Others, in black shirts with grey letters – in old-style fonts, of course – read "Let the good times of the Dark Ages roll".'

'Sam, I do believe if you were to rewrite history, it might be a lot more fun to read.'

'History is more than chronicling the doings of kings and queens –it's the people themselves,' Sam said, 'such as right here in this ancient town. Tonight I feel I'm travelling back in time.'

Walking farther on and looking up at the old buildings, Sam saw the gargoyles. Some were laughing, and some were crying. He selected a few of the friendly smiling ones to award his greeting, waving his hand at them. Their carved stone faces returned the same rigid expressions as they had for several centuries.

Sam and Penny arrived at the town's ancient, towering cathedral. In front of its spires and Gothic façade, stark temporary bleachers had been erected, impolitely demeaning the ornate architecture. Town dignitaries and invited guests showed tickets to a policeman, who directed them to their seating. The locals, wrapped in their warm coats, soon added texture to the sterile bleachers, humanizing them.

'This must be where the procession starts,' Sam said.

Shivering in the spring night coolness, Penny said, 'I'm cold. Why can't we have some live music to warm up the crowd?'

Sam enveloped her within his arms and said, 'This is a place with centuries of history. On its own merits, its heritage is sufficient to warm the heart.'

Still shivering, Penny said, 'We're supposed to be looking for Hans Kubler.'

Sam craned his neck, looking not for Hans but searching for Felicia, hoping somehow she might be there.

'Our poor Swiss banker may be in pain,' Penny said. 'We must find and comfort him.'

Some people positioned themselves on balconies. Others lined the narrow streets, pressing forward against ropes strung to block onlookers from entering the passageway reserved for the procession.

Sam said, 'It was easier finding folks on Grand Turk.'

'Are you pining for your little museum on that island in the middle of nowhere?' Penny added, 'Wanting to be a big fish in a little pond?'

Sam replied, 'The Caribbean isn't exactly a little pond. It's what you do, not where you do it.'

'Speak for yourself,' Penny retorted. 'I'd rather be listed on the New York Stock Exchange than over the counter.'

Suddenly the street lights were turned off. Shop-owners dimmed their lights. Patrons milling around inside the little establishments grew quiet, anticipating the start of the festival.

Penny said, 'The only light is coming from those holy billboards.'

'Shh,' Sam warned, 'the dignitaries in the stands are settling down. They're getting their video cameras ready.'

'You're right,' Penny said, 'I do believe something is about to happen.'

A trumpet blew. Its solemn sound echoed among the ancient buildings along the twisting streets. And the Pageant began.

As he watched, Sam caught a movement up behind the stands. He recognized Dr Giannini emerging from the cathedral carrying two boxes and moving in great haste. Sam nudged Penny and said, 'Look up there, it's the Swiss coroner. He's hurrying down into the crowd. He must have retrieved those boxes from the church.'

Following the direction Sam's arm was pointing, Penny saw him and concluded, 'Yes, that's the evidence. He hid it away in the cathedral. Come on, we've got to follow him,' Penny said.

'In this *melee* of people?'

'We've got to get our hands on that evidence, have it examined by someone independent. Someone honest. We must know the truth about Trevor's fertility.'

'Never has one man's sperm been wanted by so many,' Sam said.

They heard the clippity clop of horses' hoofs coming along the old cobble-stone streets. The trumpet sounded once more.

'The crowd is so thick we can't get anywhere,' Sam said, restraining Penny. 'And the police are lining the route of the procession, holding people back.'

Leading the Pageant and slowly passing in front of the stands was a cast of teen-age choirboys wearing long white robes with red velvet capes. They carried poles displaying religious emblems in ornate gold leaf. The standards' heavy weight, steadied by both hands, were borne in pouches incorporated into their leather belts.

A hush came over the crowd of spectators, except for the mischievous friends of the boys, who teased them as they passed. In return, the marchers stifled smiles, trying to maintain the required demeanour of the Pageant.

The traditional procession of costumed players was a vivid scene even in the dim light. Heads peered over Penny and around Sam as those behind tried to take everything in.

As he watched, Sam became immersed in the magnificent pageantry of the colour, the music, the people. In the mood of the moment he felt he was a participant in the drama that had unfurled two thousand years earlier, a watershed event for western civilization. History, he concluded, was a force so strong this stupendous event had to be carried out. There was to be no choice. History could not be thwarted. By anyone. Man, woman or deity. And he asked himself how many of the ancient people had felt its importance at the time.

He wondered, too, if any of those participating this evening sensed the significance of the Pageant's historical theme. Sam had an urge to hand out fliers to everyone telling how the history of the western world had been forged by religious fervour.

Then Sam thought of Felicia. He could see her face in each of the decorative canvases as the procession passed underneath first one, then another. She was even more radiant in the glow of the illuminated scenes. Becoming confused in his fantasy, he couldn't distinguish her angelic effigy from the sacred icons of the Pageant. Felicia seemed to blend into the holy theme, a saint watching over.

Mounted Roman soldiers, trying to control their skittish, side-stepping horses, brought Sam back to reality. Pungent fragrances of leather saddles and wool horse-blankets filled the night-time air. The most elaborately costumed equestrian, Sam concluded, was Pontius Pilate. Behind him walked those who mourned the death sentence he had decreed, the imminent crucifixion of Jesus of Nazareth.

Shouldering the heavy timbers of his cross came a fatigued Jesus, often stumbling under the oppresive weight, but each time picking himself up again to move slowly ahead. A crown of thorns, mocking his role as the purported king of the Jews, ringed his head. From time to time the Roman guards levelled their spears at his accompanying disciples, restraining them from comforting the condemned holy man.

But one of the Roman soldiers appeared to be overacting his role. Instead of wielding a spear he was chasing one of the mourners with a large olive branch, whipping him unmercifully at every opportunity.

Penny cried, 'Sam, it's Hans, and that soldier is not play-acting. He's beating Hans. You and I are witnessing an assassination. And no one else realizes it.'

To protect himself, Hans raised his good arm as he dodged among the crowd of players, trying to avoid another blow. The Roman doggedly pursued him. Onlookers and participants viewed the episode as merely another act of the Pageant, and no one became alarmed. Suddenly Hans stumbled and fell in front of Pontius Pilate's horse.

'Hans'll be trampled,' Penny shouted. 'We've got to save him.' She ducked under the restraining rope, followed quickly by Sam. A policewoman blew her whistle at their intrusion into the procession's sacred path. But its shrill was lost in another crescendo from the trumpet.

The actors stared in surprise at Sam and Penny, regarding their uncostumed intrusion as unwelcome. Others, close by, seeing Hans now lying in the path of the horse, rushed to help Sam and Penny pull

251

him away as one of the animal's forelegs was about to come down and surely crush his skull.

Affectionately Penny held Hans's head, speaking softly to the trembling banker, asking, 'Are you all right, Hans?'

Hans looked up into Penny's eyes and said, 'You came,*fräulein.*' In a frightened voice, he added, 'That Sicilian with the olive branch is trying to kill me.'

The Roman soldier was standing over them, his arm raised, holding the branch high above his head. His cruel eyes were intent on Hans, and Sam saw the long knife the soldier was trying to conceal in his other hand.

Suddenly Pontius Pilate turned his horse. To avoid the huge animal, the crowd, murmuring a blend of surprise and fear, edged back in unison, pressing themselves against the stone façades of the medieval buildings. Some ducked into the crevasses and crannies of the streetscape.

Pontius Pilate shifted the grasp on his spear from ceremonial to combat. The soldier, his exposed arm muscles bulging, brought his branch down, intending to deliver the fatal blow upon Hans. In a quick responsive motion, Pontius Pilate thrust his spear forward.

The Roman ruler seemed to know precisely where in the soldier's body to insert the spear's knife-sharp tip, for his jab pierced deeply into the chest of the disguised Mafia man. As he slumped, his knife clattered to the cobble-stones. The large olive branch fell across his face, concealing the shame of his failed mission.

Staggering to his feet with Sam's help, Hans took Penny's arm with urgency in his voice and said, 'We are safe for the moment, but we must run.'

'Who is Pontius Pilate?' Sam asked.

Hans said, 'He's my friend, the coroner. We're always in the Pageant. *Ja.* Year after year.'

Sam exclaimed, 'Dr Giannini?'

'*Ja.* He's a good horseman, and all of you have saved my life.'

Hans pressed them both gently from behind, urging, 'Move on, we must keep moving.'

'We'll look out of place if we stay in the Pageant,' Penny whispered. 'People will see we're not in costume, laugh at us . . . call the police . . . .' She asked, 'And what about the dead soldier?'

With his good arm Hans reached over, ruffled her hair, unbuttoned the top buttons of her blouse and rubbed charcoal from his own face onto hers, doing his best to make her look like a player in the Pageant.

Smiling, he said, 'It is not easy to make you look plain.'

'Really?' she replied as the procession swept them along.

'And you'd better take off your hat, Sam,' Hans said.

'But the soldier?' Penny pressed.

'People will think he's part of the play . . . at least for a few minutes while we make our escape,' Hans said.

He pulled Sam and Penny aside. 'Come with me into this little café. They won't look for us here.'

Together they ducked under the police rope and entered a small coffee house. The lights had been turned out so patrons could view the Pageant. Most people were at the window, holding cups and saucers, all watching.

Hans said, 'Very briefly, I will explain. Then we must run on.' With his good hand he gently patted the bandages beneath his tunic. He whispered, 'I have the money under here – enough to exercise the warrants and make the purchase of the stock in Amrbosiana Limited.'

Penny looked surprised.

Sam's whistle was drowned out by another trumpet blast.

'It is the cheque for all the billions of dollars – hidden under my bandages.' He looked proud as he explained, 'The company – the treasurer of Ambrosiana – deals only in dollars, you know, not lire or any of those other weaker currencies. Dollars speak a universal language.'

Amazed, Penny looked at him, exclaiming, 'But how'd you manage to get a cheque for so much money in such a short time? I thought you couldn't get your hands on sufficient money to exercise the warrants.'

'Ja. The warrants expire tonight,' Hans replied, adding, as he pushed them out of the café door and back into the procession's flow, 'we must get to Campione before midnight. Hurry.'

As they rejoined the procession, Penny said, 'But how did you do it?'

'I sold all the other positions in Mr Thomson's portfolio – bonds of three dozen companies – earlier today, all of them. I've bet the entire portfolio on this one transaction. Believe me, I am very nervous about completing this purchase.'

Penny replied, 'So, that's what caused the market to crash earlier today in Frankfurt and Wall Street, too.'

'Ja. I sold.' He smiled at the impact he'd made on the world bond market.

Penny was still puzzled. 'But how'd you get the cheque?'

'For cash on the Frankfurt bourse and a few hours later on Wall Street. It can be done. You can sell for cash, you know. Instant cash. You take the discount and have the funds wired. It can be done. *Ja.*'

'Hans, that's very clever of you,' Penny said, and she kissed him.

Reacting with a broad smile, he looked deeply into Penny's eyes for a moment and said, 'My boss doesn't realize it yet – what I've done. He'll be furious, fire me tomorrow. But if I hand the money to the corporate secretary of Ambrosiana by midnight tonight, I'll control . . . .' He looked at Sam and said, 'I mean, Trevor's estate – you, Mr Thomson, and your beautiful sister – will control Ambrosiana Limited. And when I hand over the certified cheque, the secretary – and he is here tonight – will sign for me the employment contract, hiring me at a nice salary. And that will be my reward.'

Penny hugged him, exclaiming, 'You've done it, Hans!'

'*Ja,* now we must get out of here without any of us getting killed.' The Swiss banker urged them onward through the spectators and along the edge of the procession.

The street widened a bit and the crowd thinned. Sam guessed they were close to the edge of the medieval city. Up ahead he saw Pontius Pilate. As they came closer, Sam noticed smoke seeping from beneath the blanket on the Roman ruler's horse. He exclaimed, 'Penny, look! See the wisps of white smoke coming out from under his horse-blanket.'

Penny stood on her tiptoes and said, 'That's dry ice under there.' She tugged at Sam's arm and added, 'I'll bet it's Trevor's fluids being kept frozen. We've got to get them away from Dr Giannini.'

Sam said, 'OK, I'll run after him. You take Hans to the train station and I'll meet you there.' Sam began to follow the horse through the crowd of players.

Hans yelled, '*Ja.* We meet you there. But remember, we must get to Campione before midnight.'

Sam saw Dr Giannini make an exaggerated move, first extending his legs, then digging them into the horse's tender sides. Sam yelled back, 'Dr Giannini's making a break for it.' But Hans and Penny were nowhere in sight.

Sam ran, threading his way between the edges of the procession and the police restraining rope. He jostled spectators who were pressing forward to watch. He was running in one of his races, nearing the finish line. With a burst of energy he passed slower runners, making for an imaginary banner ahead. But instead, the finish line – in this case the form of Pontius Pilate on horseback – kept moving away from him.

Sam ran even faster, weaving a course between the choirboys. He passed the Roman soldiers controlling the followers of Jesus. He was beside Jesus bearing his cross, and was surprised to hear words of encouragement, 'Run forward, run fast, conquer the winds of fear.'

Sam gave a thumbs-up to Jesus. Beside Jesus, also wearing wreaths of thorns and shuffling with the crosses they bore, walked two convicted criminals, plodding on towards their crucifixion. Sam dodged them as he tried to catch Pontius Pilate. He wasn't losing much ground, because every time the horse broke into a gallop, Dr Giannini had to rein up to avoid still more costumed players ahead of him.

Suddenly the rider pulled back on the reins. His horse neighed. Something was in front, startling it. Sam redoubled his efforts, running faster as the coroner frantically tried to control the frightened beast.

Coming up in a sprint, Sam saw the two boxes fall from their bindings under the blanket as the horse reared up on his hind legs. An outfielder deep in centre field making a diving catch, Sam dived forward, both hands outstretched, his belly scraping the rough cobble-stones. With palms up, he caught a box in each hand. He heard the spectators cheer, seeing Sam make the final out in the ninth inning, winning the game for the home team.

The rider apparently hadn't realized he'd lost his cargo, Sam concluded as he picked himself up from his awkward position in the middle of the street. Fleetingly he thought how glad he was it was cold and he'd worn his heavy shirt and jacket, providing some protection for his poor body from the cobble-stones. He could sense the cuts, and he winced with pain where the rough pavement had scraped his vulnerable ribs. Yet he had held onto the boxes, whiffs of white smoke seeping from them.

They were at the last part of the procession's route, and the crowd was less numerous, so Sam wondered what had caused the horse to bolt.

Then he saw her. It was Felicia. She was standing in front of the horse, daring it, challenging it, not giving ground to the beast. She was yelling at the rider, 'You double-crossing coroner. We had a deal, but you sold out to a higher bidder!'

Could there be someone else, Sam asked himself, another pretender for Trevor's fortune, outbidding Felicia for the coroner's testimony?

The horse neighed.

Dr Giannini, trying desperately to control his horse as it writhed, shouted back, 'No, you misunderstand . . . .'

'I understand perfectly,' Felicia shouted.

The horse returned to all fours, its eyes bulging with the untoward events, and now, out of control, charged Felicia. Its move was so abrupt all Pontius Pilate could do was to grasp the animal's neck and hang on, his cloak falling away from his head as he did so. Sam saw the horror-stricken look on the face of the Swiss coroner.

Terror filled Felicia's face as the horse, its hoofs rising high, loomed over and started to descend upon her. In one motion Sam set the boxes down on the cobble-stones and, forgetting his bruises and dodging the horse's hoofs, raced at top speed towards the frightened Felicia. Just as the animal's hoofs descended, he reached her. It was his second chance to loop his arm around her midriff, which he did, pulling her aside as the horse's hoofs struck the bare pavement, missing the two of them by inches.

Felicia's long hair fell across his now tattered coat as she collapsed into his arms. He picked up his hat from the cobble-stones and affectionately placed it on her head. Add a cavalry uniform, he thought, and she'd become a sexy 1880s woman Buffalo soldier.

52

The choirboys who were leading the Easter Pageant reached the terminus of the procession, which was at the edge of the medieval section of town. There the streets widened and the crowd of spectators thinned. Hans gently guided Penny down the street leading to the railway station. He said as he urged a quickened pace, 'Come on, Penny, we've barely time to catch the last train from Mendrisio.'

'To Lugano?'

'Ja. But we'll get off at Campione.'

Penny remembered and said, 'That's where Ambrosiana's main office is located.'

'Ja, most of their people work at the big plant in Milan, but the corporate secretary and treasurer are both in Campione – across the lake from Lugano. It's an Italian city surrounded by Swiss territory. The treasurer – that's Count Ambrosiana – wants to be close to the banks in Lugano. And, if the truth were known, he also likes to gamble some of the family money at the casino.'

'But we're not going there to gamble.'

'Nein. To see the secretary – he is Willy and you will meet him in a moment. He's the one with whom we will officially exercise the warrants.'

'What about the Mafia men? Aren't there others, and won't they follow us?'

'No, they never take the train. They'd rather drive their big Mercedes.' He laughed. 'It's more prestigious.'

'But, Hans,' Penny asked, 'why didn't you take care of this transaction earlier today – seeing the Ambrosiana Limited secretary, I mean, and delivering the cheque?'

'There was no time. After I'd sold all those bonds it was time to catch the train to Mendrisio for the Pageant. Willy was also in the Pageant. Everyone in our canton of Ticino, well almost everyone, participates. It's our annual tradition.'

'The secretary was watching?'

'No, participating. He was Jesus in the procession.'

Penny said with surprise, 'Jesus?'

'Ja. Come on. I'll introduce you and explain. Here he comes now.'

Penny saw a tall figure with a flowing robe and long hair walking hurriedly towards them. She remembered him walking bent over and carrying his cross. Up close, she expected to see a halo circling his head and the stigmata on his hands and feet.

'Leave the beard on,' Hans said to Jesus. 'It may get us a seat on the train.' He smiled and introduced the holy man, saying his name was 'Willy Koster'. Hans added proudly, 'He is a good German boy.'

Willy, appearing ill at ease in his costume with the Pageant being officially over, shook Penny's hand and said to Hans, 'So, I finally meet the sexy American investment manager you've been talking so much about.'

Penny was surprised. 'Me?' she said, blushing.

'We must hurry,' Hans insisted.

The street was still closed to traffic and bustling with people leaving the Pageant: tourists, participants and locals.

'Are you OK to walk to the station, Hans?' Penny asked, concerned. 'Can you make it, or should we try to get a taxi?'

'The station is not far and I always have a problem getting a taxi,' Hans said, picking up his pace. His good arm encircled Penny's waist, coaxing her gently onward. 'The most important thing now,' he added, 'is to catch the last train so we get to Willy's office in Campione with my cheque before midnight – he must validate the stock certificate with his time-clock.'

'To make the transaction official?' Penny asked.

'Ja.'

As they approached the lighted station, people cast curious glances at the robed and bearded figure. Some nodded their recognition, others backed off, a little frightened, still others offered respectful greetings.

Inside, in the warmer waiting-room, people who recognized Willy from the Pageant rose and offered their seats to the holy personage. Penny helped Hans ease onto the bench. He was beginning to look weak, and her concern was growing.

While Hans's face was pale, he was still alert as he eyed everyone in the waiting-room, searching for the tell-tale look of another assassin. His fear was contagious and Penny, with Jesus on her other side, also scrutinized each of the passengers.

Penny tried to sort out who were tourists and who were locals, whether they had participated in the Pageant or were spectators. In doing so, she sought out the aberration, the one who was out of place, not tired from standing to watch the Pageant, not cold from the chilly night. All the while she worried about Sam, if he would get there on time. She expected him to come running into the waiting-room any moment.

Right on time, the station-master, his voice blaring over the loudspeaker, announced the arrival of the train from Chiasso and the Italian border. He advised everyone it was the last train from Mendrisio to Lugano until morning.

No one wanted to miss it. Rapidly everyone made for the platform. Down the road from the old town, ran tourists panicking at the thought of trying to find a hotel room this late at night in an unfamiliar town, and they were joined by locals who lived in Lugano and had jobs to attend the next morning. Penny, holding onto Hans, hesitated, looking for Sam.

Willy urged, 'Come, Ms Bailes, we must board the train.'

Automatically people parted, making way for Jesus and his two accompanying apostles, some even offering a hand up the steps into the train. Growing weaker, Hans welcomed their help, politely thanking each of them, until he saw a man at the top step who was watching him with cold, hard, threatening eyes.

Hans was sure he knew the man who now confronted him, blocking his passage into the coach. It was, Hans was certain, Angelo Luciano. With alarm he remembered the Mafia man bragging how his criminal family was going to take care of him one way or another. Hans hoped his disguise as a player in the Pageant, plus the presence of the costumed Jesus, would conceal his identity. But he was wrong.

'Hans Kubler?' Angelo Luciano said, his voice ninety per cent certain, only a fraction questioning. It was the same voice he'd heard in the Unlucky Lady. Hans froze. Trying to be assertive when fear consumed him, he drew on his remaining strength and replied in German, 'Nein.'

Penny, on the step behind, quickly realizing the situation, shouted out the first German name coming into her mind, 'Heinrich, get on the train, lots of people are waiting behind us.'

The Mafia man looked confused. He knew if he made a mistake, such as killing the wrong man – an innocent man from the Pageant – the press coverage would upset his family's *padrone*. His job might be in jeopardy, maybe even his life. He hesitated, attempting once more, 'Aren't you

Hans Kubler?' Demanding confirmation, he added, 'From the Trans-Swiss Bank in Lugano?'

Penny laughed at the Mafia man, the potency of her demeanour and the force of her voice surprising her, 'He's a borrower, not a lender. You've got the wrong man.'

Hans quickly nodded.

The train official, standing in the flood of illumination from one of the station overhead lights, held high his green and white disc, ready to signal the driver. He looked at his watch, shaking his head slightly. The train was already a minute late in leaving Mendrisio. And throngs of passengers were still waiting to board.

Watching Angelo's movements, Hans knew in advance there was a gun under the Mafia man's black leather jacket, and it was pointed his way. In that tender millisecond, the Swiss banker knew he would pull the trigger. Instinctively Hans acted. Lowering his head and drawing upon his last reserves of energy, he shoved himself forward into the man, tackling his legs, pain shooting through his tender shoulder so sharply he cried out.

The gun went off.

Penny screamed.

By her side, Willy slumped.

Instantaneously Penny reached out to catch him. As Jesus fell into her arms, blood flowing onto her jacket, Penny heard more screams from the crowd. She sensed people behind her either running for cover or falling down onto the station platform as everyone sought a protected place.

It was all she could do to support Willy, the holy martyr, but others quickly came to her rescue. One man gestured violently at the Mafia man, his fist clenched, shouting in Italian, 'Christ killer.' Another lunged for the hit man, pinning his arms behind him while Hans, despite the pain, clung tightly to Angelo's legs.

For a brief instant, Angelo Luciano thought about killing himself with his own gun, for he now realized, having shot Jesus, the outcome of this affair was going to reverberate across the morning press and be seen on European television. As a result, his would be a fate worse than death. He envisioned newspaper headlines in Rome and Zurich, and Lugano too: 'Mafia Hit Man Kills Jesus'.

But, as one who yearned for public recognition in a profession in which it is eschewed, he spared his own life. He knew he had to see the newspaper story and his picture on television. He fantasized ranking right up there in history, as famous as Pontius Pilate.

He also realized he was doomed. He would be friendless. No one would dare take his side, and worse, no one would be paying for his legal defence – the Mafia would disown him. His ultimate death by hanging would be assured. Fleetingly, he wished there was a charity to come to his rescue, to save him at the last minute from the death penalty. But he realized not even the right-to-lifers would come forward to support the continuance of his life on this earth.

The policeman who promptly arrived, weapon drawn, wrenching Angelo's from his hand, confirmed the Mafia man's worst fears. He said, 'You're a dead man, if not tonight by crucifixion nailed to one of those crosses from the Pageant, tomorrow by sentencing from Judge Romano.'

The train conductor, watching the station clock click off the seconds, now coming up on five minutes behind schedule, was furious. He waved his arm frantically, motioning for people to get on the train. In his mind it was an unforgivable situation – regardless of the reason – in Switzerland's perfectly-run train subculture, even if it was Jesus who had been shot.

Having lashed Angelo's hands with handcuffs to the train's unisex washroom door, the policeman attended to Willy. Penny and Hans pulled him up the last step as the train got under way.

'We'll take him to the hospital in Lugano,' the officer said.

'No,' Hans quickly replied. 'His doctor is in Campione, and he has a special condition . . . ah . . . allergic to gauze, so he must get off there.'

'But, Hans,' Penny protested.

Willy groaned, then mumbled, whispering in Penny's ear as she bent over to listen, 'It's all right, Ms Bailes, Hans and I must conduct our business before midnight.'

'But you're shot . . . .'

'Not badly, I don't think,' he said, passing out in Penny's arms.

53

The hint of fear and the lines of stress lingered on Felicia's face. Sam desired to comfort her and erase her anxiety with his kiss. He took off his jacket and folded it. Bending over, he carefully placed it on the cobble-stones under her head.

As spectators huddled round, a man came up to Sam, gesturing. He wore a black cap, across the front of which were white capital letters announcing 'TAXI'. He spoke in Italian. Sam got the message from his hand movements: the taxi man had scooped up the two boxes and returned them to Pontius Pilate. The taxi-driver made motions indicating the horseman had ridden off into the night.

Sam rushed out with, 'Where is your taxi?'

'Taxi, *si, si*,' the man replied eagerly.

'I want to hire it!'

The man looked questioningly at Sam.

Sam tried, 'Taxi, taxi.'

The man nodded and motioned for Sam to follow. Sam bent over, trying to pick up Felicia in his arms, but the hurt from his bruised ribs was too much for him. He cried out. Several onlookers came to his rescue, gently lifting her into his arms. Seeing the problem, the taxi man ran to his nearby vehicle and promptly drove it alongside the waiting couple.

With the driver's help Sam eased Felicia into the back seat, climbing in beside her, one arm propping up her head. Pointing ahead down the road, he commanded, 'Follow that horse.'

The taxi driver accelerated. But then he turned around and looked at them, his attention totally off the narrow road. His hands in the air, palms upward, signified to Sam that he didn't know which way to drive.

Felicia stirred, opened her eyes and looked into Sam's. Smiling faintly, she snuggled close enough to excite him; his adrenaline was racing.

Sam said to her, 'Which way did he go?'

'Who?'

'Dr Giannini. On his horse. Which way did he go?'

The taxi drove on in the moonlight along the winding street, its driver still looking back at them, awaiting further instructions. Ahead, as the vehicle sped down the narrow road, Sam saw its headlights illuminate first one house, then another, each a black and white photograph mounted in an album.

Felicia thought and said softly, 'He's going to the Muggio Valley.'

The driver nodded, repeating 'Muggio.' He looked forward, thank heaven, Sam thought, turning the wheel in time to dodge a group of terrified locals poised to flee the oncoming taxi.

'Where is that . . . .' Sam began as he and Felicia were pitched together into a corner of the back seat.

Felicia murmured, 'It's close by. We were going to meet there after the Pageant. He has a lab in his house, I think. He was planning to conduct more tests, take my blood sample, and give me a certified statement of the results. I paid him off, you know – my attorneys gave him a lot of my own hard-earned money.'

Sam nodded.

Felicia went on, 'He said he'd supply me with the lab tests – in writing, for the court, but he insisted I must come alone. He told me he didn't trust attorneys. Said he broke out in a sweat when they were around.'

Again Sam nodded, drawing her closer.

'But then,' she went on, her spunk returning, 'he sprung a request for even more money. He said someone had upped the ante for his so-called services.' She looked at Sam, moved away a bit and said, 'I figured it was you.'

'But I didn't.'

'You didn't?'

The taxi swerved, missing a bicycle with no lights, and the move thrust her back into his arms. This time he didn't let her go, but held her tight, tilting her head backwards as his lips pressed hers.

The driver exclaimed, *'Avanti!'* And with each straight stretch of road, he accelerated, only to quickly brake when another of the road's ubiquitous curves loomed ahead.

They were soon out of Mendrisio and climbing into the mountains, the narrow road clinging to the edge of a great, gaping valley. The dark moon shadow of their taxi rushed along beside the speeding vehicle in parallel progress. Now and then when the taxi came close to the edge of the road and there was nothing but emptiness beyond, the loyal shadow vanished.

Sam whispered to Felicia, 'The moon over Mendrisio makes it all seem quite mystical.'

She ran her hand through his brown curls, her red nails dark in the moonlight.

The deep valley yawned below. Medieval stone houses, clustering together for companionship in this remote valley, hugged the side of the road on those stretches where it didn't cling precipitously to the mountain. Rows of more houses climbed up the hillside above the road. Most were dark, their occupants long since in bed.

The taxi took another sharp corner, throwing them apart. Sam winced with the pain in his ribs.

Felicia said, 'You've hurt yourself playing your game of catch back there on the cobble-stones.'

Sam nodded.

'You're very brave.' She added softly, 'You've saved me from that awful horse – saved my life.'

Sam said, 'I couldn't help it. I've had these dreams. They won't go away. They're about you . . . .'

Felicia said, 'And you believe in fantasies turning into reality?'

'That's why humans are blessed with imagination.'

Felicia's reply was interrupted as the taxi turned sharply, tumbling the two of them together into the other corner of the back seat.

Gesturing ahead with both arms, hands letting go of the steering wheel, the taxi-driver yelled, 'Horse!'

The taxi's headlights picked up the animal galloping along in the moonlight. Its eerie rider, Dr Giannini, his hood raised, appeared to be the headless horseman as he held onto his two boxes with each arm. Puffs of vapour from the dry ice floated amorphously behind him.

Up ahead Sam saw a straight stretch of narrow road. The taxi-driver accelerated, pulling up beside the horse.

Suddenly he exclaimed, 'Mamma mia!' Both of the driver's legs rose together and with both feet he stomped on the brake.

The taxi's headlights stared out into vacant space. No houses, no rocks, no trees picked up their beams.

Frantically down-shifting the automatic transmission into the lowest gear, the driver's combined actions practically stood the vehicle on end.

Uncontrollably Sam fell forward, hitting the back of the front seat.

Felicia tumbled down on top of him.

The moonlight illuminated the scene as Dr Giannini, clutching his two boxes, whiffs of white smoke streaming behind him, flew forward over the neck of the horse as the animal, too, stopped abruptly in its last possible moment of self-preservation.

Sam managed to open the door and climb out, Felicia following, shaking, fear flushing her face.

By their side the riderless horse, standing by a small railing, neighed, asking for instruction as to what it should do next. Beyond the low railing was the valley, its almost bottomless chasm beneath them, its appetite for the Swiss coroner and his two hand-held pieces of baggage having been satisfied.

They heard the coroner's body thud onto the rocks below. Consecutive little pops followed as the two vials hit the rocks, their precious contents, far, far below, joining the annals of unwritten history.

Looking around, Sam said slowly, 'It's a bus turn-around, off the main road, cantilevered over the valley, but unmarked and unlit at night.' He added, 'Because the buses don't run this late.'

'Dr Giannini didn't see it, but the horse did,' Felicia said quietly. 'Even our driver didn't see it until the last minute. Thank God he did.'

The taxi-driver pulled a small flask from the glove compartment. Shaking with fright, he quickly inserted the uncorked end into his mouth, tipping its bottom towards the full moon. He drank thirstily.

Quivering from the cold and the terrifying experience, Sam and Felicia stood together. His arm pulled her towards him. In the cool, cool night the moonlight reflected off her long silky hair and he kissed her, and she him.

He said to the taxi-driver, 'Is there an inn up in this mountain valley?'

'Inn?' he asked, wiping his mouth with his sleeve. '*Si.*' He pointed farther up into the valley.

Sam rolled his hand in a circle, gesturing in the same direction. He commanded '*Avanti*' as he eased Felicia back into the taxi.

54

Within a few minutes the train arrived at the Campione station. Hans looked at his Swiss watch.

'We won't make the deadline in time, will we, Hans?' Penny asked.

'*Ja!* If we hurry.'

Together they helped Jesus along the platform. Hans, an arm raised and waving, summoned a taxi. It promptly pulled up alongside.

'The casino is still open so there are taxis at the queue,' he said with relief as he instructed the driver to take them to the Ambrosiana Limited executive offices.

There, inside his lavish private office, Jesus revived long enough to accept the cheque denominated in US dollars after Hans extracted it from under his bandages.

His blood dripping onto the corporate records, and now caking in his beard, Jesus noted the exercise of the warrants. 'Five minutes to midnight on the date of their expiration.'

Hans said, 'Wow, I wouldn't want to cut it any closer.'

'How do you want the stock certificate made out?' Jesus asked, his voice barely audible.

'Have you any brandy, Willy?'

Jesus nodded, painfully opening his desk drawer.

Hans took out the flask and handed it to him. 'Here, take a swig or two. Penny revived me with it in the Caribbean. It should work for you here.' He asked, 'How many shares?'

Willy drank, coughed, and drank again. 'I make it twenty-five million shares. Now you own the majority of all the shares issued and outstanding – and that equals control.'

Penny whistled.

Hans said, 'We'll take a bearer certificate.'

Penny protested, 'But isn't that dangerous, Hans? Anyone who gets their hands on that piece of paper in effect will have control of

Ambrosiana.'

'*Ja.* But not where I'm going to put it.'

'In another vault?'

Hans said, 'No, it will be in sight of everyone.'

Willy produced the certificate, asking Penny to date it and write in the number of shares. She practised once on a blank sheet of paper to be sure she had the correct number of zeros before she made out the stock certificate.

Jesus lit a match, heated some red wax and applied the seal, placing a red ribbon over it. With all his remaining strength he affixed the elaborate Ambrosiana corporate imprint into the warm wax.

'There, it's official,' he said weakly, 'and just in time.' From his desk drawer he took out a sealed envelope, handing it to Hans. Even more unsteadily he said, 'This is your employment contract. You'll have the last laugh with Herr Oberman. You're now in charge of finance for Ambrosiana . . . .' His voice faded.

Penny hugged Hans and said, 'You get to decide which bank will receive the Ambrosiana deposits. Just think, all those billions of dollars, francs and Deutschmarks.'

'*Ja,* and pounds sterling, Finnish markkas, Japanese yen and . . . .'

Penny threw her arms around him. The kiss she planted on his Teutonic lips blocked his ongoing recital of world currencies.

Hans said, 'Now Hugo Oberman will have to pay attention to me. For I will control all the money of Ambrosiana. This is my reward.'

'But where are you going to put the stock certificate?' Penny asked.

Hans smiled and said, 'Framed on the wall of the Thomson-Columbus Museum on Grand Turk. Truecoat has a security system. It will be safer there than anywhere else.'

Willy said, 'And what about the monthly dividends?'

Hans replied, 'Wire them to Charles Fountain for Sam and Judith's new offshore trust in Turks and Caicos.' He saw Penny's look of amazement and added, 'Loyalty runs deep.'

Penny said, 'I must call the ambulance for Willy.'

Hans said, '*Ja! Ja!* Here, I will do it, you don't know the number.'

Willy slumped in his huge leather office chair as Hans made the call.

Speaking softly to Penny, Hans said, 'As soon as they come for Willy, I want to show you the view of moonlit Lake Lugano. It is mystical with ine mountains surrounding it.'

Penny nodded, glowing with a radiance.

His arm encircling her waist, Hans said gently, 'And once inside my villa, I will show you my valuable collection of framed F bonds. Some of them date way back in history.'

'F bonds?' she managed to ask.

'Yes, those are the bonds of companies, down through the years, that have failed.'

He's going to show me his etchings, Penny silently mused, allowing herself to be snuggled into his enveloping embrace. She told herself, There's going to be a place for me among his valuables – much closer to the exciting Eurobond market.

55

The little inn in the Muggio Valley was dark. The single light-bulb illuminating the weathered sign was no longer lit, the hour being long past its regular closing.

Only the moonlight shone as Sam stooped to avoid hitting his head on the hand-hewn header above the low entry door. His insistent banging finally raised the proprietor, who came to the door holding a single candlestick. He was slightly stooped and elderly. In a raspy voice, still full of sleep, he welcomed them. With a jerky wave of his night-shirted arm, he bid them enter.

Following him, Sam and Felicia passed through a small pub. The fire in its ceramic stove still glowed.

'But the horse,' Felicia whispered, adding, 'and the police, and the doctor, and the vials . . . and . . . .'

Sam raised his hand, his fingers covering her mouth. As he accepted the key to their room from the proprietor, he whispered to her, 'First you and I.' Sam bunched her long hair behind her ear and whispered softly, 'For this once, let's attend to our personal priorities.'

Felicia looked into his eyes.

In the candlelight, her hand in his, he led her up a narrow flight of stairs and into the moonlit bedroom of a real Swiss chalet.

Sam said, 'And I mean priorities other than those set in motion by Trevor Thomson.'

'You mean, it's high time we began to chart our own course?'

Sam nodded and said, 'I think we should merge . . .'

'I'm for that.'

'. . . our efforts towards a common objective.'

'You're thinking of all those children in Cockburn Town. I remember little Edward,' Felicia said, reminiscing about their run together. She went on, 'And his sister, Sherry – she was so adorable with her braided hair and the little sea shells – but the squalour in which they were living, and there is your new museum, and . . . .'

.us lips smothered her words. He said softly, 'Yes. So, shall we share our objectives with each other? And build anew?'

'Ever see the sun rise over the Muggio Valley?' Felicia responded, a sparkle in her eyes as bright as the mountain night.

'No, but I know it's going to be glorious.'